D0953083

The Secrets We Left Behind

The Secrets We Left Behind

SUSAN ELLIOT WRIGHT

A Novel

A Herman Graf Book
Skyhorse Publishing

Library of Congress Cataloging-in-Publication Data is available on file.

Cover design by Laura Klynstra
Cover photo credit Thinkstock

Print ISBN: 978-1-63220-708-1
Ebook ISBN: 978-1-63220-994-8

Printed in the United States of America

For Emma and James
And for Francis

The Secrets We
Left Behind

PROLOGUE

Sheffield, October 2010

The clocks went back last weekend so it gets dark even earlier now. She curses herself; she should have left more time. She drives a little too fast because she wants to get there before the light goes completely, and if she misses them today, it'll be another week before she can be sure of seeing them again. The sky is darkening rapidly by the time she's parked the car and walked through the old stone gateway to the park. It is unusually cold for late October, and the smell of wood smoke is in the air. The autumn colours are particularly vibrant after the rain, and the wet leaves smell fresh and earthy, though they're slippery and she almost loses her footing more than once as she hurries down through the woods.

Although she once loved this park, she keeps her head down now, avoids looking around. She has walked these winding paths so often in happier times that it is almost painful to come here, but this is the only real opportunity she has to catch a glimpse of them without being seen, and she must take it. She walks alongside the pond, but there's no sign of the ducks or moorhens that live around it, nor of the pair of grey herons that sometimes appear on the opposite bank. Today the pond is still and silent, and in this light, the water looks almost black. There is something about dark water that she finds achingly lonely and depressing.

She makes her way down behind the café to where the stepping stones cross the stream, taking care to stay behind the trees. Most of her clothing is black, but the scarf she's wearing is a pale, silvery colour; it's unlikely that it would show up in the darkness, but just in case, she pulls it from her neck and slips it into her bag. There are a few mothers and children in the play area and she strains her eyes as she searches their faces, but it's immediately obvious: they aren't there. She glances at her watch; surely they should have arrived by now?

To her left, a small black-and-white cat slinks through the metal railings that surround the swings before hunkering down, ears back and tail flicking as it spots some real or imagined prey in the undergrowth. She watches it for a moment, briefly distracted by the intense, snowy whiteness of its paws and whiskers. It's a pretty little thing, barely more than a kitten and yet already practising its skills as a hunter. The cat pounces, then examines the dry leaf it has caught between its paws.

At that moment, she spots them, just coming into the play area. She recognises their voices and she instinctively moves nearer so she can hear them more clearly, but then she stops. This is as near as she dares be to them now. If she is spotted, as she was once before, they'll stop coming here and then she may never be able to find them again, so she must content herself with lingering in the shadows for the time being.

CHAPTER ONE

Sheffield, 21 December 2009

I listened to the squeaky crunch of my boots as I walked to work. It was a sharp, crisp morning. The sky was still dark, but the whole of Sheffield was hidden under a blanket of snow and I was struck by the contrast of the white rooftops and church spires against the inky blackness. There had been another heavy fall overnight and there weren't many people about yet, so it all looked new and perfect with only my own dark tracks spoiling the pristine whiteness. Today was the winter solstice, and it was also my fiftieth birthday, though no one knew that. As far as my family was concerned, my fiftieth was three and a half years ago when we celebrated according to the date on my birth certificate – which by a bizarre coincidence was the summer solstice. It felt strange, knowing that it was such a significant day and not being able to tell anyone. As a child I thought it terribly unfair that my birthday fell on the shortest day of the year. *Tell you what, chicken,* my mum said in the end, *we'll have another party just for you in the summer; you can have two birthdays, like the Queen.* And now I really did have two birthdays, except I didn't get to celebrate them both. I was used to it now, but it was hard when it was a special one, one with a zero on the end. I sighed as I walked, watching my breath crystallise in the morning air. No point in dwelling on it.

It was my last day at the Young Families Project until after New Year. I was sure they'd rather I worked up until Christmas Eve, especially as I'd already had a week off, but they knew my daughter had just had a baby and they were pretty flexible. I usually finished at noon on Wednesdays, but after what felt like a particularly long morning, I realised that I still had some case notes to write up and I didn't want to leave them until after Christmas, so I just got my head down and carried on until everything was done.

It was gone two by the time I was ready to leave the office. I wished everyone a merry Christmas, put my welly boots on and headed out into the snow. I turned off Queen Street and trudged up the steep, narrow, cobbled road towards the cathedral. This was a pretty part of the city, and the little Georgian square where all the solicitors' offices were looked particularly attractive in the snow; the fairy lights in the windows and the old-fashioned lamp-post in the middle of the square made it look like a Christmas card.

As I walked into the warm fug of the veggie café where I usually had lunch, the lunchtime crowd was beginning

to thin out and the tea-and-carrot-cake brigade was starting to drift in. I recognised some of the other customers.
It tended to be the same faces here, mostly a mix of
students and academics from the two universities –
colourful, arty women and what my husband Duncan
sometimes called *weird beards*. Like me, they came mainly
for the organic food, but with its wooden floors, scarlet
walls and free newspapers, this café was a popular place
to hunker down away from the busy town centre, especially on cold, grey days like today.

While I waited in the queue, I glanced around to see
which tables were free. There was a blast of cold air as a
figure in a huge dark coat opened the door and disappeared out into the greyness of the street. I did a double
take. For a moment, something in the walk seemed familiar, but no, it couldn't be.

'The butternut squash and walnut risotto, please,' I
said when it was my turn. I put the plate on my tray with
a bottle of water and carried it over to the cashier. I was
about to rest the tray on the counter when I heard a male
voice exclaim, 'Jo!' I dropped the tray, and it crashed to
the floor, flipping the plate of risotto upside down. The
plate broke into several pieces and the risotto splattered
over the floorboards. For a split second I froze, unable to
breathe. I looked around in a panic, but the voice belonged
to a bearded, rotund little man who was greeting a young
woman with purple hair enthusiastically.

Briefly, the background hum of conversation stopped.
'Are you okay?' someone said.

'Yes,' I nodded. 'Yes, thank you. I'm sorry about the mess; the tray slipped.'

Shakily, I tried to help to pick up the broken plate, but the girl behind the counter insisted I sat down while they brought me another risotto. 'Not your fault, love,' she said. 'Them trays are always wet.'

It was years since I'd been that jumpy; an old reflex I thought had long gone.

*

I'd finished most of my Christmas shopping but I wanted to buy something special for Hannah, some earrings, perhaps, or a bracelet. I told Duncan I wanted to mark the fact that she was now a mum herself, but if I was honest, it was more a celebration of the fact that she'd got through the birth and she was okay. People didn't realise how dangerous childbirth can be, but I did. As I sat on the packed bus into town, I wondered whether she'd have another baby in a year or two, and how I'd cope if she did. Duncan hadn't wanted me to go to the hospital when she was in labour. 'Marcus'll call as soon as there's any news,' he'd said. 'There's nothing you can do so why not stay here and watch a DVD or something rather than pacing up and down a hospital corridor?'

'If I want to pace, I'll bloody well pace,' I told him, more sharply than I meant to. I just wanted to be there; I needed to at least be near by. And so I sat on a plastic chair outside the delivery room, praying to every god I could think of and somehow managing to keep from beating the door down. Poor Duncan; I knew he was worried too, but I was in such a state I couldn't even talk to him until I knew she was going to be all right. In the end, after a long night of worrying, it all went reasonably well, thank God, and now we were look-ing forward to our first Christmas as grandparents.

After I got off the bus I cut through the glass-roofed Winter Garden with its huge cacti, exotic ferns and giant palm trees, and I realised there were quite a few little children around who appeared to be showing an interest in the plants. What I hadn't noticed before were the larger-than-life-sized models of snakes and lizards skulk-ing in the undergrowth – a good way to attract kids. I came out of the Winter Garden and walked past the Peace Gardens where, in the summer, children in swimming costumes and sun hats ran squealing in and out of the fountains. It was a shame that none of this was here when Hannah was little, but I couldn't wait for the time when she and I would be able to bring Toby here so we could picnic on the grass and watch while he played with the other children in the foaming jets of water.

It was Christmas Eve and the city centre was predict-ably busy with some shoppers looking anxious, others looking plainly bad-tempered. Although most of the students had now gone home for Christmas, some were still here, working in the shops and bars or just enjoying the town, like the group of Chinese girls wearing Santa hats who were queuing for the Sheffield Eye, holding hands and giggling while they waited. The Wheel had gone up in the summer, and I had to admit, now it was all lit up for Christmas it looked spectacular, especially at night. Next to it was a giant Christmas tree decorated with blue lights and looking very pretty with the snow still on its branches.

As I walked along Fargate towards Marks & Spencer's I noticed a woman a few feet ahead pushing a buggy laden with shopping. A child of about four tottered along beside her, trying to hang on to the handle, his little arm stretched up high to reach past the carrier bags bulging from the sides. As I watched, the little boy stumbled and fell smack onto the icy pavement. The mother turned, hand on hip. She was heavily pregnant and I was just about to step forward and help him up so that she wouldn't have to bend, when she said, 'For fuck's sake! I haven't got time for this, Aaron, I really haven't. Get up!'

The child, bundled up in a blue padded coat and red woolly hat, was still lying face down on the ground, the soles of his Spider-Man wellies facing upwards. He began to wail.

'I said get up,' the woman yelled. 'Now!'

'For God's sake!' I scooped the poor thing up by the armpits and set him back on his feet.

'Mind your own fucking business,' the woman snarled, letting go of the pushchair and coming towards me. I braced myself but then the overladen pushchair tipped up and the baby inside began to cry. The mother turned. 'Now look what you've done,' she shouted, though it wasn't clear who she was shouting at. She grabbed the little boy by the sleeve and yanked him towards her, making him cry even harder. 'Come on, you little bastard,' she said, righting the pushchair. 'And don't think you'll get any Christmas presents if you keep up wi' that roaring,' she shouted, her voice hard as a slap. Then, dragging the crying boy alongside, she walked right in front of a tram, causing it to brake and sound its horn, before she headed off across the square and down towards Castle Market.

I stood there for a few moments. The sound of crying became fainter and the red hat got smaller as they disappeared into the bustling crowd. I felt my throat constrict and hot tears threatening. For a second I fantasised about sweeping the child away from his wicked witch of a mother and taking him home to a proper, warm, happy Christmas. Some people shouldn't be allowed to have babies. But I remembered the training I had before I started at the Young Families Project: don't make judgements; you don't know the background; you don't know the circumstances. And it's true, some of the families I supported had huge and complex problems, but if I was honest, I knew that the majority of them loved their children, and sometimes they just needed help and guidance to get back on track. It was hard, though; sometimes, I wanted to pick all those poor kids up and take them home with me so that I could make it all better.

The automatic doors to Marks & Spencer's glided open and I felt a puff of warm air as I stepped inside out of the cold. In the Christmas section mothers were buying shiny, glittering things, watched closely by wide-eyed children at their sides. I paused there for a minute, trying to wipe the memory of that horrible woman from my mind, but I couldn't seem to shake off a feeling of gloom. I shouldn't be feeling like this; after all, Hannah would be coming on Boxing Day and staying until the following evening. It'd give me a chance to look after her and pamper her a bit. I stayed with them for a few days after Toby was born, but Duncan was worried I'd outstay my welcome. 'They need to find their feet as parents,' he said. 'If you're there for too long, it'll make it all the more difficult when you go and they're on their own again. And we're only a phone call away if she needs us.' Maybe he was right. I knew I had a tendency to overprotect Hannah – I always have. But she looked so tired.

In the Food Hall there was quite a queue of people collecting their pre-ordered organic turkeys. That reminded me – I needed to ask Duncan to call into the butcher's to pick up the turkey crown I'd ordered. I couldn't go into those places myself. I could just about cook poultry even though I no longer ate it, but I couldn't deal with butchers' shops or meat counters, and I especially couldn't bear the blood any more; the sight of it on the butcher's apron and on his hands; the dark smears on the wooden chopping block, and the thought that behind the counter or out the back where you couldn't see it there would be blood pooled on the floor, sticking to his shoes and making the sawdust stick together in clumps.

I wandered along the aisles, throwing crystallised ginger and Turkish delight into my basket but resisting the pack of chocolate tree decorations because last year Monty, who doesn't care that chocolate is bad for dogs, snaffled the whole lot up, foil wrappers and all, and had sparkly poo for two days afterwards. As I made my way to the checkout, I spotted a man disappearing behind a display of mince pies. A jolt of recognition shot through my body; he was almost bald and he was wearing a huge dark coat that looked too big for him, but there was something so familiar about that walk. He appeared briefly at the end of the aisle. I only caught a glimpse of the side of his face but I could see that he was wearing heavy framed glasses and that his skin was unusually pale. Scott had had an olive complexion; he had long dark hair and he didn't wear glasses, but there was something about this man that reminded me so much... The man half turned towards me and for a moment I was unable to move. It was him; it was Scott and he was here in Sheffield. I couldn't hear anything except a rushing in my ears; I couldn't feel my own body. Then someone touched my arm. 'You all right, love? Here, come and sit down for a minute, don't worry about your shopping, duck. We'll sort that out.' I wasn't sure what she meant at first, then I realised I'd actually dropped the shopping basket, and now I could see a shop assistant and another woman picking everything up as I was led, by an elderly lady, to the chairs they put along the wall to be sat on by elderly ladies.

'I'm sorry,' I said. 'I'm fine. Really.' Then I was sitting down and someone was offering me a glass of water. The old lady had her arm around me. 'Do you want us to phone anyone, duck? My daughter's got her mobile if you—'

'No, I'm all right now, but it's very kind of you.' I gulped the water and took my bags from the shop assistant. 'Thank you. I felt a bit faint, that's all – didn't have any breakfast.'

I looked around for the man as I joined the queue for the checkout but there was no sign of him now. It couldn't have been Scott, I told myself. Scott's in New Zealand. He was taller, anyway. And heavier; and he had long hair. But then, the last time I saw Scott was when Hannah was eight months old and that was over thirty years ago. Of course he'd look different now; I looked different too. Back then, my hair was dyed red and I'd cut it short soon after Hannah was born because it was easier when I was looking after a baby all day. Now it was back to its natural colour, not grey enough yet to warrant regular treatments, but not the rich, velvety brown it was when I first met Scott and Eve. I paid for the items in my basket and went out into the street. I couldn't think about present shopping now, so I'd have to pop back later. I started to make my way home, eyes darting around, scanning the crowd for a balding man in a big dark coat. I felt raw and exposed and I was shivering so much that my teeth were chattering. As I waited for the bus, I remembered that Duncan had an early surgery today – it was only routine vaccinations, mostly cats and dogs, so he'd probably be home by now and he'd wonder why I was back so soon. I could have said I had a migraine coming on, but I didn't want to lie; I'd never lied to Duncan, only about things that happened before.

CHAPTER TWO

I was up early on Boxing Day morning and by seven o'clock I was showered, dressed, and in the kitchen making coffee and toast. Yesterday had been nice; Duncan cooked – beef Wellington for himself, caramelised onion tart for me, followed by home-made chocolate truffle ice cream. Then we watched Christmas telly, drank port and ate mince pies. It was a good day, and I was touched at the trouble he'd taken to make it feel festive. But today was the real deal; the proper Christmas.

I ate my toast standing up and drank my coffee as I took things out of the fridge. There was a lot to do. I had to prepare the turkey crown for Duncan and Marcus, make apricot and parsley stuffing and finish the cashew nut and almond loaf for Hannah and me.

'Okay.' Duncan came into the kitchen, hair still damp from the shower. 'Give me a job.'

'Peeling, please.' I handed him the peeler and a carrier

bag full of potatoes and parsnips, and he kissed my cheek before setting to work. 'Cheer up,' he said. 'We're going to have a lovely day.'

I'd felt a bit down yesterday. I knew it was selfish of me, but I wanted them here, my daughter and grandson. 'I don't begrudge Marcus's parents.' I added cranberry jelly and a pinch of ground cloves to the red cabbage and grated apple as it simmered on the back of the hob. 'But I thought, you know, Toby's first Christmas . . . And it's not even two weeks since she gave birth. Wouldn't you think tha—'

'Darling.' Duncan cut the potato he'd just peeled into four. 'They'll be here soon and they're staying until tomorrow night. Can't we just enjoy having them? They were only at Marcus's mum and dad's for a couple of hours, so I think we got the better deal, don't you?'

'I know, but—'

'Oh, come on. You're not saying you'd rather have had them here for Christmas lunch than staying overnight?'

'No, I suppose not,' I sighed. 'I'm just a bit worried about her, that's all. I get the feeling something's not right. Do you know what I mean?'

'She was a bit quiet when I saw her, but that was just after she'd had him. And when you think of what she's been through . . .' He paused and looked up at me, his eyes suddenly dark with concern. 'Do you really think there's something wrong? Seeing the look on his face reminded me of how much Duncan cared for Hannah. He loved her, as he promised he would, as though she were his own child. I sighed. 'Probably not. I expect I'm worrying over nothing.' I kissed the top of his head. 'Sorry.'

*

It was what had really sealed our relationship. I could never have made a life with someone who didn't love my Hannah as his own. The first Christmas we spent together, I'd been worried how a man who wasn't used to children would cope with a seven-year-old waking him up at four in the morning to show him the presents he'd already seen and had helped to wrap the night before. But he was enchanted, and he took the whole business very seriously, even suggesting we hire a Santa costume in case she woke up and saw me filling her stocking.

On Christmas Eve, we found Hannah a pair of stretchy old boot-socks so she could hang one at the end of her bed while I smuggled the other into the living room. We stuffed the spare sock with tiny gifts, chocolate coins, pink-and-white sugar mice, shiny pennies and a satsuma until it bulged and rustled tantalisingly, then we crept into her room together to swap it for its limp, empty partner. 'I love Christmas Eve,' Duncan had whispered. 'Do you remember waking up and feeling the weight of that knobbly stocking on your feet and thinking, *he's been!*' I did remember, but for me, those happy Christmases had come to an end too soon. 'Hey, look at this.' Duncan stooped to pick up an envelope that had slid off the bed and onto the floor. 'I didn't know she'd written to Santa.'

'Neither did I.' We took the letter, along with the mince pie, the glass of sherry and the carrot for the reindeer, into the sitting room. All around the edge of the page, Hannah had drawn bauble-bedecked Christmas trees, holly, and twinkling stars. *Dear Father Christmas, if you are real, please wake me up when you come to my house. If you do not wake me up, I will not believe in you. Your friend Hannah Matthews. PS. I hope you are well and I hope you have a happy Christmas.* And then she'd added several lines of kisses. 'Oh my God,' I laughed. 'I can't believe this – my daughter is blackmailing Father Christmas!'

Duncan smiled. 'Clever! But do you notice, she hasn't actually asked for anything, just wished him a happy Christmas.' He put his arm round me and kissed me on the nose. 'What a very nice, well-brought-up little girl.'

We had a lovely time that year. Duncan loved putting up the fairy lights, decorating the tree, and reading *The Night Before Christmas* to Hannah on Christmas Eve. 'It's like being a kid again,' he said. 'It's magical.'

'It's what a child's Christmas should be.'

I still played Santa right up until Hannah went to university; it was a bit of a joke by then and it was one gift instead of a filled stocking, but I'd wanted to keep it magical for as long as possible.

*

Hannah and Marcus were due to arrive at one, and by 12.30 almost everything was done and the house was filled with the fragrant smells of roasting turkey, herby stuffing and the warm, spicy aroma of red cabbage. Duncan had lit the fire in the dining room and laid the table with a crisp white cloth, tall candles and proper napkins with napkin rings. While he was out the front clearing snow and ice from the path, I cut a small sprig from the Christmas tree and slipped out into the garden, as I had done every Boxing Day for the last ten years.

I found the spot under the plum tree at the end of the garden, marked by a small wooden cross, only just visible now through the snow. I crouched down and brushed the snow away. This one had almost made it; the last of my ghost babies. Thirteen weeks, a perfectly formed little boy, about two and a half inches long. None of the others held on past eight weeks, and I didn't like to think about what may have happened to their tiny bodies. I should have looked; I should have overcome my horror and put my hands down in the blood and found them, my babies that never were; then I could have put them all out here under the plum tree and visited them whenever I needed to remember. This little cross would be surrounded by snowdrops in a few weeks' time, but for today I placed the sprig of pine in front of it. 'Merry Christmas, sweetheart,' I whispered.

The first eight weeks had been agonising; every time I felt a twinge I'd worry that it was happening again. But the weeks went on, I had regular scans and I felt good; we started to hope. Once we passed the magic twelve-week point, we relaxed. We were so sure it was going to be okay this time that we even started to tell people and to hell with the comments. Yes, we were both in our forties; no, we didn't want to 'enjoy our freedom' now Hannah had left home. We still had a lot of love to give and we both wanted this child – *our* child – desperately. But on Christmas afternoon, the pains started and I knew immediately. Hannah was there with Nick, her boyfriend at the time. She sent Nick away and she and Duncan spent the next few days trying to be supportive, and trying not to cry. I wanted Hannah to go back to Leeds where she shared a house – a daughter shouldn't have to see her mother in the midst of a miscarriage. But she insisted on staying with me. Then only a few years later, it had been me trying not to cry through each of her miscarriages.

I felt a hand on my shoulder. I looked round, and Duncan was standing behind me. He pulled me gently to my feet and wrapped his arms around me. We stood there in the snowy garden holding on to each other, not speaking.

CHAPTER THREE

Monty's frenetic barking announced Hannah and Marcus's arrival and they tumbled into the house in a bluster of bags and rucksacks and nappies and general baby paraphernalia. Hannah looked shattered. Marcus carried a sleeping Toby, still strapped into his car seat, into the kitchen and placed him on the kitchen table. His little body jolted due to the heightened startle reflex, and he opened his eyes briefly but then closed them again. Duncan enfolded Hannah in a big hug, then turned to Marcus and shook his hand. They got on well, Duncan and Marcus, and I was glad. My family was so small that every now and then I was gripped by a sense of absolute terror that something might happen to destroy it. I looked at Toby's red, scrunched-up face and I marvelled at how clever Hannah had been to produce him. My grandson.

'Right,' Duncan said, rubbing his hands together and smiling. 'How about a Christmas drink?'

'Huh! I wish,' Hannah said. 'There's a bottle of wine in that bag somewhere, but I suppose I'd better not have any. Any coffee going?'

'Are you supposed to drink coffee?' Marcus asked.

'For God's sake, it's Christmas!'

'But won't it—'

'One cup, Marcus.' Her voice was unusually sharp.

Marcus put his hands up in mock defence. 'Okay, okay.' He grinned. 'Sorry. The lady wants coffee, the lady gotta have coffee.'

I made the coffee with hot milk, just the way Hannah liked it. 'So, how are you feeling?' I asked after Duncan and Marcus had gone through to the dining room.

'Totally and utterly knackered.' She sighed and sat down, pushing the car seat away so she could lean on the table and rest her head in her hands.

'It'll get better, you know. The first few weeks really are the worst. Is Marcus pulling his weight?'

'He's doing more than his share, to be honest.' She put her hands round the coffee and blew lightly on the surface. 'He's very good with him.' She sounded a little sad. Then Toby woke up and started to cry.

'I'll take him, you drink your coffee.' I fumbled with the catch on the harness that kept him in his car seat. It seemed so much more complicated than the clips I remembered.

'Here.' Hannah leant across, snapped the clasp open easily then sat back with a sigh as Toby's cries increased in intensity. 'He can't be hungry again, surely? I only fed him a couple of hours ago.'

'Come on, sweetheart,' I murmured as I lifted him from his chair and held his warm little body against my chest. He looked so sweet in his Christmas-red baby-grow and the navy cardigan that Hannah knitted when she was pregnant. We had a hell of a job finding those ladybird buttons, but Hannah knew exactly what she wanted. She had such a good eye for that sort of thing. 'He's perfect,' I said. 'And so tiny and compact.' I almost commented on how like Marcus he was, but something stopped me. 'Shush.' I swayed back and forth with him as I walked around the kitchen trying to settle him. 'Shush, my little pickle; let your poor mummy have her coffee. Shush-shush.'

'Oh, shit.' Hannah looked down. 'I'm leaking again.' She grabbed a wipe from the quilted bag next to her and started dabbing at two wet spots that had appeared on her jumper. 'This keeps happening when he cries.' She held her arms out. 'Better give him here.' She lifted her jumper and held Toby in place until he seemed to sense or smell her milk and started to root frantically for the nipple. Then, after several attempts, he latched on and Hannah winced.

'Sore?' I asked.

She bit her bottom lip as she nodded. 'The health visitor said it was like breaking in a new pair of shoes, but either she's never had a baby or she wears shoes made of broken glass.'

I felt a flash of anger towards the health visitor. 'That's not very helpful, is it. Isn't there any cream they can give you?'

She nodded. 'But it doesn't get much of a chance to work, does it? It's like there's no escape; he's either clamped to my nipple or he's crying and making me leak so I couldn't get away even if I wanted to.'

'What do you—'

Hannah shook her head. 'I don't mean I really want to get away from him; just . . . well, he's less than two weeks old and it's as though he's been here for ever. He seems, I don't know, so *determined*; it's as if he knows what he wants and he knows how to get it, whether I like it or not.' She looked up at me and smiled weakly. 'I sound ungrateful, don't I?' She looked down at her son, whose eyes were now closed as he sucked blissfully, his tiny fingers curling and uncurling as they rested against her breast. 'I don't mean to,' she said quietly. 'It's what I wanted, after all. But I can't even remember what it's like to walk around without my arms aching from carrying him, or to get into bed without holding my breath, waiting for him to start crying. '

I looked at her again. My poor Hannah; she was pale, and there were deep, dark shadows in her face. And yet she'd looked so well while she was pregnant.

Despite having just been fed, Toby cried a lot while we were having lunch, so Marcus, Duncan and I all took turns walking around with him so that Hannah could eat. When we'd finished the main course, I got up to clear the plates and Hannah followed me into the kitchen, loaded the plates into the dishwasher and then sat at the table while I found matches to flame the

Christmas pudding. She picked up the bottle of brandy and sighed. 'I could really do with a large one of these right now.' I got the impression she was only half joking when she added, 'Perhaps it'd make him sleep a bit longer.'

'Listen, how about if I come over again for a few days? Just to take the pressure off for a bit? I'm not at the Project again until after New Year, and I can easily . . .'

'Thanks, Mum, but you've helped out enough already. Marcus still has another week's paternity leave, and anyway, I need to get used to coping on my own at some point.'

'Yes, but there's nothing wrong with having a little help, you know. Your body's been through a major trauma, your hormones are all over the place and your routine's changed beyond recognition. It all takes a while to get used to.'

She appeared to think about it for a minute, then shook her head. 'No, I need to . . . I'll be fine. We're still getting used to each other, I suppose. Come on, let's go and set this pud alight.'

We finally managed to settle Toby in his Moses basket and had just started eating when the phone rang. I noticed the almost fearful way Hannah glanced at Toby but mercifully, he stayed asleep.

'My mum,' Duncan said. 'Bound to be.' He looked at his watch. 'Earlier than usual, though.'

I smiled. 'Give her my love.' Estelle always called on Boxing Day. She went to her widowed sister for Christmas every year, then called us as soon as she got back to tell us how much Gina waffled on about her grandchildren, how the colour of her hair was less and less convincing and how much Gina drank before, during and after Christmas dinner.

'Hello, Merry Christmas!' Duncan said cheerily into the handset. 'Hello?' he said again. 'Hello?' He looked at the phone and then said 'Hello' once more before shrugging and hanging up. 'Probably a wrong number.'

'Do 1471,' I said. Hannah looked up sharply and I realised how anxious I sounded. 'I mean, this is the second time, isn't it?'

Duncan tapped out the numbers. 'The caller withheld their number,' he repeated, putting the handset back in the charger. 'I'd better ring my mum, just in case.' No one spoke until we heard him talking to Estelle and explaining why he'd rung her rather than waiting for her to ring us as usual.

*

After lunch, I suggested Hannah and I go for a walk, leaving Duncan and Marcus to finish loading the dishwasher and make the kitchen look less like a bomb had hit it. Hannah put her coat, woolly hat, scarf and mittens on and then she stood at the door with her hands in her pockets while I got my boots on. It was still quite snowy outside. Toby was beginning to stir; I could hear him making little snuffling noises. 'Aren't you bringing the baby?' I picked up my keys from the yellow ceramic bowl that Hannah made at school. Her 'sunshine bowl', she called it.

'What? Oh, yes, I suppose so.' She took her coat off again, lifted him out of the Moses basket and laid him on the changing mat, then pulled a tiny coat from her bag and started trying to feed his arms into the sleeves without much success. She was biting her lip.

I hesitated for a moment – I didn't want her to think I was trying to take over, but she looked increasingly exasperated so I asked if she'd like some help. 'Thanks,' she sighed as she moved aside so I could get to him. 'How on earth am I supposed to get him dressed if he keeps wriggling like this? It's impossible.'

'Try reaching into the sleeve from the other end rather than trying to push his arm all the way through. Like this.' I bunched the sleeve up with both hands then gently reached inside the cuff with my fingers and guided Toby's hand through.

Hannah looked tearful. 'Why didn't I think of that? I'm so crap at this.'

'No, you're not.' I put my arms around her. 'You're doing fine. There's no reason you'd know to do that unless somebody told you. An Italian lady I used to work for showed me how to do it when you were tiny; someone else probably showed *her*.'

She sighed again.

'Come on, sweetheart. You can't know everything from the word go, you learn as you go along.'

She nodded but didn't look at me. Nor did she make any move to pick Toby up.

'I wish you'd let me do more to help.'

'You could take him in the sling, if you like.'

She knew that wasn't what I meant, but still. 'Come along, my little pickle.' I stretched my arms out to lift him and I held him against my chest while Hannah sorted out the complicated wrap-around carrier. Then she clipped Monty's lead on and we set off.

It was dark now, and we walked in companionable silence, breaking it only occasionally to comment on a pretty Christmas tree in a window, or an over-the-top display of lights. Monty paused every few metres to sniff at something interesting beneath the snow or to lift his leg against a tree. We turned into the narrow walkway that took us alongside the Porter Brook to the General Cemetery, a high stone wall on one side and the snow-covered bank leading down to the water on the other. The soft orange light from the lamp-posts spilled across the snow, giving the scene a slightly Dickensian feel. It started to snow again as we walked up through the cemetery towards the ruined church where we stopped for a moment to watch the flakes falling against a backdrop of ancient headstones and holly trees, complete with berries. I was conscious of the warm nugget of Toby against my chest. It was so quiet, all I could hear was the sound of Monty snuffling in the snow. 'It's beautiful, isn't it?' I said, but as we stood there watching the silent snow settling like a quilt around us, I was aware of a sudden feeling of desolation. Here I was with my daughter and my new grandson, about to go back to a warm house and a husband who loved me, and yet I felt as though a cold, black fog had enveloped me; the awful sense that nothing was safe. What if I lost all this? What if it was all taken away? I looked over my shoulder and back towards the church, but everything looked the same. Why then, did I feel so unsettled?

CHAPTER FOUR

While Hannah and I were out with the baby on Boxing Day, Duncan and Marcus had cooked up the idea of a small New Year's Eve gathering. I wasn't much of a party person, but I found I was enjoying myself, and having lots of friends and family around made up for not being able to celebrate my real birthday. For my fake fiftieth, Duncan took me to Edinburgh; a boutique hotel with an enormous bed, luxury toiletries and fluffy white bathrobes. We did the touristy things – a whisky-tasting, a guided literary walk, a ride in an open-topped bus, and then a meal in a restaurant where the food was so beautiful we weren't sure whether to eat it or admire it. He said I looked fabulous, that he could hardly believe I was fifty; then he gave me a pair of pearl earrings and told me that marrying me was the best thing he'd ever done. I had to turn away then; I felt nothing short of treacherous. Duncan was a good man, and, although I tried to be a better person these days, I knew I didn't deserve him.

Hannah was talking to our old friends Marina and Paul. She still had dark circles under her eyes, but she'd put on some make-up, and she was dressed in a purple cable-knit jumper over a green miniskirt with purple tights and black suede boots; she looked a lot better. Marina held her arms out to take the baby and Hannah obliged, then came over to us. 'Bloody hell,' she whispered. 'If one more person tells me how much he looks like his father, I'll scream.'

'Well, he does,' Duncan said and I shot him a look.

'I had hoped my children would look like me, at least a little bit.'

At that point, Duncan got it. 'Sorry, Han.' He patted Hannah's shoulder. 'That was insensitive.'

Hannah shrugged. 'Forget it.'

'You okay?'

Hannah nodded and managed a small smile, though her face was tense and full of shadows, just like it had been a couple of years ago during that horrible time when they were trying to find out what was wrong, when her sweet young face had been lined with worry and haunted with fear. She'd rung me as soon as they left the consultant's office and she was crying so much it was difficult to make out what she was saying. 'They said . . . they said I've got . . .'

For one awful moment I thought they'd told her she had something terminal. Fear shot through my body like a steel bolt, pinning me to the spot. 'Darling, please tell me. What did they say?'

Marcus came on the line. He sounded pretty shaken. 'They reckon she's got something called premature ovarian failure. It means that her eggs are—' Then I heard Hannah take the phone back again. 'Mum, I'm going through the fucking menopause. I'm thirty-one, for fuck's sake. And my eggs are . . . are dying.'

I felt tears spring to my eyes. 'Oh Hannah. Oh darling, I don't know what to say.' I could hear her trying to stifle her tears. 'They say it can run in families, but you managed to get pregnant when you were forty-three. Hang on.' I heard her blow her nose, then sigh. 'Sorry, I didn't mean . . . I shouldn't have brought it up.'

I tried to gather myself; I was still trying to take it in. 'No, no, it's fine.'

'Mum, can we come round?'

They sat in the kitchen, pale and red-eyed from crying. Monty positioned himself at Hannah's feet and laid his head in her lap while she absent-mindedly played with his ears. I made tea, remembering to add lots of sugar. Once, when Hannah was five, she pirouetted off the table in our bedsit and broke her collarbone. The landlady drove us to the hospital, stayed with us and drove us home again, and then while I put Hannah to bed, she made me a cup of tea. 'There we are, love, nice and sweet.' In a still-shaky voice, I thanked her but told her I didn't take sugar. 'You do today,' she said. And I remembered

Scott making us both sugary tea that time all those years before, and I remembered that it helped.

'How old was your mum when she died?' Hannah said, sipping the tea and grimacing at the sweetness.

'Forty-one.'

'And did she . . . ? Was she still . . .'

'I'm sorry, darling,' I sighed. 'Mothers and daughters didn't discuss things like that back then. And my mum had other problems, as you know, so it was difficult to talk about anything.' I felt dizzy so I pulled out a chair and sat down. Nothing could change the situation, so what was the point of talking about family histories?

'I'm glad we can talk about things,' Hannah said. 'Most of my friends just moan about their mums.'

'I'm glad, too.' I took a gulp of my tea, burning my mouth. 'So . . . is there anything they can do? I mean to help you have a baby?' I'd often half hoped that Hannah wouldn't want kids, because much as I loved the idea of grandchildren, I couldn't shake off the crippling anxiety every time I thought about her giving birth. My greatest fear had always been of losing Hannah – my precious only child. I couldn't bear seeing her like this. I remembered my own misery each month when my period came, and when it didn't come, the delirious happiness, followed by the utter despair when the pains started a few weeks later.

'Seems like we've got two options,' she said. 'We can adopt, but there's a long wait for babies, or we could try to find an egg donor.'

'But . . .'

'IVF. We'd still use Marcus's sperm, but my eggs are no good, apparently, so we'd need donated eggs.'

'Which is expensive,' Marcus added, ' and might not work.' He was leaning forward in his chair, head down, twisting his car keys round and round in his hands. He was the same age as Hannah but he looked incredibly young and vulnerable at that moment.

We all sat in silence while I digested this. Hannah appeared to have stopped crying, but every now and again she swiped at her face as another tear slid down it.

'We'll help with the money,' I said. 'If you want to go ahead?'

She nodded and reached for Marcus's hand. 'We do,' she said, 'we really do.' Tearful again but smiling, she got up and put her arms round me. 'Thanks, Mum.'

Duncan had agreed, of course. He'd just been made a partner in the practice, which was on the outskirts of Sheffield and had business from farms and riding stables as well as the usual cats, dogs and hamsters, so he'd had quite a big pay rise, and he was delighted to have something worthwhile to do with it. And when, after the first attempt failed, the second resulted in a single pregnancy that was still perfectly healthy four months on, Hannah's happiness was the supreme reward. Pregnancy suited her, too, especially in the later stages when she positively glowed with health. The way she looked, the way she carried herself in those last few weeks was almost majestic.

Looking at her now, it was hard to believe that this was the same person as that smiling, energetic young woman.

Someone called to Duncan from the kitchen and he went off to do hosting duties. 'Marina says,' Hannah continued, 'that all babies look like their fathers. She says it's something to do with nature protecting the young, or something.'

'I read that somewhere, too. The idea is that, if a child looks like its father, the father has proof of his paternity and is more likely to stay around to protect the child, less likely to bugger off and leave the mother to it.'

Hannah nodded, looking thoughtful. 'Do I look like my father?'

This floored me for a second; she hadn't mentioned her father for years. An image of that man in Marks & Spencer's the other day flitted across my mind. He reminded me so much of Scott that I found I'd been thinking about the past much more than usual. I looked at Hannah, her hair, which she'd had cut into a sleek bob before she had Toby, was dark but not coal-black like Scott's had been; her tall, slim build was the same though, and so were the almond-shaped eyes, cornflower-blue rather than the brown you always expected with dark hair. I swallowed. 'Yes, you do a bit.' I braced myself for her to ask more but she just nodded, then rolled her eyes when she realised that Toby was crying again and went off to see to him.

CHAPTER FIVE

Sometimes I almost forgot Duncan wasn't Hannah's real dad. Partly wishful thinking, I suppose – I *wanted* him to be her father; I wanted to forget Scott had ever existed. Hannah had started calling Duncan 'Daddy' when she was eight or nine. We'd been married for over a year, but we'd only just moved into our first real home together. We were all in the sitting room, still surrounded by boxes of books and CDs and videos, eating the pizza we'd had delivered. Hannah wrinkled her nose as she looked at her slice of pizza. 'It's got mushrooms on it,' she said in disgust. 'I hate mushrooms.'

'I used to hate mushrooms as well.' Duncan's face was deadly serious. 'When I was a little girl like you.'

Hannah listened in earnest for a moment, then grinned. 'You're silly.'

'Come on then, pipsqueak.' He held his plate out. 'Give us them here. I'll swap you for the capers – you like capers, don't you?'

Hannah's face fell and she shook her head before wrinkling her nose again and announcing, 'They're like bogies!'

'Yum!' Duncan said, picking up a caper and popping it into his mouth. 'That's why I love 'em.'

'Yuk!' Hannah squealed, but she was giggling.

Later, when Duncan and I had gone back to the unpacking, Hannah came down in her pyjamas. Usually, she'd say goodnight to Duncan, then I'd go up with her to read her a story and tuck her in. But that night when she shuffled into the room with her thumb in her mouth, she came over to where I was kneeling on the floor unpacking a box of books, took her thumb out of her mouth and leaned across so that her mouth was almost against my ear. 'Mummy,' she whispered.

'Yes?' I whispered back.

'Can Duncan come and tuck me in tonight?'

'What?' I whispered in mock horror. 'Instead of me?'

She shook her head vigorously. 'No. *And* you.'

I smiled. 'Only teasing. Yes, I'm sure he will. You go and hop into bed and we'll be up in a minute.'

She nodded. 'Okay. And Mummy.' She was still whispering, although it was a bit of a stage whisper by now.

'Yes, darling?'

'Duncan's my daddy-by-marriage, isn't he?'

'Yes. He's your stepdad.' We'd gone through this before the wedding, with the help of some useful story books. Then last year, when her friend Amber's mum had had another baby, we'd had a bit of a birds and bees discussion in which I'd explained that her biological father lived a long way away and that we hadn't seen him since she was a baby. I wasn't sure how well she understood why he was so far away, but what she did understand was that Duncan did all the things a dad would do, and that he loved her.

'My stepdad.' She nodded again, earnestly. 'So am I allowed to call him *Daddy*?'

'Oh darling, of course you're allowed. Do you really want to?'

She nodded.

'Well, I think Duncan would be very pleased to have you call him *Daddy*.' I smiled as I glanced at Duncan, who by this time was looking curious as to what conspiracies were taking place on this side of the room.

'Okay,' she whispered again, and then she walked over to Duncan and said, clearly and confidently, 'Daddy, will you come and tuck me in, please?'

I watched Duncan swallow and cough to disguise the break in his voice. 'Course I will, pipsqueak,' he said, ruffling her hair. 'I'll be there in a minute.'

'Bloody hell,' he said after she'd trotted happily back upstairs, thumb in mouth. 'That's a turn-up for the books.'

'I think you've cracked it.' I put my arms around him.

He squeezed me back and kissed my head.

*

'Come on, everybody,' Duncan shouted. 'Can we all move into the garden, please. Time for some big bangs!' We weren't waiting until midnight to do the fireworks because it would have been too late for the younger children, and Estelle needed to go to bed before then anyway. She was nearly ninety, but still stood almost as tall as Duncan and never appeared in public without carefully applied make-up and a string of pearls. People were surprised when they learned that she was his mother. Duncan was, Estelle always said, *a change baby – unexpected, but very welcome.* We all shuffled outside. There was still snow here and there but it wasn't as bitterly cold as it had been recently. Duncan and Marcus were down at the end of the garden by the shed, and we all stood in huddles on the terrace with our drinks, waiting while they set up the first fireworks. There was a scratching sound on the glass behind me and I turned to see Monty sitting the other side of the sliding door in his 'I'm a good dog' position. 'No,' I shouted through the glass. 'You won't like this; go and lie down.' His brown eyes looked up at me as he listened intently to what I was saying, then he turned and padded back to his bed where he slumped down and rested his head on his paws with a resigned expression. He did everything I asked him to because he trusted me implicitly. Sometimes, even the dog could make me feel unworthy.

'Here we go, folks!' Marcus shouted, jogging over to where the rest of us were standing. We all made lots of 'ooh' and 'aah' noises as the fireworks started to fizz and spit, then there were whistles and bangs; a Roman Candle shot a red flame that changed to green and orange and purple, and a few feet away a Silver Fountain was spilling millions of twinkling stars down onto the grass. Everyone smiled and clapped, and for a moment I pretended this was my fiftieth and we were celebrating my birthday and I didn't have to tell lies any more.

'Cheers!' Duncan appeared beside me and clinked his glass against mine. 'This is great, isn't it? We should make more of New Year in future. Let's hope this year is a good one for all of us.'

Despite my thick coat and woollen scarf, I was over-taken by a sudden shiver so violent I spilt my drink. 'Steady on.' Duncan moved behind me, opened his big winter jacket and pulled me close, wrapping it around me. 'How's that?' he said into my hair. 'Better?'

I nodded and snuggled into his warmth.

The fireworks were a huge success. Just after eleven, Estelle declared she was a little tiddly and blew everyone kisses from the door before heading up to bed. I loved Estelle, really loved her. I'd had a few other boyfriends before I met Duncan, but even if they were okay about Hannah, their mothers weren't. Estelle, on the other hand, had adored her immediately and insisted she call her *Grandma* from the off. I'd felt almost as much pride in reporting Hannah's progress and achievements to Estelle as I would have to my own mum, had she been alive. When I was little, my parents addressed their mothers-in-law as 'Mum' because it was considered good manners in those days; I'd have been happy to do the same with Estelle.

The remaining guests were chatting and laughing in the kitchen, so I nipped into the sitting room, plumped the cushions and put more logs into the wood burner. A bluesy jazz CD was playing to an empty room, but we'd be putting the radio on soon so we could hear the chimes. I glanced at my watch, and just as I registered that there was a little over ten minutes to go, the phone rang. My stomach crawled; a call at this time of night could only mean trouble. But then I realised that all the people I loved were here, safely under this roof. I looked around for the handset, but the ringing stopped. Then I heard Duncan come out into the hall, away from the hubbub of chatter in the kitchen. 'Hello?' he said, his voice still carrying the trails of laughter from his last conversation. 'Hello?' He sounded upbeat, cheerful, as if he was still chatting to friends. 'Hell-o once more. No? Okay then, silent caller. It's not midnight yet, so if you've called to wish us a happy New Year, please call again. By-ee.' He hung up and went chuckling back to the others. Definitely a wrong number, then. It wasn't that unusual, I supposed, someone calling their family on New Year's Eve, hearing an unfamiliar voice and ringing off rather than wasting time with an explanation. He'd left the handset on the stairs. I picked it up and dialled 1471. I could hear my own heartbeat as I held my breath. *You were called, today, at 11.49. The caller withheld their number.*

*

That night I dreamt that Hannah was dead. She was in tiny pieces and I calmly collected them all up, put them in a shoebox and took them to the hospital, where I was convinced they would simply fix her, put her back together again. When the nurses looked inside the box and shook their heads, the enormity of it began to dawn on me: my Hannah was dead; it was *final*. Even though I knew in the dream that I hadn't killed her, I also knew that I was responsible and that I could never, ever go back and change what had happened. I woke with a jolt and my eyes snapped open. My breath felt trapped in my lungs and I could feel my heart thumping away as if it was trying to escape from my chest. It was only after I'd been downstairs for a glass of water that the horror began to dissipate and I started to feel calmer.

'Hey,' Duncan murmured as I slid back into bed beside him. 'What's the matter?' But his eyes were still closed.

'Bad dream,' I whispered, moving closer, comforted by his warmth, the safe, man-smell of him. Soon, he was breathing evenly again and I was alone, trying to work out why I felt so edgy. It was that still, timeless moment before the dawn, when reality and dreams merged together like sea and sky on a misty morning. I tried to empty my mind, but as soon as I started to drift towards sleep, my thoughts became images and for some reason I found myself back there, in the Hastings house. For a fraction of a second, instead of lying on a comfortable bed in a centrally heated, carpeted room, I was back on the battered mattress that Eve and I found on a skip, looking up at the dream-catcher hanging from the ceiling in front of the window. No thick, light-blocking curtains then, just an Indian cotton wrap, the red one with the gold embroidery, turning the sunlight crimson as it flooded the room, warming the floorboards and filling the air with the smell of old wood.

I looked around in the dark. I could make out the familiar shapes of my dressing gown hanging on the back of the door, the wardrobe with Hannah's old teddy bear still sitting on top, and the chest of drawers with Duncan's squash racquet resting up against the side. *I am lying in bed with my husband,* I told myself, *in a proper house with a mortgage and respectable neighbours. Hannah and her little family are safely asleep in the next room; all is well.* I turned over to go to sleep but my mind wouldn't slow down. It was as though there were several films running in my head at the same time, all in colour, all with the sound turned up. I curled onto my side, threw the covers off and then felt chilly and pulled them back up again. I could feel myself beginning to drift but, although I kept slipping in and out of dreams, I was still aware of the sleet smattering against the window and of Duncan breathing steadily next to me. I sighed and changed position yet again, and that's when I saw it. At first, it was a giant crow standing over me, tall and black and sinister. Then it moved slightly and it became Scott; he was wearing a black top hat and a dark cloak folded around his body like wings. 'Go away,' I said, only the sound didn't come out, and I realised that my eyes were still closed. I knew that, if I could only open them, he'd be gone.

CHAPTER SIX

I went back to the Project a few days into January, mornings only this year because I wanted to make sure I could be on hand for Hannah if she needed me. My first day back was pretty depressing. Christmas had plunged many of my families into hideous debt, and they were so bogged down by financial worry that the day-to-day business of parenting became even more difficult and exhausting. We could help them keep their creditors at bay and navigate their way through a hostile benefits system, but we couldn't do much to help them significantly in the long-term. What most of them needed more than anything was someone to offer practical help; another pair of hands, someone to absorb some of the responsibility. Sometimes, I wanted to ask where their mothers were.

Some of my colleagues said they found their clients resented them, or at least, resented their middle-class, financially comfortable lives. But I could honestly tell my families that I knew what it was like; I'd been there; I understood how it felt not to know where next week's rent was coming from and to be dealing with it on your own. But I could also tell them that it didn't have to be that way for ever, that things could change, life could improve. They looked at my clothes and my car and they assumed money had never been an issue for me, so I told them about when Hannah was a baby and we'd lived in a grotty flat above a shoe shop where I worked on the days Scott didn't, and how he'd buggered off leaving us with no money the day before the rent was due. I was seventeen. We paid ten quid a week for that flat – two rooms and a shared bathroom. I spent the next three weeks hiding from the landlord until I managed to find a job where they'd let me take Hannah with me. It was easier in those days, though, before this obsession with health and safety. I pushed her in her pram up and down the high street, going in and out of all the shops until I ended up at a coffee bar called the Continental. The owners, an Italian couple called Mr and Mrs Sartori, fell in love with Hannah and said they'd set up a playpen for her in the back room where I could keep an eye on her and where she could play safely when we were busy. You wouldn't get that now. Mrs Sartori was brilliant. She adored Hannah, and she treated me like one of her own daughters. It was she who taught me to cook, really. I still make her minestrone soup and the crispy little bread rolls flavoured with rosemary and olive oil to go with it. But the best thing about Mrs Sartori was the way she helped me with Hannah, and how she always knew the right thing to do. She showed me how to sponge her down to reduce her temperature when she had a fever, and how to keep her upright to reduce the pain when she had an ear infection. And if I was tired after a bad night with Hannah, she'd take her out in the pram so I could get some sleep, because, she said, *The tired mamma not a happy mamma, and bambini not-a happy if the mamma not-a happy.*

This morning, I'd found Lauren, a young mum who had her second child just before Hannah had Toby, in floods of tears because the baby had a sore bottom and she blamed herself. She was so tired when she got up in the night to change him that she hadn't noticed his nappy rash and so hadn't put any cream on him, and now, the way she saw it was that her child was suffering and it was all her fault. Lauren was only just getting used to being on her own with her two kids, the dad having left her when the baby was three days old. The poor girl was on her knees with tiredness, not to mention financial worry. Where was her mum, that's what I wanted to know. We weren't supposed to probe too deeply into our families' back-grounds, but it seemed Lauren's mum was retired and only lived about half an hour away, so why couldn't she spend some time helping her daughter? I was still think-ing about this as I drove home, and there was a tight ball of anger in my stomach, possibly because Lauren reminded me a little of Hannah. I was suddenly overcome with an urgent desire to see my daughter. I flicked on the indicator, pulled over and took out my phone. 'Are you in?' I said when Hannah answered. 'I'm on my way home and I wondered if you needed any shopping or anything.'

She sounded a bit fed up. She didn't know what she needed from the shops, she said. She couldn't even think straight at the moment because they'd been up half the night with Toby – he had colic. She was shattered.

'Listen,' I said, pretty sure she'd say no – I knew how hard it was for new mums to let their babies out of their sight in the first few weeks. 'I'm having lunch with Grandma today; can I persuade you to let me take Toby with me? Dad says the car seat will go in my car easily enough. Grandma would be over the moon, and it'd give you a couple of hours to get some sleep.' To my surprise, she said yes almost eagerly. She'd feed him now, and she'd thaw some expressed milk in case he needed a top-up.

*

Estelle's face lit up when she saw I'd brought Toby. I kissed her cheek and, as always, the smell of Nivea triggered a wave of longing for my own mother. As usual, Estelle was fully made up and dressed as though we'd be eating in a restaurant. I always felt flattered that she'd made so much effort, and I tried to dress nicely whenever I visited her in order to return the compliment. Today she was wearing a floral skirt with a contrasting green jacket and a carefully chosen pink silk scarf. She radiated a calm beauty.

Hannah had said Toby would be bound to want feeding again before too long, but he was quiet for the moment, so I put the kettle on for coffee while Estelle prepared the lunch. 'Nothing fancy,' she said, 'just a bit of bread and cheese.' We sat at the kitchen table where she cut up a fresh baguette and put it into a basket, then arranged the selection of fine cheeses she'd bought from Waitrose onto a board and even added bunches of black grapes so that it looked like something you'd order in a good restaurant. Toby was dozing peacefully in his car seat, which I'd put at the other end of the table so we could keep an eye on him. 'Goodness,' Estelle said, leaning towards him. 'Look at the length of his eyelashes! He'll make the girls jealous, that's for sure.'

I smiled, and as we gazed at him, his lashes fluttered in his sleep. I used to spend a lot of time watching Hannah sleep. 'I wonder what babies dream about?' I said as his raspberry-pink mouth twitched into a windy smile and then relaxed again; there was a tiny white blister on his upper lip.

'Milk, probably,' Estelle said, with an air of resignation. 'I seem to remember that the business of caring for young babies has a great deal to do with putting food in at one end and cleaning up what comes out of the other! Goodness, I don't know how we get through it, any one of us.' She gave an exaggerated shudder, then tilted her head to one side as she looked at me. 'It's hard, isn't it? Watching your child struggling with her own baby; it brings it all back.'

'Yes, it does a bit,' I sighed. 'I know it's a cliché, but they grow up so fast, don't they?' I went to the cupboard and took out the yellow cups and saucers that Estelle liked to use for coffee. 'I have to stop myself from telling Hannah what to do. In my head, she's still about eight.'

Estelle nodded. 'Especially daughters.' She cut pats of butter from a half-pound pack and put them into a ramekin. 'Julie was only twenty when she had her first, as you know.' She knew I got on well with my sister-in-law, and I think she imagined that we'd shared confidences. 'But she fell into it like an old hand. She was a good little mother, like you were.'

'Hey, what do you mean, *were*?' I teased.

'Sons are a different kettle of fish, you see.' She shook her head and chuckled. 'Truth be told, I think John and Duncan would have still had me tying their shoelaces at that age if they could have got away with it.'

I smiled. 'Hannah was the opposite. She was trying to dress herself at the age of two and she'd get very cross with me if I tried to help.' I set the cafetière down on the table and pulled out a chair. I enjoyed these moments of womanly camaraderie with my mother-in-law. 'You know, I don't think I realised I'd still be worrying about her even now; I think I sort of assumed—'

'Oh, you don't get off that lightly.' She chuckled again. 'I still worry about all three of them, and here's Duncan, a grandad himself now.'

'And John and Alice have a grandchild due in the summer, don't they?' I reminded her.

Estelle gave another of her famous shudders. 'Two sons who are grandfathers – as if I didn't feel old enough already!' But then a faraway expression settled on her face and she absent-mindedly twiddled her rings, which all hung loose on her fingers but were kept in place by the swollen knuckles. On her wedding finger were her engagement ring and a gold band so thin now that it looked as though it could snap; on her middle finger were three eternity rings – Duncan's dad had bought her one on the birth of each child. I poured the coffee and pushed it towards her, together with the sugar bowl. She added a spoonful of sugar and stirred it round several times before tapping the teaspoon twice on the side of the cup and placing it neatly in the saucer. She looked thoughtful.

Toby shifted in his seat and screwed his face up but didn't open his eyes. We both looked at him and waited, but then his face relaxed and he made a few sucking motions before drifting back to sleep.

'You know, dear, I sometimes think motherhood is the best and worst thing that can happen to a woman.'

'How do you mean?'

'Life is so very short, even when you reach a great age, such as I have.' Her hand was shaky as she raised her cup to her carefully painted lips and took a sip of coffee. I waited for her to continue, but she seemed to drift for a moment, as though some unexpected memory had slid into her mind.

'Estelle, what did you mean?'

Her eyes focused on me again. 'I'm sorry, darling?'

'About motherhood being the worst thing that can happen to a woman.'

'Oh, yes, well. I just meant that it's all so temporary, you see; the joy of it. One minute, you're a brand-new mother with your brand-new baby that you grew inside you – you're the centre of one another's worlds, and you know you will do anything for your child. It's the most complete and perfect type of love. And then the next minute . . .'

She had that faraway look again. I'd seen photographs of Estelle as a young mother, and then as an older mum after she had Duncan. She'd always been a good-looking woman, not pretty, exactly, but handsome. And in all the pictures, whether she was posing in a studio, perfectly groomed and wearing a hat and gloves while holding a freshly washed and combed child on her lap, or whether she was on a beach in an old skirt and with her hair tied back while the kids built sandcastles, she positively glowed with love and pride as she looked at her children. *A complete and perfect love.* The thought triggered a memory of the exact moment I'd realised how important Hannah was to me. I'd been giving her a bottle and she had her hand curled around my little finger; I looked into those cornflower-blue eyes and I suddenly knew that, if I had to, I would kill with my bare hands to protect her.

'Your children have your love and devotion for ever, you see, until you die. But you only have theirs for a limited time. Now, I don't mean that they stop caring about you, but I've learned this, and so must you.' She looked over her glasses at me almost sternly. 'Once your children have their own children, the balance alters. And it's only right and proper that it should.'

'Yes, of course.' I knew she was right, but I wasn't ready to acknowledge it yet, not really. 'But Hannah still asks for my advice.'

Estelle smiled and shook her head. 'There, you see? That's what I mean about it being the best and worst. Heavens, I still worry about my children and two of them are grandparents! But although they look after me,' she rested her dry, cool hand on my arm, 'you all do; you're all so very good to me – they don't ask for my opinion or advice any more; if something goes wrong, instead of asking me what they should do about it, they hide it from me so I shan't worry.' She tutted and took another sip of her coffee, and a little of it ran down her chin but she didn't notice.

'But that's because we love you. Of course we don't want you to worry.' But she was right; we kept things from her that maybe we shouldn't.

'Of course, dear, I know *why* it happens – it's the natural order of things. But that's what I mean about the balance altering. When they're young, we care for our children, we protect them and we pass our wisdom on to them; in return, they adore us and look up to us; we are the very centre of their world. But gradually the way it works changes; our children start caring for us, taking responsibility and protecting us. And then we realise we have no more wisdom to pass on because the world has changed and our wisdom is out of date. And then they have their own babies, and we realise that our children are now the ones who must pass down wisdom and be looked up to and adored, and we, sadly, are slowly fading from the picture, making way for the next in line.' She sighed a little shakily. 'Goodness, whatever's the matter with me. I'm becoming all maudlin, and we haven't even had a sherry yet.'

*

When I got home, Duncan was standing in the hallway with the phone in his hand and a slightly perturbed look on his face. He smiled when he saw me, and nodded towards the handset. 'That was another one. Another funny phone call. You haven't got yourself a secret lover, have you?' he said affably. 'You know, "if a man answers, hang up"?'

'Did you do 1471?' I tried to sound light, but I realised that there was an edge to my voice.

He shrugged, then picked up the handset again and punched in the numbers. 'Hmm, withheld number.'

I felt my blood cool.

CHAPTER SEVEN

On Sunday afternoon, we were getting ready to head off to the woods for a walk with Monty. I tried to persuade Hannah to join us but Marcus had taken Toby out so she was going to go back to bed for a while. Her voice sounded dull and flat; she hadn't been herself at all since Toby arrived. I'd always assumed she'd take motherhood in her stride. So had she, I think; my poor Hannah. I'd seen a lot of tired new mothers, but I'd begun to wonder if it might be more than that.

I was trying to tie the laces of my walking boots when a violent surge of nausea rose up inside me. I sat back heavily on the stairs; I could see slivers of light shooting downwards at the edge of my vision.

'Darling, are you all right?' Duncan was at my side in an instant. 'You've gone grey.'

It took me a moment to answer because I was concentrating on not throwing up. 'I'll be all right in a minute. I think it's a migraine tuning up. Could you grab my pills.'

He put his hand on my forehead, like I used to do with Hannah when she was little and I was checking for a fever. 'I didn't know you still got migraines.'

'I haven't had one for ages. I don't know why it should start again now.'

Duncan handed me a pink pill and a glass of water. Usually, that was enough to stop it, but if the pink pill didn't do the trick, I had to take one of the yellow ones.

Monty was walking round and round in circles, his claws click-clicking on the wooden floor. Duncan hadn't put his boots on yet and was standing there in his socks, looking concerned.

'I'd better stay here,' I said. 'You go ahead. I just need to lie down for a while.'

Duncan looked at me for a moment. 'You sure you'll be all right?' Again he rested his palm on my forehead and it was so soothing, I wished he could keep it there.

'I'll be fine. Hopefully it won't get a grip. A couple of hours lying down in a darkened room'll sort me out.'

Monty started to make impatient little noises. 'Okay, fella.' Duncan picked up the lead and Monty began leaping up to try and catch it in his mouth. Then he started jumping in ecstatic circles until Duncan told him firmly to 'sit!' which he did instantly, tail thumping the floor, mouth open and smiling as he looked excitedly from one to the other of us. Duncan caught hold of his collar and clipped his lead on, at which point Monty almost pulled him off his feet in the rush to get to the door.

I stayed where I was until the front door closed behind them and silence settled around me. Then I turned and climbed the stairs slowly, on my hands and knees. I couldn't move too fast because I could sense rather than feel the actual headache, there on the edge of my brain, poised like a predator ready to strike. I felt as though I was pitched against it, that if I could just crawl into bed without making any sudden movements I might avoid its wrath, but if I tilted the thing into action, it would attack, knives slashing at my head without mercy.

In the bedroom, I turned back the duvet then lowered my head carefully onto the pillow and shut my eyes. Little pinpricks of light popped and fizzled around the edge of my vision, even though my eyes were closed, and the nausea rose and fell, rose and fell. I lay there, motion-less, grateful for the thickness of the curtains and the stillness of the afternoon, willing the pills to kick in. So far, I still wasn't feeling actual pain, but the tentacles were sliding ever nearer and I tried not to think about the possibility of a disabling three-dayer.

I wasn't sure how long I'd been lying there when the phone went, each ring jabbing into my poor fragile brain. I lay still and tense, willing it to stop and trying to remember how many times it would ring before the voicemail kicked in. When it stopped, the silence sort of twinkled for a moment, and I felt my body relax. The phone rang again almost immediately, causing my body to tense and the nausea to start swirling inside me. I held my breath and counted the rings, six, seven, eight. Then blissful silence, but only for a few seconds before it started again. Slowly, I levered myself up using my elbow. The room was darker than before, but it wasn't completely dark outside yet, which meant Duncan hadn't been out for long. Maybe something was wrong. The ringing stopped again, and this time I simply braced myself for it to resume, cursing the fact that I hadn't brought the handset from downstairs and put it next to the bed. A sequence of pictures flashed though my head: Hannah had collapsed with an unknown illness; the baby wasn't breathing; Duncan had had a heart attack or slipped on the ice and broken his leg; Monty had chased a squirrel into the road and been run over. Sure enough, the ringing started again. Still moving slowly, I swung my legs round and put my feet on the floor, then I stood up and walked across the room.

'Hello?' I was aware that my voice sounded anxious. Duncan was always telling me off about it. He said I always sounded like I was expecting bad news.

'Jo?'

I froze. No one had called me by that name for over thirty years. My fingers gripped the phone more tightly as another thick wave of nausea swayed inside me. I wanted to hang up but I was paralysed. I wasn't sure if I was going to be sick or if I was going to faint, but right at that moment I felt very, very ill, like I might die. I leant back against the wall as my knees buckled and I allowed myself to sink down onto the carpet.

'Jo?' he said again. 'Look, I know you're there.'

I recognised his voice, even though it sounded softer, weaker than I remembered. So it *was* him I saw in Marks & Spencer's that day.

'Listen, please don't be scared. I know your husband has gone out—'

I hit the *End call* button and slammed the handset into its cradle, the sudden movement sending a missile of pain deep into my skull. He must have been watching the house. Oh dear God, why? What did he want? I sat there on the landing with the warm carpet thick and comforting beneath me and I put my hands out to steady myself as though I was on a boat that might tip me into the freezing water at any moment. I could feel my heart thudding and panic rising in my throat. The phone rang again. I stared at it until it stopped, eight rings. But then it rang again, and again. I could have unplugged the main phone downstairs, but something told me he wasn't going to give up, and if he knew where I lived . . . On the next ring, I picked up.

'Don't hang up,' he said. 'Please, Jo. We have to talk.' He sounded desperate.

'We can't talk,' I said. 'Ever.' And I was about to hang up again when he said, 'Jo, for God's sake listen.'

'That's not my name,' I breathed. 'You know it isn't.'

'You might have to get used to it again,' he said.

'Wha—'

'Look, I need to see you. I have something to say and I need to say it in person. When can we meet?'

'Scott, we can't meet. We agreed when you left. I have

a husband; I have a completely new life. I thought you did, too. I thought you were in New Zealand.'

'I did; I was. But I've been back in the UK for a few years now. I was in London for a while, but now . . . Jo, I'm dying.'

I half laughed. It was the sort of thing he'd have said when he'd wanted one of us to roll him a joint or make him some tea.

'I mean it. I'm ill; cancer. There's a tumour in my stomach and there's nothing more they can do. I have a few months at most, maybe less.'

I was listening now, of course I was. He wouldn't lie about such a thing, would he? The pain throbbed behind my eye as I tried to guess what this meant. He'd sworn he would never . . . but if he was dying . . .

'Jo? Are you still there?'

'Scott, I'm sorry, but we agreed, no contact, no matter what—'

'I know that's what we agreed, but things change, Jo, and anyway—'

'Don't keep calling me that.'

'And anyway, that's not what I want to see you about. Listen, he'll be back soon, your husband.'

I felt the anger rise in my throat. I wanted to scream at him but my head would explode if I shouted so I tried to control my voice. 'You've been following me around the town and now you're watching my house? You're *stalking* me? Look, Scott, I'm sorry if your life hasn't worked out—'

'I'm not quite dead yet.'

'I didn't mean that. I meant, look, I've made a good life for Hannah. Duncan has been a good father to her, and you . . . you said . . .' I could feel my voice rising and I had to make a conscious effort not to lose control, not to scream and shout and cry. 'You said you wouldn't do this. You swore you'd never contact us – *Tell her I'm dead,* you said. The only reason I didn't is because she'd have probably wanted to see your grave.' A big boulder of pain rolled to the front of my head with a thud.

'I know.' He spoke quietly, calmly. 'But things are different now. When can we meet? Do you have a free day this week? Or an afternoon?'

'No. I'm not meeting you. You have to go away; you have to leave me alone.'

'Or what? You'll call the police?' There was a silence that felt full up, like swollen black clouds before a thunderstorm. 'Jo.' His voice was gentle, almost tender. 'I'm sorry, but I'm not going to let this go.'

I was still hanging on to the carpet as though I might fall off the landing into thin air. Neither of us said anything, but I could sense him there on the other end of the line, waiting. After a few more seconds of silence, I realised why he was waiting so patiently – it was because he knew there was nothing I could do; that I really didn't have any choice. 'All right,' I said, and as I spoke, I felt a sudden stab of vulnerability, as though I'd just unleashed something destructive and must now brace myself for the consequences. I took a breath and tried to steady my voice. 'I suppose I could meet you at lunchtime on

Wednesday, or any time on Friday – I'm off work then, anyway.'

'Friday's cool. As long as you don't have anything else to do in the afternoon, because I think you're going to need some time to yourself afterwards. You'll want some time to think.'

'Scott, I'm sorry you're ill.' I paused. He was only a few years older than me; early fifties at most. And the last time I'd seen him – well, apart from when I saw him in town before Christmas – he'd looked so strong, so *alive*. 'I mean,' I said more softly, 'I really am sorry. But can't you just tell me what this is about?'

'Not on the phone, not when your husband's due back any minute. Trust me.'

'Oh, for heaven's sake. All right. Make it Friday morning.'

'Okay. And listen, we'd better swap mobile numbers – I'm guessing you'd rather keep this between us for the time being?'

My instinct was to refuse but on the other hand I didn't want him calling the house again, so I gave him my number and wrote his on a Post-it note which I peeled off and put in my pocket.

'Cool. I'll meet you at ten. There's a church I go to sometimes—'

'A church? Which—'

'I'll text you the address. See you at ten, and Jo, if you don't turn up, well, as I say, I'm not letting this go. It's in your interests to hear what I have to say. See you there.'

And he rang off.

CHAPTER EIGHT

I found myself looking at the phone as if there was some answer hidden in there somewhere. Finally, I replaced it in its holder and walked carefully back into the bedroom. The migraine was kicking in properly now, flashing lights and all. I sank down against the cool pillows and closed my eyes. It hurt to think, but my mind wouldn't be still. What on earth could it be that he couldn't tell me on the phone? 'Oh God,' I murmured aloud, but the effort of making a sound called up another bombardment of pain, so I said it in my head: *Oh God oh God oh God*. I raised myself up on one arm and shifted my body so that I could bury my face in the pillow but the pain sliced behind my eyes again. Just then I heard Duncan's key in the door, followed by the sound of Monty's lead being hung up and then his claws on the kitchen floor as he trotted over to his water bowl. I heard Duncan coming softly up the stairs. He paused at the bedroom door. I realised I was holding my breath. After a few seconds, he whispered, 'Are you awake?'

For a moment, I considered pretending to be asleep, but then I raised my hand slowly and waved. Duncan came over and sat on the bed, gently pulling the duvet back so he could see my face. 'How are you feeling?' he said. 'You still look rough.'

'Awful,' I whispered. 'It's a bad one.'

'Right, you stay there. Can I bring you anything? Pills? Tea? Water?'

'Water, please, and could you bring me the yellow pills.'

'Oh dear. That bad?' He kissed me on the top of the head, covered me up with the duvet again and went downstairs. For a moment, I was overcome with longing for my mother. Not as she was at the end, but as she'd been when I was little and I had mumps or measles or something, and she'd sit by my bed, tucking the duvet around me, stroking my hair and making sure I was comfortable. I sighed and closed my eyes again. I tried to empty my mind by picturing Scott and then drawing a black velvet curtain across the image so that there was nothing there but blackness. But then I remembered it was Eve who taught me how to do that, so then of course I started thinking about him again.

*

On Thursday night, I couldn't sleep. The shock of Scott's call had faded a little, but now, knowing it was Friday tomorrow, it was all coming back. I'd been in a state all day. This morning I took the toast out of the toaster and put it in the dishwasher instead of on a plate, and I was so distracted at work that the poor woman I was talking to actually asked me if I was all right, when she was the one whose child had just been diagnosed with leukaemia. This evening, Duncan caught me checking out of the window to see if Scott was watching the house. 'What you looking at?' he said, sliding his arm around my waist as he stood behind me. 'Or are we being nosy neighbours?'

But there had been no sign and apart from sending the address of the church by text, he hadn't been in touch again either. I looked at the numbers on the digital clock; it was almost two, and the alarm was set for seven, so even if I went to sleep within the next half-hour . . . Oh, stop it, I told myself; watching the clock like this only made insomnia worse.

I kept wondering what would happen if I didn't turn up, but then I remembered how desperate Scott had sounded and how he'd laboured the point that he wasn't going to let this go, whatever it was. As I lay there in the darkness, I kept turning it over in my mind. My first thought had been that he was going to demand to see Hannah, but if that was it, why wouldn't he have just said so? And would he bother to talk to me about it first anyway? He'd managed to find me easily enough, so I was sure he could find Hannah. Maybe he just wanted to know what I'd told her about him? Duncan snored softly and turned onto his side, facing me. I tried to put Scott out of my head as I moved closer to Duncan and curled into his warmth. Duncan had always made me feel safe. He slipped his arm around me without waking, and amazingly, I drifted into sleep.

In the morning, I felt calmer. Somehow, I'd managed to convince myself that I'd misunderstood, or misinterpreted, and that it was a simple matter of him wanting to leave Hannah something in his will. He may not even want to see her. Perhaps he didn't want to storm into my life and wreck everything after all. Bright winter sunshine streamed into the kitchen as I sat, still in my dressing gown, drinking coffee, as Duncan got ready to leave for work. 'What are you going to do with your day off, then?' he said, after he kissed me goodbye.

'I thought I'd go into town, have a wander round the shops.' I did plan to do this while I was there, so I wasn't lying. 'And it's a lovely day, so if it's not icy I might put Monty in the car and have a drive out to the moors for a walk.'

'That'll be nice,' Duncan said, and I could see that he was thinking the same thing – the same thing we always say, that we should drive out there more often; to the moors, to the hills; we live so close to the Peak District and yet we hardly ever take advantage of it. The last time we'd been out there together must have been months ago. In fact, it must have been in the spring, because I remembered the moors had been covered with heather in various shades of pink, lilac and purple. We'd held hands as we stood looking at the view across the valley. Monty was sniffing around in the undergrowth and the sun was beginning to set, casting a golden glow over the fields. 'I know we always say this,' Duncan said, and then I joined in so we spoke in unison, 'but we really should do this more often.' We both laughed, and then I found myself thinking about a colleague whose husband had just died of a heart attack at the age of forty-two. 'Yes, we should make the most of every day, shouldn't we?' I'd said. 'You never know what's going to happen; when things are going to change.'

And as I thought back to this now, I felt a ripple of apprehension. It was the same feeling I'd had just after my mum died; a sense that I had absolutely no control over what was about to happen; that I was completely powerless, as though I'd been swept off the shore and was being carried out to sea.

CHAPTER NINE

Newquay, Cornwall, March 1976

Jo wiped her eyes with the scented tissue the ward sister had given her. 'Is there someone we can ring for you, Joanna? Grandma, perhaps? Or an auntie or uncle?' Jo shook her head. It hadn't occurred to her how small her family was until now. Her auntie Margaret had died of a burst appendix a week before she was born, and Granny Pawley, her mother's mother, had had a massive stroke just after Christmas last year. She hadn't seen her father since she was ten and anyway, he'd moved to the other side of the world with his girlfriend.

'It's a hard thing to cope with at your age,' Sister said, patting Jo's shoulder. 'I lost both my parents when I wasn't much older than you. It'll get easier with time.'

Jo nodded and thanked her for all she and the other nurses had done, then she picked up the small bag of her mother's possessions and half ran out through the double doors and along the corridors into the weak sunshine.

People were parking in the hospital car park; how many would get back into their cars newly bereaved, remembering the previous visit's complacent 'See you tomorrow'? On the bus home she was aware that her eyes were red and puffy from crying, so she picked up a newspaper someone had left on the seat and paid her fare without looking at the conductor. *Wilson resigns*, the headline read. She stared at the pictures of Harold Wilson on the front page, but although she read the paragraph underneath twice, the words wouldn't register; it could have been in Greek for all she could take in. She tossed the paper onto the seat next to her and turned to the window, leaning her forehead against the cool glass and closing her eyes for the rest of the journey.

She couldn't face going straight home, so she went to the beach and headed down to the shoreline, where she knew the sound of the waves breaking on the sand would soothe her. She stood, looking out across the slate-coloured ocean. The sun had gone in now; the sky was the same hue as the sea and the clouds were swollen, puffed up with rain. She didn't move when the rain began to fall, a few large drops at first, then more, falling at a slant, fast and sharp, like a million needles piercing the surface of the dark water. She unfolded the death certificate. *Chronic liver failure*, it said; and *alcohol-induced hepatitis*. Her hands itched to rip it up, to pull it to pieces and throw it down onto the sand and stamp on it. But the sensible part of her knew she'd need it to arrange the funeral, so she folded it again and shoved it back into the pocket of her parka before it got too wet.

Before her mum had become ill, they'd talked about moving, not just away from Newquay, but right out of Cornwall. It was great living near the sea, but this place didn't have much else going for it; it was dead all through the winter, and in summer it was swamped with tourists who spoke to you like you were scum. A few seagulls were standing around in the rain, looking as though they didn't quite know what they were supposed to be doing. Why didn't they fly off; they had wings, didn't they? Stupid birds.

As she stood watching them, the realisation began to creep over her that she needed to make plans, think about what to do next. She could stay here in Newquay, or she could pack up the flat, draw her savings out of her Post Office account and go somewhere different. It was her decision. Maybe she should try London; she'd heard it was easier to get a job there and the pay was better, and it would be good to see what it was like to live somewhere other than this shithole. The possibilities tumbled around in her head, but she couldn't seem to distinguish her thoughts; she couldn't think straight. Perhaps she should talk to her mum about it? But then she remembered.

It was late afternoon now and it was starting to get dark. She could feel the rain running down the back of her neck so she reached behind her and pulled the hood of her parka up over her head. Her legs felt heavy as she trudged along the rain-dimpled sand, past clumps of black seaweed with shards of wood, plastic water bottles and other bits of rubbish tangled into it. She carried on walking towards the wooden steps that led up onto the road. At the bottom of the steps she paused and took a few lungfuls of the clean sea air, noticing the salty taste of it, the sharp tangy smell, then she looked back at the sea, shrouded now, and smothered in a grey blanket of rain. She wiped her eyes with the sleeve of her parka and headed up the steps, across the road and homewards through the town.

The rain was hammering the pavements and the noise it made drowned out any other sound. Coming down in stair-rods, Granny Pawley would have said. People were hurrying, trying to get home from work before they got too wet. Jo didn't change her pace; she was wet now anyway. As she walked, she watched the pattern the rain made in the puddles, circles that appeared and disappeared; bubbles that bloomed then popped. She kept her head down; she didn't want any of the neighbours seeing her and asking after her mum. Not that anyone was likely to want to hang around and chat in this weather, and come to think of it, people tended not to ask these days, anyway. Her mum had borrowed money and failed to return it too many times. The rain hit the pavements so hard it bounced off again and created a mist which gusted along the black tarmac. Wide, rippling streams of water ran noisily along the gutters. It felt right somehow. It felt like an ending.

For the last few years, they'd lived on one of the tattiest roads in Newquay, and today it looked even worse than usual. There was as much furniture outside on the street as in the houses, by the look of it. She passed a double mattress propped up against the wall and a ripped armchair with an old reel-to-reel tape recorder on the seat, all getting sodden in the rain. Sometimes, she struggled to remember what things had been like before, when they'd lived in a nice house in a nice road where people mowed their lawns on Saturdays and washed their cars on Sundays. She couldn't even picture her bedroom in that house now.

When she let herself back in, it felt like she'd been away for ten years rather than ten hours. Time was all wrong in hospitals. The flat felt cold and damp, more so than usual. She stooped to pick up the post, walked through to the kitchen and switched on the light, waiting while the fluorescent tubes flickered into life, then she turned on the radio – a reflex action – just in time to hear Abba joyfully singing the chorus of 'Mamma Mia'. She turned the radio off, threw the post onto the table and went over to the sink where the pan from last night's spaghetti Bolognese was soaking in the bowl, a greasy orange scum floating on top of the cold washing-up water. Apart from the tea and biscuits they'd given her at the hospital this morning, she hadn't eaten a thing since last night, so still in her coat, she opened the fridge, ate some corned beef with her fingers, then poured a glass of milk and drank it straight down. She felt in her pocket for the tiny lump of hash Rob Trelawney had given her yesterday, then took her coat off and sat at the table to roll a spliff. She wasn't very good at it, not like Rob, but then he smoked all the time. To Rob, spliffs were like cigarettes. She lit the thin, inexpertly rolled joint and took a deep drag, letting the calm wash over her. It definitely numbed things a bit. That's what her mum used to say about drinking. 'It's only a drop of sherry, Jo-Jo, just to take the edge off.'

Some of the post was for her, some for her mum. There was a reminder to take her books back to the library, and a pink envelope in Sheena Smith's handwriting. Sheena was one of the few girls she'd kept in touch with from school. She opened the envelope; Thank You card for the tights and bath salts Jo had given her for her birthday. There was a gas bill and a letter from the hospital, both addressed to her mother. The gas bill was a red reminder; Jo slid it between the salt and pepper pots to remind herself to phone them tomorrow. And she should phone Mr Rundle, the landlord, too, and the Social Security; and there would be loads of others. She'd better make a list. The hospital letter sounded like a telling-off because her mum had 'failed to attend' for her fortnightly blood test. Another appointment had been made and would she please notify them if she was unable to keep it. The letter went on about wasting time and using up an appointment that another patient might be able to take blah blah blah. Jo snatched up a green felt tip pen that was lying in the fruit bowl on top of some wrinkled apples, turned the letter over and scrawled on the back, *I did not attend the appointment on the 26th because as you should bloody well know, I've been in your stupid hospital for six weeks and anyway I died this morning. Hope that's a good enough excuse for not attending the next one. Yours, Marie Casey (deceased).*

She read what she'd written, then tore the letter into shreds and tossed it into the sink. How could it be that, just last night, she'd been sitting in the living room watching *Top of the Pops*, and now, twenty-four hours later, she no longer had a mum? She took another toke on the spliff and ignored the tears that were rolling down her cheeks. She'd been almost relieved when her mum was admitted to hospital; at least the nurses would know what to do. Also, it meant that, for a while, she could pretend her mother wasn't an alcoholic, that she was in hospital for some normal reason, like gallstones or piles or a hysterectomy. Jo had gone in to see her most nights, but her mum was often so drugged up she was barely conscious. Last night, she'd seemed a bit better, although her skin was a sickly yellow and there were brown shadows under both her eyes. She'd even talked about a holiday in Spain. 'We'll save up,' she'd said, her voice stronger than it had been for weeks. 'I'll get a little job when I'm back on my feet. I was a cashier before I met your dad, you know; I did double-entry bookkeeping for two years, so I'll be able to find something.' Then her eyes had filled up and she reached for Jo's hand. 'You shouldn't have to be the one who goes to work, not at your age, not when you're such a clever girl. You should have stayed on at school and done your A levels. Oh, Jo-Jo.' She turned her head away on the pillow. 'What sort of mother have I been?'

For a fleeting moment, she wanted to say, *A lousy one, if you want to know the truth. A really bloody shitty one.* But she knew that wasn't entirely fair. When she was little, she'd thought her mum was wonderful, the best mum in the world, and that had given her a dilemma, because although she knew she wanted to have her own babies as soon as she grew up, she couldn't imagine living in a different house to her mum. So when she was old enough, she'd decided, she would buy a big pink house and she and her children and her mum would all live there together. She hadn't given much thought to a husband; she didn't think she'd need one.

She realised her mum was crying.

'It's all right, Mum.' Gently, she pulled her hand away and stood up. 'Listen, I'll come and see you again tomorrow, okay?' She kissed her mum's clammy forehead and walked out of the ward, keen to be home in time for *Top of the Pops*.

Then in the middle of the night, the ward sister had telephoned and told her that her mum had taken a turn for the worse. The minicab cost almost two pounds, but it got her there quickly. She'd sat next to the bed for nearly three hours, listening to her mother's laboured breathing and leaning in closer every time her eyelids flickered. And then at just after five in the morning, her mother had smiled for the first time in weeks, a warm, beatific smile that came more from the eyes than the mouth, and then she'd closed those once-pretty green eyes for the last time, and died.

Jo gathered up all the envelopes, opened the pedal bin with her foot and threw them in, thank-you card and all, then she put her hand in the cold, greasy washing-up water, fished out the torn-up pieces of the hospital letter and threw them in on top. She finished the spliff then walked across the hall and into her mother's room. The last time she'd been in here was the day the ambulance came. She pushed the door open slowly. The room felt chilly and smelt stale, like unwashed clothes. The laundry basket in the corner was full, and she felt a pang of guilt. She could have taken this lot to the launderette, couldn't she? Six weeks. She could have come in here and changed the bed, at least. There was a sticky glass and a Kellogg's Corn Flakes mug on the bedside cabinet, along with a jumble of pills, a box of tissues and a pot of Nivea face cream. She slid open the top drawer; more pills, more creams and ointments. She picked up one of the tubes and smiled when she read the label. She remembered her mum's voice, incredulous: '*Anusol*, I ask you! Why not call it *arsehole* and have done with it?'

When she was a little girl and they'd lived in Padstow, she'd loved going into her mum's room because it smelt nice and there were pretty bottles on the dressing table and necklaces hung over the mirror, and sometimes, her mother would let her try on her shoes and clip-clop about in them like a grown-up lady. But this room bore no traces of that mother. There was still a perfume bottle on the dressing table, but it was covered with dust; her mother hadn't worn perfume or jewellery for years. Under the bed there were two carrier bags full of bottles, mostly sherry or Martini, which was what her mum drank in the evenings; during the day, she'd sometimes slip some vodka into her tea when she thought Jo wasn't looking. Those damn bottles. She remembered wondering why her mum always took a clinking carrier bag with her when she went to the corner shop, and one day, she watched out of the window as her mum stopped at a litter bin, glanced around and then lifted the carrier bag and tipped the bottles into the bin. It was only when Friday came around and Jo saw the dustmen taking the lids off the bins all along the road that she understood. That was back in the days when her mum still cared what people thought.

Jo tried to think of the old mum, the mum who used to know so many songs that you could say any word you thought of and she'd know a song with that word in it; the mum who used to fold a sheet of paper, make little cuts or tears in it and get Jo to tap it with her finger and shout *Abracadabra* and then, magically, open the paper out to reveal a string of paper dollies holding hands, or a beautiful peacock with a fanned tail, or a swan with its wings outstretched. For a second, the memory was so strong that her mum, the funny, happy, laughing mum, felt intensely real and present, but then it was gone, leaving an imprint on the air like when you've just blown out a candle. For the first time since she was a little girl, she climbed into her mother's bed and cried herself to sleep.

*

Mr Rundle was very sorry to hear of her mother's death. She was welcome to stay in the flat until the end of March, he told her, and she wasn't to worry about the two months' rent they owed. 'You'll have enough to think about, young miss.' His craggy forehead wrinkled as he lit his pipe. 'I'm not short of a few bob these days, and your mum was a good tenant, mostly.' He asked about the funeral and Jo admitted she had no idea what to do, so he and Mrs Rundle took over the arrangements, much to Jo's relief. A week later the three of them, together with Rob Trelawney and his parents, her friends Sheena and Jackie, a nurse from the hospital and Miss Bradwell, her mum's social worker, sat round on chairs and packing cases drinking weak tea out of disposable cups; Jo hadn't realised you were supposed to provide tea and cakes after a funeral and she'd given away most of the crockery. There hadn't been a lot to get rid of. The WRVS and the Salvation Army had taken most of the household things, and Mrs Rundle had helped her bag up her mum's stuff for the church jumble. It fitted into four dustbin bags; not much to show for a whole life. Apart from clothes, her mum owned very little. She'd sold most of her jewellery ages ago, except for a Victorian cameo brooch that had belonged to her own mother. It was the only thing Jo wanted to keep; it would remind her of her mum and of Granny Pawley at the same time. Her own things, the stuff she wasn't taking with her, filled another two bags and a couple of packing cases – her old record player, the cassette recorder, her books, records and tapes, a few old toys she'd hung on to. Once she'd made the decision, getting rid of her things was easier than she'd expected. She'd hung on to too much; those things were all part of her childhood, and that was behind her now.

The tiny funeral party picked at the ham and tomato sandwiches, mushroom vol-au-vents and fairy cakes that Rob's mum and Mrs Rundle had made that morning. No one said much, and no one stayed for long.

She gave a week's notice at the Co-op and told Carol and Geoff, who owned the pub where she worked three evenings a week, that she wouldn't be back, then she wrote notes to Sheena and Jackie promising to stay in touch. When she'd seen Rob and his mum out after the funeral, she'd said she'd pop round to say goodbye, but she knew she wouldn't. She hated goodbyes, especially as she still quite liked Rob. She was going to stay with her mum's cousin in London, she told them all. No one questioned her, not even Miss Bradwell. Only Mr Rundle had any doubts. Being a dyed-in-the-wool Cornishman, he was suspicious of Londoners who, he said, had no consideration. 'Noisy beggars, they London folk,' he grumbled when he came to collect the keys. 'Come down here in summer with their cars and motorbikes, playing their transistor radios on the beach and leaving all their mess behind. Never see sight nor sign of 'em come wintertime.' He shook his head. And London itself, he told her, was a filthy place, full of people you couldn't trust. 'Streets paved with thieves and blaggards.' He puffed furiously on his pipe. 'Steal a wooden leg from a cripple, they

Londoners.' When he dropped her off at Newquay station with her duffle bag and her mum's only good suitcase, he pushed a five pound note into her hand. 'You look after yourself, my lover; 't ain't right, a young maid all alone up there in that place.'

CHAPTER TEN

Jo stashed her suitcase in the luggage rack, then settled with her duffle bag on her lap. It was a long journey, over six hours, and she'd barely slept the previous night. The last time she'd been on a train to London was when she was nine; she hadn't slept the night before that journey, either. Her dad was working in London and renting a bedsit in Green Park because it was handy for the City. He came home on Fridays and left again on Sunday nights to get the train back. Just before Christmas, her mum decided to take the train up and surprise him. 'We'll travel up on the Thursday,' she said, 'then we can go out to dinner with Daddy in the evening, get up early on Friday for Oxford Street, do some shopping, have lunch, then come back with Daddy on the four o'clock train. So when he phones tonight'– she put her finger to her lips – 'not a word, okay?'

Jo nodded eagerly, pleased to be trusted with keeping the secret.

The night before, she'd been so excited she'd lain awake for hours, and in the morning she was up and dressed long before her mother. She wore her new navy corduroy pinafore dress with a white jumper underneath, white socks and black patent shoes. She knew you needed to dress smartly for London. Into the beige suede handbag Granny Pawley had given her, she put *The Lion, the Witch and the Wardrobe* to read on the train, a mini pack of tissues, a notebook and pencil, a packet of Spangles and her purse with eighteen shillings for her Christmas shopping. She could barely keep still as she sat on her parents' high iron-framed bed while her mum applied lipstick in the same cherry-red colour as her trouser suit. 'You wait until you see the lights in Regent Street, Jo-Jo; the best Christmas lights you'll ever see.' She twisted the lipstick down again and put the lid back on, pressed her lips together and then blotted them with a tissue. She leaned into the mirror and turned her face first to one side, then the other. Apparently satisfied, she took her new fun-fur coat out of the wardrobe. 'Come on then, Jo-Jo,' she said with a mock-impatient smile. 'Are you going to laze around here all day or are we going to London?' Jo jumped down off the bed and ran to get her own best coat, which was plum-coloured with gold buttons and a black velvet collar.

'I expect we'll see some real choirs, too,' her mum said as they hurried to the station hand-in-hand. 'Real choirs singing proper carols that we can join in with. And if you're really good'– she looked down at Jo – 'we'll go and see Father Christmas in Selfridges tomorrow.' She smiled. 'How would you like that?'

Too overwhelmed to speak, Jo nodded eagerly and skipped the rest of the way to the station. On the train, they played I-spy for a while, then they ate their liver sausage sandwiches and butterfly cakes, and then Jo settled down to read her book. Before long, her eyes grew heavy, so she laid her head down on her mum's lap and went to sleep. She was still sleepy when they arrived, so they took a taxi to the bedsit. It was five o'clock and her dad should have only just got back from work, but he answered the door wearing a woman's dressing gown, a glamorous, silky affair in pink and dove grey. Jo had never been so embarrassed in her life. All she could think about were his hairy legs poking out under the grey silk. The dressing gown, it turned out, belonged to Elena, his beautiful Spanish secretary, who was waiting for him in the bed at the other end of the room.

Jo's mum stood in the doorway, not saying anything at first. Jo held on to her hand but it felt weird, like she wanted to let go but didn't know if she was allowed to. She remembered her dad looking uncomfortable and running his hand through his hair, but she couldn't remember what he said, only her mum's response, and she remembered that clearly, word for word. Her mum had flipped, yanking her hand away from Jo's and hitting her dad in the chest. 'Have a drink?' she screamed. 'Have a drink? Would that just be you and me or is your whore going to drag herself out of your bed and join us? Dear

God above, I don't know which is worse, the betrayal or the . . . the *fucking* cliché.' Jo had gasped. She'd never heard either of her parents swear, but somehow she knew that her mother had just said a really bad word. She couldn't remember exactly what happened for the rest of that day, but they never got to go Christmas shopping in Oxford Street, and she never saw Father Christmas in Selfridges.

And now here she was over seven years later, the train pulling into Paddington station once more. It was gone six thirty now and already dark outside. She yawned as she stood up. Her legs felt stiff and her neck ached, and when she pulled her duffle bag down from the luggage shelf, it still felt heavy, even though she'd eaten the sandwiches and the Wagon Wheel and drunk both cans of Coke. Her suitcase was fairly heavy as well, so she hoped she wouldn't have to carry them far. Outside the station, it was chucking it down, but she needed to find a cheap room so she headed straight out into the wet evening. With the five pounds Mr Rundle had given her and the twenty-two pounds from her Post Office account, she had enough to last for a few nights, at least, and after that, well, by that time she'd have found a job.

The shops were closed now, but there were still loads of people around, all with their heads down, walking quickly in different directions, determined to get where they were going and not looking at anyone else. It was just like her first day at Harfield Grammar, when all the other girls appeared to know where they were supposed to be and how to get there, and none of them seemed to notice her as they passed by; she'd felt like an intruder, a gatecrasher who nobody wanted to talk to. She felt a bit like that now, an outsider who really shouldn't be here. She was surprised at how different everything was; not only did it look different, it smelled and sounded different. She hadn't realised before now just how much she'd taken for granted the smell of the sea and the sound of the seagulls screeching overhead.

She wandered around the streets near the station, not knowing where she was going and increasingly conscious of the weight of her suitcase and duffle bag, but there was nothing but expensive-looking hotels. In Newquay, there were lodging houses or bed and breakfasts on almost every street. The rain was getting heavier and she was soaked through, as well as exhausted from so much walking. She was almost in tears. It was getting late, and people were beginning to settle down in shop doorways. The thought of sleeping on the streets was scary. She looked up at the grubby front of another hotel, which didn't look quite as grand as some of the others; she went in.

The receptionist looked bored as he ran through the prices. The cheapest room was £7.50 a night – twice what she'd expected to pay, and that didn't even include breakfast. But she was wet and cold and tired. 'Okay,' she said, aware of how weary her voice sounded. The receptionist handed her the key and then came round from behind the desk to take her bags. 'No, it's all right,' she said. 'I can manage, thank you.' She'd never stayed in a proper hotel before, and all she knew about how to behave was from what she'd seen on television. In *Crossroads*, when David Hunter carried someone's bags, they gave him a tip, and she didn't want to risk having to do that. The receptionist looked at her oddly, shrugged, and went back behind his desk. 'Suit yourself. Third floor, fifth room on your right along the hallway at the top of the stairs.'

When she'd finally managed to haul herself and her bag up six flights of narrow, creaking stairs, she used the communal bathroom before letting herself into her room. It was expensive, and it wasn't very nice, but she'd done it, she'd found a place to stay and she'd paid for it. She had a fleeting thought about telling her mum, showing her how very grown-up she really was. This kept happening – she'd imagine running home to tell her mum something, and then she'd remember. She sighed as she hung her dripping-wet parka over the back of the chair, climbed into bed fully clothed and fell into an exhausted sleep.

CHAPTER ELEVEN

The following morning, she ate the remaining food in her duffle bag – a sausage roll and a couple of squares of Fruit and Nut – drank a few mouthfuls of water from the tap in the bathroom and set off in her still-damp parka to find a cheaper place to stay. The weather continued to be cold and drizzly, but it wasn't raining heavily now, and she felt a lot better after a night's sleep. Things seemed so much more possible in daylight, even if that daylight was still slightly grey, and as she was looking for somewhere to buy a newspaper, she spotted a sign on a building across the road, *Hostel: women only*. How the hell had she missed this last night? She crossed the road and rang the bell.

It only cost £1.20 a night. There were eight beds to each dormitory, but it was clean and fairly quiet and you could get a cooked breakfast for 15p and a dinner in the evening for 35p. All you had to do was take your turn in the kitchen for two hours every day helping the cooks or doing the washing up.

The hostel manager showed her to her dormitory, which was on the first floor. The walls were painted a dark greenish-blue, which made the room a bit gloomy, but on the other hand, the colour reminded her a little of the sea. Some of the pictures on the walls reminded her of home, too, especially the one of two children playing on a sandy beach, the sea twinkling in the sunshine behind them. 'There are only three other girls in the dormitory at the moment,' the manager explained, 'but we could fill up at any time. Barbara' – she addressed a thin, dark-haired girl with a sullen expression who was sitting on her bed, varnishing her nails – 'this is Jo; she'll be staying with us for a few days.' Barbara nodded to Jo but didn't smile or say hello. Then the manager introduced Karen, who had masses of wild, frizzy red hair and looked as if she was in her thirties, so not really a girl at all, and Hilary, who was probably about the same age as Jo, but was quite overweight and had clearly been crying. After saying hello, Hilary climbed back into her bed, turned to face the wall and pulled the covers over her head. Karen chatted to Jo while she unpacked her rucksack. As she'd guessed, Karen was in her thirties – thirty-three, in fact; it was one of the first things she told Jo before asking how old she was, whether she had any brothers and sisters, what her favourite TV show was and a lot of other things as well. She talked quickly and flitted from subject to subject like a small child; she even had a slightly childlike voice. Jo smiled and nodded but eventually Karen lost interest and wandered back to her own bed.

Jo's first shift in the kitchen was that afternoon, helping to prepare the evening meal. She had to lay out sausages ready for the oven and prick their skins three times with a fork; then she had to grate an enormous block of cheese, after that she was on potato-peeling with two other girls. She enjoyed working in the kitchen. Some of the girls had been there for quite a while, but she would only be staying a night or two, she told them – it was only until she found a job. She was looking for something clerical to start with, but she could always fall back on bar work if she had to.

After she'd been at the hostel for four days, she began to lower her sights. Anything would do for now – bar work, waitressing, cleaning; anything so that she could get a proper room, then she'd think about what she was going to do long-term. 'I might train to be a nanny one day,' she told Tina, who'd just arrived and had been given the next bed. Jo had her feet up on her own bed and was flicking through the job ads in the paper. 'I love kids. I want to have my own as soon as I get married, but until then, I'd like to work with them, if I can.'

'They took my kids off me,' Tina said, pushing her greasy blonde hair behind her ear. 'Bastards. Here' – she pointed at Jo's pack of No 6 which was open on the bed – 'let's have one of them fags.'

Jo picked up the pack and did a quick count. There were nine left; she supposed she could spare one. 'There you go.' She tossed a cigarette to Tina, then leaned over to pass her the lighter. 'How many kids have you got?'

'Three.' Tina threw the lighter back. 'Louise is five, Darren's three and Dean's one. But I ain't seen them since before Christmas. Fucking social workers won't let me.'

Jo didn't say anything. Had Tina hit her children? Starved them? She didn't like to ask.

'Go on, then.' Tina lifted her chin in defiance and narrowed her eyes as she blew out a column of pale grey smoke. 'Ask me why they took them off me.'

Jo shook her head. 'No, it's all right, you don't have to —'

'Wacky baccy.' She mimed rolling a spliff. 'Bit of acid. Nothing too heavy. Not like I was doing H or nothing. But they said I weren't fit to look after me own kids, then they kicked me out of me flat, so now I ain't got nowhere for them to sleep anyhow.' She took another big drag of the cigarette, then leaned forward and whispered, 'You got anything on you? Some grass? Little bit of hash?'

'No, I haven't. I smoked the last of mine before I came to London. Can't afford to buy any more.'

'Come on,' Tina said, she was smiling, but it wasn't a friendly smile. 'Posh bird like you must be able to afford a bit of smoke?'

'Posh?' Jo laughed. 'I'm not posh. And I've hardly got any money left, which is why I'm looking for a job – and why I'm staying in this place.'

'Yeah, right.' Tina rolled her eyes. 'Me heart bleeds for you.'

Jo swung her legs down onto the floor, picked up her duffle bag and her cigarettes, and told Tina she'd see her later. Tina had been nice at first, but now it looked like she wanted an argument and Jo just didn't have the energy.

By the evening, Tina wanted to be friends again. Although it was only ten past nine, Hilary had already turned in for the night and Karen was busy trying to read her creased copy of *Jackie*, her lips moving steadily and her finger sliding back and forth along the pages as she followed the words. 'Psst! Jo!' Tina whispered. 'Want some of this?' She nodded towards her open rucksack, which was on the floor between the two beds. Jo looked down and could see that inside the rucksack was a carrier bag containing two bottles. 'It's cider,' Tina said. 'Have some – it'll make up for all the fags I've been poncing off you. Careful.' Jo looked over her shoulder. You were allowed cigarettes in here, but if they found alcohol, you could get thrown out.

'It's all right. Those two won't say nothing. Fuck me, you've got to do something in this place to cheer yourself up.'

Jo glanced round the room again. Hilary was asleep, and Karen was far too absorbed in her magazine to notice what anyone else was doing. 'Go on, then. Thanks.' She took the bottle from Tina and took a surreptitious swig. 'Bloody hell, that's strong!'

Tina smiled. 'Too right, it is.'

*

When Jo woke the next day, she couldn't remember much about the previous evening, only that Tina had kept passing her the bottle until she'd been unable to talk without giggling. By the time she realised that Tina herself was barely drinking, it was too late: the room was spinning and she didn't feel giggly any more, she felt ill. She had a vague recollection of Tina's face very close to her own at some point in the night, and she also thought she saw Tina get up to go to the loo.

As soon as she opened her eyes, she was aware of feeling extremely sick and desperately thirsty, but it was only when she sat up that the pain behind her eyes intensified and the full savagery of her headache became apparent.

She turned her head carefully to the left, but Tina's bed was empty and her bag had gone. Only the empty cider bottles remained. The dormitory supervisor, who came round first thing to get everybody up and to make sure that nobody had smuggled a man in overnight, seemed to take great delight in finding that Tina had absconded without paying for her bed and that Jo had been 'consuming alcohol on the premises'. She had no option but to report it to the hostel manager, she said, and bustled off to do that as quickly as she could. The hostel manager herself was nicer about it. She believed Jo that it was Tina who'd brought the cider in, but said she would still have to ask Jo to leave – rules were rules, after all. But she did give her the address of another hostel not far from

Trafalgar Square, and she also said there was no hurry – Jo could have breakfast before she left, and she could also stay and have a bath if she wished.

'Thank you,' Jo murmured, trying not to cry. It wasn't fair; just when she'd begun to feel a bit more settled. She took up the offer of a bath hoping it would make her feel better, especially as she'd slept in her clothes. But it didn't really help, and as she stood on the cold tiles of the bathroom floor to get dressed, she was overcome by a powerful longing for her mum. It kept hitting her afresh: her mum was dead, she wasn't coming back; Jo was on her own now, completely on her own.

When she went back to the dormitory, the supervisor and the hostel manager were both there, ready to escort her from the building, no doubt. She could hardly bear to look at them; she just wanted to pay for the previous night and get out of there. She reached for her purse. 'Oh my God,' she said as she rummaged through her duffle bag. 'I can't find my purse. It's got over nine pounds in it.' She could hear the edge of panic in her voice. 'It must be here somewhere.' She saw the hostel manager and dormitory supervisor exchange a look. 'I'm not trying to get a free night, honest,' she said, taking things out of the bag and stuffing them back in again. 'I've paid for all the rest, it's just I can't find my purse.' She slid her suitcase out from under the bed; maybe she'd put it in the zip pocket, but no, the pocket was empty, and anyway, she was almost certain her purse had been in her duffle bag. She pulled everything out, tipped it upside down and shook it out onto the bed. Her hands were trembling as she went through her belongings more slowly, just to make sure the little brown purse hadn't got caught up in one of her jumpers.

She heard the hostel manager sigh heavily, then she felt the woman's hand resting gently on her arm. 'I know you're not trying to get a free night. I think I know what's happened.' She looked pointedly at Tina's empty, unmade bed. 'I think you've been robbed. It's another reason we don't allow alcohol on the premises. It's happened before, you see. An easy way to make money – they come into the hostel looking for someone like yourself, someone who's new to all this.' She gestured around the dorm. 'They offer you a drink to make out they're being friendly, get you so drunk you pass out, then once you're unconscious, they pinch all your money.' She picked up one of the cider bottles and sniffed it. 'Thought so.' She passed it to the dorm supervisor, who also sniffed it and nodded. 'No wonder you're feeling rough; there was meths mixed in with that.'

Jo sat down on the bed and bit her lip. How could she have been so stupid? But it was only after she went through her things one more time that she was unable to stop the tears; not only had Tina stolen her purse, but her mum's cameo brooch was gone, too.

CHAPTER TWELVE

The hostel manager was sympathetic and said she could stay for one more night if she liked, but she just wanted to get out of the place now. She still had almost five pounds – there were three pound notes in the pocket of her jeans, which she'd been wearing because she'd been too drunk to get undressed, and there was well over a pound in loose change in her parka which had been crumpled under her shoulder as she slept. But that was it. They said she could leave her bags at the hostel while she looked for work, but after several hours of going in and out of shops and knocking on hotel doors, she still hadn't found a job. None of the hotels had anything at the moment, though a couple of them did say she could try again next week. It was late afternoon by the time she went back to collect her bags, and although her hangover had gone, her feet ached and she was getting a blister on her heel. She was hoping the hostel manager would still be in her office, because she was dying for a cup of tea, and she was pretty sure the manager would let her have one. But it was the dorm supervisor who opened the door, and she left her standing on the doorstep while she fetched the bags.

It was two and a half miles to the other hostel, but she didn't dare spend any more money, so she walked, despite having to grit her teeth and make a conscious effort to ignore the pain from the blister on her heel. She only had enough left to pay for another two nights, three at the most; what if she couldn't get any work tomorrow? As a last resort, she could sign on, she supposed, but she really didn't want to do that. Not only would it be admitting failure after less than a week in London, but she probably wouldn't be able to get anything anyway – Rob said you could only get the dole if you'd paid a proper stamp, and you couldn't get Supplementary Benefit unless you had an address. Rob knew about all that, because he'd left home once after a row with his mum, and he'd ended up sleeping on the beach. He'd tried to sign on until he got a job, but they said he wasn't entitled to anything because he had 'no fixed abode'. She bit her lip now as she thought of the beach at home. Somehow, the idea of sleeping on the beach didn't seem that bad at the moment. She tried to remember the sounds she was so used to: the waves gently washing over the sand, the constant cry of the seagulls. Their shrieking often used to drive her mad; who'd have thought she'd end up missing it? But she did, especially now when all she could hear was the perpetual noise made by the cars, buses and lorries that crammed the London streets.

By the time she got to Trafalgar Square, having got lost despite the map the hostel manager had drawn for her, she was limping and hungry. It was getting on for seven, and she hadn't eaten since breakfast, so she spent another 15p on a bag of chips which she ate sitting on a bench near Charing Cross station, then she bought a cup of tea to warm herself up while she counted out her remaining money. She had £4.67 left, and this hostel was £1.40 a night. How on earth was she going to survive? She began walking along the Strand without really thinking about where she was going. People had begun to arrive for the theatres. The women in their fur coats and high heels seemed to move around in a haze of hairspray and perfume, while in shop doorways, men and women prepared to bed down for the night. She slowed her pace, watching as they spread their possessions around them, marking their territory, establishing a temporary home. They weren't all scary old tramps, she noticed. In fact, some of them were quite young. She spotted a girl who looked about the same age as herself sitting up in a sleeping bag with a plastic sheet spread over the bottom, reading a small, grubby-looking book. 'Hello.' Jo tried to sound as friendly and nice as she could. 'All right if I sit down next to you?' When the girl looked up from her book, Jo could see straight away that she was no more than fifteen, possibly even younger. 'No,' the girl said, reaching out and pulling her holdall closer to her. 'Fuck off.'

Jo was so surprised, she didn't move immediately. 'Go on,' the girl said. 'Fuck off away from me or I'll make you.'

'Okay,' Jo said. 'I'm going.' Her legs felt shaky as she hurried away. There were homeless people back in Cornwall, but they weren't so . . . so hostile. She decided not to risk talking to anyone else, but the thought of spending almost all her remaining money on a bed in a hostel where she might end up getting her stuff nicked anyway was looking less and less attractive, so when she found a tiny unoccupied doorway in Neal Street, just round the corner from Shaftesbury Avenue, she squashed herself into it, even though there was barely room to sit down. It was starting to rain again, and she was cold and tired. This would just have to do until tomorrow. She huddled in the doorway, watching the rain hitting the dark pavements but too nervous to actually close her eyes. Then she saw two police uniforms further along the road. They didn't seem to be doing anything other than talking to the people in the doorways, but she still didn't fancy having to explain herself, so she gathered her stuff and, with her head down against the rain, walked back the way she'd come to find another spot.

She moved four times during the night, finally settling behind some parked cars at the rear of a building where warm air was blasting out of a heating vent. If only she could have a cup of tea. But she hadn't a clue where to get one, and even if she had, it would probably be stupid to give up her spot.

*

The city began to come back to life at around 5.30, and at last the rain had stopped. She wasn't sure if she'd actually slept at all, but she got stiffly to her feet and set off to find a public toilet. God, she was desperate for a wee. She'd been too scared to leave her warm spot so had been holding it in for hours. In Berwick Street, she found a public toilet which had soap and hot water, so she gave herself what her mum used to call a 'cat's lick and a promise' and then headed back in the direction of Trafalgar Square, which was probably the only place in London she was sure she'd be able to find.

She was sitting on the steps of Nelson's Column, eating a soggy Wimpy and wishing she had some gloves when she realised someone was standing over her. Her experience with Tina and Mr Rundle's warning about wooden-leg-stealing Londoners jumped into her mind and she pulled her suitcase and duffle bag closer as she looked up. The woman wore a long maroon velvet coat with a floor-length chunky-knit scarf in bottle-green wound around her neck. Those long scarves had been all the rage at school a couple of years ago. You made them by using big thick knitting needles and double strands of wool. Jo had made one herself, though not very well – it had somehow got wider as well as longer and had ended up almost twice the width at one end as at the other. The woman's hair was partly hidden by a crocheted hat, but dark strands poked out from beneath the mustard-yellow wool and her stripy shoulder bag matched the hat and the scarf, with one tassel in green and one in yellow.

'My name's Eve,' the woman said, crouching down. 'Are you okay? You look so . . .' She frowned and stroked a strand of hair away from Jo's forehead – her hands were encased in sheepskin mittens. 'So very lost.' She sounded quite posh, Jo thought, but she didn't look well-off.

'I'm not lost,' Jo said. 'I mean . . .' She looked around the square. 'I mean I know where I am.'

'But you don't really know who you are, do you? How old are you?' Eve said, in an I-know-what's-best-for-you voice that reminded Jo of her mum's social worker.

When she looked more closely, she could see that Eve was younger than she'd thought, probably only three or four years older than Jo herself. Her skin was peachy-coloured and her complexion was completely clear. She wore no make-up but there was a hint of rosiness to her cheeks, as though she was wearing blusher.

'Nineteen,' she said. She'd had to lie to Carol and Geoff when she'd started working at the pub, and it came out almost automatically now. People often took her for older than she was anyway; Sheena said it was the way she talked and behaved, especially since she'd been running the house and looking after her mum. Her final school report described her as *a sensible and responsible pupil who is surprisingly mature for her age.* Granny Pawley said it was because she was an 'old soul'.

'I sense,' Eve said, drawing her dark brows together,

'that you've been having a difficult time; I'd say you need some time to heal.' She undid the toggle on her shoulder bag and opened the flap. Jo's instinct was to get up and walk away; her mum would have said Eve was *one of those airy-fairy hippy-types*. She did seem a bit weird, and after the week Jo had had so far, she could do without any more weirdness. But there was something about her that made Jo feel safe, so she carried on sitting on the cold steps while Eve mumbled to herself and rummaged in her bag. 'Ah!' she said, smiling with her wide mouth. 'Here we are. Rose quartz.' She pressed a little pink stone into Jo's hand. 'It'll be perfect for you. Rose quartz can heal your heartache and ease your loneliness. And it'll help you find inner peace.' Her smile suddenly turned to a frown. 'Oh don't worry, it's absolutely free. I can tell when someone's in dire need of healing, and when that someone looks as frightened as you do, well . . .' She looked away and began fiddling with the woven-leather bracelet she wore on her wrist. 'I suppose you remind me of myself not so long ago.' Jo didn't know what to say to that, so she just stared back, then Eve started telling her all about how she'd discovered the amazing healing powers, not only of crystals but of aromatherapy oils, of meditation, and of course, of a healthy, nutritious diet. She was reading up on crystal healing, she said, and was making a little money selling crystals for their healing powers as well as in jewellery. 'Come to think of it, maybe you should look into getting hold of some lapis lazuli, especially if you're thinking of starting a new life.' She

THE SECRETS WE LEFT BEHIND

looked right into Jo's eyes. 'Are you?' she said, and she brushed another strand of hair from Jo's face. She'd taken her mitten off this time and her hand felt dry and warm. 'Are you trying to start a new life?'

Jo nodded dumbly for a few seconds, like one of those stupid dogs they have in the back of car windows, then she burst into tears like an idiot. She felt Eve's arms go around her and then Eve began to rock her, and she was transported back through the years to when she was little, when she woke up with tummy-ache, or a nightmare, and her mum would rock her and stroke her hair until she felt better and was able to go back to sleep. She could feel the silkiness of Eve's velvet coat and the slightly damp coldness of the fibres against her ear, but there was a warmth too, almost tangible, that seemed to seep through Eve's clothing. It made her feel – she tried to pin down the feeling – soothed.

'Come on,' Eve said. 'I'll buy you a cup of tea.'

As they sat in a café near Charing Cross station, Jo admitted she'd come to London without giving any proper thought to what she was going to do and where she was going to stay. She told Eve about not being able to find any work, and about Tina stealing her money and the cameo brooch, and about how she'd ended up sleeping in a doorway last night.

Eve listened closely and nodded sympathetically.

'And I know it seems stupid,' Jo continued, 'and I really don't want to go back there, but the noise and the fumes from the traffic are really making me miss the sea.'

Eve smiled. 'I love the sea,' she said. 'Especially when the weather's windy and stormy and the waves get really high. I grew up here in London, but I hated it, so now I live quite near the sea with my boyfriend. I only come up here now and again to buy the bits and pieces I need for the jewellery. I can get crystals and beads and things locally, but not the clasps and settings. We're in Hastings, on the south coast. Do you know it?'

Jo shook her head. 'I'm from Cornwall – Newquay.

'Ooh, lucky you,' Eve said. 'I went to Cornwall when I was little, with my mum and dad. They're dead now.' A dark cloud floated across her face. 'Are your parents still there?'

'They're both dead, too,' Jo said. It didn't feel like a lie – she wanted nothing to do with her father, and she felt like an orphan, anyway. 'My mum . . .' She felt her throat tighten and the tears beginning to gather behind her eyes. It was the first time she'd actually had to tell someone. She took a breath. 'My mum died three weeks ago. She had . . . something wrong with her liver.'

Eve's eyes widened. 'Just three weeks ago! Oh my goodness, you poor, poor thing. It's so awful to lose your mum. And your dad, of course, but . . .' She sighed. 'I was ten when my mum died. It was so' – she looked away and then back – 'so *unfair*. And then it was only a year later when my dad . . .' She shook her head. 'Sorry. I shouldn't be going on about myself. We were talking about you.'

'That's it, really. My dad, well that was ages ago. But my mum . . . I still can't really believe it.'

Eve was looking right at her, as though she was waiting for her to say more, but Jo didn't want to talk any more today. Eve's eyes were a deep violet colour and they were huge, so big that when she blinked it took a long time for the lids to make their way over the surface of her eye and back again. Jo wished she had eyes like that.

'So,' Eve said, after a few moments. 'Do you have anywhere to stay tonight?'

Jo looked at her tea. Part of her wanted Eve to think she was capable of sorting herself out, of getting everything organised; but the other part was desperate to admit that she was actually quite scared. In the end, she didn't even need to answer.

'Look,' Eve said. 'Why not come back to Hastings with me? Scott won't mind. It's only a squat but it's fairly civilised. You can see how you feel after a few days. Stay if you want, go if you want. What do you say?'

Overwhelmed by gratitude and relief, she bit her lip and nodded, not trusting herself to speak in case she started crying again.

CHAPTER THIRTEEN

They hitchhiked as far as Crowhurst and took a train from there, but now they had to walk from the station. Jo's suitcase felt as though it was getting heavier by the second and the handle of her duffle bag was cutting into her shoulders; the sea wind was harsh and bit at her face. They paused for a breather before continuing up the hill past a sign saying *Unadopted road*, which Jo thought sounded rather sad and uncared for – another orphan. 'Is it much further?' she asked.

Eve shook her head and pointed to a flight of concrete steps that led up to more flights of steps and eventually to another road. 'Just up here. Come on,' she grinned. 'It'll be worth it; just visualise putting your feet up with a lovely hot cup of tea.'

By the time they reached the top, Jo's heart was pounding. 'Nearly there,' Eve said as they turned into a wide, tree-lined road with big detached houses that were set back from the street. Most had cars in the driveways and heavy curtains at the windows. Jo turned to look behind her – they seemed quite high up. There was the sea, a grey-green strip, slung like a hammock between a gap in the rooftops. Just seeing it made her feel better.

'That's the one,' Eve said, pointing to a huge Victorian house with steps up to the peeling front door. The house had once been white, but now it was stained with green where moss had grown on the damp parts. It was the last one on the street, bigger than the rest, but in the worst condition, with chunks of the rendering missing, rotting window frames and a massively overgrown front garden. It looked higgledy-piggledy; the House that Jack Built. On one corner, a turret with windows that went all the way round jutted out from the house. The main roof sloped this way and that, with several chimneys poking up in the middle and a little wall running around the edge. Were those gargoyles looking down from the corners? They looked gruesome, although most of them were broken, so they weren't as frightening as they could have been. She turned to Eve. 'This is a squat?'

Eve smiled. 'We've been living here since last autumn. Gorgeous, isn't it? Like our own castle. Come on. We go in round the back.'

The broken wooden gate squeaked as they went through into a large walled garden that was badly overgrown. An old, chipped bird-bath poked out from under the ivy that covered one of the walls and had started to creep across the ground, and in the middle of the muddy, patchy grass stood a stone plinth supporting a sundial, which, like the bird-bath, was chipped and battered but spoke of better times. Jo tried to imagine what the ornamented garden would have looked like before the house lost its grandeur.

They walked past sacks of builders' rubble piled against another wall alongside two broken bentwood chairs, an old armchair and a shopping trolley containing a plastic bowl and a headless Sindy Doll. 'We're trying to clear this bit.' Eve gestured towards a patch of partly dug soil. 'We're going to plant tomatoes, onions, potatoes, cauliflowers and peas. And maybe some runner beans along that wall. There are allotments up the road, but we've got our own vegetable patch right here.'

Jo nodded. Her dad had grown runner beans; she remembered her mum making her a wigwam in the garden out of the bean poles. She followed Eve down some stone steps to a wooden door, where Eve pushed the ivy aside and opened the door with a new-looking key. 'First rule of squatting,' she smiled. 'Fit your own locks.' The door opened into a dank, low-ceilinged room with a hole in the floorboards that must have been four feet across. 'Mind where you tread.' Eve flicked a switch as she took Jo's hand and pulled her inside. An un-shaded light bulb dangled from the ceiling, casting a sickly light over the room.

'How come there's electricity?'

'Oh, it's perfectly legal. We just had a meter reading and got it turned back on. They're not allowed to refuse to connect services just because you're squatting. Some people tap into the meter and steal the electricity, but we

don't think you should do that unless you absolutely
have to do. Although we did give a false name for the
bills.' She giggled. 'Just in case. Anyway' – she gestured
with her arm – 'this is it, home, sweet home.'

Jo could feel the cold air on her face as she picked her
way across the rotting floorboards. The smell of damp was
overwhelming. There was an orange fungus growing on
the walls and the ceiling had collapsed in one corner, leaving a hole where the joists showed through and a pile of
rubble on the floor beneath it. She shivered; God, it was
cold in here. That shop doorway was starting to seem
attractive compared with this mouldering basement. What
had she done, coming here? Eve didn't seem the sort of
person who would live somewhere like this. But then they
went up some stairs and through another door into a large,
bright hallway. The few remaining black-and-white tiles
on the hall floor were cracked and broken, but you could
see it must have once been quite impressive – it reminded
her of Eaton Place on *Upstairs, Downstairs*. A huge wardrobe had been pulled across the front door, which had
planks of wood nailed across it anyway. Eve took off her
coat, revealing a long, emerald-green skirt with a man's
white shirt belted over the top. The black-velvet choker
around her neck completed the romantic, gypsy look. She
wore DMs, too; Jo was glad she'd worn her own DMs and
not the red platform boots with the black stripe down the
side; she'd been so tempted to bring them, but they took
up too much space and anyway, they hurt her feet, so
they'd gone in the jumble with the rest of her clothes.

'This is the living room,' Eve said, parting what looked at first like a bead curtain, but which, when you looked properly, turned out to be made entirely of tiny shells.

Jo took hold of one of the curtain strands and ran her fingers along its knobbly length. 'There must be hundreds of shells here. I bet it would take ages to thread them all onto strings like this.'

Eve nodded. 'It did, but I think it's rather pretty, don't you? Definitely worth the effort.'

'You made this?'

'Created with my own fair hands.'

Each individual shell had been painted in graduating shades of yellow through to a deep, russety orange, and they'd been strung so that, when you looked at the whole thing together, it resembled the flames of a bonfire. 'It's fab. It must be brilliant to be able to make stuff like that. To *create* something of your own.'

Eve smiled. 'I make loads of things – jewellery, bags, scarves, candles. It all sells well at the markets, especially in the summer. I've always loved making things, ever since I was a kid. I used to make *everything* they did on *Blue Peter*. Drove my mum loopy.'

Jo smiled and stepped through the curtain into the living room. The floorboards were bare here as well, but they looked dry and in good condition, and with the squares of carpet here and there it felt almost cosy. She walked over to the fireplace and looked into the mirror that was propped up on a wooden fire surround. What a state she looked. Her hair was greasy and there were dark smudges under her eyes. She'd barely thought about her appearance for the last couple of weeks, but Eve was so pretty she felt dull in comparison.

In the fireplace stood a black iron grate in which were the remains of a fire – a few burnt-out lumps of coal, some charred wood and a lot of ash. To one side was an old tea chest full of wood and newspaper and with a guitar resting against it, and on the other, a Calor gas heater, which Eve managed to light on the third attempt, filling the room with the smell of Calor gas. Eve flopped onto the sagging sofa in front of the huge bay window, which had one cracked pane with a criss-cross of black tape holding it together, and old-fashioned wooden shutters on either side. Jo had always wanted to live in a house with shutters, ever since her mum used to read her 'The Night Before Christmas' in a whispery, excited voice: . . . *Away to the window I flew like a flash, tore open the shutters and threw up the sash . . .*

'It's not . . . what I expected. You know, for a squat.'

'There's no need to live in squalor, not unless you have to.' Eve adjusted the brightly coloured scarves and shawls draped over the back of the sofa so that they covered the worn bits. 'The addicts who lived next door to us in St Leonards; they lived in squalor, but I suppose if you're out of it half the time . . .'

Jo nodded. Her mum had been 'out of it half the time'. They hadn't lived in squalor, but things had changed. Her mum still wiped the kitchen table, ran the carpet sweeper over the living-room floor and cleaned the loo, but it was Jo who'd kept the place generally clean and tidy for the last couple of years. Her mum still cooked, but it was usually beefburgers or sausages with beans or chips. Now and again, she'd have a good day and fill the freezer with Bolognese sauce and chicken casserole. But a day's proper cooking always meant she'd start drinking earlier because she felt she deserved a 'reward', and by the time *Coronation Street* came on she'd be slurring her words. It seemed like a completely different lifetime when they'd all lived in a nice house and her mum and dad had given dinner parties where there would be white wine in the fridge, gin and tonics before the meal and brandies afterwards. She liked the smell of alcohol on her parents' breath when they came up to tuck her in; it meant nice things, men in smart jackets, women wearing perfume and bracelets, flowers in the dining room and leftover pudding in the fridge the next day. After her father left, her mother still had a gin and tonic before dinner, and on Sundays, she'd buy a bottle of Blue Nun and even let Jo have half a glass with Sunday lunch. Later, when Jo was fourteen, she was allowed a glass of sherry or a Martini and lemonade on Friday nights, which became Pizza Night. They'd buy cheese and tomato pizzas from Bejam and pep them up with olives and capers and little bits of ham. There was no telly on Friday nights – it was their night for talking, her mum said, for spending time together. They'd sit in the kitchen with the cassette player between them on the table, singing along to Bonnie Raitt or Joni Mitchell, and they'd be having a really nice time, then something would change very suddenly, as though her mother had become a different person. One night, her mum had been crying and trying to sing at the same time, the tears running down her face and twisting her mouth out of shape. Jo didn't want to have to deal with it, so she said she was going to bed. Her mum grabbed her wrist. 'Not yet, Jo-Jo. Don't go yet.' Her eyes were glazed and her hair was a tangled mess from where she kept running her hands through it. 'You listen to me, Jo-Jo.' She was slurring her words. She wiped the tears with the back of her hand, streaking her face with mascara, but then she seemed to forget what she was going to say. Her upper body swayed as she tried to pour more sherry from an empty bottle. 'Shit shit shit. Where's that other bottle? Sure I had another bottle.'

'You've already drunk it, Mum,' Jo said.

Her mother's eyes narrowed. 'Don't be ridiculous. You're trying to make out I drink too much, aren't you? And I don't appreciate it, Joanna, I really don't.' She picked up the empty bottle again and poured several drips into her glass. 'I think it's time you went to bed, young lady.'

'I know. I just said I was going to bed, but you said—'

Her mum banged her hand down hard on the table, making the glasses jump and rattle. 'Don't try to be smart with me, missy.'

'I wasn't, I . . .' But she stopped because her mum was crying again.

'Jo?' Eve's voice broke in and rescued her from the memory.

'Sorry, I was miles away.'

CHAPTER FOURTEEN

She followed Eve up two flights of stairs and along a dingy passageway where the plaster was bulging in some places and coming off the walls in others. Most of the rooms on the top floor were unused. In one, there was nothing but a dressmaker's dummy and a grubby brown armchair with straw spilling out of a tear in the seat, in another, a couple of empty suitcases and some boxes of old toys. 'Oh wow.' Jo walked across the room. 'Spirograph, Monopoly, Beetle Drive – I used to have all these.' She rummaged in the box. 'Oh look, a Tressy Doll!' She fished the doll out, pressed the button in its back and tugged on a section of hair, which then lengthened, appearing to 'grow' from the top of its head as if by magic. She remembered the advert on television: *Tressy from Ideal; her hair grows!* Granny Pawley had bought it for her that first Christmas after her dad left, the one where her mum hardly stopped crying. Jo had been thrilled with the doll, especially as it came with its own brush, comb and curlers. But when she showed her mum how the hair could change from a neat bob to flowing tresses at the press of a button, her mum had wrinkled her nose. 'Ugh. Take it away, Jo-Jo, it's creepy.'

'This is my work room.' Eve opened the door to a large room with two tall, uncurtained windows that let in lots of light. 'It's where I make my jewellery and suchlike – things we can sell at markets and summer fayres – brings a bit of money in.'

Along the wall under the windows were two pasting tables set up as a work bench and a pain-spattered step-stool. This was a treasure trove; there were different types of crystals, shells, bits of coloured glass, beads, feathers, squares of leather, paints, dyes, glues – Jo had never seen anything like it. She took a piece of clear crystal and held it up to the light, then she spotted some coloured feath-ers. She picked one up and brushed its soft fronds against her cheek. 'What are these for?'

'I'm making a dream-catcher,' Eve said. 'It's nearly finished – look.'

It was a beautiful thing, a tea-plate-sized wooden hoop with an intricate network of purple threads woven across it like a spider's web and decorated with tiny silver beads that caught the light; red and purple gull's feathers hung down on silver cords, weighted with more silver beads at the end. 'Tell you what, you can have this one when it's finished, if you like.'

'Really? Wow, thanks.'

She followed Eve back along the passage past a minia-ture flight of five stairs leading to a little square door, which led to a storage cupboard. On the next floor down, Eve pointed to various doors. 'Bathroom on the left. A bit ancient but everything works. We use an immersion heater for hot water, but it's expensive, so we try to be careful. That's my and Scott's room, and the one right at the end next to the stairs, that's the thinking room – it's got windows all round and you can see the sea. And this' – she flung open the door to an enormous, high-ceilinged, bay-windowed room – 'is yours.'

She felt a twinge of disappointment. The floor was strewn with empty beer cans and newspapers – mainly the *Hastings Observer* and the *Sun*. A grubby orange sleep-ing bag had been thrown across a couple of wooden pallets; next to it was an overflowing pub ashtray. The room smelt faintly of feet.

'Oh my giddy aunt,' Eve said, 'I completely forgot. We had another friend staying recently, and I haven't been in here since he left. Elliot – he's an actor. An absolute sweetie but a filthy pig to have around the house. He got a part in *Z Cars*.'

Something about the way Eve talked made Jo smile. She hadn't heard anyone talking about giddy aunts since Granny Pawley caught her trying to hide the cat under the bedclothes. Eve was smiling too, but quizzically, as though waiting for Jo to explain, but she couldn't. Eve was just . . . funny. The room, though; the room was disgusting. Could she realistically tolerate living in this smelly, male-haunted space? But there was something about the way Eve said *another* friend that made her feel comfortable, as though she already belonged here.

'It's a good house.' Eve moved around the room, stuffing papers and beer cans into a black rubbish sack. 'But the neighbours are a bit square – they called the police when they saw us moving in, so we keep ourselves to ourselves now. The police got in touch with the owner, so he knows we're here, and he said that, as long as we look after the place and don't cause any trouble, we can stay until he's ready to sell it.'

'When do you think he'll want to sell it?' Jo was already worrying about when she might have to leave.

'I don't know. He's got a few other houses, I think, and he lives abroad now anyway, so he's not in a hurry. He'd have to do it up and sort out the damp in the basement, and that'll cost a fortune so it'll probably be yonks before he gets round to it. And all the time we're living here, it's being heated and no one's going to break in and mess the place up.'

It was lovely listening to Eve talk, no matter what she was saying. She had the sort of voice that was so clear you could hear every single, separate word. Jo had a sudden flash of memory: her mum, back in the days when she still laughed and sang, sitting at the piano wearing a pale lemon jumper and with a matching cardigan slung over her shoulders. They'd been to the pictures to see *The Sound of Music,* and now her mum kept singing all the songs. 'Come on, Joanna-Pianna,' she said, pearly-pink-tipped fingers poised over the keys. 'Let's see what we can do. *Let's start at the very beginning,* she sang, trying to sound like Julie Andrews. *A very good place to start . . .'*

Once more, it struck Jo painfully and powerfully that she would never hear her mother's voice again, ever. How *could* that be possible?

'Right, that's a bit more like it.' Eve tied up the rubbish bag she'd just filled and surveyed the room. 'Mind you . . .' She picked up the sleeping bag between her thumb and forefinger and held it away from her like it was covered in dog shit. 'You absolutely can't sleep in this. There's a clean one in our room, and extra blankets, too. You'll be snug as a bug in a rug.'

Jo smiled. Every time Eve opened her mouth, she reminded Jo of her mum or of Granny Pawley.

'At some point we'll need to talk about practical matters, of course.'

'I don't have much money left, but I'm sure I can get a job soon. I —'

'Tomorrow.' Eve waved her hands around as if she was shooing the words out of the window. 'We'll talk about the boring part tomorrow. Scott'll be back later. He's working in the hotels at the moment – kitchen porter. He started training as a teacher but he's a musician really, so he's concentrating on that now. He does a bit of busking and he's got a couple of gigs over the weekend. Once the summer comes, the busking goes really well, and there are the summer fayres, too, so there are plenty of ways to make a few pounds.' She started to walk towards the door. 'Come and talk to me while I make us some dinner.'

The kitchen was enormous with a rickety wooden table in the middle. A floor-to-ceiling cupboard in one alcove was painted a pale yellowy-brown, like the Wimpy Bar French mustard that Rob said was really cat poo. The tiles behind the sink were a similar colour and mostly cracked or broken, as were those in the large recess cut into the chimney breast. 'Did this use to be a fireplace?' Jo looked up at the brickwork. 'It's bigger than me!'

'Probably. Humungous, isn't it? Makes a brilliant cooking area.'

On one side, tucked into the recess, was a red-topped Formica table with two rusty-looking Baby Belling cookers resting on it; on the other, an enamel-topped table served as a work surface. There was an old leatherette armchair to the side of the fireplace and a couple of fireside chairs on the opposite wall near another Calor gas heater. The room reminded her of Granny Pawley's dinette. She settled herself in the armchair and watched while Eve took tomatoes, onions and mushrooms from a cardboard box under one of the tables, and then set to work chopping and slicing. Jo was mesmerised as she watched Eve deftly peeling the onions and then chopping them in no time before starting on the mushrooms, and lastly the tomatoes. It was as though there was no effort involved; it would have taken Jo ages to do the same thing, but Eve just made a few smooth, graceful movements and, bingo, the job was done. Eve opened the window. 'Here.' She tossed Jo the pack of Cheddar cheese she'd taken from the windowsill. 'You could grate that and open a tin of beans if you like. We haven't got a fridge yet, but it doesn't matter this time of year. I'm sure we'll find one before the weather turns warmer.'

While Jo grated the cheese, she watched as Eve fried the onions, mushrooms and tomatoes and tipped them into a pie dish. Then she whisked up the eggs and poured them in as well, sprinkled cheese over the top and put the whole thing in the Baby Belling. 'There,' she said. 'An oven omelette. Stick those beans in a pan and then we can relax.' Jo emptied the beans into a saucepan and was about to throw the can away when Eve grabbed it and peered inside. 'Wait,' she said. Then she nodded. 'Oh, that's okay. You have to leave at least three beans in the tin, you know. One would be lonely, and two might fight. So it must be three.' She looked up at Jo and grinned. 'Always three.'

CHAPTER FIFTEEN

After they'd eaten, Jo borrowed Eve's key and popped out for cigarettes. She could smell the sea and, although it was almost dark now, she had a sudden yearning to see and hear the waves, so she took a detour along the coast road where the wind coming in off the Channel made it feel even colder. A few spots of rain hit her face. Hastings was very different to Newquay. It was a pebble beach for a start, and it sloped down to the sea in stages, like shelves. The beach in Newquay was sandy and flat and wide, whereas this was divided by wooden groynes at regular intervals all the way along to the pier, giving the impression of many smaller beaches.

With no distinguishable horizon to break up the grey, the vastness of sea and sky was magnified, and as she looked at the pier in the distance, she began to feel the sadness swell inside her again. The lights on the pier should have cheered her, but although they looked quite festive, she found her eye drawn downwards, away from the flashing lights and the promise of fun and good times, down beneath the creaking boards to the darker underside of the ageing structure, where the rusty, barnacle-covered supports stood resolutely in the cold water, forgotten and unnoticed.

She looked at her watch. She hadn't thought about her mum or about home for almost three hours. Home; she must stop thinking like that. Aware of a powerful need to be inside, in a room where there was someone she knew, she headed to the newsagent's, bought ten No 6, then began to make her way back up the hill towards the house.

She could see a light on in the sitting room, and as soon as she went in, she could smell the Calor gas. A man was standing in front of the heater with his back to her. He was wearing a black top hat and a long black cape which made her think of the Dracula films. His hair was black too, and he'd tied it into a ponytail with a band of plaited leather. He turned to face her. 'I'm Scott,' he said, removing the hat, which had a red-silk flower tucked into the rim, and then the cape. 'Sorry about the get-up. It's my busking uniform – adds a bit of theatre.' Underneath the cape, he was wearing ragged-looking black jeans and a Bob Dylan T-shirt with an ice-blue denim shirt open over the top. 'I'm guessing you're Jo.' He sat down on the settee, stretched his long legs out in front of him and began rolling a joint. He looked up at her and smiled. His skin was pale but with an olive tinge to it that suggested it would go very brown in the summer, and his nose was too long and slightly twisted, but he was nice-looking in a poetic, hippyish sort of way. A tiny black beard sat in the middle of his chin and his eyes were bright blue, like cornflowers, and all the more striking because of his raven-black hair, which, he explained later, was something to do with his ancestry – his father was half-Chinese on his mother's side, whereas his mum was a typical English rose.

He licked along the edge of the Rizla and carefully sealed the joint, then held it up in front of his face as though admiring it. 'I deserve this, man.' He placed the joint between his teeth and reached into each of his front jeans pockets, then started feeling around the back.

'Here,' Jo said, offering her lighter.

'Cheers.' He leaned forward and, rather than taking the lighter from her, looked at her pointedly until she flicked it into life. He used his hand to steady hers and she noticed the fine black hairs on the backs of his fingers, which smelled of tobacco and very faintly of lemons.

'Coffee, Jo?' Eve called from the kitchen.

'Could I have tea, please?' she called back.

Scott smiled. 'Polite. That's nice, man.' He nodded slowly. He moved a several-days-old copy of the *Guardian*, a pouch of Old Holborn and a pack of Rizlas off the settee and patted the cushion beside him. 'Come and sit down.'

Was he flirting with her? A strand of greasy hair fell over her eye and she tucked it quickly behind her ear. There was something about him that made her feel shy and silly and very conscious of how she looked. But he was Eve's boyfriend.

When Eve came into the room, Scott's attention turned entirely to her, and his features seemed to relax and soften as he looked at her. Maybe he hadn't been flirting after all. He smiled at Eve and thanked her when she handed him a plate of food – the last of the baked omelette, which she served cold with salad. When she went to the fireplace to start laying a fire, he stopped her. 'Leave it, Evie. You're tired, man; I'll do it when I've had this.' And when Eve smiled back at him, Jo noticed, she somehow looked even prettier. This was a couple who were in love, Jo realised. There hadn't been this sort of love between her parents, not even when she was little, and seeing it now filled her with a sort of sweet sadness. On the one hand, it was strangely comforting to watch them exchanging glances, nods and smiles as they talked, and she loved how proud they were of each other: *Scott's a brilliant guitarist, and you should hear the songs he writes; Eve's so talented, she can make beautiful objects out of anything, even bits of old junk . . .* On the other hand there was something about their closeness that induced in her a piercing loneliness she hadn't been aware of before.

'Our plan,' Scott was saying as he rolled another joint, 'is to grow as much as we possibly can while we're here.' They'd been talking about their plans for the garden. He paused and nodded towards his plate which was still on the floor next to him. 'You know, if we kept chickens, and if we could make our own cheese, we could produce this meal without having to pay for anything except the electricity to cook it. That would be so cool.'

'I'd love to keep chickens, but I think cheese-making might be a bit beyond us,' Eve said. 'Although, who knows what might happen in the future.'

Scott turned to her and grinned. '"Who knows what might happen in the future"? I thought *you* did.'

Eve was grinning, too, and Jo looked from her to Scott and back again.

'Scott doesn't believe me, but—'

'Eve has magical powers.' He put on a spooky voice. 'She can read your palm, gaze into a crystal ball—'

'Oh Scotty.' Eve shoved him playfully on the arm, then turned to Jo. 'I've no idea how to read palms, and I don't have a crystal ball. But I can read tea leaves. Scott thinks it's a load of rubbish, but my grandma showed me how to do it.' Her face brightened. 'Tell you what, I'll read yours later if you like.'

Jo just smiled.

'Anyway,' Scott continued. 'As I was saying, our ethos is simple. Live off the land and off your skills and talents where possible, consume less, and reuse things.' He gestured vaguely around him. 'Most of this is other people's leavings, things we've found in skips or at jumble sales. It's perfectly good stuff. The waste in our society is unforgivable, man. You just have to be on the lookout; tune in to what people throw away. We all have too many possessions, anyway.'

123

'You're like Tom and Barbara,' Jo said. 'You know, on *The Good Life*.'

Scott nodded. 'We've seen it a few times at a mate's; we don't have a television here, though.'

'I love Tom and Barbara,' Eve said. 'And Margot and Jerry. Oh, wouldn't it be cool to live like that.'

'I've got a lot of time for the whole self-sufficiency scene,' Scott agreed. 'Even if they did start it in this, like, massive pad in suburbia. Anyway' – he turned to Jo – 'what do you think?'

'Um, about what?'

'About staying here for a while. It's totally cool with us; we like having people here – well, one person, anyway. Sometimes there'll be more, but it works best when there's just two or three of us. We lived in this squat once where it was, like, some sort of open-house commune scene.' He shook his head. 'That was not cool, man.'

'Do say you'll stay,' Eve said. 'The only rules are, you contribute your share of food and bills – that means the electricity bill and the gas cylinders – and you take an equal share of the communal work. The way it usually works is . . .' And she reeled off a list of house rules.

Jo felt a beat of disappointment at the realisation that she was simply one of many, a temporary house guest rather than a special friend. She nodded. 'I don't have much money left, so I'll need a job. Is there anywhere—'

'There's plenty of casual work about,' Scott interrupted. 'Bar work, mostly, cash-in-hand.'

'Okay then, yes, I'd love to stay,' she smiled. 'Thank you.'

'Good! That's settled, then.' Eve stood up. 'I'll make tea.'

Scott was rolling another joint when Eve returned with a teapot and a bottle of milk, then she went out of the room again and came back with two mugs and a cup and saucer. 'You have to leave about half an inch of tea in the bottom,' she explained as she poured the tea and handed the cup and saucer to Jo. 'Hold the cup with your right hand if you want to see the future, or in your left if you want to understand the past.'

'Here she is,' Scott said, his tone gently mocking. 'Mystic Madam Eva. Your destiny revealed . . .'

'Shut up, Scott. I just have a knack for it, that's all. I've always been able to see shapes and symbols in the leaves, and they all have meanings. I . . .' She looked down as if she was embarrassed. 'I just know how to interpret them.'

When Jo had finished her tea, Eve told her to turn over the saucer and place it on top of the cup, then swirl the cup around three times, clockwise, before tipping it up and allowing the remaining tea to drain down into the saucer for a minute or so.

'Now, let's see.' Eve peered into the cup. 'A lot of leaves; that indicates a full and busy life. Oh dear. There's a drop of tea left on the side of the cup – that means tears, but that's probably because of your mum. Ooh look, see this cigar shape? That's the symbol for new friends, and it's right at the top, near the rim, which means it relates to the immediate future.' She smiled. 'So it probably means Scott and me.'

Jo smiled as she looked into the cup. It could be a cigar shape, she supposed, but to her it just looked like a line of tea leaves. 'What about that?' She pointed to a very clear flower pattern near the bottom.

Eve's face lit up. 'A flower! Lucky you – it means you'll have a happy marriage, but not for a while. You have to read the leaves from the top of the cup to the bottom, you see, and the further down the cup the symbol is, the further away the event it represents.' She pointed to a tiny clump of leaves about half an inch down. 'Now this little fan usually means a flirtation or an unexpected kiss.'

It did look a bit like a fan, Jo had to admit. In fact, the more she looked into the cup, the more she could see little pictures in the leaves. 'Is that a bird?' She pointed to a shape about halfway down the side. Eve didn't say anything for a moment. 'A raven,' she mumbled, turning the cup around. 'And that looks like . . .' She blinked a couple of times. 'No, I think I must be doing it wrong.'

'What is it?' Jo reached for her cigarettes. The whole thing was starting to seem a bit silly. 'Come on, tell me.'

'Did you swirl it with your right hand, or your left?'

'Oh, come on,' Scott said. 'That's enough.' He sounded annoyed.

'Right,' Jo said. 'At least, I think it was.'

'No, I think it must have been your left. I'm seeing the loss of someone close to you, a long-lasting grief – it must mean your mum.' She put the cup back on the saucer and stood up. 'Perhaps we'd better try again another time.'

*

By eleven, Jo could barely keep her eyes open. With Eve's help, she set the mattress on the pallets and made up the bed.

Eve put her hands on her hips and looked up at the window. 'Now all we need is a curtain. Elliot never bothered covering the windows, and he used to wander around in the nuddy sometimes. I didn't know where to look! Oh, hang on – won't be a tick.' She hurried out of the room, then came back with a handful of drawing pins and a huge, bulging dustbin bag from which she pulled a length of red cotton fabric with swirly patterns in gold stitching. It looked Indian, like a sari. She stood on a chair and pinned it up over the glass. 'That'll do for tonight.' She got down and nodded towards the bag. 'That bag's full of clothes. I don't know if there's anything there that might be any good to you, but it's all in fairly good nick. Some of them belonged to Sapphire – she was the girl who moved here with us last year. Until she ran off to live in a caravan on the Isle of Wight, that is. But most of it's stuff that's a bit tight on me now. Everything shrinks when you wash it, doesn't it?' Eve grumbled. 'Either that or I'm getting fat.'

'Thanks,' Jo said. 'I didn't bring much with me, so . . . well anyway, thank you. It's very kind of you to . . .' Then she felt her lip wobble and she didn't trust herself to say any more.

Eve tipped her head to one side. 'You're tired. You'll feel better after a good night's sleep. Night-night.' She switched off the light and Jo could hear the floorboards creaking as she went back downstairs.

Jo fell asleep immediately, sleeping deeply and dreamlessly until two in the morning when her eyes snapped open. For a few seconds, she didn't know where she was, but then the dark shape of her duffle bag next to the bed came into focus and she remembered. She could feel the swish of her eyelashes moving on the pillowcase as she blinked. But there was another noise coming through the pillow, a sort of rhythmic thumping. She could hear someone moaning. A woman; she sounded like she was in agony. Eve! Jo jerked her head up, her heart suddenly pounding hard and fast. Then she heard a man's voice as well, a sort of grunting. 'Oh shit,' she murmured as she realised what the noise was. She lay back down and pulled the covers over her head.

CHAPTER SIXTEEN

Sheffield, January 2010

I'd never been inside this church before, despite having walked past it for years. I went to church a few times when Hannah was a baby, but I didn't find what I was looking for. What was I looking for? Forgiveness, I suppose. But maybe I'd never found it because I didn't think it was God who needed to forgive me.

I stood looking up at the stained-glass image of Mary gazing adoringly at her baby son. Hadn't she only been about sixteen when she conceived the son of God? She looked older here, as though she already knew that no good could come of it. For a moment, I was so lost in the scene that I forgot why I was here, then I heard the big old door being pushed open, and there he was, leaning on a wooden walking stick. I could see immediately that he was telling the truth about his illness. It was hardly surprising I hadn't been sure it was him when I saw him in town; his eyes were sunken with sludgy brown crescents beneath;

his skin was pale and stretched-looking with a greenish tinge around the mouth, and he was so thin that I could see the exact shape of his skull. I had no doubt that I was looking at a dying man.

'You came,' he said in an almost resigned way.

'Did I have a choice?'

He nodded in recognition. 'I know. I'm sorry about that. I had to make you see how important this is.' He used the ends of the dark wooden pews for extra support, resting his hand on each as he passed.

'How are . . .' I stopped myself from asking the ridiculous question. 'I can see you're not well,' I said instead, 'and I'm sorry. It must be . . . I don't know, frightening.'

He shook his head, then motioned to a pew. 'Do you mind if we sit? I'm not feeling too good today.'

'Of course.' I watched his knuckles turn white as he grasped the back of a pew and lowered himself slowly into the one behind. I had to tell myself again, this is Scott. *Scott.* For a few moments, we didn't speak. For myself, it was because I had no idea what to say. But in Scott's case, I suspected it was because the sheer physical effort of walking towards me and sitting down had taken it out of him.

'So, how are you managing?' It was what I said to parents at the Project, and I heard the professional tone in my voice, brisk and slightly distant; it was the tone I used when I was trying to show that I cared without getting too involved.

'I used to feel frightened,' he said. Then he looked at

me sideways and smiled. 'I was scared I might have cancer. But now I know for sure, well, there's nothing to be scared of any more.'

I forgot about the professional voice. This was Scott; this was Hannah's father. 'But . . . but aren't you afraid of actually . . . you know, of —'

'Of dying? You can say it, you know. And no, I'm not, not really. I don't want to feel pain, but they tell me they can make sure I don't.' He smiled at me again. 'I'll be getting some *serious* drugs when the time comes, man. But dying? No. It's weird, but once you know it's going to happen, you sort of accept it.' His tone was vaguely superior, as though I couldn't possibly understand. Although, thinking about it, I suppose he was right.

'Do you come here often?' I said, completely oblivious until he laughed.

'The old ones are the best, aren't they? But I can't say I ever got far with that line.'

'Oh God, I mean, I'm sorry.' I felt myself colouring. 'I meant —'

He was still smiling. 'No worries, I know what you meant, and yes, I do. Well, not here, necessarily. Probably a bit late to save my soul, but there's nothing to lose, I guess. Anyway, I think I should tell you why I wanted to see you.'

I wanted to ask how long he'd been going to church, whether it was because he was dying or whether he had been going ever since it all happened. I wanted to know the answers to these questions, but I was also stalling for

131

time, trying to put off the moment when he told me something that was going to blast my life apart. He wasn't smiling now.

'The thing is, I want us to own up; to tell the truth.'

I stared at him. I didn't want to hear this; I would not hear this.

'It's been haunting me for years,' he said, not looking at me. 'We should have spoken up at the time . . . well, soon after, anyway. I suppose I thought it would come to light eventually.' He looked up at me now, and his eyes were glistening as though he was holding back tears. 'I think that's one of the reasons I left when I did, to be honest. I kept expecting a knock at the door. Even when I was in New Zealand with my parents, I couldn't stop thinking about it. And now . . . well, now I just want to try and put things right.'

I tried to speak but my mouth was dry. I felt all the blood in my body rush down to my feet and my bowels started to shift and I wondered if I was going to suddenly need the loo. I had to get away, to get out of this place and away from what he was saying. I didn't realise that I'd actually stood up until I felt his hand on my arm. 'Sit down,' he said quietly. His voice had a certainty to it, as though he felt totally confident what he was saying. Without wanting to or knowing why, I sat.

'We've got to tell them, Jo. Hannah, your husband, the police – everyone.'

'I . . . I can't,' I stammered. 'We can't, not now, not after all these years.' I could hear and feel my voice rising, but

I couldn't seem to do anything about it. 'You're mad,' I said, getting to my feet again. '*Put things right*? How can we possibly put things right? You're crazy. Just ... just leave me alone.'

He took my hand. 'Stop. Listen to me for one more minute.'

I snatched my hand away just as the door swung open again and an elderly woman came in. She looked at us, caught in mid-confrontation in this holy place, but she didn't seem to notice anything amiss because she nodded and smiled before sliding into one of the pews and bending her head. I sat down again and this time I spoke in a whisper. 'One minute, then.' Scott leant closer and spoke quietly. 'I have nothing to lose now,' he said wearily, looking down at his hands again. 'The guilt is eating me away as much as the cancer. In fact, I've often wondered if they aren't one and the same thing.' He looked up at me. 'What about you, Jo? Don't you feel guilty?'

'Of course I bloody do,' I snapped, still whispering. 'But I've had Hannah to bring up; I've had to be practical. It wasn't easy, you know, stuck in that awful flat, living on next to nothing while you swanned off to the other side of the world to pick up where you left off.'

I waited for him to argue with me, to justify once more why he left us in that flat, why he'd convinced me that it would be better if we never saw, mentioned or spoke to each other ever again. But he didn't. He looked at me calmly, and when he spoke, his voice was quiet and steady, but with a steely edge. 'But you're all right now, aren't you? You've got a good job – good money and worthy at the same time.'

'Yes, I'm all right now.' I ran a hand through my hair for the third or fourth time and wondered if I was developing a nervous habit. 'I was lucky enough to meet a good man, one with a sense of responsibility.' The elderly woman looked up from her prayers. I made a conscious effort to lower my voice again. 'But that was years after you left. Before then I had to do endless shitty jobs so I could pay the rent and feed and clothe us both; I didn't have parents I could run back to; I barely had time to think.' I sighed. 'I'm sorry. But having Hannah to consider meant I had to get on with things, and it was years before I was able to earn any reasonable money, and even then it was only because Duncan was prepared to support me while I studied. He cares about us both, even though Hannah isn't his.'

Scott nodded slowly. His eyes were closed and I could see the blueish-grey lines under the skin of his eyelids. There was so little skin stretched taught and shiny over his face that I wondered how there could be room underneath for veins and blood and flesh.

'You've done well, Jo. But the thing is, I don't have long left, and I've made up my mind. I wanted to give you the opportunity to tell your family first. Then, when you've told them, we'll go to the police together. I doubt Hannah will want to meet me, but I'd like to see her, just once. If—'

'No!' I stood up and tried to move away so he couldn't

touch me again, but my scarf caught on the end of the pew. My hands trembled uncontrollably as I tried to untangle it.

'Well, maybe we'll worry about that later. I'm sorry, Jo, but if you won't tell them, I will.'

'Stop calling me that,' I yelled as I ran down the aisle, past the old woman who looked up with a quizzical expression as I passed. She probably thought it was a lovers' tiff. I wrenched the huge door open and stepped out into the sharp, cold sunlight. I ran blindly through the milling shoppers and didn't stop running until I got back to the car. Breathless, I threw myself into the driver's seat and pulled the door shut quickly behind me as though I could shut out everything that had just been said. I could feel the tears building up; I rummaged in the glove compartment for tissues, and pulled out an unopened bag of dog treats, an *A–Z*, a thank-you card from a client, the mini umbrella that Hannah had left in here weeks ago, and a pocket-sized book of short stories that Duncan gave me a couple of years back after the car broke down and I had to wait forty minutes for the breakdown people. 'Stick it in the glove compartment and leave it there,' he'd said, 'then if you break down again, at least you'll have something to help pass the time.' I found the tissues and blew my nose before piling all the stuff back in and starting the engine. I headed south up Ecclesall Road, past the restaurants and bars that were packed with students most nights, past the park and the tall Victorian houses that overlooked it, and out to where the houses became even grander before the buildings began to fall away and the countryside stretched out in front of me.

The things in the glove compartment had made me feel even worse, somehow; evidence that I had a normal life, a good job, a nice house, a husband and a daughter and a dog. I had a family that loved me and had no idea that I'd deceived them all these years. In the distance, the hills were still covered with snow. This was officially 'high ground', and conditions were different up here.

I drove another couple of miles and pulled in to the lay-by we usually parked in when we brought Monty out here on the moors. I felt a stab of guilt as I realised that Monty was still at home in his basket, probably bored and waiting for me to come and take him out. I should have gone home and picked him up, made things normal. I climbed out of the car anyway. A walk might clear my head, help me to think properly. There was still a fair bit of snow around up here, although it was in clumps where the deeper snow had thawed. The air was sharp and clean and the sky seemed wider as I walked through the woods and into a clearing which then gave out onto vast open moorland. In front of me was a large, flat rock where we sometimes sat in the summer, eating our sandwiches and marvelling at the view across the moors, over the rooftops of Sheffield and out towards the hills.

There was something poking out from behind the rock, and when I moved nearer I saw that it was a dead fox. Its soft, red-brown fur was mostly still covered with snow, but I could see the white tip of its bushy tail and its lovely serene face only partly revealed by the thaw. It wasn't very big, but it didn't look like a cub so it was probably a vixen. Her glazed eyes stared vacantly upwards and her mouth was open, revealing beautifully white, pointed teeth, so perfectly smooth; so elegant. I wondered how long the poor thing had been lying out here under her blanket of snow, and whether she'd died of natural causes or had been hit by a car and slunk here through the trees from the road. Did she have babies somewhere, slowly starving as they awaited her return? But no, it was probably too early in the year. She could have been pregnant, of course. I reached down and touched her cold face with my finger, feeling gently around her ears, stroking the white fur on the tender underside of her chin and noticing for the first time that it was stained with a single line of darkened blood. And that was when I couldn't hold back tears any more. At first they fell silently, rolling down my face one after the other, but soon I found myself sobbing like a child, noisily and without restraint. I felt as though an icy hand was poised around my heart, reminding me that I had everything to lose, that if I wasn't careful, the life I'd built so assiduously was about to come apart.

CHAPTER SEVENTEEN

I stood under the shower for a long time but couldn't seem to wash away the smell of the church, a mix of lavender-scented floor polish and musty old hymn books. After my shower, I lay down on the bed for a while; I was exhausted after the conversation with Scott, emotionally wrung out. But when I closed my eyes, all I could see was that poor dead fox.

The sound of Duncan's key in the door, usually so welcome, tonight made my stomach shift. I felt exposed, as though he'd be able to know everything that had happened today just by looking at me.

'Hey.' He kissed me in that slightly distracted way that told me he'd had a bad day – an ill-treated dog, perhaps, or a distraught owner having a beloved cat put to sleep. His lips were cold and I could smell the chill of the outside on his coat. I should have poured him a glass of wine, asked if he wanted to talk about it. But I couldn't look at him for fear of what he might see in my face. 'Hey, yourself.' I turned back to the hob where I was boiling water for spaghetti, and I opened a jar of pesto because I couldn't think calmly enough to plan a proper meal. Duncan did a double take. We usually made Friday nights a bit of an occasion, and if we weren't eating out, I'd cook something nice, something a bit more interesting than pasta and pesto, anyway. Duncan didn't say anything. He swung his rucksack off his back and then crouched down to make a fuss of Monty, who was frantically wagging his tail and greeting him as if he'd been gone for weeks. 'Hello, Monty matey. Yes, I've missed you, too. Good boy.' He stood up. 'What time are we eating?'

'It'll be about ten minutes.'

He nodded as he took his coat off. 'You all right?' he said. 'You look a bit stressed.'

'Just tired, that's all.'

He smiled. 'Was it hard-going?'

I snapped my head up. 'What? What do you mean?' My voice sounded sharper than I intended. Had he been in town today? Had he seen me with Scott?

His smile disappeared and he looked at me oddly. 'Are you sure you're okay? I meant the walk. Where did you go in the end? Did you make it up to the moors?'

As I reached for the spaghetti, I knocked the pesto jar and a wooden spoon off the worktop. It took another second or two for me to remember that, this morning, I'd told him I might take Monty for a proper walk. 'Oh, sorry, I see what you mean.' I bent down to pick up the jar, which wasn't broken, thank goodness. 'Yes, it was good. There's still a fair bit of snow up there, you know.' At least I actually had walked on the moors, so, technically, I wasn't lying. I wanted to tell him about the fox, but somehow I couldn't; it was too sad.

'Bet he had a nice time.' He nodded towards Monty who was in his basket, resting his head on his paws and watching me carefully, lest I should drop some food.

'He certainly did. Didn't you, Monty?' So it had come to this; I'd stooped to making the dog complicit in my deception.

'So, what else did you do?'

He knew I usually packed my days with activity. He expected me to say I'd had coffee with a friend, wandered around the Millennium Galleries or maybe even seen a film at the art deco cinema near the station. He was waiting for me to answer but for a moment I couldn't think of a single thing to say. Part of me wanted to collapse sobbing into his arms. I was tired; unbelievably, bone-achingly tired. I already knew I didn't have the strength for this.

*

I was shattered. After we'd eaten, I told Duncan I was going to lie down and that I thought I had another migraine starting – one more lie, but it was the only way I could think of to shut myself away from his worried expression, the tender sympathy in his eyes. But despite

140

my exhaustion, I couldn't switch my thoughts off and I just lay there staring at the ceiling. I dropped off eventually though, because when I woke, my face was wet and I realised I'd been crying a split second before I remembered why. This was what used to happen in the early days after we'd left Hastings. I'd wake up sobbing in a way that I couldn't allow myself to while I was awake. Scott would lean over and stroke my hair, trying to soothe me, but his attempts were clumsy and it never quite worked. Then I'd get up and walk across the cold lino to the other side of the room where Hannah slept in a second-hand carrycot, and I'd put my finger in front of her nose to make sure she was breathing. Sometimes, I'd pick her up just so I could feel the warmth of her solid little body in my arms, then I'd bury my face in that delectable hollow at the back of her neck and smell her sweet, talcum-powder scent.

The door opened slowly and Duncan hovered in the doorway, the light from the landing behind him. 'It's okay,' I said. 'I'm awake.'

He smiled, came across the room and leaned down to look at me. 'How're you feeling?'

I was touched by the way he automatically spoke softly when I had a migraine, but his being nice to me only made me feel more guilty. I wanted to go downstairs and drink a large glass of red wine, but then he'd have known for sure that something was wrong, and anyway, I wouldn't have done that if I really did have a migraine. I needed time to think, but I also knew that I couldn't keep this up for long. 'I still feel pretty rough, but it's going off a bit, I think. ' I closed my eyes again. 'I'm sure I'll be all right in the morning.'

'Okay. Anything I can get you?'

I could hear the disappointment in his voice. Friday evenings were special – the start of the weekend. Usually, Friday evenings meant good food and wine, a fire in the grate, a DVD perhaps, or some music and a chat and then an early night for some comfortable, reassuring sex. But instead, he'd had a crap dinner and now he'd end up watching *Casualty* with the dog before creeping into bed carefully so he didn't disturb me. 'No, thanks; I just need to sleep, so I'll say goodnight now.' And I turned over, lying bitch that I was, because I was finding it hard to keep the tears in.

But I couldn't get back to sleep, and now it was two o'clock and I was sitting in the kitchen, composing a reply to Scott's text, which I'd only noticed by chance because I'd left my phone on the table. When I checked, I saw that the text had come earlier, after I'd gone upstairs. *Just a reminder*, it read. *Think about it, but not for too long.* I should have taken my phone up with me. What if Duncan had seen it? But then I cursed myself – when had Duncan ever read my texts? *I need to talk to you,* I typed. *Can we meet next week? Same place, 1-ish Mon or Tues?* I pressed *Send* and was astonished when my phone pinged and there was an immediate reply. I changed the setting to *Silent* straight away. *Tues 1 pm?* it said. *Fine,* I replied. *See you there.* I didn't know what I was going to say yet, or even if I'd turn up, but at least if we had a time fixed it'd stop him from calling or texting. For some reason, before I pressed *Send*, I added, *Why you up so late?* The silent reply came back: *I don't sleep much.*

I drank a cup of hot chocolate in the hope that it would help me sleep, then crept back upstairs and into bed. I was still awake at four, still trying to think of a way out. Slowly, I began to turn over an idea in my mind. Scott was too ill to work, which probably meant he was on benefits. He must have hated that. But Duncan and I, we had savings. I started to calculate how much I could withdraw without him noticing, and before long, I drifted off to sleep.

I woke feeling slightly more positive, and when Duncan asked me sleepily how I was feeling this morning, I told him I was much better. He yawned and stretched expansively, lifting the covers as he did so and causing a blast of cold air to hit my bare shoulders. I pulled the duvet up around my neck and tried to recapture the cocoon-like warmth for a few more minutes. Duncan's arm slipped around my waist and he moved nearer; I could feel his warm breath on the back of my neck and his penis nudging at my buttocks. This was my cue to turn over and wrap my arms and legs around him, but I couldn't. Much as I craved the comfort of his body, the sex could sometimes be too real, too truthful, and I was scared of what I might reveal. 'Sorry, darling. I'm still feeling a bit queasy.' I felt his arm tense.

'I thought you said you felt much better?'

'I do. Much better, but still a bit, you know . . .'

He sighed, lifted his arm off me and moved away, and I wanted to cry out and pull him back, but instead I just said, 'Sorry.'

*

I made coffee and fired up the laptop. Duncan had been quiet. He was still a bit put out, I think, and I couldn't shake the feeling that he knew something was up. He came into the kitchen wearing trainers, jogging bottoms and a sweatshirt. 'Going for a quick run,' he announced, and he left without kissing me.

Having lied to Duncan about feeling queasy I found I now did feel quite sick. My stomach was unsettled and I felt weak and shivery, as though I had a fever. I tipped the coffee down the sink and made myself some ginger tea instead. Eve always called it 'tea', but really it was an infusion; you took an inch-long lump of ginger, peeled it, sliced it finely and steeped it in a mug of boiling water for five minutes, then you sipped until the nausea disappeared.

We had four bank accounts between us, a personal account each, a joint household account and another joint one for other expenses – holidays, Christmas etc. If I juggled things around, I reckoned I could scrape together about £4,000 without Duncan knowing. Fortunately, the finances had always been my job, so he hardly ever looked at the accounts. I'd have to think of some way of replacing it, but I could worry about that later. I felt a slight thrill at the thought that this was something I could try; it was a plan. If Scott really didn't have long to live, then some money might make his last days more comfortable. His *last days*; briefly, sadness pierced my thoughts, despite the fact that he was threatening everything I loved.

While I moved the money around, I tried to ignore the little voice telling me this wouldn't work, that it wouldn't make any difference. I was about to shut the laptop down when Duncan came back from his run, breathless and looking a little sweat-dampened but healthy none the less. 'I need to do this more often,' he said. 'I've only done a couple of miles and I'm knackered.' He took his trainers off and flung them in the corner. 'Just going for a shower.' He nodded towards the laptop. 'What are you up to?'

It was a casual, non-threatening question, but I snapped 'Nothing' too quickly and he flinched at the sharpness of my tone. 'Only asking,' he said.

'Sorry, I didn't mean to snap. I was wasting time, that's all. Seeing what's on telly tonight, looking at eBay.' I was a despicable liar and I hated myself.

I saw his face relax. He nodded and headed off for his shower.

CHAPTER EIGHTEEN

It took daily trips to the cashpoint to withdraw the money, but after a few days I finally had £4,000 in cash. Tuesday was admin day at the Project so I was in the office rather than out on a visit. At eleven, my phone pinged. It was a text from Scott. *Feeling bad, can't travel. Pls come here.* He gave an address not far from the city centre. I felt a flash of irritation that he was telling me what to do rather than asking, but then I reminded myself that he was dying, and even if he hadn't been, he definitely had the upper hand.

I knew roughly where the road was – I'd lived a few streets away when I first moved to Sheffield. London Road was busy as always, and as I drove along it, past the scruffy pubs, the PC repair shops and the many restaurants and takeaways, I felt like I was playing one of those simulated driving games where hazards pop out at you every few hundred yards. Today I narrowly avoided a cyclist who turned in front of me without signalling, a Staffordshire bull terrier who was running in and out of the traffic and a woman who pushed a double buggy out in front of me twenty yards from a zebra crossing.

When I saw where Scott was staying, I felt quite hopeful about persuading him to take the money. It was a dump, one in a row of terraced red-brick houses, all with satellite dishes like ugly growths sprouting from their walls. Some of the windows were boarded up, while others framed filthy net curtains or had blankets nailed across. A broken television lay outside one house, its guts spilling out onto the pavement; the whole street was littered with empty pizza and burger boxes, beer cans, cigarette ends and dog shit. Number 89 was smaller than the others, stuck on the end as though the builders had found they had a few bricks left over and thought they might as well use them up by throwing together one more tiny house to finish off the terrace, like a makeweight. There was an overturned wheelie bin in the front yard and a scrawny-looking black cat chewing vigorously on a bone from a KFC box. The cat hissed as I approached, eyed me warily for a moment, then carried on chewing, the tip of its tail flicking sharply from side to side. There was no doorbell, so I knocked hard on the peeling front door and waited. Just as I was about to knock again, my phone pinged: *Come round the back. Door open.*

You had to go through a shared gennel to get to the back door, which opened into the kitchen. I could immediately smell incense – patchouli; it was so evocative I almost expected Eve to appear and offer me a cup of chamomile tea. On the windowsill was a plastic tray of dried-up soil that had shrunken away from the sides, and a saucer containing a rusty key, a couple of corks and an open packet of seeds, mung beans, by the look of it. An old image flashed up: egg boxes crammed onto the kitchen windowsill in Hastings, the tender young shoots of cress, mung beans and alfalfa sprouts, bright green sparks of life pushing their way up through the soil and into the light.

'Hello?' I called.

'In here,' came the weak reply. He looked dreadful, thinner, if that was possible, than he had last week, and his eyes seemed yet further sunken into his face. He sat in an armchair, his feet up on a wooden stool with a woven canvas top. I wondered if he'd made the stool himself; it was the sort of thing he used to do.

'So, how are you?' Usually when we asked this question, we didn't really want to know the answer, but I did want to know now.

'Had better days,' he said. 'Had worse, though.' There was no colour left in his voice. My eyes strayed to the guitar that hung on the wall in one of the alcoves. I wondered when he'd last been able to sing. 'A long time since I've made music,' he said, as if reading my mind.

The wallpaper in here was dark, with an old-fashioned leafy pattern, and there was a torn and faded poster bearing the words: *If God gives you lemons, make lemonade* stuck to the chimney breast with Sellotape. A coal-effect gas fire sat in the fireplace, chucking out heat and swallowing up oxygen.

'I can offer you nettle tea.' He nodded to the flask on the floor next to him. 'Or you can go through and make yourself something else.' He gestured towards the off-shot kitchen.

'I'm fine.' My eyes flicked around the room. There were a few books and CDs here and there, a couple of dry-looking cactus plants on the windowsill. It wasn't particularly homely, but it was reasonably clean and tidy. He read my mind again. 'My landlady lives next door. She comes in a couple of times a week to do my laundry, a bit of cleaning and so on.' His eyes closed when he stopped speaking and his body appeared to deflate, as though the effort of speaking had taken all his energy.

'What about meals?' Why was I asking this? Why should I give a damn?

It was a second or two before he opened his eyes. 'Takeouts, mainly, and Brenda – the landlady – brings me meals when I ask her to. I pay her, obviously.'

I looked at him. 'Scott, I've been thinking about what you said.'

He met my gaze without speaking. His eyes had lost their sharp cornflower colour and were paler now, a weak, sickly blue.

'And I need to talk to you.'

He waited.

'You're not going to like—'

'I told you, Jo, I'm not letting it go.'

'Just hear me out. And don't call me that.'

He opened his mouth to interrupt again but I put my hand up. 'Look, I listened to you, now listen to me.'

He sighed and his body sort of slumped. 'Go on then, say your piece.' He closed his eyes again.

'Thanks.' I was slightly thrown at how easily he gave in. 'I understand why you feel the way you do. Believe me, I've dreamed of unburdening myself ever since it happened, but it's not that simple, is it? I could walk into a police station now and tell them everything, and I'm sure I'd sleep easier if I did, but what good would it do? It won't change the past or make anything better; all it can do is make things worse.'

'For you, maybe. But do you only think of yourself?' He opened his eyes and turned towards me. 'Look at you. You've come a long way since you turned up on my doorstep looking pathetic, haven't you? '

'*Your* doorstep?'

'Nice house, nice car, nice clothes. I bet your husband's nice, too. Good, solid provider-type.' He shook his head dismissively.

'I've been lucky, I know that. I told you, Duncan's a good man and he's been a good father to Hannah.'

'She's my daughter.'

'But you didn't want to know.' I slapped my hand down on the arm of the chair and stood up. 'You can't pull that one on me now. You don't care about her; you haven't even asked about her life.' I felt tears threatening, but they were tears of frustration and anger. 'You don't know anything about her,' I shouted at him. 'Whether she's married or single, whether she's happy, what she does for a living. You don't know whether she was bullied at school, whether she had chickenpox or mumps or measles or . . .'

He tipped his head back and closed his eyes again. 'She married in 2008; husband's name, Marcus Wilson, a physiotherapist, I believe. She's a qualified acupuncturist and reflexologist, and they work together at an alternative healing centre on the outskirts of the city. Their baby' – he opened his eyes and looked at me defiantly – 'my grandson was born not long before Christmas.'

'How the hell—' But I stopped myself. He'd found me easily enough, I supposed he was bound to look Hannah up as well. 'Bastard,' I muttered as I rummaged in my bag for a tissue. 'Not your grandson, actually.' But I didn't know if he heard that. How dare he! How dare he turn up after all this time hell-bent on ruining our lives. 'You've got a nerve,' I said, anger making my voice falter. 'Have you been following her as well? Making anonymous phone calls to her in the middle of the night?'

He shook his head slowly. 'No. And I never called you in the middle of the night, either. Well, I know it was late on New Year's Eve, but I knew you'd be up then.' He looked at me. 'Listen, I needed to make sure I spoke to you, that's all. I didn't want to follow you to work, or creep up on you in the park.'

'Well, how very bloody generous of you.' I walked over to the window and looked out, glad to have turned my back on him. 'I haven't "come a long way" as you put it; all right, I made a good marriage, but only after years of struggling on my own.' I snapped round to face him again. 'You've no idea what it was like for me. I'm the one who fed her and clothed her on next to nothing, bathed her cuts and grazes, sat up all night with her when she was screaming with earache – you haven't a bloody clue, have you? Being a parent is not just about providing the sperm, you know. You can't spend your life mooning around in the sunshine with your guitar and then think you can suddenly come back and decide to play at being a father because, I don't know, because you feel unfulfilled or something, or because I have a family and you don't and you're jealous.' I ran out of steam, and there was a silence when I stopped speaking. Scott still had his eyes closed and his head was tipped forward now so that his chin was almost on his chest.

'I know what it is to be a father,' he said, without opening his eyes. 'I had a daughter – I mean, another daughter. I had a family.' He still didn't look at me. I waited. 'Alice, my little girl, she was killed.'

The room was silent, but I could hear the whine of a rubbish-collection truck outside in the street. I knew I was staring at him and that my mouth was open; I closed it and swallowed, trying to gather my thoughts. 'I'm sorry to hear that.'

He sighed heavily. 'She was only twelve when it happened, and Kara – my wife – she couldn't . . . we couldn't ... after the funeral, we stayed together for about eighteen months, but ... '

'What ... ?' But I couldn't bring myself to ask. 'I'm sorry,' I said again.

'It was a hit and run.'

I shook my head, and now I sighed, too. I looked at my nails, then I looked out of the window where the orange light from the rubbish truck flashed steadily as the bin men made their way down the street. 'I really am sorry, Scott. It must have been awful for you. And for your wife. But ... but that still doesn't make it all right for you to come here and stir up our lives like this. Surely having been a father you can see that?'

'I think Hannah should know the truth, that's all. And I want her to know about me.' He bent forward to pick up the flask and stopped halfway, drawing in a breath. His face was twisted in a grimace and I noticed that he was gritting his teeth and a film of sweat had appeared on his pale forehead. He let out a breath and his face relaxed again.

'Look, Scott.' I took the fat brown envelope out of my handbag and thrust it towards him. 'There's £4,000 here; I know it's not much, but it would mean you could afford some more help.' I gestured vaguely towards next door. 'Perhaps get someone professional in; a qualified carer.' He was paying attention now, so I warmed to my theme. 'I could even help you to find someone. It might make life a bit, I don't know, more comfortable, I suppose.' I waited for him to say something, but he didn't, and then I saw that he'd closed his eyes again.

I saw a flicker of movement in his jaw as he drew a deep breath, but he still didn't speak.

'So, what do you think, then?'

He shook his head slowly. 'My God, you certainly have come up in the world, haven't you?'

'Sorry?'

'If you think four grand is *not much.*'

'I meant in terms of—'

'Hush money. You think money would make a difference?' His voice was stronger now. 'You think I give a *toss* about money now?'

'Well, what *do* you want then?' I leapt to my feet. 'Drugs? Sex? Just tell me what I can do to—'

'Stop, for fuck's sake.' He put his hand up, palm facing me. 'And calm down.'

'Calm down? How dare you tell me to calm down! Do you really not see the implications of what you're asking?'

'Of course I do. That's why I haven't gone to the police yet. I want you to tell her what happened; it would be better coming from you. And whatever you may think, my aim isn't to totally fuck up your life. I want her to know the truth, and I want to see her – I don't want to interfere in your precious, comfortable life, I just want to meet my daughter once, so she knows who I am.' He looked down. 'Or who I was.'

CHAPTER NINETEEN

Hastings, 1976

Although she'd only been living with Scott and Eve for five weeks, it seemed longer. It felt like they'd all known each other for ages. She felt comfortable here, and every now and then, she'd catch herself laughing, forgetting that her mum was dead, that she'd watched the coffin being lowered into the ground. And then she'd feel ashamed.

Scott had been right; there was plenty of cash-in-hand work, and within a week, she'd managed to get regular shifts at a pub in the town centre. It wasn't as nice as some of the quaint little pubs in the Old Town but the money was okay and meals were thrown in so she was able to pay her way and have enough left over to buy a few bits for her room. Eve had dragged her along to help at a jumble sale on Saturday because the helpers always got first pick. She'd bought a rocking chair for 50p and a red lava lamp for 20p; the stand was chipped but the lamp worked perfectly and looked lovely in the corner of her room. Scott and Eve had been so kind, giving her things, listening while she talked endlessly about her mum, and on the few nights she wasn't working at the pub, even cooking her meals. Today, she was determined to do something for them. She hadn't done that much cooking before, but she was good at making Granny Pawley's cheese hotpot. It was the first proper meal her mum had taught her to cook. It was Granny Pawley's own recipe, made from layers of sliced potato, onion, tomato and grated cheese, and sometimes topped with crispy bacon for a special treat. The trick was to slice the potatoes thinly so they cooked right through and to season every layer, then you had to cook it for a couple of hours so that the potatoes and onions softened into the melted cheese. The salty, savoury tang of the cheese was perfectly offset by the sweetness of the tomatoes. The only trouble was, it was the sort of meal that was really best eaten on chilly winter evenings, but today it was sunny and very warm, especially for the second week in May. Oh well, she didn't suppose it mattered.

The hotpot was soon bubbling away in the Baby Belling and a rich, savoury aroma drifted through the house. After clearing the kitchen and setting the table, she went up to the thinking room to read. She was about to check on the meal when she heard the door at the top of the basement stairs open and close. 'Hello,' Eve called up the stairs. 'Anyone home?'

'Yes,' Jo called back. 'Coming.' She was smiling as she went down into the kitchen, expecting Eve to comment on the wonderful smell that was wafting through the house. But Eve was standing in the middle of the room with a frown creasing her forehead. She wrinkled her nose. 'Is that . . .' She paused, took another sniff. 'Is that bacon?'

Jo stopped, realisation dawning fast and hard. They were vegetarian! Of course they were. All at once, it was as though she could see every meal they'd eaten together floating before her eyes; hear every conversation they'd had about food whispered into her ear. There was never any meat, never any mention of meat. It was so obvious, now she thought about it. It took her a moment to find her voice. 'I wanted to make you a special dinner, to say thank you. But . . . but I forgot . . . I didn't think . . .'

Scott appeared in the doorway. 'Something smells good,' he said.

Jo felt her bottom lip tremble, so she bit it. 'You're vegetarian, aren't you? I'm sorry. I'm such an idiot. You don't even need to make it with bacon, it's just that's what my granny used to do for a special treat.'

Eve's face relaxed into a smile. 'It was very sweet of you.'

Jo looked up hopefully. 'The bacon's only on the top; you could take it —'

But Eve shook her head. 'I'm sorry, Jo. I'd be able to taste the flesh lingering on the vegetables. Thank you for the thought, though. And don't worry about us; we'll get ourselves an omelette or something.' She went over to the sink and tipped out a carrier bag full of leaves. 'And look what I picked – nettles and wild garlic. We can have a lovely salad with it. She turned the tap on to wash the leaves, then began opening cupboards to look for something to eat. 'What do you fancy, Scott?'

Scott smiled sadly at Jo as he walked across the kitchen to look in the cupboards. As he passed behind her, he whispered so closely in her ear that she could feel his breath, 'Shame, because it smells delicious.' She turned to look at him, but he was already talking to Eve.

*

By the end of May, the temperature had hit the eighties, and by the start of June it was too hot to wear anything in bed. Last night had been so uncomfortable that she'd thrown the covers off, but it was still too hot and sticky to sleep. She dragged herself reluctantly out of bed and pulled on the white peasant blouse and the orange gypsy skirt Eve had given her. What on earth would she have done for clothes if Eve hadn't put on weight? All she'd brought with her was winter stuff. She moved aside the red fabric she was still using as a curtain. The window was shut – no wonder it was like an oven in here. She could feel the heat searing through the glass onto her bare arms and warming the floorboards so that they gave off a rich, biscuity smell. She pulled the sash window up as far as it would go and leaned out. The garden below looked battered by the heat; everything that grew there appeared dull and limp, yet the park on the other side of the wall was lush and vibrant thanks to the sprinklers that had been set up last week. If you turned to the right, you could see the whole of the park with its sweep of emerald grass punctuated by regimented flower beds; if you looked to the left, beyond the park and over the rooftops, you could see the sea, the blazing sun reflected in the water. The punishing heat burned the top of her head and there wasn't a breath of air. Above her, the dream-catcher Eve had made for her hung perfectly still in front of the window; even the feathers didn't move. She stood back to admire the way the silver beads sparkled as the sunlight bounced off them. She'd had a go at making one herself, but it hadn't turned out very well.

'Jo!' Eve's voice called from downstairs. 'Jo, are you up? It's gorgeous outside. Let's go for a swim.'

'I . . . I don't have a costume.'

'That's all right.' Eve was coming up the stairs. 'You can have my old one – it's too small for me now, anyway.'

'Oh, okay,' Jo said slowly. 'Thanks.' Usually, when people said they wanted to go for a swim, they meant they wanted to paddle or play about in the water for a bit, so she probably didn't need to say anything.

Eve's old costume was made out of a slightly shiny, sea-green material and it had five metal rings going up each side so it looked like it was only held together by chains. It was a bit big on the bust, but she didn't look too bad. Not as good as Eve, though. Eve had a bit of a tummy but she was so curvy anyway that it suited her. They'd just stretched their towels out on the pebbles when Scott came crunching down the beach towards them in cut-off jeans and with a towel rolled up under his arm. 'I didn't know Scott was coming,' Jo began, but Eve was already bounding down to the water.

Scott spread his own towel alongside theirs, reached down behind his neck and pulled his T-shirt off over his head, then stretched out on his towel. Feeling suddenly self-conscious standing there in Eve's swimming costume, Jo sat down next to him, drew her knees up and held them to her chest as she watched Eve wade into the sea.

Scott turned on his side to face her. As he moved, she caught a faint trace of his hot, male smell. He was so close that she could feel the heat coming off his skin.

'You going for a swim, then?'

She shrugged. 'I might, in a minute.'

'I think you should, you know,' he said. 'Because if you sit here much longer in that swimming costume' – he fixed her with his eyes as he put his finger through one of the metal rings – 'you're going to end up with five ring-shaped burns on each side.'

She could feel herself going red. His finger was still touching her skin, and now she could feel the metal rings, which were indeed getting hot.

'Come on, Jo!' Eve shouted from the sea. She was already in up to her thighs, jumping up and down and squealing with the cold.

'Go on,' Scott said, moving away from her and lying on his back. 'I'll watch your stuff.'

As she hobbled down the shingle, she could feel the

hot stones burning the soles of her feet and the midday sun cooking her skin, which was already sore from spending too long in the garden. She went in gingerly as far as her ankles and at first it felt quite warm, but then a step further and she shivered as the chill nipped her calves. When the water reached mid-thigh, she stood up on tiptoe so the lapping waves didn't get any higher. It was a weird sensation; her legs were turning red with the cold, while the drops of water that splashed on her shoulders sizzled as the sun bore down onto her skin.

'Come on, Jo. Straight in up to the waist! You've got to get your aunt Minnie wet quickly or you'll never do it.' Eve was grinning as she splashed Jo with the flat of her hands.

'Pack it in,' Jo yelled, but she was laughing too as Eve continued to whoop and shriek as she went further and further in.

'Look – this is what you do.' Eve leapt up, holding her nose, and plunged her shoulders and head right down under the water, springing up again, wide-eyed and gasping as she shook the silver droplets from her flattened hair. 'Ooh, shit and sugar! It's bloody freezing.' But then she dived down like a mermaid and disappeared, bobbing up again about six feet away. 'You, Joanna Casey' – she grinned, putting her icy wet hands on Jo's burning shoulders – 'are going to get your hair wet.' And she started to push Jo's shoulders under the water. The weight of Eve's hands knocked her off balance, and the moment she felt that her feet weren't connected with the ground, that she wasn't firmly rooted, the panic began to rise up through her stomach and into her chest. Her arms shot out in front of her but there was nothing solid to hold on to, and she could feel herself going under. The shouts and shrieks of the other people on the beach became distant and echoey as the icy water closed over her head. She scrabbled frantically with her feet, trying to find the sharp pebbles she knew were there, but her panicked kicking had thrown her into a chaotic backwards somersault. She felt a burning sensation as the water went up her nose, then her shoulder bumped against the sea bed and she clutched at the shingle with her fingers. At that moment, she felt hands go under her arms and she was being pulled upwards.

'It's okay,' Eve was saying. 'Jo! It's okay. You're all right.' Eve had her arms around her but she was still kicking, imagining that Eve was doing a life-saving technique, then she realised that Eve was standing and the water was only just higher than her waist.

At last her feet touched the ground and she regained her balance. She was gasping, her heart was thumping and her nose and throat stung with salt water.

'I'm sorry, Jo,' Eve said. 'I didn't mean to knock you over.' She still held on to Jo's arm, and was looking at her with a mixture of alarm and curiosity.

'I should have told you,' Jo said, still panting. 'Can't swim.'

'You can't swim? Oh Jo, why ever didn't you say?'

Jo coughed, wincing at the pain. 'Can we get out?'

Eve held her hand as they waded through the water back to the shore.

Scott was sitting up now, watching them, his arms draped loosely over his bent knees. She avoided his eyes as they walked up the beach, the tips of her fingers tingling with embarrassment; he must have seen the whole thing. But all he said as they drew near was, 'Is everything cool?' And when Eve assured him it was, he lay back down and closed his eyes.

'So how come you can't swim?' Eve said as they dried themselves. 'I thought you grew up a stone's throw from the sea?'

'I did. I just never learned. My mum couldn't swim, either. My dad always said he was going to teach us but, well, he never got round to it.'

Eve spread her towel out on the shingle then lay down so the sun could finish drying her off. 'But what about school? That's where I learned – I was in the school team.'

So Jo told her about Mrs Watkins, the sadistic PE teacher who'd singled out the three non-swimmers in the class and made them line up at the side of the pool – the deep end – trembling with fear, their toes curled round the edge as they tried to cling on to the broken tiles. 'She walked up and down behind us a few times, then she pushed us in, one at a time, saying, "Sink or swim, girls, sink or swim." I sank.'

'What a bitch, man,' Scott said without opening his eyes or changing position.

'How awful,' Eve said. 'What a horrible, cruel woman.

So many teachers really are bullies, aren't they?' She propped herself up on her elbow. 'I know! I'll teach you to swim.'

'I'm not sure . . .'

'It'll be okay,' Eve insisted. 'I won't let go of you until you're ready, I promise.'

So over the next week, on her days off or before she started her shift at the pub, Jo went with Eve to Covehurst Bay, a quiet beach further along the coast, and she learned to swim, initially just enjoying the way the incoming waves would raise her up, lifting her almost off her feet before setting her gently back down again, and finally, after days of thinking she'd never get the hang of it, realising that she was moving her arms and legs confidently through the water and that Eve was no longer holding her. She was swimming!

Whether it was due to the exhilaration of achievement, or to the sudden realisation that she'd never be able to tell her mum, she didn't know, but before she could stop herself, she burst into tears. Eve's arms went around her and held her while she cried. She breathed in the warm, salty sea smell of Eve's hair and skin, and in a moment of absolute clarity, she knew that Eve was the most important person in her life.

CHAPTER TWENTY

By the third week in June the temperature had hit the nineties in some places, and Jo had never known it so hot. The summer fayre was coming up in a couple of weeks and Eve had been busy making jewellery and tote bags. Scott had made some picture frames and little wooden boxes decorated with tiny painted shells and bits of sea-smoothed glass, and Jo herself had been plaiting strands of leather to make bracelets and chokers; the house was a hive of industry.

Today, she'd volunteered to make candles, but now she was beginning to regret it, given that it would require having the electric rings on for goodness knows how long. This kitchen was sweltering as it was. She took out the two old saucepans that Eve kept for the purpose, filled the larger one with water and the smaller one with tiny white pearls of paraffin wax and set them to heat on the Baby Belling. She added a disc of beeswax, which looked like Wright's Coal Tar Soap, because that helped the candles to burn for longer, apparently. While the wax was melting, she prepared the moulds as Eve had shown her. They were using polystyrene cups this time – Eve said you could use almost anything as long as it was clean and waterproof, something she'd discovered a couple of years ago during the three-day week and the power cuts. 'We used to sell them to the local shops,' she explained. 'It didn't matter what size or shape they were, someone would buy them. We couldn't make enough of them. Almost makes me want the power cuts back!'

Jo threaded lengths of wick through holes in the bottom of each cup, then she placed a cocktail stick across the top and tied the wick around it so that, when you poured the wax in, the wick would stay in the middle. With the moulds all lined up ready, she added some dye to the melted wax, a little red, a touch of blue, the right amounts, she hoped, to create a lavender colour – she was going to scent these ones with lavender oil and she wanted them to look right, too, because apparently you could get 35p each for the scented ones.

The lavender oil was in a miniature wooden chest of drawers in Eve and Scott's bedroom, so she turned off the heat while she went upstairs. Their room was next to hers and, though she'd walked past the open door many times, she'd never been inside. Now she peeped tentatively around the door even though she knew they'd both gone out hours ago. The air was still and warm, and it smelled of patchouli and of hot wooden floorboards and tobacco.

There was another smell that she recognised but couldn't quite put her finger on, a strong, spicy aroma; reminded her of Christmas. Cloves! That was it; oil of cloves. Then she remembered that Scott had a toothache and Eve was treating it by dabbing clove oil onto the tooth with a cotton bud. Eve didn't believe in dentists.

There were two windows overlooking the garden and fixed across them were lengths of the same red fabric with gold embroidery that Eve had given her that first night. They had the effect of bathing everything in a warm red glow as the sun shone through them into the room. Jo's eyes were drawn to the bed which, like hers, was a mattress resting on several wooden pallets, except of course it was a double, and instead of a continental quilt pulled neatly over like her own, there were rumpled orange sheets and blue blankets and a lot of pillows strewn around, like the aftermath of a pillow fight. Scott's guitar stood against the wall next to an empty cider bottle and a glass jar full of pennies and half pennies. The mini-chest was on top of the tallboy, and as she walked past the bed to get to it, she caught the faintest whiff of naked-ness. On the floor with the pillows were a couple of burned-down incense sticks and a hairbrush, swathed in strands of Eve's thick, dark hair. She picked up a couple of pillows and put them back on the bed. What must it be like to sleep with someone every night? Tentatively, she pulled back the bedclothes and got in, swinging her legs up and curling into a foetal position. She tried to imagine what it would feel like to wake up and see Scott's face next to hers, then she turned over and buried her nose in the pillows. They smelt of patchouli, but with a salty, warm-hair smell underneath. Eve's face swam into her mind. She sat up. The room reeked of intimacy.

She found the lavender oil. She should go back to the kitchen and get on with the candles, but there was something enticing about this space; being in it made her feel closer to Eve, and to Scott, as though the essence of them was more accessible in here. One of Eve's cloth bags was hanging on a drawer knob; she couldn't resist it. She lifted it off, undid the toggle and lifted the flap, releasing a new, intense waft of patchouli. There was a packet of Aspro, a fountain pen that had leaked a violet stain onto the brown lining, a couple of Lil-Lets and a *Blue Peter* badge. In the inside pocket was an envelope; she peeked inside. When had she become such a nosy-parker? There was a National Insurance number card, some photos, and . . . Eve had a driving licence! But she'd never said anything about being able to drive. Eve was her friend, her *best* friend, but there was so much she didn't know about her. She flicked through the photos, feeling a pang of jealousy at the photo-booth pictures of Eve with two other girls in school uniform, all pulling silly faces. There was a colour photo of a tabby cat curled up on a cushion, and one of a couple with a little girl. There was no mistaking the young Eve; those huge eyes with their double layer of lashes were so distinctive. The woman, clearly Eve's mum, was heavily pregnant and wore a dark-coloured maternity smock with a large white bow at the neck. So Eve must have a younger brother or sister. Where, she wondered? Eve was one of those people who encouraged you to talk about yourself but rarely discussed their own lives; she really must ask Eve about her family. She thought back to that day they'd met in London a little over three months ago; although it often felt like they'd known each other much longer, she knew so little about Eve's background that it sometimes seemed they'd only just met. That day in London, Eve had obviously wanted to talk about her dead parents, but had stopped because Jo herself had been so upset about her mum. She would make a point of asking; it would probably set her off thinking about her own mum again, but so what? She looked again at the photo. Eve's mum was smiling down at her, resting a hand on her shoulder. Eve's dad was tall and almost bald but with a full, dark moustache nestling under his nose. He too was smiling, and looking at his wife. The only one looking at the camera was Eve. Jo felt her throat tighten as she remembered a similar picture of herself with both her parents, and how her mum had ripped it in two after her father had left.

She closed her eyes for a moment and tried to remember her mother's face, but yet again she couldn't get it quite right. It was like a jigsaw with bits missing. She could see her mum's eyes, sometimes an olive-green, and sometimes a brighter and more sparkly green, like emeralds, or she could see her mouth, or her nose or the purple birthmark she used to cover with make-up before she stopped caring. But she couldn't ever seem to see her mum's whole face in one go. Everyone should be able to remember their own mum, shouldn't they?

She put the photos back, all except the one of Eve with her mum and dad which she slipped into the pocket of her skirt. She looked in the envelope again; she really shouldn't be doing this. The birth certificate she pulled out was folded into three; she unfolded it. 'Genevieve Christiana Leviston,' she read aloud. It sounded so pretty, so much more interesting than her own names, Joanna Margaret – Margaret after her auntie who died just before she was born. What had happened to Eve's parents, Douglas and Audrey Leviston? She and Eve had such a similar background, they should be sisters. She returned the envelope to the bag, which she put back where she'd found it.

She just wanted a quick look at Eve's clothes, and then she'd go back downstairs. She lifted the sheet that hung from a curtain wire across the alcove. The metal rail was bowing under the weight of long floral-print dresses, cheesecloth skirts and shirts, embroidered peasant tops, velvet jackets and heavy knitted cardigans that came down past your knees. They were the sort of clothes she'd started wearing herself now, things that didn't fit Eve any more, or things that Sapphire had left behind. Her own clothes, she now realised – the short suede skirt, the white trousers, the blue tank top and cardigan twinset she'd bought from C&A – now felt far too neat and tidy; far too *square*.

God, this room was hot. She held up a long cream cotton dress smothered with pink roses; it had a deep, scooped neckline and was ruched over the bust. When Eve wore it, she didn't wear a bra, and you could see her nipples as clear as anything. She looked amazing in it. Without thinking, Jo took off her blouse and skirt, relishing the sensation of breeze as she did so, then slipped the cool cotton dress over her head. As an afterthought, she pulled the elasticated top down so she could slip off her bra. There was only a head-and-shoulder mirror in here, so she was about to go along the landing to one of the empty rooms where there was a wardrobe mirror propped against the wall when she heard a movement downstairs. She froze.

'Anyone home?' Scott's voice called out.

She could feel the panic rising up through her body as she tried to calculate whether she had time to sprint back to her own room before replying.

'Hello?' he called again.

Her room was only next door, so perhaps he wouldn't be able to tell from her voice. She decided to risk it. 'Hello,' she called back. 'Down in a sec.'

She grabbed her skirt and blouse from the floor and was about to nip into her own room when, to her horror, she heard him bounding up the stairs. She'd only taken a few steps when he appeared in the doorway. He stopped, half smiled and then appeared to register what he was seeing.

'I . . .' Jo started, but couldn't think what else to say.

'That dress.' Scott was looking at her curiously, as though he wasn't sure who she was. She'd expected him to be angry. 'It's Eve's, isn't it?'

Jo nodded. 'I'm sorry, I just came in for the lavender oil but it was so hot and —'

And then his mouth was on hers and she could smell his cigarettes and the oil of cloves, and she could taste the coffee on his tongue which was feeling its way around her mouth and making her insides liquefy. It was only when he slipped his hand down the front of the dress and touched her bare breast that she pulled away. He immediately let her go. 'Sorry,' he mumbled. Then he pushed past her, grabbed his guitar and bounded back downstairs and out of the house. She stood still for a moment, aware of the tiniest ripple of disappointment.

CHAPTER TWENTY-ONE

The day of the summer fayre dawned. The radio news said that record temperatures had been reported over the last few days. It was much hotter than usual for this time of year, and there was more to come, according to the long-range weather forecast – a proper heat wave. Jo had woken early and taken her toast upstairs into the thinking room, but she'd found the early morning sun and glittering sea so enticing that she'd decided to go for a walk on the beach. She'd worn a floaty white halter-neck dress – another hand-me-down from Eve – and the slight breeze had felt delicious on her bare neck and shoulders, but by nine o'clock, she could feel the heat prickling her skin and, by the time she walked back into the house, her shoulders had definitely reddened.

'Oh, there you are.' Scott barely glanced at her as she walked into the kitchen. Things had been a bit strained between them since he'd come home and caught her wearing Eve's dress, but neither of them had mentioned it. She'd tried to say something the following morning. He'd been in the living room, restringing his guitar, when she went in; he looked up and nodded, then went back to what he was doing. She said good morning, then sat on the settee and watched him for a while, wishing she'd thought about what she was going to say before she came in. Then she found she couldn't take her eyes off his hands. She kept staring, looking at the way those pale slender fingers moved as he twisted the fret keys to tighten the strings; the tiny black hairs that grew just above the knuckle. What would it be like to feel those fingers moving over her body? She stood, but made no move towards the door. Scott looked up, and for a moment she could feel his eyes resting on her. Then he went back to what he was doing. 'Haven't you got something to be getting on with?'

'Yes. Sorry. I was . . .' She looked around in vain for something to pick up, then changed her mind. 'I just wondered if you wanted a cup of tea or anything. While I'm making one?'

'No,' he said, without taking his eyes from his guitar. 'No thanks.'

So she'd walked out of the room and hadn't made any attempt to mention it since. He obviously wanted to forget all about it, but she wished he didn't make her feel as though it was her fault. After all, it was he who'd kissed *her*; she certainly hadn't done anything to encourage him. *An unexpected kiss*; the phrase jumped into her mind and she remembered Eve reading her tea leaves the first night she stayed here, but hadn't Eve said it referred to the past, not the future? Oh what did it matter? It was all mumbo-jumbo anyway.

There were still quite a few boxes piled up on the table. They'd filled them yesterday with all the merchandise for the stall – shell necklaces and earrings, leather bracelets, knitted tote bags, hand-stitched felt bags, decorated picture frames, and of course, candles. Scott was packing some of the boxes into a green tartan shopping trolley, like the one Granny Pawley used to take to the butcher's every Friday morning for her weekly order: chump chops to be grilled that evening, skirt of beef for pasties on Saturday, leg of pork to roast for Sunday lunch and to have with cold pickles on Monday, sausages with mash and baked beans on Tuesday, brisket for the Wednesday pot roast, and mince with gravy and boiled potatoes on Thursday. So much meat! Since that awful day with the hotpot when it had finally dawned on her that Eve and Scott were vegetarian, Jo had made a conscious effort to avoid meat herself, but now suddenly she craved one of Granny Pawley's plump, tender lamb chops with crispy roast potatoes and mint sauce; or her home-made Cornish pasties, rich, peppery and savoury; or even mince and gravy, which she'd hated as a child. She tried to put thoughts of food out of her mind. Last night, Eve had made a stack of sandwiches for them to take for their lunch, but they were all cheese and pickle or egg and salad cream.

Maybe she could sneak off and buy herself a ham sand-wich at some point.

Scott finished filling the trolley. 'Right, that's mine done.' He straightened up, reached behind him and pulled another shopping trolley over to the table, then another. One was red, also tartan, and the other was made of a soft, tan plastic and had clearly seen better days. 'Take your pick.' He was looking at her as though he was waiting for her to say something. 'What's the matter?'

'Nothing's the matter. They're just a bit . . .'

'How did you think we were going to get the stuff there?' He turned away, shaking his head. Why was he so snappy with her these days? Perhaps he thought she wasn't pulling her weight. Eve had been working hard to get everything ready for the fayre, but that wasn't Jo's fault, was it? 'Can I help?' she said, moving nearer to the table.

'Well, all this lot's got to fit in there somehow, so you might have to repack some of it in smaller boxes. There are a few more in that cupboard.' He nodded towards the built-in cupboard and then looked back at Jo. 'That dress . . . is it one of—'

'Eve gave it to me. She said it didn't fit her any more.'

Scott continued to look at her until she started to feel quite uncomfortable. What had she done wrong now? She hadn't *asked* for the dress; Eve had just given it to her.

'Cool,' he nodded. 'Suits you.' He turned back to what he was doing, muttering, 'Where the hell is she, anyway?'

Jo could feel herself starting to blush. It was the first time he'd said anything nice to her in a long time.

Scott went to the kitchen door. 'Eve?' he shouted up the stairs. 'Evie, come on, man. We need to get a move on.'

Jo started putting stuff in the trolley while Scott went upstairs to see what was keeping Eve.

'She's not feeling well,' he said when he came back in. 'We'll have to set up without her.'

'What's wrong with her?'

'Feeling dicky again.' He patted his stomach to illustrate. 'She says she'll be all right once she's had some breakfast, but she needs to take it slowly.' He pulled the last trolley towards him and started to pack it. 'We'll have to make a start with what we can, then she can bring this lot along later.'

Would he have been so sympathetic if it had been she who'd felt ill, she wondered?

The trolleys were surprisingly heavy, and although Jo managed to get hers down the stairs, manoeuvre it through the basement room and out of the back door, she struggled to get it up the stone steps, causing her to feel even hotter as she felt the sweat break out on her forehead and prickle under her arms. When she finally drew alongside Scott, she hoped he couldn't smell her. She pulled her trolley along the promenade, grateful for the suggestion of a breeze that was coming at her in intermittent puffs of warm air on her face. As she walked, she looked out to sea; it was a deep blue for a change and twinkled and sparkled beneath the vivid, startling blue of the sky. There wasn't so much as a wisp of cloud and the scene looked like something from a postcard.

By the time they arrived at their pitch, people were busily setting out trestle tables all along the stretch of grass that ran between the beach and the promenade. There were many stalls selling all sorts of things: clothes, second-hand books, records, wooden toys, wind chimes, seed-bead necklaces, pottery, jams, pickles, cakes and even plants. Scott took a white cotton bed sheet out of his trolley, shook it out and draped it over their table. Jo began taking stuff out of boxes and arranging it in what she thought was an artistic way, but she obviously wasn't doing it properly because Scott kept moving it all around. When the stall was completely crammed, Scott pushed the half-full boxes under the table so they could top up when necessary, and Jo went round to see what it looked like from the front. She had to admit, he did seem to have a knack for making everything look more inviting. 'When we start to sell things,' he said, 'don't replace them too quickly; if the stall looks too tidy and completely full, people will think we're not selling stuff, and if they think we're not selling stuff, they'll think we're too expensive.'

'Okay.' Jo wasn't really paying attention; she could feel the sun burning the top of her head as she watched the woman opposite filling her stall with enormous artificial sunflowers. She couldn't tell if they were made of paper or fabric, but they looked brilliant. Eve would love them.

'Right,' he said. 'Bacon sandwich?'

'Bacon? But I thought— '

He put his finger to his lips. 'Don't tell Evie – she'd be so disappointed in me. I've tried to be totally veggie, but I lapse every now and again. You do dig meat, don't you? Usually, I mean?'

'That's funny – I haven't missed it up until now, but I've been really fancying a ham sandwich today. You know, thinly sliced white bread with salty butter, crumbly ham and Coleman's Mustard.'

'Sounds cool, but I think they only— '

Jo shook her head. 'No, I didn't mean – I mean, yes, please; I'd *love* a bacon sandwich. And my lips are sealed.' She felt absurdly pleased at the conspiratorial nature of this exchange. An illicit sandwich with Scott; it felt like they might be making friends again at last.

Scott smiled as he handed her a tobacco tin heavy with coins. 'Right, there's about a pound's worth of change in there, and a list of all the prices; if there's anything I've missed, use your common sense.' And with that he turned and walked off along the front. Jo watched him go; there was a dark patch where his T-shirt was sticking to his back, and she could see the shape of his shoulder blades. He'd tied his long hair back with a bootlace today, and his ponytail bounced as he walked. She was still watching him when a voice said, 'Excuse me, how much are the shell bracelets?'

She opened the tobacco tin and looked at the list. 'Ah, here we are – the varnished ones are 20p and the painted ones are 25p.'

She took the money and was just putting it away when

another customer asked about the candles and the jewellery box. By the time Scott came back with the bacon sandwiches wrapped in serviettes, she'd taken almost two pounds and was beginning to enjoy herself. Eve arrived at midday looking pale and drained. She'd brought more shell necklaces and bracelets and some lovely pairs of crystal earrings. She'd also brought some more candles, but they decided not to put them out because the ones that were already there were beginning to go soft in the heat.

They took turns minding the stall so that each had a chance to wander around and look at what else was on offer. Jo bought a strawberry Mivvi from the ice-cream van and stood for a while listening to a bare-chested man with a mahogany tan and a shark's tooth pendant playing the didgeridoo; then she walked along to the Stade where a group of morris dancers were leaping about, ringing their bells and knocking wooden sticks together. How on earth could they jump about like that in this heat? She paid 10p for three goes at the hoopla, where the prizes were ice-cold cans of Tizer and bottles of Pepsi, but she missed every time; then she saw a stall selling paper concertina fans for 12½p, so she bought one for herself and one for Eve.

When she got back, Eve was sitting on the grass with her head tilted forward. 'She nearly fainted,' Scott explained, his voice thick with concern.

'I'm all right,' Eve said, lifting her head. 'It's the heat. I just need to lie down.'

'Why don't you go home,' Jo said. 'Scott and I can manage, can't we, Scott?' She looked at him expectantly, eager for an opportunity to show herself to be competent, able to adapt in a crisis.

Eve nodded wearily. 'I think I will, if you don't mind.' She tried to stand but swayed sideways and had to sit down again. She looked awful.

CHAPTER TWENTY-TWO

Scott went with Eve back to the house, worried that she might pass out in the street. Once they'd gone, Jo took her suntan lotion out of her bag. She hadn't wanted to use it in front of Scott because there was something so sensual about smoothing lotion into sun-warmed skin. The plastic bottle felt hot, and when she squirted some of the lotion into her palm, that felt hot as well. She undid the ties of her halter-neck dress and smothered the exposed parts, aware that her shoulders were already burning and that there were two much paler lines where the ties had been.

It was lunchtime now and she could smell fried cod and hot, vinegary chips. She took an egg and salad cream sandwich out of her bag, ate half of it and then threw the rest of it onto the grass behind her for the seagulls. Warm egg wasn't very nice. She leaned back in the canvas chair and watched the people milling past. A group of friends, girls not much younger than herself, chatted happily together as they clustered around a stall selling denim hot pants. It was a long time since she'd been out with a group of friends like that. Even when she was back home in Newquay, she didn't see her mates all that often, because it had become more and more difficult to leave her mum alone. And she couldn't have brought anyone back to the flat. She picked up the little fan she'd bought and waved it in front of her face, but even the air she was moving around was hot.

She watched the pairs of lovers holding hands and smiling dreamily in the balmy heat; a couple wearing fringed black-leather jackets and carrying crash helmets were looking at the plaited leather bracelets. 'Cool,' the woman said. The man nodded. 'Cool,' he agreed. 'How much?' he asked, looking at Jo from behind his sunglasses. '95p,' Jo said. 'They're real leather.' They must be sweltering in those jackets, she thought, and she must have been staring, because the biker, who was holding out two pound notes and two of the bracelets, waggled his hand. 'Hello?' he said, smiling. 'Anyone in?' Jo looked back at him. 'Sorry.' She took the notes and gave him 10p change. 'Aren't you boiling in those jackets?' They both smiled and shook their heads. 'Keeps the heat out,' the man said, and they wandered off again, still holding hands. She put the money in the tobacco tin. They were doing pretty well – there were pound notes, lots of silver, and even a couple of fivers. And some of it had come from her candles. It felt so satisfying to sell something you'd actually made yourself. Perhaps she'd ask Eve to show her how to make some of the other stuff, too, then next time she could contribute more than just a few leather bracelets and candles that melted in the heat.

The beach was crowded, and there were loads of people splashing about in the water. She should have brought her costume. She enjoyed swimming now – could hardly believe she'd waited so long to learn. The sea looked silver in the sunlight and the air shimmered in the heat. She loved this weather; the sun always made her feel happier, lighter. But as she sat there, she became aware of a slow, creeping sadness as she watched the families, the fathers with toddlers riding on their shoulders, the mothers straightening sun hats, wiping melted ice cream from sticky hands and kissing grazed knees, and most of all, the mother who held open a white towel and enfolded her little girl in it, kissing her nose and hugging her tight after she emerged dripping from the sea. Mothers and fathers with their children; friends; lovers; everyone had someone.

The stalls were getting busy again. People were coming up off the beach to buy drinks and ice creams, putting on shirts and T-shirts over their swimming gear and browsing the stalls to give their bodies a break from the blistering heat. Almost everyone was tanned or reddened by the intense sunshine of the last few days, and quite a few of them had overdone it, by the look of them. When Jo was little, her mum had drummed it into her that the sun was something to be not only enjoyed, but respected, even feared. She could picture her mother now, the younger, stronger mother who used to care for her, not

the sickly, drunken mother who had herself needed looking after.

It's a lovely sunny day and they're at the beach with a
tartan blanket to sit on and a basket containing ham sandwiches wrapped in greaseproof paper, Battenberg cake,
lemon-barley water for Jo and a flask of tea for her mum.
They'll be going for a paddle later, so Jo is wearing her
brand-new swimming costume, which is navy-blue with
a white anchor on the front and a white pleated skirt-bit
around the bottom. Her mum reaches into her bag for the
Ambre Solaire. 'When you're big enough to do this yourself, Jo-Jo,' her mum says as she smears the thick white
sun cream onto Jo's arms, legs and face, 'always use lotion
or cream, because oil just makes you fry. There, all done.'
She wipes her hands on a towel and reaches for her cigarettes. 'We won't stay out for too long today, chicken; you
need to build up gradually, a bit longer each day.' She
lights a cigarette and then blows the smoke out in a
smooth white line. 'Not like the tourists,' she says, shaking her head as she looks around the beach. 'Look at
them, the lobster brigade. First time they've had their
clothes off all year, and they rub oil on themselves then
lie under that ball of flame so they cook like sausages on
a grill.' She looks at Jo and grins. 'Fat, porky sausages,'
she says, because she knows it'll make Jo laugh.

The memory faded.

She became aware of a child crying. There were so
many people milling around she couldn't tell where the
sound was coming from at first, but then she saw him,

about two or three years old with white-blond hair, his head turning this way and that and a look of mounting panic on his tear-stained face. He was wearing white shorts, a red-and-white-striped T-shirt, with red-leather sandals buckled over chubby feet. He was trying hard not to cry but his face kept crumpling in distress. Jo looked around to see if she could see who he belonged to but no one seemed to be paying him any attention. She stood up and went round to the front of the stall. 'Are you lost?' she asked, crouching down to the little boy's height.

He nodded solemnly.

'Who've you lost? Is it your mummy?'

Again the child nodded and a fresh wave of tears came.

'Hey, don't cry. Let's see if we can find her, shall we?' Jo stood up and the child slipped his warm, sticky little hand into hers. 'Tell you what, how about if I lift you up and let you stand on my stall, then perhaps you'll be able to see her, okay?'

He nodded and bit his bottom lip.

She lifted him up onto the table, surprised at how light he was. She stood behind him with her arms around his waist so he didn't fall. He smelled both sweet and salty; the smell reminded her of Lisa and Lynne, the twins she used to babysit when she lived in Newquay. 'Can you see her yet?' she said, catching a whiff of Johnson's Baby Shampoo. He shook his head and gave a shuddering sigh, but at least he'd stopped crying. 'What's your name, chicken?'

He turned towards her and spoke for the first time. 'I not a chicken,' he said with the ghost of a smile.

Jo smiled back. 'True,' she said. 'My name's Jo. What's yours?'

'Andrew.'

'Okay, Andrew. Let's see if we can find that mummy of yours, shall we?'

He nodded again, and allowed her to pick him up and rest him on her hip. It felt so easy and natural to be carrying a child. She knew she'd be a good mother; like her own mum had been in the early days. She couldn't wait to have her own babies. Once, after she'd slept with Rob the second time, her period had been ten days late. She'd been terrified, wondering what on earth she would do if she was pregnant. She'd written all sorts of embarrassing things in her diary, and had even written to the problem page in *Jackie*, asking them to please print the reply instead of writing back because she couldn't risk her mum finding the letter. But then her period came, and she tore those pages out of her diary and threw them away in a bin in the park. It was only then that she allowed herself to think about what might have happened if she actually had been pregnant. Of course, her mum would have been furious, but she was not the sort of mother who would throw her out – that's what all her friends at school were worried about: getting 'chucked out'. When Norma Wilson had got pregnant in the fifth year, although her mum had apparently gone berserk at first, she'd calmed down in the end and even looked after the baby, who was called Luke, while Norma studied for her O levels. Maybe, Jo had wondered, her own mum might have changed back into a proper mother if there had been a little baby to look after. But she hadn't been pregnant after all, so there was no point in thinking about it.

She was about to head off into the crowds with Andrew when she remembered the tobacco tin full of cash, which she'd almost left open on the table. She grabbed the tin and asked the girl on the next stall to keep an eye on the stuff. As she walked among the stalls with Andrew on her hip, she wondered what would happen if they couldn't find his mum. She'd have to take him to the police station, she supposed. When she was about thirteen, there had been a story in the paper about someone finding a newborn baby in a shoebox in the park. For ages after that she'd fantasised about finding a baby and had even made a point of walking through the park on her way home from school, looking under all the hedges and bushes, in all the shelters and under the benches in the swing park. If she did have to take Andrew to the police, perhaps they'd at least let her look after him for a while; after all, he trusted her – see how he was cuddling in to her now, his weary head resting on her shoulder? She turned and gave him what she hoped was a reassuring smile.

Just then, she saw his mother. She knew instantly because of the woman's expression, which was one of agonised panic, and she had that same white-blonde hair, cut in a neat bob. Any thought that Andrew's mother didn't care about him disappeared now as she saw the terror and pain etched on the woman's face. Andrew himself obviously hadn't spotted her yet, but Jo was about to shout and wave when his mother saw them. Jo smiled but the woman's expression turned to fury as she barged through the crowds. 'There you are!' She pulled Andrew roughly from Jo's arms, causing him to begin crying all over again. 'What have I told you about going off with strangers?' And then, to Jo's horror, the woman slapped Andrew's leg twice, making him cry even louder. 'You stay with *me*,' she yelled, but then her voice broke and she clutched him to her, her face a study in anguish. 'I thought you'd gone,' she said, stroking his hair. 'It's all right, darling; shush, shush. But you *must* hold Mummy's hand, okay?'

Andrew nodded, sniffed, then took his mother's hand and trotted off happily with her towards the ice-cream van. Neither of them looked back at Jo, who was still standing in the same spot feeling unaccountably tearful and embarrassed, her hip aching with a melancholy lightness. She didn't know what she'd expected, but she'd have thought a distraught mother might have managed a 'Thank you' to the person who'd helped her child, a child that she, the mother, had allowed to wander off in crowds of people, any one of whom could have taken him away. But she'd looked at Jo as if she was the one in the wrong; as if she'd been trying to kidnap him. Maybe it was how all mothers would react; maybe real mother-love made you do irrational things, even hurt someone you really cared about.

CHAPTER TWENTY-THREE

As she made her way back to the stall, she reflected on how poor little Andrew had instantly forgiven his mother for slapping him, and then her thoughts returned to her own mum. Had she properly forgiven her? It was easy to forgive the irrational, drink-sodden arguments, the being sick in the bathroom, the embarrassment of her mum's drunken attempts to banter with her friends. But what hurt the most was the sense of abandonment, the sense that she'd only really had a mother until she was twelve or thirteen, because by that time the booze had definitely become more important. Once, Jo had deliberately stolen a Miners eye shadow and lipstick from the counter in Woolworth's, half hoping she'd get caught, because she wanted to make her mother *do* something for her, even if it was only coming to pick her up from the police station.

She slipped back behind the stall and sat down. People were walking past with towering pink mounds of candyfloss, and the sugary smell was making her feel sick. Scott had been gone a long time; she wished he'd hurry up – she was dying for a cold drink. There were still quite a few people stopping to look at the jewellery. An old lady was fanning herself with one of the same fans Jo had bought earlier. She smiled at Jo and pointed to a pair of lapis lazuli earrings. They'd taken Eve quite a long time to make, and they were beautiful – deep blue stones with a gold vein, in good-quality settings. Probably quite expensive compared to the other earrings, which were mainly made using shells or glass stones with cheap metal settings.

'Those blue ones are so pretty, aren't they? It's my daughter-in-law's twenty-first coming up and they're definitely her sort of thing.' The woman held them up and looked more closely. 'How much are they, dear?'

'I'll have a look.' Jo opened the tobacco tin to check the price. A fat, oily bluebottle landed on her arm and she batted it away. The price list wasn't there. It must have fallen out. Perhaps she'd knocked it onto the grass. 'Just a sec,' she said to the customer as she lifted the tablecloth. She knelt down and looked under the table, certain she'd see the piece of paper covered with Eve's neat handwriting resting there in the dry grass, but no. Surely it couldn't have blown away? There was barely any breeze.

'I'm sorry,' she said to the woman. 'I can't seem to find the price list—'

'Shall I pop back a bit later, then?'

She hesitated. If she let the woman go now, she might not come back. 'I think they're about . . .' They weren't cheap, she knew, because Eve said there was a good profit on them, but they were quite expensive to make and she only ever made a few pairs at a time because she didn't sell a lot of them, not like the other earrings, which were selling like hot cakes at a pound and £1.50 a time. Use your common sense, Scott had said. They'd both be impressed if she managed to sell an expensive pair of earrings. 'I'm almost certain they were £4.75.' She held her breath. That was more than three times the price of the others – was it way over the top? Why hadn't she paid more attention when Eve was talking about the prices? 'They're lapis lazuli,' she added. 'And the settings are pure silver.'

'I'll take those then, please.' The woman began rummaging in her bag for her purse while Jo carefully wrapped the earrings in the pink tissue paper that was only for the more pricey items. 'There we are, dear.' She held out the exact money – four pound notes and 75p in silver. She put the earrings carefully in her bag and then waved as she headed off into the crowd.

There was still one pair of the lapis earrings on the stall, and Jo took another pair from the box under the table and laid them out alongside them. Eve had told her to try and keep two pairs out at a time, because then people tended to notice them more easily.

'How much did you say them earrings was, darlin'?' A middle-aged bald man with no shirt on and a badly sunburnt chest appeared in front of her. He wore huge mirrored sunglasses and was smoking a cigar, which he didn't take out of his mouth when he spoke. '£4.25, was it?'

'£4.75,' Jo said.

'They'll put a smile on my old lady's face, I reckon. Here, I'll give you four quid.' He took a handful of silver out of his shorts pocket, and began counting it out onto the table.

'Sorry, I can't take four pounds, because they're not even mine to sell. I'm minding the stall for a friend.'

'"Minding the stall for a friend",' he mimicked, making her sound uptight and prissy. 'Are you, darlin'?' He puffed on the cigar and a cloud of blue-grey smoke billowed out around him. 'Well, I'm sure your mate told you it's normal to haggle, didn't she?' He was smiling, but there was a hint of menace in his tone. 'Look, I tell you what, me old mum would probably like them earrings as well, so I'll give you nine quid for both pairs. How's that? Bulk order discount.'

When she didn't reply, he puffed on his cigar again. 'Your mate'll be a bit cheesed off if she finds out you're not playing the game, won't she? Nine quid, cash – that's a good price, you know. Wha'd'ya say?' He began drumming his fingers on the table.

'I'm not sure . . . ' That would make it £4.50 a pair; it was only a bit cheaper than she'd sold the others for. It would probably be all right. 'Well, perhaps —' But before she could say any more, the man thrust six pound notes into her hand and pushed a pile of silver towards her.

'There you go, babes; nine pounds exactly.' He winked at her, pocketed the earrings and was gone, disappearing into the crowd before she could do anything to stop him. She opened her mouth to speak, but there was no sign of him. With a bit of luck, she'd overpriced the earrings, anyway. She started counting the money he'd pushed towards her, but there was only £8.50 there; so he'd managed to beat the price down *and* diddle her. Not only that, but he'd made her feel like an idiot. Horrible man. It was at that moment that she spotted Scott weaving his way towards her.

'Hey.' He looked cheerful. 'Brought some refreshment.' He swung his green canvas bag off his shoulder and took out two bottles of lager. He took the caps off with his teeth and handed her one of the bottles. It was wonderfully cold. 'Cheers.' He clinked his bottle against hers. 'How's it been? Business still booming?'

Jo went to speak, but without warning she felt tears spring to her eyes. Scott put his beer down. 'Hey, what's the matter?' He put his arm around her shoulders and drew her towards him. She could smell a mix of salty sweat and tobacco. 'Come on now; tell Uncle Scott.'

'God, I'm sorry,' she sniffed, wiping her face. 'I'm being stupid. It's nothing at all, really. Just this horrible man beat me down on the price *and* diddled us out of 50p, and he made me feel as though I was thick, like some silly child. Oh, I don't know, he was just so, *slimy,*'

Scott sighed and patted her arm. 'That's shit, man. But listen, it's not a fortune, right? These things happen. And on the whole, it's a good scene, yeah? A good payback for all the work we've put in. We've sold a lot of the lavender candles you made – chicks really dig those.' They both looked at the box of candles that had begun to melt in the heat. 'Anyway.' He picked up his beer again. 'What else have you sold while I've been gone?' His gaze began to rove across the stall. 'Where are the lapis earrings?'

'Oh, I sold three pairs.' She brightened. 'Although two were to that horrible man, so we're short on each of those. I wasn't sure of the exact price – the list got lost, but I got £4.75 for the first ones and £9.00 for the other two – well, £8.50 because he disappeared before I could count what he'd given me. Anyway, I sold three pairs. Was that okay?' She waited for his approval.

He turned towards her slowly, his eyes now cold with anger. 'For the lapis earrings?'

The sickening certainty that she'd got it badly wrong rendered her silent.

'High-quality lapis lazuli, set in sterling silver, and you thought you'd let the whole lot go for less than fifteen quid?' He banged his fist on the table, making everything jump and rattle. 'Fuck!'

A few people turned round, and a man in light flannel trousers and a straw hat stopped in front of the stall. 'Steady on, chum,' he said. 'There's ladies present, you know.'

'Eve wrote you out a bloody list so you'd know exactly what to charge. And what do you mean, it "got lost"? Things don't just get lost on their own.'

She explained about Andrew and how she'd had to

grab the tin in a hurry and so maybe she'd dropped the list at that point, but Scott's eyes got even wider. 'You mean you left the stall unattended?' He looked back at the things that were still laid out on the table. 'You're bloody lucky nothing was stolen.'

'The girl on that stall was watching it for me. And I couldn't leave a toddler wandering around lost, could I?'

But his face didn't soften. He spoke slowly, through gritted teeth. 'Of course you couldn't, but how could she watch two stalls? Look, she's busy with her own. Didn't it occur to you that things could be nicked?' He turned away from her. 'Christ, Jo.' He shook his head. 'I honestly thought you had more sense, man.'

'I'm sorry, I really am. But nothing *was* nicked, was it?'

'More by good luck than good judgement.'

What a shitty day this was turning out to be. First she'd felt humiliated when Andrew's mother had snatched him from her arms as though she was some sort of child molester, then she'd been hoodwinked by that nasty, slimy man. And now this.

'I've said I'm sorry. I don't know what else to say.'

Scott picked Jo's bag up off the ground and handed it to her. 'Go.' He turned away, shaking his head and waving in the direction of the beach.

'But—'

'Those earrings cost five quid a pair just for the materials.' His voice was cold and he still wouldn't look at her.

'I'll make up for it,' she said. She could actually feel her legs beginning to tremble. 'It'll take a while—'

He glanced at her. 'Please, Jo, not now. I don't want to say something I might regret.'

She nodded, trying not to cry. 'What about the packing up? Do you want me to—'

'Just go.'

CHAPTER TWENTY-FOUR

Sheffield, 2010

It was four in the morning and I hadn't slept a wink. I felt sick with misery, physically sick. Duncan was breathing deeply and heavily, so I slipped carefully out of bed, then tiptoed downstairs and switched on the electric heater in the dining room. I paced the room for a while, wishing I still smoked. For the first time, I allowed myself to consider what might happen if I did have to tell them. I remembered Granny Pawley saying that if you were worried about something happening, the best way to deal with it was to work out what you would do if it did. So now I started to wonder how I might go about telling them. I tried to practise the conversation in my head, but I couldn't make the words come. Maybe if I could see them written down . . . I took a pen from my bag, grabbed a handful of paper from the printer and sat at the dining table.

Duncan, I don't know how to tell you this. What I have to say will shock you, and may make you turn away from me. Before I say any more, I want you to know that I love you. If it's even possible, I love you more as each year passes, and I always will. I know you love me, too, but what I have to tell you now may change that. You already know a little about Hannah's father, and about how we met, but I need to tell you

I sighed; this was rubbish. And anyway, I was still avoiding the main conversation. I tore up the paper and started another sheet.

My darling Hannah, I wrote, then I sat there for a full minute. This was ridiculous; I tore that sheet up as well and shoved all the pieces in my bag before reaching for the laptop. This wasn't something I was going to be able to do in one draft. *My darling Hannah,* I typed. *There is something I have to tell you, and I'm too much of a coward to tell you face to face, so I'm* . . . I deleted what I'd written. *My dearest Hannah, this will come as a shock, and I am going to have to beg you to forgive me.* I deleted the second part of that sentence. *As you know, your biological father left us when you were a baby to go to New Zealand. You soon began to regard Duncan as your 'real' dad, so we've never talked much about* . . . I deleted that, too, and put my head in my hands. I had never imagined myself having to tell anyone this; I couldn't find words that wouldn't cause them pain. Telling Hannah would be like physically hurting her. *I love you so much, and I need to tell you something, but I want to prepare you first.* I stopped, because tears were pouring from my eyes so fast they were dripping all over the keyboard. I couldn't do this, I *couldn't*. I rummaged in my dressing gown pocket and found a screwed-up tissue to mop my face. There was a creak behind me and my heart thudded, but it was only Monty, who'd just realised I was there. He was going a bit deaf. He yawned as he stretched his forelegs in front of him and went down on his elbows with his rump in the air and his tail wagging ecstatically. It was like he was worshipping me. 'Hello, Monty.' I leaned down to press my cheek against his soft, warm fur and he tried to lick away my tears, which made me cry all the more. I tried to control myself and sat back up at the table, while Monty settled himself at my feet, gazing up at me with a worried expression. I blew my nose and turned back to the screen to read what I'd written, then I highlighted the whole thing and pressed delete.

I stared at the blank document for a while, marvelling at how easy it was to erase the words, to make it as though they had never been written. If only you could wipe out the past that easily. I tried to imagine what life would have been like if it hadn't happened, but then again, if it hadn't . . . I closed down the program and switched off the laptop, then I knelt down on the floor with Monty, whose tail thumped appreciatively as I put my arms around his silky neck. 'Oh Monty, Monty.' He licked my face once, then stared at me as if he was trying to read my thoughts. His eyes were a deep, rich brown, like conkers, and they shone with trust, faith and adoration. 'I don't deserve it, boy,' I said, and he thumped his tail again, then I looked into his eyes and I whispered my confession.

'What's up?' Duncan said, making me jump so that I bashed my shoulder on the underside of the table. I hadn't heard him come downstairs but now he was standing in the doorway looking at me. I froze; could he have heard me?

'Sorry,' he said, 'I didn't mean to startle you. I woke up and you were gone.'

'I couldn't sleep.'

'Hey, you're crying.' He came over and put his arms around me. He was warm and he smelled of sleep, and I hated myself.

'No, it's just a cold coming, I think. That's why I couldn't sleep – blocked nose.'

He pulled away slightly, looking perplexed as he searched my face with his eyes. 'Okay,' he said after a bit. 'If you say so. You coming back to bed?'

I nodded. 'In a minute.'

There was a question in his expression before he turned away. 'Okay.' He walked slowly towards the door and I could feel him hurtling away from me.

*

Even though I hadn't finished the book, I went to my book group tonight – Duncan knew I rarely missed and he'd have thought it odd if I'd skipped it. It was at Marina's, and we were doing *Wuthering Heights* this time.

Most of us had read it before, but we were all up for reading it again. Eve loved this story, and I remembered how she'd romanticised Heathcliff, who was, after all, a cruel obsessive. 'Just think, Jo,' she said one evening, her eyes alight with the passion of it, 'imagine a man loving you so much he'd try to dig you up when you were dead.' The idea gave me the creeps, but Eve had been moved and excited by the sheer intensity of Heathcliff's love for Cathy. Eve was a bit like Cathy in that she needed to live somewhere where she could be close to nature. She liked the idea of the windswept moors as much as she loved living near the sea, and when she talked about how being out in the elements made her feel more alive, she made me want to be out there, too. Whenever I thought about that summer in Hastings, I thought of Eve as a sun goddess, but I'd forgotten how she used to love going out in all weathers, how she'd climb up the East Hill cliff so she could stand at the top and feel the wind and the rain on her face. She often talked about travelling to Yorkshire, to see Top Withens on the Pennine Moors, the place where *Wuthering Heights* was set. Now I thought about it, that was probably one of the reasons I'd moved up north after Scott left – that and the incredibly cheap rent. I never did go to Top Withens, though, even though it was only a few miles from where I lived in Halifax. Sheffield was more tame. Eve would have said it was Yorkshire for wimps; even Duncan sometimes called it Yorkshire Lite, but then he'd grown up near Harrogate where the winters were much colder. The slightly milder climate was one of the reasons Estelle moved here after Duncan's dad died, that and to be nearer to us, of course.

'Thanks, Marina.' I kissed her as I stepped out into the chilly night. 'Good discussion.'

'It was, wasn't it?' Marina said, smiling as she saw us all out. 'See you next time.'

It had been a good evening, and even though I'd been thinking about Eve, my thoughts had barely strayed to the Scott situation for the last two hours. But as soon as I was in the car, it all came crowding back. I rooted around in my bag for my phone so I could tell Duncan I was on my way home, but then I had a sudden memory of seeing it plugged into the charger and lying on the kitchen worktop.

There were no lights on in the bedroom as I pulled up outside, so I assumed Duncan was asleep already, but as I opened the front door I saw that there was a light on in the kitchen. He was sitting at the table with a two-thirds-full bottle of whisky in front of him, and my phone next to it. He took a swig from his glass and banged it down on the table.

'Hello,' I said. 'Having a bit of a nightcap?' He didn't look at me. 'Duncan?'

He raised his glass again, and I saw his face shift as if he was grinding his teeth. He put the glass down without taking a sip. 'How long has this been going on?'

'What? What are you talking about?'

'This "S" character, whoever he is.' He nodded towards my phone. 'Who is it? How long have you been seeing him?' He stood, pushing the chair back roughly behind him. 'Christ, I've been so stupid. I should have twigged, shouldn't I? The headaches, the late-night emailing, the days off when you couldn't quite remember where you'd been or what you'd done. Have you been with him tonight?'

I shook my head vigorously. 'No, and, Duncan, it's not what you think.'

'Ha! Not what I think! God, that's such a fucking cliché.'

'I know it's a cliché, but it happens to be true. This really isn't what you think.'

He turned to face me; his eyes looked bloodshot. 'How could you?'

'I have been meeting . . . someone . . . but I'm not sleeping with him, I swear.'

'What is it then? Cosy little dinners? Days out on the moors?'

I'd never heard Duncan use this sneering tone before and it felt horrible to be on the receiving end of it. 'Duncan, please . . .'

He took a gulp of his drink and banged the glass down so hard I feared it might shatter.

'I thought we were happy,' he said quietly, looking into his glass. 'I thought we had the perfect . . . ' He flicked his head savagely and muttered something unintelligible.

'Listen to me!' My tone made him start and he looked up sharply.

'It's . . . it's Scott; Hannah's father.'

For a moment he looked blank, then it appeared to sink in. It was a good ten seconds before he said, 'Her father? But I thought . . . I thought he'd cut himself off completely.'

'Yes, so did I. But he's changed his mind, apparently, and he's been back in this country for a few years.'

'So how long—'

'Oh, he only contacted me a few weeks ago.'

He sighed. 'How did he find you?'

'I don't know. I suppose it's not that difficult these days – he'll have searched my maiden name, found my married name—'

'And now he wants to see Hannah?'

And that's not all he wants, I thought, but I just nodded.

Duncan stood up and went over to the kitchen window, hands in his pockets. 'Christ.' There was another pause before he said, 'Well, he can go fuck himself, can't he?' He turned. 'Those anonymous phone calls over Christmas—'

'Yes, that was him.'

He shook his head, then he looked at me, his eyes searching mine. 'What have you said? I hope you've told him to forget it?'

I nodded. 'Of course. But he won't let it go. Thing is, he's ill. I mean, very ill. He says he only has a few months to live.'

Duncan made a 'huh' sound and shook his head dismissively.

'No, it's true, I've seen him. It's some sort of cancer. I haven't asked details but I can see he's telling the truth.'

Duncan didn't say anything for a minute, then he walked back to the table and poured himself another drink. He sighed as he sat back down. 'Why didn't you tell me?'

I looked away. 'I . . . I suppose I thought he might give up and leave me alone. I didn't want to let him into our lives.' I turned back towards him, hoping he wouldn't see that this was only half the truth.

'And you've been to meet him?'

'Only twice.'

'Twice?' He shook his head again and sighed; it was a sad sigh. 'I can't believe you didn't tell me about this. Why didn't you trust me to try and help?'

I could hardly bear to see the pain in his eyes. We'd shared so much since we'd been together; I was desperate to let him know that this was no rejection, that I didn't feel any different. I should have just told him that Scott wanted to see Hannah; there was no reason he'd have thought there was any more to it than that. But I was deluding myself, thinking he'd never need to know. 'I'm sorry. I just . . . I don't know, I suppose I hoped I could just make him go away.'

He sighed heavily. 'Want one?' He nodded towards the bottle, and I said yes, because this was Duncan acknowledging that I was worried, and that he was with me again, back on my side. I had a problem to deal with, therefore *we* had a problem to deal with, and he'd help me to sort it out, just as he always had done. Only this time I couldn't tell him why I needed that drink. He took a clean glass down from the cupboard, poured a couple of centimetres of the rich, honey-coloured Scotch and handed it to me. I took a sip. It was a single malt, the one that Hannah and Marcus had given him on Father's Day, and it tasted good. I felt the soothing warmth burn down my throat and into my stomach like an instant anaesthetic. That one sip was so dangerously full of promise, the potential for oblivion. It was only in recent years that I'd really begun to understand how my mum ended up like she did.

He swirled the whisky in his glass. His face was more relaxed now, though still distressed. He'd thought I was seeing someone else; I felt chastened by the pain I'd caused, horrified by my power to hurt him. I was relieved that he knew I hadn't cheated on him but I wanted to say no, don't be too relieved; don't think I'm good after all, because I'm not. I'm really not. I took another mouthful of whisky. What if I told him the truth? The whole truth? The idea zipped through my mind. He loved me; he would understand why I did what I did, wouldn't he?

'To be honest,' he said, 'I find all this quite hurtful. I mean, when did we start keeping secrets from each other?'

'I'm so sorry,' I whispered.

'Anyway,' he sighed. 'What do you think?'

'What do I think?'

'About him meeting Hannah. Have you said anything to her?'

'Of course not! He can forget it, like you said. He can't just turn up and disrupt our lives after all this time.'

'Well, yes, but I suppose if the man's dying—'

'Duncan, you can't be serious? I'm sorry he's dying, but why should that give him the right to—'

'I'm not thinking of him, I'm thinking of Hannah. It was different when he was the absent father on the other side of the world, but if he's here now, and if he really is dying, don't you think that she—'

'No. I don't. Look, my own father did much the same thing, didn't he? Buggered off to Oz and virtually forgot he had a daughter. If he'd suddenly turned up after twenty, thirty, forty years, I wouldn't have wanted anything to do with him, because as far as I'm concerned he doesn't count as my father any more. He forfeited that connection, and Scott has forfeited his connection with Hannah. *You're* her father, for God's sake.'

'I know, of course I am. But what about her need to know her roots? Everyone wants to know where they come from, don't they? And what if she found out that he was here, in the same city as her and at death's door, and that we hadn't told her? She might not want to meet him, but I don't think she'd be too impressed that she'd been denied the opportunity to make up her own mind about it.'

'Oh God,' I murmured as I covered my face with my hands. He was right, and I couldn't see any way out of it. 'I can't think straight; I don't know what to do.'

'You've got to tell her, surely? Then she can decide. And if she says no, he'll have to leave us alone. If he doesn't, we'll get the police involved.'

I let out a half-sob. He stood up, scraping his chair back, and came and put his arms around me. 'Hey, come on.' He kissed the top of my head. 'It's not good that he's turned up after all this time, and it's bound to unsettle Hannah, but she's a strong girl, and we're a strong couple. What's the worst that can happen?'

CHAPTER TWENTY-FIVE

Every couple of days, Duncan asked whether I'd said anything to Hannah. 'Not yet,' I kept telling him. 'I can't just dump this on her; I've got to wait for the right moment.' I was stalling for time, I knew, still hoping I'd be able to think of something.

I made a point of trying not to call on Hannah too often because I didn't want to be one of those mothers who was always sticking her nose in, but as I parked the car I realised I'd not spoken to her for three days and it had been almost a week since I'd seen her. I'd been too preoccupied with Scott, and also with Duncan knowing that Scott was around. She hadn't rung me, though, so I assumed things were okay, but when she opened the door, I could see immediately that they weren't. She was still in her pyjamas, her hair unwashed and un-brushed, and her eyes were red and puffy. She looked weary and anxious.

'I didn't know you were coming,' she said as I followed her in.

'I was going to phone, but I thought you might be in the middle of feeding or something.'

'Sorry about the mess.' She gestured around the kitchen, which did look a bit chaotic, even for Hannah, then she sat down heavily at the table, slumping in her chair.

'Where's—'

'Marcus has taken him for a walk round the park. It was supposed to be so I could go back to bed, but I can't sleep anyway so there's no point.' She was looking down as she spoke, not making eye contact.

'Hannah, are you all right, darling? You look—'

'Like shit. I know.' She still didn't look at me.

I paused, not quite sure how to handle this. It was so unlike her. 'Shall I make us some coffee? Or a cup of tea?'

She shrugged. 'If you like.'

I squeezed her shoulder as I went past her to fill the kettle. Why hadn't I come round before? I could have kicked myself for leaving her this long. She was ill, depressed; I was certain of it now. I made the coffee slowly so I had time to think. I knew from some of the young mums at the Project that you had to be careful what you said.

As I carried the mugs back to the table, I could see that her shoulders were shaking. I set the mugs down and put my arms around her. 'Oh sweetheart, what is it? Whatever's the matter?'

It was a few moments before she could speak. I tore off some kitchen roll and handed it to her so she could blow her nose. 'I don't know what I'm doing wrong,' she managed to get out between sobs. 'But he never seems to stop crying.'

'Have you talked to the health visitor?' I asked gently. 'Or the doctor?'

She shook her head.

'They might be able to suggest something that would help.'

'Yes, but I don't want them knowing I'm so rubbish at this.'

I laid my hand on her arm. 'Listen, darling. You're not rubbish at this; it's just taking a while to get used to, that's all. Do you think you might be depressed? It's quite common, you know. And it can be fairly easy to treat.'

But I wasn't sure she was listening. The tears were streaming down her face as she balled up the kitchen towel in her hands. 'You know,' she said, 'I used to think it would be great to push the pram round the park in the afternoons, but he cries and cries the whole time, and then people look at me like I should be doing something about it but if I've fed him and changed him and he's still crying, what else am I supposed to do?' She looked at me. 'I had to get Marcus to take the day off today because I don't think I could have got through it on my own.'

'Darling, why on earth didn't you call me? I'd have come over straight away, you know I would.'

'Yes, but you've got work and stuff and anyway, I've

got to learn to deal with it some time, haven't I?' She wiped her eyes and sighed a shuddering breath.

I stood up and put my arms around her again. 'No, darling, you don't have to deal with this on your own. I'm so sorry – I should have come before, or phoned you at least.' How could I have been so preoccupied? How could I have not seen this coming? There was no way I could lay any more on Hannah's shoulders now. 'Have you talked to Marcus about how you're feeling?'

She shook her head vigorously and pulled away from me. Her eyes were glassy, the tears brimming. She reached behind her and grabbed the kitchen roll from the worktop, reeling off a few sheets and holding them to her eyes to catch the rapidly spilling tears. My poor Hannah; my poor girl.

'I wanted a baby so badly,' she sniffed, 'but I look at him and . . . and he doesn't feel like mine. I'm trying, I really am, but, oh God, this feels such a terrible, shitty thing to say, but I don't think I love him.' Her eyes slipped cautiously in my direction, checking my reaction. 'At least, not *really*; not as much as I'm supposed to.' A fresh wave of tears overtook her and her shoulders heaved as she collapsed against me.

I held her tight and stroked her hair. 'Oh Hannah.' Instinctively, I rocked her as though she was still a child, and I did so until her crying subsided a little. After a minute or so, she sat up, reeled off some more kitchen towel and blew her nose.

'Don't tell Marcus, will you? He'll think I'm a monster,

that's if he doesn't already.' She looked up at me, then looked away. 'You must think so, too.'

'Of course I don't! And Marcus won't, either. Having a baby is a massive disruption, not to mention the trauma of giving birth.' I could hear my professional voice creeping in. I saw this happen so often among the young mothers I looked after, but this was different, this was my own Hannah.

'I mean, I want to do things for him, to look after him properly and stuff, but I don't seem to be able to do anything without messing it up somehow. I can't even feed him for more than a couple of minutes because it hurts so much. And – and I don't think he really likes me, anyway.' She sighed a shaky post-tears sigh. 'I know it sounds bonkers, but I keep thinking it's because he knows.' She wiped her eyes with another sheet of kitchen paper and then twisted it between her fingers as she talked without looking up. 'He's all right with Marcus. The minute Marcus picks him up, he stops crying, and when he baths him or changes his nappy, he doesn't cry at all, but when I do it, he screams. He just senses that Marcus is his real daddy and I'm not his—'

'You are. You're his real mummy – don't even consider thinking anything different! Listen,' I said gently. 'You need to trust yourself a bit more. I know it's easy to say and not so easy to do, but try not to worry so much.' I had a sudden flash memory of watching her with him a couple of weeks ago, her jaw set tightly as she washed and dried him, then fastened him into a new nappy, quickly, efficiently, and silently. Why the hell hadn't I spotted it then? 'Hannah, sweetheart, I think there's a good chance that you have proper postnatal depression. I think we should get you to a doctor.'

She looked up at me and her eyes started to fill. 'But what if they take him away? Marcus adores him; he'd never forgive me.'

'Darling, nobody is going to take him away, but you need some help now. You're not well and it's not your fault. '

She began to cry again. 'I've wanted a baby almost since I was old enough to have one.'

'I was the same.'

'But I feel like . . . like I've cheated, or something; like I'm not really supposed to have him. If you're not meant to be a mother, I mean, if nature decides you're not, then how can—'

'Being a mother isn't just about being biologically connected, you know; nor is being a father. Look at your dad; he couldn't be any more your father if he had the same genes, could he?'

She nodded. 'I know, I know.'

'And your – I'm not going to say "real" – father, well, he couldn't have been much less of one, could he?' I heard myself and I knew what I was doing, but seeing Hannah's distress only made me more angry that Scott thought he could just turn up and cause havoc without any thought of the consequences. 'It's about what you do, how much you care. You're bound to make mistakes

– we all do. But we can only do what we think is the best thing at the time.'

She didn't say anything, and my words seemed to ring in the air as though they were hanging around to taunt me. Who the hell was I to talk about being a good mother? I summoned up the professional voice again, because in this I was justified: I was a good family support worker.

'Hannah, trust me. You will be able to love him properly, I promise, and it'll almost certainly start happening as soon as you stop worrying about it *not* happening. But you need to get some help first. Let me talk to Marcus. I can come to the doctor with you if you'd like me to, and I can come and stay for as long as you need me.'

She mopped at her eyes again. 'I bet this didn't happen to you, did it? I mean, you've always said you loved me the moment I was born.'

'Yes, I did. But that doesn't mean . . . Well, it certainly doesn't mean I did everything right.'

'What sort of things did you do wrong, then?' She sniffed. 'I've never even asked you about feeding and stuff. Did you breastfeed? I bet you didn't feel desperate to give it up.' She shook her head. 'Do you know what? I went and bought a steriliser unit and bottles from Mothercare the other day, but I felt so guilty for even considering it that I just chucked them in the back of the cupboard and didn't even tell Marcus.'

'Oh darling, not everyone can breastfeed for long. Some women aren't able to do it at all. It's nothing to feel guilty about. And you've given him a good start, anyway.'

'So how long did you breastfeed for?'

At that moment, we heard Marcus's key in the door, swiftly followed by the sound of Toby crying. Marcus jiggled him as he brought him into the kitchen. 'Hey, look, buster! Grandma's here. There you go, Grandma.' I took him automatically. 'Hello, my little pickle,' I murmured, enjoying the welcome weight in my arms but suddenly aware that I could help more by sacrificing that simple pleasure. 'I could hold you all day, but I think your mummy needs a cuddle now.' Hannah hesitated for a second, then took him.

'Why, what's up?' Marcus asked, concern flooding his face.

'I'm fine,' Hannah said, perhaps more sharply than she needed to. Then she looked down at Toby and burst into tears.

*

I was still on the phone to Duncan when Marcus came back downstairs. He looked weary. *She's asleep,* he mouthed. *Good,* I mouthed back, then turned to the phone again. 'Marcus says she's asleep, so there's not really much point in you coming over right now. I'll call again when I've spoken to Marcus. Speak to you in a bit.' I put the handset back in its cradle.

'Duncan says to give her his love.'

Marcus nodded, ran a hand through his hair and shook his head. 'I didn't notice how bad it was getting. She's

217

been a bit weepy, but I honestly didn't realise it was serious. I should have seen it earlier. '

'I keep telling myself the same thing.'

'Yes, but I live with her. There's no excuse.' He walked over to the crib where Toby was sleeping and looked down at him, then turned to me. 'All this stuff about her not feeling like his mum – I had no idea she felt like that. I thought that the fact he grew inside her, that she gave birth to him . . . I don't know.' He ran his hand through his hair again. 'I thought that would do it, you know?'

I nodded. 'You can't predict these things, though. You just can't know how you're going to feel in advance.'

He sighed. 'She's agreed to see the doctor, at least.'

'Well, that's something. If I'm right, if she does have postnatal depression, things may look very different once she's being treated.'

'What, like antidepressants, you mean? I'm not sure I want her taking happy pills.'

'Marcus, you listen to me. Antidepressants are *not* "happy pills"! And you should know better, for goodness' sake.' I didn't often tell my son-in-law off, but this fear of antidepressants made me so angry. 'I've seen enough depression, postnatal and otherwise, to know that it takes more than a *Cheer up and pull yourself together* to recover,' I told him. 'She may need some counselling as well – you both might – but I think the doctor is going to recognise that she needs help now, and that may well mean getting her on a course of medication as soon as possible.' I thought fleetingly of my mother and her fits of despair; I wondered whether things would have been different if she'd been prescribed antidepressants when she needed them.

Marcus nodded and mumbled, 'I suppose you're right.'

'Marcus,' I said gently. 'It's a difficult time for you both, and it may take a few weeks before things improve; I think it might be an idea if I were to come and stay again, at least for a few days. Duncan's offered to do the same – he said to just let him know what he can do that'll be the most helpful. We can both take time off work, so we can sit with Hannah, take Toby out, cook, shop – whatever's needed.'

And to my surprise, he looked grateful. 'Thanks,' he said. 'I appreciate that.'

*

I was just leaving the house to pop home and pick up some clothes when my phone beeped a text. *Need to talk urgently. S.* The flash of anger I felt was sudden and intense. How *dare* he intrude at a time like this? I stabbed out my reply: *Can't talk now. Hannah not well. Will be in touch soon.* And I pressed *Send*. It was true that he had the upper hand, but I felt so angry right now that I wasn't going to jump the moment he said jump.

CHAPTER TWENTY-SIX

Just as Hannah's GP had said, the medication took ten to fourteen days to kick in, but now it appeared to be making a huge difference and things were starting to get back to normal. I sighed as I reached for my phone; I had to admit, Scott was being fairly patient but I knew I couldn't put off going to see him for much longer. I'd had two more texts from him, but I'd explained that Hannah was ill and promised to contact him as soon as I could. *Hannah slightly better*, I typed now. *I can come tomorrow*. I pressed *Send*. He rarely went out any more, so I was sure he'd say yes. I was going to tell him that he *couldn't* say anything to Hannah, not yet, at least. If I could get him to understand just how ill she'd been and how fragile she still was, surely he'd realise how much telling the truth would hurt her? Thinking about it all stirred up my anger again. Quite apart from the postnatal depression, she only gave birth a couple of months ago, for Christ's sake. How could he be considering this, just to try and absolve himself of guilt? It was selfish, pure and simple.

The GP had been supportive and sympathetic, thank goodness. PND was far from uncommon for mums in Hannah's situation, she said, and the sooner she started treatment, the better. She also referred her for urgent counselling and recommended a couple of support groups. I was impressed – the NHS didn't always run that smoothly. The only hiccup was that when the GP said she didn't recommend breastfeeding while taking antidepressants – she made a point of putting it that way round, Marcus told me – Hannah said she wouldn't take them. She was worried that it was 'another failure' on her part; how could she be a proper mother if she couldn't even feed Toby from her own body, was how she put it. But the GP, a young woman about the same age as Hannah, eventually managed to reassure her. In some cases, she said, bottle feeding was definitely the better choice for mum and baby.

My colleagues at the Project were very understanding about me taking more time off to look after Hannah, but they were pleased to see me back at work. Duncan, Marcus and I had taken time off on a rota basis to make sure there was someone with Hannah constantly, even if it was just so we could hold the baby while she went to the loo. It was important that she didn't feel responsible for him for every single second of every day. With this in mind, Marcus had reduced his working hours for the foreseeable future. Marcus had impressed us over the last couple of weeks. We'd always liked him, but he could sometimes be a bit too laid-back and we'd never been quite sure he'd be able to take care of Hannah properly. But he'd really stepped up to the plate this time, and he seemed suddenly much more aware of the magnitude of being a parent, something that Hannah, even though she struggled with it, had appeared to be aware of immediately. What was mildly annoying, I thought as I checked my phone again, was that it seemed that it took a crisis to make men see that you couldn't just play at being a father. Although that probably wasn't fair; it wasn't Marcus who'd made me angry, it was Scott. I felt a fresh surge of bitterness at the way he was behaving. Well, the way he'd been behaving up until now, anyway.

It was unusual for Scott not to reply immediately, and when his text came through an hour later, it was a bit of a shock. Yes, I could go and see him tomorrow, but he wasn't at home – he was 'spending some time' in a hospice. He gave the address. Hospices were for what they called 'end-of-life care', weren't they? I remembered him saying they'd give him 'serious drugs' so there wouldn't be too much pain at the end. This must mean that the end was near. I felt a bit shaky as I filled the kettle for tea. I wasn't sure why – it had been clear from the moment I saw him that he wasn't lying about his illness, but the thought that his death might be imminent . . .

I poured boiling water into the mug with the milk, but realised I'd forgotten the tea bag. My hands were trembling and my stomach felt sore, as though it was flooded with acid. I was still angry with him for turning up like this after all these years, for meddling and upsetting things; but on the other hand, I couldn't help but feel ashamed of myself – how could anyone be angry with a dying man? Worse still was the other thought that had begun to creep in, the even more shameful one; when Scott died, it would be over. I wouldn't have to worry any more. I disgusted myself; I'd almost loved him once, and now I was hoping for his death.

Later, when Duncan came home, I told him about the text. 'So, it looks like he might not have long left.'

Duncan looked down at his lap. 'Well,' he said. 'I can't pretend it wouldn't be something of a relief.'

'Really? But I thought you thought—'

'I thought you should tell Hannah about him, that's all – I still think so. But that doesn't mean I relish the fact that he's turned up. I don't want that joker turning our lives upside down any more than you do.' He took a mouthful of the coffee I'd just poured. 'But look, this makes it all the more important that we tell Hannah.'

I spoke carefully, aware that he was likely to find what I was saying unpalatable. 'Thing is, if he dies soon . . . well, we won't need to tell her at all, will we?'

He didn't look as shocked as I expected, but he flicked his head in irritation. 'Of course we will. We can't pretend this never happened, and after all, he is her flesh and blood. She might decide she wants to find out more about him, especially since he finally bothered to come looking for her.' He said the last bit with disdain.

SUSAN ELLIOT WRIGHT

'I don't understand how you can be so pissed off with him and yet still want to do the right thing.'

'I keep telling you, I want to do the right thing for Hannah, not for him. No matter how lousy a father he's been, and however much we wish he'd never turned up, he *is* her father and he did turn up, and it's her right to know that. And now, if he's at death's door – and I can't say I'm sorry if he is, to be honest – then it's all the more reason to tell her. Imagine if she looked him up later and found out he died here in Sheffield? Then if she found out that we knew about it, how's she going to feel about us not telling her?'

'All right, I see your point. But think about it. She's not seen him since she was a baby; she's never shown the slightest interest in him or desire to find out anything about him – or anything more than I've already told her, anyway.' I had a sudden memory of New Year's Eve, when she asked me if she looked like her father. 'And anyway, she's not strong enough to deal with something like this yet.'

He nodded thoughtfully. 'Yes, that *is* a worry. But she'll want to know more about her roots at some point, especially now she's had her own baby. We'll just have to be careful how we tell her. Perhaps we should speak to Marcus first?'

'No, she'd hate that.' I sighed. 'Duncan, she's been through so much. What with the early menopause, then the IVF. And you know she's still struggling to come to terms with the fact that they had to use a donor.'

224

Duncan nodded. 'I know. Poor Han.'

'I know the treatment seems to be working, but I still don't think we should dump this on her, not when she's in such a fragile state.'

Duncan loved Hannah; he wouldn't want to risk making her ill again, I was sure. He was looking at me intently and I could see him turning it over, weighing it up. He folded his arms and looked down at his feet while tapping his thumb rapidly on his upper arm as he thought about it. 'You're right,' he said, looking out into the shadowy garden. 'I suppose there's no point in risking setting her back again.' He sighed deeply then stood up, put his hands in his pockets and walked over to the window. 'But I'm still uncomfortable about keeping something like this from her.'

*

My stomach was doing somersaults as I walked into the hospice. I'd never been inside one before, and I expected it to be like a hospital, only, I don't know, *more* so. I thought I'd find Scott in bed, attached to various tubes and wires, drugged up to the eyeballs and clinging to life by a thread. I felt hot and breathless as I followed the nurse. What would I say to him? Would he even be conscious? And if he wasn't . . . could this actually mean that it was over, that I didn't have to worry any more? The nurse led me along a corridor where the walls were painted a cheery yellow and hung with modern framed prints of brightly coloured flowers. 'I'll just check for you,' the nurse said as we came out into a carpeted area with sofas and coffee tables and the nurses' station in the corner. 'Visitor for Scott Matthews,' she said to the nurse behind the desk. 'Is he still in the smoking room?'

Apparently he was. She must have noticed the look on my face. 'Patients and visitors are permitted to smoke in the designated areas. Would you like to join him in the smoking room today, or shall I ask him to move into another day room?'

'No, don't move him. I don't smoke any more, but it doesn't really bother me.'

'Here we are, then.' I could smell the cigarettes even before she opened the door to a large, light room with armchairs dotted around and a table in the corner where three people were playing cards. There was quite a fug of cigarette smoke hanging in the air and it was only when he turned round that I realised that one of the card players was Scott. He nodded at me, excused himself from the game, then stood, with the help of his stick, and walked slowly to a group of chairs at the other end of the room, gesturing for me to join him.

'You look . . .' I paused. 'Not *well*, exactly, but . . .'

'Not as bad as you expected?' His voice was weak and he was skeletally thin, but the darkness around his eyes wasn't quite as bad as it had been the last time I saw him. I nodded.

'Morphine is a truly wonderful thing.'

'But I thought a hospice was—'

'So did I before I was ill. But you can come in for short stays as well. It's respite care, really – some decent pain relief and a break from having to look after yourself, or for whoever else is looking after you. I'm only in for a couple of weeks while Brenda's away.'

'Brenda? Oh yes, your landlady. She's still helping out, then?'

He leaned back in his chair. 'She comes in every day now. I rely on her almost completely for shopping and cooking – I don't really go out any more because I can only walk about twenty yards before I need to stop and rest.' He took a tobacco pouch out of his pocket and put it on the arm of the chair along with a packet of Rizlas. Slowly, with an old man's hands, he rolled a thin cigarette. 'So, you said Hannah's been ill?' He offered me the tobacco pouch.

I shook my head. 'I haven't smoked for years. And surely, I mean, should you be—'

He gave a tight smile. 'Not going to make much difference now, is it? Anyway, Hannah. Is she better?'

'A little, but there's a long way to go before she'll be back to normal. She's had postnatal depression. It's been bad. I mean really bad, and we've all had to take time off work to look after her. She couldn't cope with the baby, or the house, or anything, really, and she's still very fragile, so you see, I can't possibly – you can't, I mean . . . There's no way she's strong enough, so you mustn't . . . ' I was babbling.

Scott was nodding his head slowly. 'Has she seen a doctor?'

'Yes. They've given her tablets. And she needs to have counselling. Scott, you've got to leave her alone. She can't take it, okay?'

'What do you mean, "leave her alone"? I've told you. I think *you* should tell her. Or tell your husband first and you can tell her together, I don't know.'

He sounded irritated; I hadn't heard him like this before. His voice was stronger although he was still speaking quietly, even though we now appeared to be alone in the room.

'Jo, be realistic. I'm not going to just walk up to her and say, *Hey, I'm your dad and by the way, there's something else you should know,* now am I? Not unless I have to; not unless you absolutely refuse.'

I could feel a tightening in my chest, as though I couldn't take a breath. 'Scott, don't you understand? She's ill; she can't take this.'

'But she is getting better, right?'

'Oh my God!' I was on the verge of tears. I put my head in my hands. 'Scott, can't you just . . .'

'Listen, two weeks, okay? I'll be back home by then. Well, for the time being, anyway.' He leaned forward again. 'Jo, it's the right thing to do, you know it is. And I do think it's better coming from you. And tell her . . . tell her I'd really like to see her, just once.'

CHAPTER TWENTY-SEVEN

Hastings, 1976

Jo wandered around the Old Town, waiting for the summer fayre to be over. She didn't want to see any more morris dancers, or jugglers or smiling people with ice creams or candyfloss. Usually, she loved this part of town, with its little flights of steps in odd places, the alleys and passage-ways running between the streets and the Tudor houses, higgledy-piggledy timber-framed dwellings with an over-hang jutting out over the pavement below because their upper floors were bigger than their ground floors. But today, she barely noticed its charm.

She could feel the skin on her shoulders prickling as she trudged up All Saints Street and past the strange, wedge-shaped house known as 'piece of cheese cottage'. She ought to stop and put some more sun cream on, but she couldn't be bothered. Scott had been so much nicer to her today until he found out about the earrings; it seemed doubly cruel that he was so pissed off with her now. She carried on walking aimlessly until she noticed that the pubs were beginning to open. Briefly, she wondered whether to risk going back to see if he'd calmed down yet, but it would be unbearable if he was still furious with her. Instead, she took a deep breath and walked up a flight of stone steps into the pub. She'd only ever walked into two pubs alone before, the one where she'd worked in Newquay and The Crown where she worked now – but she couldn't face going there today because they'd know she'd been crying and would want to know why. And anyway, they all knew she was supposed to be doing the fayre.

The cool gloom of the pub's interior was instantly soothing, and because it was only just past opening time, there were no other customers yet – there was no way she could have walked into a crowded pub by herself. A collection of tankards and Toby jugs hung above the bar, and on the corner was a model of a Babycham deer scampering past a champagne glass. A huge stag's head looked down from the wall. The girl behind the bar looked reasonably friendly, so Jo ordered a half of Double Diamond and a packet of crisps, paid the 22½p and made her way to a table in the corner. There were a couple of folded newspapers on the seat and she opened one and pretended to read it while she ate her crisps and drank her beer and wondered whether she'd still be welcome at the house after this. Had Scott meant she should go temporarily? He'd sounded so angry; perhaps he meant she should go for good. Maybe he hadn't really wanted her there anyway and now he had a good reason to ask her to leave. She felt a horrible sinking feeling in her stomach at the prospect. She'd begun to feel so settled at the house, and so comfortable with Eve, and even with Scott, although he couldn't seem to make up his mind whether he liked her or not. She cringed when she thought about the earrings. Eve had looked so pale and ill earlier; what was she going to say when she found out that so much of her hard work over the last few weeks had been for nothing? She flicked her head as if to shake the memory away. Should she go straight back to the house and apologise again, she wondered as she finished her drink, or should she try to stay away tonight, perhaps write them a letter explaining how truly sorry she was? She could wait until it got dark and put it through the door. Perhaps Scott would have calmed down by then.

As she walked to the bar to buy one more drink, she noticed the two scrawny dark shapes hanging above her head. The barmaid smiled. 'I know. Mental, aren't they? They're cats; mummified. The previous owners found them bricked up in the wall, apparently, and they reckon they belonged to an old witch who was supposed to have lived here. Tell you what, though, he's going to have to move them soon. Bits keep dropping into the bleeding drinks!' And she laughed. 'Same again?'

Eve was always saying that she liked Hastings because it was such was an odd place, and Jo thought about this as she smoked her last cigarette. Where else could you go into a pub and find a mummified cat hanging above the bar? As she walked back to her seat, a horrible memory popped up in her mind; she'd forgotten it completely until now. It happened when she was four. She'd spent what seemed like a whole morning dressing up their old ginger cat in her baby doll's clothes so she could push him round the garden in her doll's pram. She'd been so pleased that she'd been able to make Tiger look pretty – she'd even managed to tie a frilly bonnet on him without getting scratched. It was only when she proudly wheeled the pram into the kitchen that she realised something was wrong. Her dad had leapt up and whisked the pram away while her mum quickly buckled her into her sandals, took her hand and led her outside. 'Come on, Jo-Jo. No more tears, now. We'll go to the park, shall we? How about a choc-ice?' It wasn't her fault, they told her. Tiger was very, very old, and he'd probably died in his sleep. But Jo had never, from that day to this, been able to remember whether the cat had been alive when she'd first tried to manoeuvre his front paws into the sleeves of the doll's matinee jacket.

Despite the crisps, she was starting to feel hungry again and she didn't have much money left, so she finished her drink and went back out into the street. The sun no longer blazed quite so ferociously, but it was still hot outside. She set off down towards the beach, stopping on the way to buy ten No 6 and a bag of chips.

The tide was going out, and the strip of glistening wet shingle it left looked so inviting that she went almost to the water's edge, took off her sandals and walked along towards the pier with the cool water occasionally lapping over her feet. There was some movement in the air down here, but it was still so warm that it felt as if someone were opening and closing an oven door. Most of the families had gone now, but there were still people about. Further up the beach there was a group clustered around a small fire; one of the men was playing a guitar and a couple of the women were singing along to 'American Pie'. She felt a pang. On Eve's birthday just over a week ago, the three of them had built a fire down here and had sung Simon & Garfunkel songs so well that some of the other people on the beach had come over and joined in. Afterwards, everyone had laughed and clapped, and when the others had gone, the three of them had stayed on the beach, talking and gazing up at the clear night sky until the early hours of the morning. Would that ever happen again, or had she ruined their friendship for ever?

She walked on past the pier and found herself in Bottle Alley, one of Eve's favourite places. It was a stretch of the lower promenade where the rear walls had been concreted and studded with thousands of fragments of coloured glass, like an art deco mosaic. Eve had shown her this not long after she'd arrived. The light was fading now so it was difficult to see the colours of the glass, but it was still beautiful. When she came to an alcove with a bench, she sat down, lit a cigarette and smoked it slowly as she watched the sky darken even further. A huge yawn overtook her. Perhaps she could sleep here, then go back tomorrow and see how things were. As she sat looking out across the darkening water, she felt heavy, weighed down by sadness. With a sigh, she took her sunglasses and cigarettes out of her bag and put them under the bench, then she plumped up her bag to use as a pillow, curled her legs up behind her and lay down to try and get some sleep. The bench was hard and her sunburned shoulder was starting to hurt, but she felt so exhausted from the heat and the anxiety that she was sure she'd be able to doze. So yet again she was 'sleeping rough'. How could she be in this situation again, especially after everything had started to feel safe at last? At least it wasn't cold like that horrible night in London, just after her mum died. She swallowed back the lump that had started to form in her throat. People said that grief would gradually lessen over time, and in some ways it did. But every now and again, Jo found herself thinking that her mum had been dead for long enough now, and it was time she came back. She knew it was a stupid thing to think, but it was the *permanence* of death that was so difficult to cope with.

The warm air moved gently over her bare arms and she closed her eyes, trying to ignore the burning pain in her shoulder by focusing on the soothing, rhythmic sound of the sea. A tear slid out of her eye, quickly followed by another, but she bit her lip to hold them back and soon drifted into a light doze.

The first thing she became aware of was the smell of tobacco and stale sweat, then she felt the hard wooden bench beneath her and, as she moved, there was a searing pain in her shoulder and the events of the day came flooding back. She tried to open her eyes but they were crusted shut with dried tears. She was aware of someone breathing and for an instant she wondered if it was Scott come to find her, but when she managed to open her eyes, it wasn't Scott's gently bearded face she saw just inches from her own, but an engorged penis and a big, calloused hand frantically pulling at it. She scrabbled to her feet, grabbed her bag and swung it at the man who jumped back, clearly startled. She only glanced at him briefly but she could see that he was an older man, his fat white belly showing through his untucked shirt and his shorts open and falling down. He'd let go of his penis and had a hand stretched towards her. 'Please, I won't hurt you,' he called after her, but she was running along Bottle Alley now, her cork-soled sandals making an echo as they hit the ground. Thank God she hadn't taken them off when she went to sleep. She ran on towards the pier, but when she glanced over her shoulder, she could see another figure coming towards her. Her feet crashed and crunched into the stones as she veered out of the alley and onto the beach. She could see the steps up to the street ahead of her, but as she ran towards them she heard more crunching footsteps behind her. It was difficult to run on a pebbled beach at the best of times, but her sunburned shoulder was killing her and she needed to pee – she could feel the beer sloshing around inside her. The footsteps were close behind her now and she could barely run any more. She was about to scream when a voice called, 'Jo! Jo, it's me, for Christ's sake. Slow down.'

Scott. She stopped and turned round just as he reached her. 'What on earth's the matter?' he said. And at that, she burst into tears and half fell onto him. 'I was asleep on the bench and when I woke up there was a man right next to me and he . . . he . . .'

'Fuck, man. Are you okay? What happened?'

'No,' she said, shaking her head and recovering herself a little. 'No, I'm all right, he didn't touch me or anything. But he . . . he had his cock out, and he was, you know, playing with himself, right in front of my face.'

'Filthy pervert bastard,' Scott said, putting his arms around her and hugging her tightly. 'You sure you're okay?'

She nodded her head against his chest. It felt so good to lean against him. She could smell a trace of beer on his breath, and tobacco, but it was different, not like the stale smell that had come from the other man. Scott smelled of Lifebuoy Soap, too.

'What the hell were you doing asleep on a bench, anyway?' He held her away from him now to look at her.

She cast her eyes down. 'I didn't know what to do, after . . . you know, everything today, with the earrings.'

Scott sighed. 'We all make mistakes. Sleeping on a bench isn't going to help, is it?'

'I didn't know whether to come back to the house; I wasn't sure I'd be welcome.' She wiped away another tear. 'What did Eve say? Was she very angry?'

He shook his head. 'Eve's never, like, "very angry". She was a bit pissed off about it, but only because they take so long to make. She's not pissed off with you, though. In fact, she had a go at me for being such a prick. And she's right; I'm sorry.'

Jo felt her heart lift. 'No. No, it's me who should apologise. And like I said, I swear to God I'll pay you back. I'm sure I can do some extra shifts at the pub, and I—'

'Jo!' Scott held his hand up. 'Cool it, man. If you want to do extra shifts that's fine; and any extra cash in the kitty is obviously good. But don't think you have to pay it back. Seriously. It's not entirely your fault. Eve pointed out that neither of us had actually, like, told you how much the earrings were. And the price list was only on a scrap of paper, easy enough to lose. Eve reckoned she might have been distracted as well if she'd been in the same situation – a lost kid and that. So look, it could have happened to any of us, really. I've accepted your apology, now accept mine, huh?'

Jo almost cried with relief.

'I overreacted, I guess.' He looked at her. 'I told you to go, didn't I? I didn't mean for good, you silly cow.' He smiled. 'Come on, let's go home.'

CHAPTER TWENTY-EIGHT

Jo woke early as usual, with perspiration pooling in the hollows of her collarbones. She longed for a proper shower, but they only had a rubber attachment that fitted on the bath taps, and anyway, they were supposed to be saving water. Once she was dressed, she went down to the basement, filled a bucket with washing-up water from the old tin bath then went outside and up the back steps to water the tomato plants before the sun rose too high in the sky. It was hot already, and it wasn't yet eight o'clock. The patch of grass Eve had planned to turn into a mini allotment was parched and brittle, the soil nothing more than dust. It was just as well that Eve hadn't felt well enough to dig it over in the spring, because anything that was planted in the ground wouldn't have stood a chance.

Scott and Eve were in the kitchen already. A huge pan of strawberries and sugar was bubbling away on the Baby

Belling and the fragrant perfume of hot, sugary fruit filled the room. They'd walked three miles to a Pick Your Own farm yesterday. It was half the usual price because the fruit was ripening too quickly, and they'd managed to pick almost twelve pounds of strawberries that were at their peak of ripeness but would probably have gone too far if left another day.

'It's busy in here,' Jo said. 'And it's only eight o'clock.'

Scott was stirring the jam while Eve scalded jars with boiling water; again there was this feeling of industry.

'I wanted to get at least one lot of boiling done before it gets too hot,' Eve said, 'and anyway, we need to have this lot completely finished by about half eleven because Scott's got a lunchtime gig in Battle, and my train's at five to twelve.'

Jo was surprised by a slight flare of panic. 'Where are you going?'

'Covent Garden. I need more supplies.'

'Supplies?'

'For the jewellery,' Eve muttered as she lined up the jars. 'I need to build up the stocks again.' She spoke quietly. She'd barely mentioned her jewellery-making ever since the summer fayre, and Jo was certain she was avoiding the subject because she knew Jo still felt guilty over those earrings.

'Oh yes, of course.' That day she'd met Eve in Trafalgar Square seemed so long ago now. 'Eve, I'm not working today; is there anything I can do to help?' She half hoped Eve would suggest she go with her, although she'd struggle to find the train fare. Maybe they could hitchhike like before? But instead, Eve asked if she'd mind going down to the beach to look for some small shells she could use for necklaces and bracelets. 'Okay,' she said, and tried not to look too disappointed.

The radio was on and the news was all about the drought and the dried-up reservoirs and how in some parts of the country people had to get their water from standpipes. The situation was becoming serious, the newscaster said, and if rain didn't come soon, the whole country was in trouble. 'Like it's not in trouble already.' Scott turned the radio off and shook his head. He lifted the pan of bubbling jam from the cooker and began filling the jars Eve had prepared. 'Honestly, I used to be worried about living in squats and not having a regular income, but at least we're not having to pay, like, a third of what we earn to the government. That makes me so fucking angry—'

'Scott!'

'Sorry. But why should we work our butts off to support rising prices and falling employment? And then they accuse us of being long-haired layabouts and communists. I may have long hair but I bet we work harder than most of those ignorant bastards who trot off to their office jobs with luncheon vouchers and a key to the executive khazi; and I guarantee they're still using hoses to wash their brand-new BMWs while the poor farmers are losing their crops.'

'You know I agree with you, Scotty,' Eve said. 'But

there's no point in being angry about it, is there?' She began wiping the sides of the jars and putting little discs of waxed paper on top of the jam.

'But the state of this country, man.' Scott shook his head as he poured the last of the bright red jam into a jar. 'It's no wonder so many people are emigrating. My parents had the right idea, didn't they? Hey, maybe we should all go to New Zealand?'

Jo and Eve both laughed. 'No,' Eve said. 'The country may be in trouble, but we're not really part of it, are we? We work, we earn our living but we don't have to answer to anybody. All right, so we don't pay tax, but we don't claim anything, either. We don't even use the Health Service, never mind rely on weekly giros.'

Jo hadn't told them that, for a while, she and her mother *had* relied on weekly giros.

'And I don't see why we shouldn't carry on just the way we are. Anyway, I like it here. Especially right here, by the sea.' Eve looked wistful for a moment. 'I hope Mr Hedman doesn't want to sell the place too soon; I don't ever want to leave this house.'

Jo spent most of the day at the beach, gathering shells for the jewellery. She also picked up a few pretty small stones and some pebbles of smooth coloured glass that Eve might be able to use. It was scorching again, but she'd been careful to apply plenty of sun cream ever since the summer fayre, when her shoulders had been badly sunburned. She'd been furious with herself because she should have known better – *did* know better. But Eve had rubbed lavender oil into her damaged skin and it had healed remarkably quickly, although it still felt a bit leathery. Now though, she was developing a deep toffee tan which she knew suited her, especially when she wore the hot pants she'd bought at a jumble sale with a white cheesecloth shirt tied in a knot under her bust.

Scott was standing at the sink when she got back, and when he turned round he did a double take, then let out a low, appreciative whistle. 'You look good,' he nodded. 'That get-up shows off your tan.'

It was only when Jo felt the little thrill of satisfaction at the compliment that she realised that it was exactly what she'd been hoping for, and was, if she was honest, the reason she'd chosen these clothes. Scott turned back to the sink. 'Do you fancy some grilled mackerel for dinner? We could have some bread and tomatoes and lettuce with it. I got talking to this bloke at the gig. He went fishing off the beach this morning, caught a load of mackerel and then got home to find his deep-freeze had packed up, so he was sharing them out in the pub and I thought as it's just you and me tonight . . . you do like fish, don't you?'

'Yes,' Jo nodded. 'I love fish. But how come it's just us? What time will Eve be back?'

'Oh, I doubt she'll be back tonight, not unless she finds another lost soul to bring back.' He looked up suddenly, a bit sheepish. 'Sorry, I didn't mean—'

'It's okay. I was a bit of a lost soul, I suppose. Does she often bring people back from London with her, then?'

She'd thought she was in some way special, that Eve had only brought her back because she'd liked her, but maybe she was kidding herself.

'Not that often, no. But we have an open-house rule – we always have, wherever we've lived. If someone needs to crash and there's room at our place, we offer them a bed for the night, and then we see how it goes, and if they want to stay, and as long as we're both cool with whoever it is, they can stay.'

'So you were both cool with me?'

He smiled. 'Evidently.'

*

After they'd eaten the mackerel and salad, they sat in the living room with the windows open, smoking the extra-long joint Scott had made to celebrate the fact that his gig had gone well and the venue had booked him for two more dates at fifteen quid a time, plus food, plus drinks. The heat showed no sign of abating, and there wasn't the slightest breeze coming in at the open window. Usually, Jo loved the hot weather, but this was getting to be a bit much, even for her. 'Phew!' she said, fanning herself ineffectually with her hand. She stuck her bottom lip out to try and blow air up onto her face, but she could feel that her skin was covered in perspiration and her hair just clung to her damp skin in tendrils. Scott was sitting opposite her, and she could see the tiny beads of sweat on his forehead, which glistened after he'd rolled a cold bottle of beer over it. Jo did the same with her beer, and it provided a few seconds' relief. They were listening to *The Dark Side of the Moon* and soon fell into a reverential silence as they wallowed in the music, the experience heightened and deepened by the cannabis.

After the record finished, they both sat there unmoving in the tingling silence. It was impossible to judge time when you were smoking hash, but they'd listened to the whole album and it was now completely dark outside, so it must have been a couple of hours. Jo knew she should think about going to bed, but it was difficult to move from the little cocoon of contentment she found herself in. She looked across to where Scott had been sitting, but he wasn't there and she hadn't even noticed him going. She closed her eyes and leant her head back. It was nice hash; it made her feel floaty and dreamy and happy. When she opened her eyes again, Scott was standing in front of her holding out his hand. 'Something to show you.' He was grinning like an excited child. 'Come see!'

Feeling slightly woozy, she allowed him to pull her to her feet and lead her out of the room, along the hall and up the stairs. In any other situation, she might have wondered if he intended to lead her to a bedroom, but his occasional chuckles suggested otherwise. He led her along the landing, past the bedrooms, then round the corner and past the thinking room, up to the second floor. Where on earth was he taking her? The only room in use up here was Eve's work room, and at first, she thought that was where they were going, but he pointed to the five narrow stairs that led up to the storage space. The door was small, only about two and a half feet square, and she'd never opened it. Eve had said it was locked, but now Scott was leading her towards it, still chuckling. 'Come on,' he said, 'but don't tell Eve.' He let go of her hand, produced a key from his pocket and unlocked the door, then he crouched down to crawl through it. Jo followed on her hands and knees and as the surface she was touching changed from carpet to hard, rough concrete, the memory of her favourite childhood book flashed into her mind, *The Lion, the Witch and the Wardrobe* – it was as though she was crawling from the house into Narnia. But when she was through the door, she was almost as astonished as she would have been if faced with trees and snow. Scott took her hand and helped her to her feet; she was standing on the roof, but it didn't feel anywhere near as scary as she'd have expected. There were lots of slopes and chimneys, but there were lots of flat areas, too, and the parapet was about two feet high and was like a little wall running right around the edge of the building so it felt safe. It was just like another floor of the house, only one with the sky and stars overhead instead of a ceiling.

Up here, even though the air was still warm, there was a slight breeze, barely perceptible. From this vantage point, instead of the thin strip of blue that was visible from the thinking-room window, you could see the sea clearly in all its vastness. It seemed so much nearer than it did if you were looking out of one of the windows downstairs. The sky was speckled with stars and the almost full moon shone a silvery white light onto the inky blackness of the water below; to their left, Hastings Castle, illuminated by tasteful golden lighting, stood majestically on the West Hill as though still watching over the town, still guarding England. Jo turned her head slowly so she could take it all in. 'Wow,' she said.

Scott was still grinning. 'This way.' He led her along one of the walkways and round to the other side of the main chimney stack. There, where a sloped part of the roof met the flat area, Scott had laid out a picnic – more a midnight feast, she supposed – on a piece of hardboard that served as a table. There was more beer, half a bottle of white wine, a wedge of cheese, a French stick cut into chunks and a pack of Anchor butter. He'd also brought up the remains of the jumbo-sized packet of crisps they'd been eating earlier, an unopened box of Cheeselets and a bowl of rather mushy-looking strawberries left over from the jam-making. 'Scott, this is . . .' She looked around her. 'I don't know what to say.'

'I figured you'd probably have the munchies after all that pot you've smoked, so I thought, well. And also' – he looked down at his feet – 'it's to make up for the way I've, like, you know, been with you lately. Come on, let's sit down and enjoy the view.'

They sat with their backs against the sloping roof, legs stretched out in front of them; Scott's feet just touched the parapet. They ate the bread and cheese then some of the squishy strawberries washed down with the wine, which was sweet and slightly fizzy and which they drank straight from the bottle. Drinking from the same bottle seemed an intimate thing to do; more intimate that sharing a joint, somehow. The wine was warm but went surprisingly well with the strawberries. She rested her head back against the slates while Scott rolled another joint and they giggled disproportionately over the fact that it was pink from the juice that stained his fingers. It was so strange to be up here, so exposed and so near the sky.

'Eve doesn't like me coming up here,' Scott said. He took another deep draw on the joint. 'But it's so . . .' He tipped his head back and exhaled, holding his arms out as if to embrace the sky. 'It's so *fucking* beautiful.'

Jo nodded. 'I've never seen anything so amazing. I didn't even know you could get up here. Why doesn't Eve—'

'She's scared I'll fall. I've told her you couldn't fall really, not unless you were being stupidly careless. But she gets nervous. I used to have a motorbike, you know, when we first met, but she was terrified I'd have an accident and get killed, so I sold it in the end.'

'Wow. You must really care about her.'

'I do. She means a lot to me, Eve does. She's, like, really cool; you know what I mean?'

'Yeah, I do. She was lovely to me even when she didn't know me. She's been ever so kind.'

'She likes having another girl around. It's not usually girls who need somewhere to crash. There was Sapphire who stayed with us when we first moved in. Eve was quite upset when she left; she missed her.' He passed her the joint; even in the moonlight she could see the sheen of sweat on his face. 'And I think she likes the fact that the two of you have so much in common, you know, having no family and that. It's one thing I can't share with her. I can sympathise, but I can't know what it's like to have lost both your parents and your only sibling.'

'I didn't know she lost a sibling as well.' Jo thought about the photograph, the one that was now hidden in her own bag, of Eve's mum, so obviously pregnant. 'I keep meaning to ask her about her family. I knew her mum and dad were dead, but—'

He turned to look at her. 'Didn't she tell you what happened?'

'No. She started to, I think, but—'

'Oh. Well, it was a bad scene. She had a baby brother, but he died not long after he was born – there were mistakes at the hospital, apparently; he shouldn't have died. Then her mum had a brain haemorrhage a few days later. She'd been complaining of headaches ever since the birth, but no one took any notice.'

'Oh my God, that's awful!'

Scott sighed. 'There was an inquiry and everything; people were suspended. But none of that was any help to Eve and her dad.' He shook his head. 'She's had a tough time, Eve has; she's lost a lot, man. That's why she worries I'm going to drop dead or fall off a cliff or something.'

'Poor Eve.' She felt a wave of sadness wash over her,

partly for Eve, but also for herself. Thinking about what had happened to Eve's mum had opened up a big, yawning hole of grief for her own mum. She blinked back the tears that had started to well up and lit a cigarette. She'd been going to ask what had happened to Eve's dad, but she wasn't sure she could take it at the moment.

They sat in silence for a few minutes, smoking and looking out to sea.

Scott had a soft, dreamy look on his face. 'I wonder where she is right now.'

She turned towards him. 'Don't you even know where she's staying?'

'She'll find somewhere; she always does. She knows where the squats are; she'll find someone who'll let her crash.'

'But—'

'We don't own each other.'

It was the same thing she'd heard Eve say again and again. 'No, but . . .' But what? What was wrong with being relaxed about what the other was doing? It was cool, she supposed; maybe she should try to be more cool about it herself. She finished the joint and flicked it over the edge, then she lay back against the slope and closed her eyes. It was quiet and still. She could hear the sea's gentle rhythm in the distance, the occasional car going along the coast road. Now and again she could hear loud voices and laughter as people made their way home from a pub or from the pier. She was feeling quite drowsy now. Apparently some people had taken to sleeping outside these last couple of weeks. What would it be like to sleep up here, under the stars? she wondered. It was still pretty warm, but there was a tiny hint of a breeze, and just feeling that wisp of movement against your skin was probably enough to tempt people up onto the rooftops.

'Look.' Scott grabbed her arm. 'Shooting star!'

'Where?' But she'd missed it.

'Keep watching, we might see another one.'

She'd never seen a shooting star, so she stared up at the silver lights in the darkness, willing one of them to go zinging across the sky. She didn't know how long she'd been staring upwards, but she became aware that Scott wasn't looking at the sky any more, he'd turned towards her and was looking at her, his face inches from hers. She didn't move. Slowly, he came closer, so close that she could feel his breath on her shoulder. 'Jo,' he whispered, 'let's take our clothes off; let's make love.'

CHAPTER TWENTY-NINE

She thought she must have misheard him.

'It would be so beautiful; *you're* so beautiful.' He ran his finger down the inside of her arm, sending a pleasant quiver through her body. 'Please.' He kissed her shoulder. 'Right now, the only thing I can think about is you, and how it would feel to make love with you up here, outside, under this beautiful sky.'

She didn't answer, didn't move. She had that same cocooned feeling that she'd had earlier downstairs, a sort of timeless stillness, as though she could stay in that moment for ever and nothing would change. Except that something *had* changed. Ever since she'd first arrived, she'd found herself wondering what it would be like to kiss Scott, even to go to bed with him. But not really, not actually, physically, *really* having sex with him. She closed her eyes, as if doing so might allow her the privacy to think. But he started kissing her eyelids. 'Wake up,' he whispered. 'Wake up and make love with me.'

She opened her eyes. 'Eve,' was all she said. 'What about Eve?'

'Eve's cool.' He pushed the damp hair back from her forehead and looked at her. 'Listen, I love Eve, and nothing's ever going to change that, okay?' And then he started kissing her face again, and she felt his hand slide up her sweat-coated back to where her bra would have fastened had she been wearing one. She put her hand on his arm. 'But it's not right, is it? I mean, Eve's your girlfriend.'

He stopped what he was doing and faced her again. 'Jo, Eve's not "my" anything; I don't own her, I love her and respect her, and the scene we've got together is cool, I mean *really* cool. But it has nothing to do with me wanting to make love with you. It's a beautiful night, we're out here in the summer air together sharing it; we've shared food and wine and we've shared hashish; why not share our bodies with each other? It's just a different form of pleasure; a deeper form of communication.' He was looking at her intently, his eyes were deep and soft. 'If you're sure, I mean, like, really sure that you don't want to, say so and I'll stop.'

'It's not that I don't want to,' she said, and at that, he let out a sort of moan, pulled at the ties of her shirt and buried his face in between her breasts. She'd only ever done it a few times before, back in Cornwall with Rob. She'd never really thought of him as her boyfriend, not in the 'going out' sense. He took her to the pictures once, to see David Essex in *Stardust*, but mostly, they hung out round his dad's house. He was just Rob. He smelled of cigarettes and motor oil and too much Brut, but he was kind and he never said anything nasty about her mum, even when he'd seen her drunk. The first time they did it, it hurt like hell and she bled all over her new button-through dress. But when he'd held her afterwards, she'd felt safe. They'd neither of them been that good at it – at sex – but there was a sense that it didn't matter, because they were practising on each other, learning what to do so that, one day in the future, when they were with a 'proper' partner, they'd know how the whole thing worked. Jo had liked it when their bodies were so close together, the feel of Rob's warm skin almost melting into her own. But apart from that, she didn't see what all the fuss was about.

But what she was feeling now was different. Scott was leading her confidently as though in a dance, and all she had to do was follow. The intensity of the pleasure she felt almost scared her and it was all she could do not to cry out. Scott did, though; he cried out so loudly she worried that people in the street below would hear, although there probably wasn't anyone around.

Afterwards, bodies slick with sweat and hearts pounding, they lay still until their breathing slowed to normal. They were lying along the flat part of the roof now, just behind the parapet. Jo's knee was stinging; she must have scraped it on the concrete without noticing. Scott lay heavily across her and she tried to shift him to the side so that he wasn't squashing her quite so much.

'That was fantastic,' he said into her hair.

There was no doubt that sex with Scott was proper sex; real, grown-up sex, man and woman stuff, not the incompetent and unsatisfactory teenage fumblings she'd had with Rob. But the joy and exhilaration she'd felt moments before was now rapidly evaporating as the sheer enormity of what she'd done started to sink in. Eve. No matter what Scott said, she didn't really believe that Eve would be 'cool' about someone else sleeping with her boyfriend while she was away for one night. Eve; lovely, kind, generous Eve. Jo felt tears beginning to spill over her lower lids. How could she have betrayed their friendship like this? She let out a half-sob and heaved Scott away from her. She was completely naked; how had that happened? Scott had taken her shirt off, but she didn't remember him taking her hot pants or her knickers off. She sat up to look around for her clothes, and felt suddenly dizzy as she did so. God, she was stoned; probably pissed as well. No wonder she didn't remember some of the details.

'Hey.' Scott reached out lazily towards her. 'Relax. There's no hurry. Let's stay up here all night.'

'No! I don't want to stay here all night.' She started to scrabble around for her clothes, pulling them on clumsily so that her shirt went on inside out and her hot pants back to front. She couldn't find her knickers at all but then had a sudden memory of tossing them joyously over the parapet and then giggling as she imagined them sailing down and landing on someone's head. Although that was unlikely, given that the part of the roof they were on mainly overlooked the garden, and anyway, it was rare for anyone to be walking past, especially in the middle of the night.

She swayed as she stood up and put a hand out to steady herself on the chimney stack. She had to get downstairs; she began stumbling along, looking for the door they'd come through, but the roof now seemed huge and with multiple slopes and stacks and recesses, and she had no idea how to get back down.

'Jo, hang on,' Scott said, pulling on his T-shirt and getting to his feet. 'What are you doing?'

'Going back downstairs,' she called over her shoulder as she walked along a flat part between the slope and the parapet. 'I shouldn't have come up here.' She was crying now. 'Shouldn't have smoked so much.'

'You're going the wrong way. Don't go past that stack—'

But she already had, and now she froze. Just ahead of her, a large section of the parapet was missing. One more step and she'd have no protection if she slipped or stumbled. Her hand still held onto the stack, and the parapet wall came way up past her knee; she tried to tell herself that it was all right, that she was perfectly safe, but six inches in front of her an open gap yawned to the left. She didn't know how high up she was, but it was a four-storey house, so it had to be at least fifty feet. Despite the heat of the night, a cold, sick sensation started to creep through her body. She became aware of the crumbly feeling of the chimney stack bricks and the softness of the moss under her fingers. She recognised the beginnings of a shiver and prayed that it would not be a violent one that would jolt her body forward even so much as an inch. She wanted to call out to Scott but what if using her body to produce a sound caused her to move inadvertently? Scott was not far behind her, she could sense him moving nearer, but did he know about the missing section? What if he didn't and he tried to barge past her? She had to tell him not to come too near, but her voice had vanished and she found herself unable to produce even the smallest sound. She half turned towards him but in doing so looked down and felt a cold lick of fear. Oh my God, she thought; I could fall; I might actually die tonight. Her fingers were sweating; what if they became so slippery that she lost her grip on the chimney stack? But then she realised she didn't actually have a grip on the bricks, her fingers were just resting against the mossy surface. Scott stopped a few feet away and she knew he'd seen the gap and realised what was happening, that she had suddenly and unexpectedly been paralysed by abject terror. The air was still incredibly warm, given that it must surely be one or two in the morning by now, but the sweat on the skin of her bare arms had turned icy. Just go back, she told herself; it's perfectly safe as long as you don't go forward. But she simply could not move. The expression *scared stiff* popped into her mind; she understood it now.

'Jo.' Scott's voice was low and gentle. 'Come back towards me; you'll be fine.'

She couldn't answer.

He took a step nearer and slowly held out his hand towards her. 'Jo, take my hand,' he said softly. It flitted through her mind that he might wonder if she was thinking about jumping, but no, she was upset, but she wasn't stupid, and nor was he.

'Jo, it's cool, okay? You're going to be fine, it's just vertigo. You know, like in that Hitchcock film. I'm going to come a bit nearer so you can take my hand and walk back, okay?'

Still she couldn't speak, and there was no point in her taking his hand because she knew that there was no way, absolutely no way she could move, not even if he was holding on to her. How long would she be standing here, she wondered? What about when she needed to pee? Or when it got light? Oh, God, it would be even worse when it got light because she'd be able to see clearly just how high up she was. Her stomach shifted again at the thought. Then she felt Scott's hand rest ever so lightly on her arm and at the same moment something small and furry flew into her. Instinctively she screamed and put both hands up in front of her face, enabling Scott to grab her wrists and pull her towards him. 'It's okay, it's okay, it's okay,' he said, clasping his arms around her. 'It was only a bat, that's all. You're safe; everything's cool.' He walked her back around the other side of the stack, along the flat walkway and down through the door into the house. It was only when he locked the door and Jo could feel the carpet beneath her feet that she began to shake.

She sat down on the step, unable to stop trembling. Maybe it was some sort of delayed reaction. Or maybe it was because it was beginning to dawn on her; not only had she slept with Eve's boyfriend, but they hadn't used anything – what if she was pregnant?

CHAPTER THIRTY

Jo couldn't concentrate. She didn't have a shift at the pub today so she was supposed to be painting some shells for Eve, but she'd barely slept and now she was just sitting in the thinking room, going over and over the previous night. She could hardly believe what had happened, and as she relived it in her mind, her feelings swung violently back and forth: one minute, she felt the most delicious thrill at the memory; the next, she was engulfed by a sense of miserable, sickening guilt.

And what if she was pregnant? She groaned aloud. Seagulls were shrieking outside the window, and for a moment the sound stirred in her a powerful longing for home, for the sandy beach at Newquay with the noisy herring gulls that woke her early every morning. They'd driven her mad there just as they did here, and many people regarded them as vermin; 'sky rats', Mr Rundle called them. But somehow the fact that Hastings had this one thing in common with Newquay made her feel nostalgic for her home town.

She lit a cigarette. Even if she wasn't pregnant, there was still Eve to worry about. The idea of deceiving Eve was unthinkable, but on the other hand, how could she tell her? She just couldn't believe what Scott had said, that Eve really wouldn't mind.

A seagull alighted on the windowsill and looked in at her with a malevolent stare, as if it knew what she'd done. She stubbed out her cigarette and lit another. Scott didn't appear to feel remotely guilty. He'd wanted to sleep with her in her room last night, but she'd refused. He'd looked disappointed but then shrugged, told her to sleep well and loped off to his and Eve's room along the hall. When she'd gone down to the kitchen this morning, he was already in there, so she'd crept back upstairs before he spotted her and had only gone back in to make her tea and toast once he was out in the garden sawing wood he'd found on a skip for the box he was making.

There was nothing covering the many windows in the thinking room, and the sun coming through the glass turned the room into a greenhouse. She picked up her mug and cigarettes and went out into the relative cool of the landing, an instant relief from the relentless late-morning heat. She could still hear Scott working in the garden, and was about to go downstairs when the sound of sawing stopped and she heard voices. Eve was home. A knot of misery tightened inside her. If only she could go back twenty-four hours and start again. She stood on the landing, listening intently, but she couldn't make out what they were saying. There was a pause at one point, and she had the powerful sense that they were kissing. Then she heard the basement door open and close and the sound of Eve's footsteps coming along the hall.

'Jo.' Eve smiled and put her arms around Jo in that familiar, comforting way. 'Scott told me what happened, and I know you're feeling bad about it, but don't, Jo. Please don't.'

She didn't say anything. Eve's hair smelled hot, and not of the sea like it usually did, but of trains and traffic and Trafalgar Square. 'It's only bodies, after all. Why shouldn't we share our bodies for pleasure?'

Jo pulled away and looked at her. 'But don't you feel . . . betrayed? I mean, I'm supposed to be your friend.'

Eve laughed. 'Betrayed? Of course not, you silly thing! I might feel that way if you'd lied to me, but how could I feel betrayed by the truth? And you *are* my friend. It's like I keep telling you, me and Scott, we don't . . .'

'I know, you don't own each other.'

'That's right, we don't. Jo, sex is a beautiful thing; it's something we should share. I'm not saying we should sleep with any Tom, Dick or Harry who comes along, but why not share it with special people in our lives?'

'I just . . . I'm not . . .'

'Jo, what are you so upset about? It's okay.' She reached up and wiped away the tear that had leaked out of Jo's eye. 'Don't you believe me?'

Jo turned and ran out of the kitchen and up to her

room. They were mad, Eve and Scott; absolutely crazy. They were just like those hippies that used to come to Cornwall for the solstice, with their Afghan coats and bells around their necks and flowers painted on their skin. She remembered walking through the park once when the hippies were having a picnic; they were all bare-chested, even the women, and one of the men was sitting between two of them with an arm round each one, his fingers idly playing with their breasts as he kissed first one, then the other. The young Jo had been shocked. *Peace, man; make love, not war*. But that was 1969; it was all a bit outdated now, wasn't it? She crawled onto her bed and stared up at the ceiling, watching the dust motes dance in the sunlight. Was it possible that Eve really, truly didn't mind? Even if she didn't, surely she was a little disappointed? Like her mum had been disappointed in her when she'd been unable to stop herself from taking one of the butterfly cakes from the table half an hour before her birthday party started. She must have only been about eight or nine, because there hadn't been many birthday parties after that, and although she knew now that it had more to do with her parents splitting up than with her own behaviour, she'd always felt that there must be something intrinsically greedy about her, something that compelled her to take things to satisfy her own desires, whether she had permission to take them or not.

She fell into a fitful, sweaty doze. When she woke, her shirt was stuck to her back and sweat was trickling down her chest. The thought of going downstairs made her stomach flip. She couldn't stay here now; she felt exposed, dirty; *embarrassed*. She could go back to London and find another squat, start again. Eve found places to stay easily enough, so why shouldn't she? And if she was pregnant, then she'd find a mother and baby home. There were bound to be plenty of those in London. She'd have to make it clear that she didn't want her baby adopted, she just wanted some support until she got back on her feet. She didn't know quite how she'd manage, but other girls her age did, so it must be possible. She stood up and started tearfully shoving things into her duffle bag. How had she managed to acquire all this stuff in just a few months? There was so much here that she could hardly bear to leave behind. All the clothes Eve had given her, for a start. She'd grown to love the cheesecloth shirts, the peasant tops, the long, floaty skirts. Now her hair was growing longer and Eve's was shorter they were starting to look more and more alike, apart from the fact that Eve was getting a bit pudgy. In fact, the man in the corner shop had taken to calling them Tweedledum and Tweedledee whenever he saw them together. She started to feel tearful again as she looked at the shelf full of books, the red lava lamp, and the other bits she'd found at jumble sales or in skips. She didn't want to leave it all behind, but how could she possibly stay? She put her duffle bag down and sat on her bed with a sigh. There was no hurry, she supposed; she could aim to leave by the weekend.

'*What?*' Eve said when Jo told her what she'd decided. 'Why?' She was hand-stitching a lace trim to the child's sun hat she was making. They were selling well on the beach – plenty of day trippers underestimated the sheer power of the sun beating down on their toddlers' heads, and an inexpensive cotton sun hat saved the day. Eve had bought up lots of remnants of cotton material, then she simply cut circles of fabric and gathered them with sheering elastic to make little mob-caps. She put down the cap she was working on and looked at Jo. Her skin had paled and her eyes glittered as though she was fighting tears. 'You can't leave, Jo. Please don't.'

'I can't stay,' Jo said. 'Not after what happened the other night.' She couldn't quite bring herself to talk about it in the open and uninhibited way that Eve and Scott did. 'I'm sorry. I know you said it doesn't matter, but even if you honestly don't mind, I still feel awful about it. I feel embarrassed every time I see you or Scott.'

'But there's no need to feel—'

'I know. But I can't help it; I do.'

To Jo's horror, tears started to spill down Eve's face. Before now, she'd only ever seen Eve cry over awful things like the Vietnam War, or the Troubles in Northern Ireland, or earthquakes where thousands of people were killed; she'd never *made* her cry.

'I'm sorry.' Eve quickly wiped away the tears and shook her head. 'I'm feeling a bit emotional at the moment. Listen, Jo, I need to tell you something and I really hope it'll make you change your mind.' She looked down at her sewing again. 'I'm going to have a baby.'

'What?' The momentary shock Jo felt was quickly

replaced with the uncomfortable realisation that, now she thought about it, the signs had been there for a while and she just hadn't taken them in – Eve putting on weight; the tiredness; the sickness she'd had until a few weeks ago. She swallowed. 'When's it due?'

'November.'

'*November*? So you're . . .'

'Five and a half months.'

Jo felt her face colour; how could she not have realised? Eve had been getting bigger and bigger every week, her clothes straining at the seams, and Jo had just been grateful for the hand-me-down clothes. It was so obvious now she thought about it. How could she have been so naïve?

'But why didn't you tell me before?' She did a quick calculation. 'You must have already been pregnant when I first moved in.'

'Yes, but I didn't know I was, not at that point. I was . . . we were going to tell you soon, but . . . the thing is, well . . .' Eve was shifting about in her seat, looking this way and that as though she wasn't sure what to say next. 'The thing is, I wanted to ask you something.'

For a moment, it flashed through her head that Eve was going to ask her if she thought she might be pregnant. Had Scott told her that they hadn't used a Durex? She waited.

'Yes. You see, I don't want to have the baby in hospital, and so I'll need some support here, some female support. Scott's marvellous, but it's not the same thing as having another woman around.'

She'd never been referred to that way before, and she felt a silly little thrill to know that Eve thought of her as a woman rather than a girl.

'You're my friend, Jo, and I was hoping you'd stick around to give me a hand, not only before the baby's born, but after as well. I think it would be lovely for the baby to have you around as well as Scott and me.'

'But why—'

'You know I don't have any family, and Scott's family is in New Zealand, so there'll just be us two. And I want my baby to have more people to love her. Or him. You'd be an honorary auntie.' She looked up at Jo again and her face was a picture of hope and trust. 'Please, Jo, please stay; I need you.'

Jo's thoughts were reeling. A baby! Eve was going to have a real, live baby, and she, Jo, was being asked to be part of it, to be involved. 'I . . . I don't know,' she said. 'I need to think.' She hurried from the kitchen and ran back up the stairs and along to the thinking room. As she opened the door, the force of the heat coming through the glass almost took her breath away. She sat on the wicker chair and put her feet up on the window seat, then tipped her head back and closed her eyes. The sun was searing her skin, but she wanted to feel its intensity. It helped her to concentrate. What would Eve say if she knew that there was a possibility Jo could be pregnant? Would she still think the whole thing was okay? She sat there with her eyes closed for a good ten minutes, wondering whether she should say anything. She could feel the beads of sweat forming on her forehead, but still she didn't move. Realistically, she probably wasn't pregnant, and her period wasn't due for another fortnight anyway, so there was no point in worrying about it now. But she needed to think about Eve. Eve really *was* pregnant; there would definitely be a baby.

Ever since Jo was a child, she'd looked forward to the time when she would be a mother herself. When she was eleven, not long after her dad left, the lady next door gave birth to twin girls and Jo had quickly become besotted with them, going next door at every opportunity, offering to help, probably making a nuisance of herself, now she thought about it. But Auntie Pat, as Jo had been instructed to call her – her mother said it showed respect – had always welcomed her and what's more, had treated her like an equal instead of like a child. One day, she'd been telling Auntie Pat that she couldn't wait to grow up, get married and have babies herself. 'Don't be in too much of a hurry,' Pat said, bending over a sink full of hot water and soap suds, her short, permed hair plastered to her face by the steam, the skin on her arms and hands reddened by the heat. 'I got married at sixteen, and look at me now.' Jo looked at her, a dumpy figure in a shapeless dress, bare legs and swollen feet pushed into grubby carpet slippers. 'Old before my time.' With a pair of wooden tongs, she lifted a greying nappy dripping from the sink and then she wrung it tightly until she could get no more moisture out of it.

'How old are you now?' Jo had asked innocently. She'd

always assumed that Auntie Pat was about the same age as her mother, and all mothers must be roughly the same age – about thirty-five. 'Eighteen,' Pat had said, wiping her forehead with the back of her hand.

Eve wouldn't be old before her time like poor Pat. In fact, Eve was looking better and better every day; her eyes were clear and bright, her skin was glowing, especially now she had a golden tan. A thought flashed into her mind; had Scott only wanted to sleep with her because Eve was pregnant? Maybe you weren't allowed to have sex when you were pregnant. She walked over to the open window and looked out. Did that make it better or worse? She shook her head; she couldn't think straight any more.

Scott was still working away in the garden, his back a deep brown colour now, almost mahogany. She and Eve had good tans, but next to them, Scott no longer even looked English. She watched the muscles in his back moving as he sanded the piece of wood he was working on. It was only when he paused to hold the curved wood against what she'd thought was to be a storage box that she realised what he was making. The curved pieces were rockers; he was making a wooden cradle. Seeing the cradle made it suddenly seem more real, somehow. There was going to be an actual baby whose arrival needed to be planned for. Jo felt her blood quicken; she'd be able to help; Eve *wanted* her to help. She could babysit again, and take it out in its pram. She felt a little thrill at the thought. Perhaps she could knit or sew something for the baby to wear. When Pat's twins were two, she'd had to make a child's garment in Parentcraft at school, so she'd hand-stitched a little sky-blue summer dress and trimmed it with white ric rac braid. She got a good mark for it, so she went straight out and bought more fabric out of her own money and made another one, and when she gave the two dresses to Pat, Pat hugged her and told her what a clever and thoughtful girl she was. Maybe that was one of the reasons Jo always spent so much time next door rather than at home with her own mum, that and the fact that she was allowed to help with the twins, obviously. She'd loved babysitting them and sometimes, when Pat and Derek were out, she would pretend that she was their mother. Even now, when she closed her eyes, she could almost feel the weight of their little bodies as she held them; Lisa's chubby legs; the silky softness of Lynne's hair as she rested her head against Jo's shoulder.

Yes, she told Eve when she went back downstairs; of course she would stay and help with the baby.

*

Over the next few days, as she thought about the impending arrival of Eve's baby, she began to wonder more and more what would happen if she too were pregnant, if she and Eve would have babies within a few months of each other. She'd watched a film at school once, when she was about fourteen, about an African tribe where each man had several wives who all lived happily together, caring for each other and looking after the children between them. The female interviewer asked a group of native women how many wives their husbands had: three, some said, or four. 'I am number one wife of five,' said one woman, her chin tilted upwards with pride. Then, giggling, one of the women asked the interviewer how many wives *her* husband had. When the interviewer explained that in England we had monogamous marriages and that bigamy was a crime, the cheerful, carefree chatter and laughter was replaced by shocked faces and a sudden outbreak of serious muttering. 'But what happen,' said one of the women, a horrified expression on her face, 'when the wife have a child? Who help with the child? Who care for the mama?'

On the surface of it, the thought that the two of them could be pregnant by the same man was absurd; but it wasn't so ridiculous in other cultures. And she found she was thinking of the possibility with increasing warmth and pleasure – hope, even. She imagined the unconventional little family they would be, she and Eve helping each other to care for their children, like sisters. Briefly, she thought of asking Eve to read her tea leaves again, but there was probably no point – the last couple of times she'd asked, Eve hadn't seemed keen.

CHAPTER THIRTY-ONE

Sheffield, 2010

As I hurried down the paved slope towards Sheffield station, spray from the fountains and the steel water-feature landed on my face, making me think of the sea. I was on my way to Hastings. The two weeks were up; today was Scott's deadline and I'd run out of excuses. Hannah was a lot better, so much so that Duncan was on at me again to tell her that Scott was here. 'As soon as possible,' he'd said last night. 'Because even if he's not staying there permanently, the fact that he's using a hospice means it won't be long.'

It was a lot of travelling in one day but I'd never been back since it all happened and now I had a powerful urge to go there, to stand on the beach and watch the waves, to see the house where we spent that summer. I suppose what I really wanted was to talk to Eve, to ask her what I should do; but anyway, I felt as though somehow just being there would help me to feel clearer.

Since I'd seen Scott in the hospice, I'd been dreaming about him every time I went to sleep. The other night I dreamt that he wasn't ill at all, that I came home from work and found him on the doorstep, talking to Duncan; last night I dreamt he was in Hannah's kitchen, sitting there at her table, telling her everything while he jiggled Toby on his knee. Hannah had been asking about him again lately, so maybe that was why I had that particular dream. It seemed Duncan had been right about her wanting to explore her roots; barely a day went past now without her asking me something about Scott or about when she herself was a baby. Some things I could answer truthfully, but every time I couldn't I felt as though I was trampling on her. Over the years, I'd told as few lies as I'd been able to get away with, and they'd been practical, functional, necessary. But these last few weeks I seemed to be wading through them like piles of dead leaves; they clung to my feet as I walked, and as the whole situation had become more complex, more convoluted, lying had become second nature.

As I boarded the train to London St Pancras, I reflected on the fact that I'd bought an expensive train ticket for a journey that was going to take four and a half hours each way, in the vague hope that, by going back there, I'd have some sort of revelation that would somehow help me decide what to do. Once I was in my seat, I sent Scott a text to say I hadn't forgotten, and that I'd be in touch later. I took the tube from St Pancras to London Bridge to pick up the train to Hastings, and before long, I was settled in a window seat with a cup of coffee and a free newspaper. *Good morning, ladies and gentlemen, this is the 13.23 South Eastern service to Hastings, calling at . . .*

I tried to read, but I couldn't take anything in, and after Tunbridge Wells, my concentration vanished completely and images from the past started jostling for position at the front of my mind. By the time the train pulled into the station, my stomach was doing somersaults. People gathered their bags and newspapers and started to leave the train. I sat there, clutching my empty coffee cup. This was crazy; why had I come here?

'This is Hastings, ladies and gentlemen,' called the train conductor. 'All change, please. All change.' He made his way down the carriage, closing windows as he went. 'End of the line, madam. All change, please.'

I was momentarily surprised at being called 'madam', but then I reminded myself that I was a grandmother now, not the young girl I'd been when I boarded the train at this station all those years ago. 'Yes, sorry. I was miles away.' I got up and put my coat on, but my legs were trembling and I fell back into the seat. The conductor walked back along the carriage towards me. 'You all right there, love?' He leaned over me. I could smell the tobacco on his breath, and see the speckling of crumbs that were lodged in his thick grey moustache.

'You all right there, love?' The porter was hurrying along the platform towards us. Scott had already climbed into the carriage and was hauling the two tightly packed shopping trolleys in after him. 'Here, let me take that,' the porter said. He

took my bag and slipped his arm under my elbow to help me up the step and onto the train. 'There you go, treacle. When are you due, then?' I opened my mouth to speak but Scott put his hand on my back and guided me into the carriage. 'Any day now,' he said to the porter, who grinned and winked. 'Best of luck to you, mate,' he said. 'Got two nippers of me own, bless 'em.' He leaned into the carriage. 'Hope it all goes well for you, darlin',' he called in. 'Yes, well,' Scott said. 'Thanks for your help.' He pulled the carriage door closed behind him and it flashed through my mind that the man must think us rude, but he didn't seem to notice, because he called cheerio and touched his cap before turning on his heel and going back along the platform, whistling as he went.

'Are you sure you're all right?' the conductor was saying.

I blinked a couple of times. 'Yes, yes, I'm okay. Just felt a bit dizzy, that's all.'

'There's a qualified first-aider on the station.' He took a walkie-talkie from his pocket.

'No, really. I'm absolutely fine, thank you.' I got to my feet and allowed him to help me onto the platform. I smiled, thanked him profusely and made an effort to look fully recovered before heading towards the ticket barriers. The station looked so different – not surprising after thirty odd years, I supposed. As I went out of the main entrance the wind lifted my hair and lashed it at my face. There was a new community college with lots of shiny glass right by the station; there were new shops, concrete planters full of daffodils; flights of steps and an underpass I was sure hadn't been there before. It seemed that Hastings had been 'regenerated'. I looked left and right but the only things that were recognisable right now were the scraggy seagulls that darted and swooped and glided across the muddy sky. Instinctively, I headed down towards the seafront, and things started to become more familiar. The old public loos were still there, but they'd been smartened up; the bikers' pub, the Carlisle, was still open, looking just the same as it had back then, with a board outside advertising the bands that would be playing on Friday and Saturday night.

The sea was as muddy as the sky, and it was flat today, uneventful, just rolling in and breaking on the shore with the gentlest sound of shifting shingle, despite the blustery wind. *Bor-ring*, Eve would have said with a mock yawn. She'd liked the sea best when it was crashing onto the beach in an extravaganza of white foam, or when the tide was in and the waves were rocking and chopping against the sea wall, making the dark water look thick and muscular and dangerous. I crunched down the beach towards the shoreline, the salty air stinging my eyes. There was hardly anyone else around at the moment. Not surprising on a chilly Thursday afternoon in March. As I walked along towards the pier, I passed a man fishing by one of the groynes and a couple of women walking their dogs. The clouds parted and for a moment a shaft of silvery winter sunshine fell on the water before disappearing again and leaving the place feeling even more bleak and lonely. It was very different from that one summer, when the beach had been so packed you could barely find space to put your towel, and even late into the evening there would be people swimming, lovers holding hands as they walked along the water's edge, groups of friends sitting on the warm pebbles until long after the sun had gone down. I felt the sadness swell inside me as I remembered the many evenings the three of us had sat here, enjoying the residual warmth of the day and the constant rhythmic wash of the sea as we talked late into the night.

Eve was always so full of enthusiasm, always so sure things would get better and better for all of us. I missed her so much. Being here, standing on the beach where we'd spent so much time talking, laughing, making plans – it did make me feel closer to her, but at the same time it made her absence all the more painful.

There was a fine mist coming in off the sea, making my hair wet and salty so that it stung as it flicked about my face. I tried in vain to push it out of my eyes as I walked, then I stopped in my tracks. The blackened skeleton of the pier loomed in front of me, its charred remains silhouetted against the murky sky. I'd heard about the fire, of course, but I'd forgotten, and I was surprised to find that my eyes filled with tears as I looked at the result. This once-magnificent structure, the proud centre of entertainment for everyone who lived here and visited the town, was now a poor, abandoned ghost. Briefly, the sun came out again and at the same moment I had the sensation of someone standing very close behind me, but when

I looked over my shoulder there was no one there. As I turned and walked away from the unbearable sight of the ruined pier, my shadow felt thick and heavy.

I headed further along the beach towards Bottle Alley, where I walked a little way through the lower promenade, looking at the patterns made by the thousands of pieces of coloured glass set into the walls, a triumph of artistic recycling. The larger panels were made using glass in the more traditional 'bottle' colours of blue, green and brown, but these were interspersed with smaller panels of pretty, multicoloured glass chippings. The effect was more striking than I remembered. But the smell of urine was more powerful and rather spoiled the experience, so after a few minutes, I made my way back up to the street and crossed the main road. The sky had turned inky-black and it was starting to rain, although there were still occasional bright flashes of sunshine, which made the white-feathered seagulls look incandescent against the dark sky. It was the sort of eerie light that often heralds an approaching thunderstorm. I wondered again why I'd come, how physically being here was going to change anything, and part of me wanted to head straight for the station and start the long journey back to Sheffield. I thought about being at home, in bed next to Duncan, the glow of the streetlamp coming in through the curtains, the ticking of the pipes as they cooled down after the central heating went off, the alarm set for 7.15, ready for the start of another ordinary day. But I knew I couldn't go home until I'd seen the house.

SUSAN ELLIOT WRIGHT

*

I wasn't sure if I would remember the way up from the beach, but as I trudged up the steep hill, I began to recognise the road names – Cornwallis Terrace was familiar, and there was the railway bridge, then Braybrook Road, and then, yes, there they were, the six short flights of concrete steps that I'd climbed almost every day when I lived here. I set off up the steps, pausing halfway to catch my breath. I didn't know what I expected when the house came into view, but it wasn't what I saw. A clean, bright, freshly painted building in good repair, converted now into flats, by the look of it. Tentatively, I walked up yet more steps to the front door. There was an intercom system with a bank of six buzzers. How could they possibly get six flats out of it? I wondered. Some of them must have been bedsits, or studio apartments, as they called them these days. I went back down onto the pavement and stood looking up at the house. There were tasteful wooden blinds in one window, vertical office-type blinds in another, some of the curtains were open, some closed. There was a light on at the very top of the house, and I wondered who lived up there, and what they were doing in Eve's work room. The gargoyles at the corners of the roof had been restored, and the gap in the parapet had been repaired, but the windows to the thinking room looked empty and forlorn. Maybe no one used it these days. That was a shame, because it was a lovely little space, despite being freezing in winter and hot as a

278

greenhouse in summer. This wasn't the only house in the road with a turret, but it was the only one where the turret jutted out and had windows on all sides so that, if you stood near any of them, you had a clear view of the sea.

I stood there for a good half-hour, just looking up at the windows; I was surprised no one reported me for acting suspiciously, but if anyone had noticed me, they were probably leaving it to someone in another flat to do something about it. The house may have looked clean and bright on the outside, but I was certain it was lonely and soulless inside, housing its six single people. It had been the other way round when we were there, broken and shambolic on the outside, but on the inside, it had been full to the rafters of warmth and love. I thought of Eve, of what she'd lost, and of how she'd taken me in and cared for me and loved me as if I were her own family. For a second, Eve's face flashed clear in my mind; I came here wanting to feel close to her, and I felt it now.

And then the image melted away, and it was Hannah's face I could see. That's when I felt the tears building behind my eyes. I hated lying to Duncan, but above all I hated lying to Hannah, especially after she'd been so ill, and especially after the conversation we'd had a few days ago. She accepted that Toby couldn't possibly know that he'd been born from a donor egg, but now she was beginning to bond with him, she was talking about telling him the truth as soon as he was old enough. 'But why do you have to tell him at all?' I asked her while she was changing him.

'How could I *not* tell him?' she said, and the way she looked at me suggested she was genuinely horrified by the idea. 'It's his right to know where he comes from. I couldn't possibly keep something like that from him; he'd resent it – he'd resent *me*.' She fastened the poppers on his babygrow.

'But there's no reason he'd ever find out, is there? I mean—'

'Mum, Marcus and I have talked about this. We believe in being honest about it, right from the word go. Yes, it would make life easier for us if he didn't have to know, of course it would.' She picked him up and handed him to me to hold while she cleared away the changing things. 'But that's just being selfish, isn't it?'

Being selfish; it was exactly what I'd accused Scott of for wanting to tell her the truth. I don't know whether it was because I was standing right outside the house, but a memory flashed into my head of the day after Scott and I slept together for the first time. I was so worried about Eve finding out, and then Scott told her and she was lovely about it. All that mattered, she told me, was that we were honest, that we told the truth.

Before I went back to the station, I walked through Alexandra Park and sat on the bench by the larger of the two ponds. I watched the pairs of swans gliding through the water; had there been swans here that summer? All I remembered was seeing the pond water shrink back further and further each day until the hidden detritus of the town was gradually revealed, half buried in the mud – shopping trolleys, car tyres and bicycle wheels, even an old pram. Soon, even the mud dried up, leaving a baked, deeply cracked crust on the surface. Now the pond was lush and green again, teeming with life. I felt calmer just sitting there looking out across the water.

I'm not sure how long I sat there, but I was thinking so hard it almost hurt. I kept coming back to that conversation with Hannah; I could see the look on her face and I could hear her words in my head. *Yes, it would make life easier . . . But that's just being selfish, isn't it?* And now, much as I hated to admit it, I understood that Scott was right; I could not keep this secret any longer. Hannah had a right to know the truth, and so did Duncan.

The journey back seemed quicker, somehow, maybe because I was so preoccupied. I'd parked the car about ten minutes from the station, not far from where Scott lived. I still hadn't heard from him, but it was only nine o'clock so I decided to call round there before I went home. I'd told Duncan I might be late back anyway. I was in no hurry to get home, and I certainly didn't want to disturb Hannah tonight; I would tell them tomorrow. My stomach flipped again at the thought.

When I pulled up outside Scott's, I couldn't see any lights on in the front of the house, so I got out of the car and walked through the gennel round to the back to see if maybe there was a lamp on or something. But the house was in darkness. I thought at first that he might have gone to bed, but then I remembered him saying that he struggled with stairs now, so he usually just dozed in his chair. Perhaps he was still in the hospice; maybe he hadn't been well enough to come home. I turned to go back to the car when the door to the next house – where the land-lady lived – opened and a tiny woman of about my age with short-cropped hair and large dangly earrings came running out, the light from her kitchen illuminating the small yard. 'Are you a relative?' she said; her face was creased in an anxious frown.

I looked back at her blankly. 'Sorry,' she continued in a rush, holding out her hand. 'I'm Brenda. Scott's landlady. Are you a friend? Relative?' She paused. 'Sorry.' She adjusted her voice. 'You're looking for Mr Matthews?'

I nodded. 'Yes, it's all right, I'm a friend of his.' I didn't know why I said that.

'A friend. Oh dear.' She looked flustered. 'I'm afraid . . . it's very sad, but . . .' She inclined her head and rested her hand on my arm. 'I'm afraid I have some bad news for you, lovey.'

I looked at her. Was she saying what I thought she was saying?

'Did you . . . I mean, are you a close friend?'

'No.' I shook my head. 'No, not close at all. Just a, you know, more of an acquaintance, really.'

She seemed relieved. 'Oh, well. In that case . . . oh dear, I'm sorry to be the one to break the news, but he passed away peacefully on Monday afternoon.' She looked anxious again. 'You did know he was ill?'

I nodded. 'Yes, yes I knew.' He was dead. Scott was dead.

'But you're not a close friend, you say? You see, I need to find . . . oh dear.' She gestured to her open back door. 'You've gone white as a sheet. You'd best come in for a minute.'

I could feel my legs trembling; I needed to get a grip. 'No. No, thank you. It's kind of you but . . . no. I need to—'

'They want to know who his next of kin is, see. He gave the hospice my name, because there wasn't no family, except for the little girl who died.' She shook her head. 'Proper tragic that, to lose a child. You don't know of anyone, do you, lovey? Only they need to see to the funeral and so on.'

'No.' I shook my head again and hitched my bag up onto my shoulder. 'No, I don't think he had any family. As I say, I didn't know him very well at all.'

'Well, leave your number anyway, then I at least I can—'

'Sorry, I have to go.' I turned and hurried away. 'Thank you for telling me,' I called over my shoulder. 'Sorry I can't be more help.'

'Wait up, duck,' she called, but I was through the gennel and into the car in no time. I stalled the engine at the first try but then I managed to get it started and I pulled away as fast as I could, in the wrong gear and without indicating. I drove round the corner and pulled up in the next street. I was trembling. I tried to unclip my seatbelt, but I hadn't even done it up. Scott was dead; he couldn't hurt me any more. I felt a rush of adrenalin as the relief hit me. This meant I was free. I'd have to tell

Hannah that he'd been here, that he'd wanted to see her, but I wouldn't have to tell the whole truth; I wouldn't have to risk losing everything. I could feel my own heart-beat and I think I was actually holding my breath while the fantasy sparkled in the air for ten, maybe fifteen seconds. Then it popped like a child's soap bubble and I started to cry. Of course I had to tell the truth.

*

I sat in the car for a while before I drove home. I wanted to be sure Duncan would be asleep, because I needed to tell them both, together. I made myself some chamomile tea – I didn't like the taste, I never had, but Eve always used to say that chamomile would help you through hard times. I went into the dining room, switched on the electric heater and sat in the comfortable armchair, where I would savour these last few hours. Monty looked up from his basket, thumped his tail a few times and then went back to sleep. In the quiet darkness, I reflected on how lucky I'd been to meet Duncan. If there was such a thing as God, he couldn't have sent me a better father for Hannah. But I wondered what would happen now.

I must have dozed for a while, because when I opened my eyes it was light outside and I could hear the floor-boards above me creaking as Duncan moved around.

'There you are.' He appeared in the doorway of the dining room and his face started to form a question as he took in my fully clothed state.

'Can you phone Hannah,' I said. 'And get her to come round without Toby – I'm sure Marcus can take him for a couple of hours. There's something I need to tell you both, something important.' I couldn't hold the tears in. Duncan opened his mouth to speak and started moving towards me, but I put my hand up and shook my head. 'No, please. I don't deserve any sympathy.'

'Darling, what on—'

'Duncan, please, just do it. I'm sorry. I'll explain when she gets here.'

*

Half an hour or so later, Hannah arrived looking anxious; was I ill? she wanted to know, her sweet face etched with worry. I shook my head quickly and took a deep breath, and then I told them. I told them everything.

CHAPTER THIRTY-TWO

Hastings, 1976

The drought worsened. The shops on the seafront were selling T-shirts with the slogan *Save water – bath with a friend!* which caused a lot of sniggering among teenagers, and some disapproving looks from pensioners. The hot summer had brought a bumper crop of day trippers and holidaymakers flocking to the area, and when Scott went busking near the pier, or in Bottle Alley, or up in the Old Town, he made more money than he'd ever made before. The dazzling sunshine made people more generous, and the sound of his guitar and the Bob Dylan or Neil Young songs he sang seemed to fit well with the long days and the languorous mood. At the house, they managed to rig up a system that channelled washing-up water from the kitchen sink straight out of the window and down to the garden where Eve was growing tomatoes, runner beans and other things in various receptacles – terracotta pots, a stone sink that they'd found hiding under mounds of ivy and even an old trunk that Jo had found on a skip. As the three of them worked together to make sure the system operated efficiently so that water went to the growing areas and didn't spill onto the hard ground, Jo began to wonder how she could ever have considered leaving the house. This was her home; Eve and Scott were her family now; they needed each other. Eve had said again and again that she was fine about Jo and Scott having slept together; in fact, she'd said it so often now that Jo finally believed her. And a few times, usually when Eve was feeling particularly tired, Scott would come to Jo's bed, sometimes just to sleep, sometimes to make love, always with Eve's blessing. And in the morning, Eve would smile and cheerfully ask each of them whether they would like tea or coffee.

The three of them had fallen into an easy rhythm, moving around the house, cooking, eating, carrying out their chores in comfortable relaxed companionship. And if Jo did turn out to be pregnant – they used condoms now, but her period was nine days late so she'd started to think about it more seriously – then somehow, they would cope, the three of them would manage and they would be a beautiful family. She hadn't mentioned it to Eve or Scott yet, but they'd be cool about it; they were bound to be. And the fact that the rest of the country continued to hit problem after problem only enhanced this feeling of joyful separateness. It was not how she'd pictured her life, and every now and then she still ached for her mum, but in many ways they were happy; they were doing all right.

When her period came on the tenth day, a vicious, heavy bleed that made her feel as though her insides were being dragged out, she felt more than a stab of disappointment; and when Eve asked her what was wrong, she was glad to be able to say truthfully that she had a painful period, and needed to shut herself in her room for the day. After twenty-four hours she felt better, relieved even. They lived in a squat – looking after one baby was going to be difficult enough; how could she have possibly thought they would manage with two? It had been fun to imagine it, though, she and Eve, pushing their prams side by side. But it was just a fantasy. She was almost seventeen and she thought of herself as an adult, but she didn't really feel grown-up enough yet to actually have a baby. But she still cried herself to sleep three nights in a row.

*

It was late August, and Jo and Eve were at the beach. Jo handed Eve an ice cream that was already melting and sat back down on a towel to flick through a copy of the *Daily Express* that she'd found sticking out of a bin. Like the radio news they listened to at the house, the paper was full of doom and gloom – inflation was higher than it had been for years while the pound had hit a record low against the dollar; water shortages were now so serious that there was rationing in some areas and people were having to use standpipes at the end of the street – the government had even appointed a minister for drought. The continuing heat wave was relentless, causing freak plagues of insects – in some places, apparently, there were millions of ladybirds, and they covered the roads so thickly that people were crunching them underfoot. Reservoirs were baked dry and cracking; the tarmac on the roads melted under the blazing sun, and forest fires swept through wooded areas and heathland that were dry as tinder. They forecast a break in the weather soon, but it was hard to even remember what rain felt like.

'It almost makes you feel guilty, doesn't it?' Jo took another large bite of her ice lolly which had started to slide off the stick. 'I mean, the whole country's going up in smoke – literally – and we're just lying around, getting tanned and being happy.' They'd been on the beach for most of the day, just reading and swimming. Scott was bringing his guitar down later, along with some cheese, French bread and black grapes. Then they were going to swim some more, eat the food, drink some cider and smoke some weed – at least, Jo and Scott were going to smoke some weed; Eve said there had been a couple of reports recently about smoking being bad for unborn babies, and even though she only smoked occasionally, she didn't want to risk it.

Eve licked her ice cream thoughtfully. 'It's terrible about the fires, and the drought and everything, but we must never, never feel guilty for feeling happy.' She absent-mindedly ran her hand in light circles over her bump, which was significant now, and with its coating of

Ambre Solaire it glowed in the sunshine like a big brown beach ball. Eve was proud of her pregnancy and refused to cover it up. Pregnancy was beautiful, she argued, a life made from love; so why hide it under ghastly, tent-like maternity dresses with neat little white collars? It was clear that not everyone agreed, but Jo no longer felt embarrassed by the disapproving glances of other people on the beach, only anger on Eve's behalf, especially this morning when one woman had stared openly at Eve's rounded belly, shaking her head as she muttered, *'Disgusting.'* Jo had sprung to her feet, incensed. 'Excuse me,' she said, hands on hips. 'But what can you possibly find "disgusting" about an unborn baby?'

The woman had looked slightly taken aback and hadn't yet managed to form an answer, when Jo felt Eve's hand on her arm. 'Leave it, Jo,' Eve had said quietly. 'You don't know what's behind it.' Jo's anger had subsided as she watched the woman continue along the beach.

'Happiness is only a cause for guilt,' Eve was saying now, 'if the pursuit of it causes pain or unhappiness to someone else. Life is a gift, and it's our duty to make the most of it.' She looked down at her bump. 'And we owe it to this little person to be happy, too. Do you hear that, baby?' She smiled, as if the baby could see her. 'You're going to be born into a gorgeous, happy, happy family.'

'I can't wait for him or her to be born,' Jo said with a smile. 'It seems like you've been pregnant for years.' She felt a tiny whisper of sadness as she thought of her own briefly imagined baby.

'It does to me, too. But it's not that long now; she'll come when she's ready.'

'What if it's a boy?' Jo teased.

'It isn't,' Eve said, finishing the last of her cornet. 'I'm going to call her Lily.'

'So anyway,' Jo lay back down again, wriggling her body into the pebbles to try and get comfortable. 'Do you know who your midwife'll be yet?' She'd spent quite a while in the library reading up on home births, and now felt quite knowledgeable on the subject, but they hadn't discussed details yet. She hoped there wouldn't be a problem with Eve wanting to give birth at home. Jo herself had been born in her parents' bedroom, and Pat next door had been going to have her baby at home until they discovered it was twins, but Eve's home was a squat. True, they had water and electricity, but even so . . .

At first, she thought Eve hadn't heard her, so she repeated the question.

There was a pause before Eve answered. 'There won't be a midwife.'

Jo looked at her. 'You've not abandoned the idea, have you?' She felt a prickle of disappointment; for all her concerns, she was becoming increasingly excited at the prospect of being so close to an actual birth. 'So . . . ?'

Eve had lain back down and given no indication that she planned to explain any further. Jo loved Eve, but God, she could be maddening sometimes. 'So,' she continued. 'What's happening then?'

Eve answered drowsily, as though Jo had woken her

unexpectedly from a nap. 'What do you mean, "what's happening"?'

'Oh Eve, for God's sake!' Jo raised herself on her elbow to look Eve in the face. 'You know what I mean.' At that moment, she spotted Scott loping down the beach towards them, guitar slung over his back, cool box in his hand. The crowds were thinning out now as people packed up their towels and picnic baskets and headed back to boiling cars for a tortuous journey home, or to their hotels or B&Bs to take cooling showers and to smooth Aftersun on sunburned skin before heading out to spend the evening on the pier or in a pub garden.

'Hey,' Scott said, his shadow falling over Eve's body. 'How are my two favourite sun worshippers then?' He set down the cool box, wincing and shaking his arm to show how heavy it was, swung his guitar off his shoulder and settled himself next to Eve before reaching down the back of his neck and pulling his T-shirt off over his head. Jo found herself looking at his hairless chest, now the deepest brown she'd ever seen on a white man. A slight flutter in her stomach reminded her that, even though they only rarely slept together now, she still quite fancied him.

'Eve's being mysterious again,' she said, trying to lighten her voice to hide her irritation.

'Eve? Mysterious?' He was grinning as he planted a kiss on Eve's swollen belly. 'Surely not.'

'I want to know what's happening with the birth, that's all, and I was asking about the midwife. I just want to know whether they're going to let her have it at home, that's all.' She saw a glance pass between Eve and Scott.

'You'd better tell her,' Scott said to Eve, his voice serious now.

CHAPTER THIRTY-THREE

'Tell me what?' Jo said, looking from Scott to Eve and back again.

Eve sighed, took off her sunglasses and sat up. 'Okay. Jo, I need you to understand something. This is my baby – our baby – and "they" have no right to tell me where I can or can't give birth.'

'But—'

'I'll be having the baby at home, with you and Scott helping me.'

Jo was silent as what Eve was saying began to sink in. 'You mean . . . no, you can't mean . . . are you saying it'll *only* be me and Scott?'

Eve nodded, then smiled and took Jo's hand. 'Don't be worried about it, Jo; it'll be fine, I promise. I'll tell you what to do when the time comes.'

'But . . . but you can't, can you? I mean, I'm sure they won't allow—'

'I told you, it'd not a question of being *allowed*; I will bear my child where I choose, attended by the people I choose to attend me.'

'But what does the doctor say?' Jo persisted, convinced no doctor would sanction such a crazy idea.

'What doctor?'

'*Your* doctor, or the hospital doctor – I don't know, wherever it is you go for your antenatal check-ups.' She knew all about antenatal check-ups from when Pat was expecting the twins.

'I don't have a doctor,' Eve said quietly. 'I don't need one. I never get ill.' Then she shrugged. 'Well, if I ever get ill, I know what remedies to use to make myself better. The cure for everything is in nature, I've told you that before. Foods, plants, oils – you just have to— '

'Yes, I know but . . .' Jo pulled her hand away from Eve's and reached for her cigarettes. 'Bloody hell, Eve. Having a baby's not like having a cold or getting toothache.' She lit a cigarette and threw the pack down onto the pebbles as she exhaled. 'You can't just have a baby on your own.'

'But I won't be on my own, will I? I'll have you two.'

Jo looked at Scott, who was sitting cross-legged, head down, his elbows resting on his knees and his hands dangling between them. 'What do you think about this? Don't you think it's crazy?'

He shrugged. 'It's not crazy. A bit out there, perhaps; but not crazy, no.'

Eve was smiling again. 'See? You just need to get used to the idea, that's all.'

Jo shook her head, took another drag of the cigarette.

'Listen, Jo, I know it *seems* mad, but that's because our society forces women to go against nature. Women give birth unaided all over the world. Sometimes they have their mothers or sisters or friends to help, and sometimes they're completely alone. And it's easier; they give birth more quickly, they recover faster and they're happier.'

Jo thought back again to that documentary she'd seen, where three wives of the same man were talking about the most recent birth among them. The woman had given birth in a mud hut, attended only by her mother and the two other wives, and had been up and about the same evening, getting ready for the many visitors who were expected to arrive later that night bearing good wishes and lucky charms to bestow on the new arrival. 'Okay,' she said, 'I can see it might be a good idea if everything goes normally. But what if something goes wrong?'

At this, Eve's expression changed and she flicked her head in irritation. 'The main reason I want to do this without doctors and midwives is that it's their inter-ference that *makes* things go wrong.' She pulled her yellow cotton sundress on over her head and started to get to her feet. 'If my mum hadn't had a midwife, then my brother wouldn't have died. And if he hadn't died, my mum and dad probably wouldn't be dead, either.'

'What?' Jo blurted out. 'How come?'

Eve's face had flushed red and she was clearly fighting back tears. 'Right after it happened, my mum had terrible headaches and she kept telling the nurses and doctors that she knew something was wrong in her head. But they just said it was the grief and she'd get over it in time.' She wiped away a couple of tears that had spilled out while she was speaking. 'After she died, they said her blood pressure must have been through the roof, and yet no one took any bloody notice.'

'Eve,' Scott said, taking her arm. His voice was full of tenderness. 'Evie, are you all right?'

'I will be.' Eve leaned against him. 'But I want to go back. I need to be on my own, just for a little while.' Scott nodded, then stood and held her silently for a moment before she broke away. 'Sorry to be a party-pooper.' She glanced at Jo and gestured towards the cool box and the bags of stuff they'd brought down earlier. 'You two stay. I'll see you later.' She smiled briefly, assured them she'd be fine, then turned and made her way slowly up the beach, just as the first few drops of rain began to fall.

'I don't quite get it,' Jo said, after she'd gone. 'I can see why she blames the hospital for her mum dying, but what happened with the midwife? I mean, it must be terrible when a baby dies, but it does happen sometimes, doesn't it? Was there something wrong with him?'

Scott shook his head, then sighed as he started to explain. A student midwife had been looking after Eve's mum while the main midwife attended to someone else. When the baby started to come, much more quickly than anticipated, the terrified student had called for help, but had then tried to delay the birth by pushing on the baby's head. The child had suffered severe brain damage resulting in cerebral palsy and had died as a result. The inquiry that followed found the hospital responsible and also suggested there may have been a link between the trauma of the birth and the high blood pressure that caused Eve's mum to have a brain haemorrhage. 'So all that was bad enough,' Scott said, 'but then her dad went into a terrible depression, packed Eve off to a relative one day and chucked himself under a train. That's why it's all cemented together in Eve's mind; her mum had wanted to have the baby at home, but he'd insisted she have it in hospital, so obviously he blamed himself.'

By the time Scott had finished telling her the story, tears were streaming down her face. No wonder Eve was terrified of doctors and midwives.

*

Rain lashed at the windows and drummed on the roof of the thinking room as Jo sat looking out at the grey sea. There was something quite comforting about the sound of the rain against the glass. She leaned her forehead against the cool window; the rain had been torrential for hours, and had brought with it a break in the oppressive heat, a slight freshening of the air. Just then a jagged fork of lightning flashed against the darkening sky, followed by a low, distant rumble of thunder. She stood up, walked back and forth across the tiny room and then opened the window a little wider. She felt restless, and she wanted to hear the rain more clearly. Maybe it was the fact that the air had cleared, but she felt invigorated all of a sudden, confident that she could help Eve deliver her baby, that Eve was right about it being a straightforward procedure if handled properly from the start. It was, after all, the same thing that the books she'd been reading were saying, only they were obviously assuming a trained midwife would be present. A movement in the garden below caught her eye. 'Eve!' she shouted down. 'What are you doing? You're getting drenched!' But the sound of the rain drowned her voice, so she went down the three flights of stairs to the basement and opened the back door. Eve was standing in the middle of what was once a lawn, head tipped back and eyes closed until Jo called her name. 'Oh, there you are, Jo,' she said, she was smiling again. 'Come out here and take advantage of this gorgeous rain.' Jo grabbed a plastic bowl that was lying on the floor and held it over her head as she went up the steps. 'Oh Jo,' Eve said. 'Put the bowl down. Just enjoy the rain on your skin – it's wonderful!' She held her arms out wide and tipped her head back again so that the water pounded her face and streamed down her neck. She was still wearing the thin cotton sundress but it was so wet that it was transparent, and you could clearly see her protruding belly-button and her swollen breasts through her dress. Jo felt a pang of envy. She'd stopped wearing a bra herself soon after she'd moved in, but her own tits looked pathetic when compared with Eve's gloriously full ones. She discarded the plastic bowl and allowed the rain to soak her through to the skin. It wasn't as cold as she'd expected, and it did feel quite refreshing. The garden smelled of warm rain and wet earth, and of the rich, earthy scent of the tomato plants. The many plants that Eve had grown in pots and tended so carefully were always limp at the end of a hot day, despite their regular diet of washing-up water, but now they were noticeably perking up after the long weeks of drought. Even in the light that spilled into the garden from the house, you could see that everything was becoming greener. And there Eve stood in the middle of it all. With her full breasts, the swell of her pregnancy, the way she was smiling as she tilted her face to the heavens, she resembled some sort of maternal goddess, like a statue erected to the worship of nature, of fertility and fecundity. Of course Eve would be able to give birth successfully; why had Jo ever doubted it?

CHAPTER THIRTY-FOUR

Over the next few weeks, they made preparations. They read everything about childbirth that they could lay their hands on; they bought waterproof sheeting and brand-new towels and they cleaned all the main areas of the house, especially the living room, which they'd decided would be the best place to deliver the baby because it was nearer the kitchen for hot water, and because the room was big enough for all three of them to sleep in if necessary. They scrubbed floorboards, wiped down the paintwork, took anything that was washable to the launderette, and made up the birthing bed – a single mattress raised up on several pallets – at one end of the room. Scott varnished the little wooden cradle and put it next to the birthing bed, where it gradually acquired a mattress made out of a foam offcut, some new-looking brushed-cotton sheets, a Winnie-the-Pooh quilt from a jumble sale, and two navy-blue shawls, one rather badly knitted but the other quite passable. Jo had found a wool shop that was closing down; there were only dark colours left but she bought a huge cardboard box full of wool and two pairs of knitting needles for 35p. The first shawl was a bit of a practice run, but the second had turned out rather well, and Eve loved them both anyway.

As Eve grew larger, she left the house less and less, finding it increasingly tiring to make the long trek down into the basement then up the back steps and round to the front again. She continued to make her jewellery and bags, and when, halfway through September, they discovered that not only was there a bumper crop of blackberries from the bushes that had all but taken over their own garden, but there were yet more in the garden of the empty house next door, not to mention fruit trees heavy with apples, pears and plums, Eve duly went into production, making pounds and pounds of jam – plum, pear, and blackberry and apple. She also used the damaged fruit and the last of the summer's vegetables to make what she called 'interesting and unusual' chutneys. Jo and Scott loaded up the shopping trolleys and sold the home-made preserves at local markets and at a stall they set up on the A21 just outside the town. With Eve's efforts and the wages Jo and Scott brought in – he was working in pub and hotel kitchens again now the season was over and the busking wasn't so lucrative – they continued to bring in a surprisingly respectable amount of money. Scott had started to talk about going back to finish his teacher training and looking for what he called a 'proper job', much to Eve's dismay. 'We'll be tied down, Scotty,' she said when he mentioned it one night. 'I don't want us to have to live like that.'

'It's all very well living this way when it's just us,' he argued, 'but once the baby comes, things'll be different. And what if we get kicked out of the house? We can't doss down in any old squat once the baby's here.' Jo watched Eve's expression change from defiance to compliance as she reluctantly agreed that things would have to change. Jo, who hadn't thought more than three months or so ahead ever since she moved here, began to wonder what would happen to her if they were kicked out of the house. Because if Scott found a flat that he could afford to rent – he'd mentioned this a couple of times – Jo was pretty sure the arrangement wouldn't include her, despite what Eve had said about the baby having three parents.

*

One afternoon a couple of weeks before the baby was due – which was the first week in November, according to Eve's calculations – Eve complained that she was fed up and she wanted to go out. After the long, dry summer, it had rained almost every day for the last few weeks and she'd barely left the house. Now the rain had eased off, she felt restless. Jo suggested they go down to the seafront for the Hastings Day celebrations. Hastings Day had been an annual festival since 1966 when it had first taken place in commemoration of the Battle of Hastings. It used to always be on the Saturday nearest to the date of the battle – 14 October – but this year, for the first time, the celebrations were spanning four days. There were marching bands, drum majorettes, live music, a medieval banquet – all sorts of things were going on and Jo had been dying to go and see what was happening, but Scott wouldn't be home until the evening and she hadn't wanted to leave Eve on her own. She enjoyed feeling responsible for Eve, who, limited by her increasing size and crippling tiredness, had started to rely on Jo more and more.

'Are you sure you don't mind coming with me, Jo-Jo?' Ever since Jo had told her the childhood name her mother had used, Eve had taken to using it too. If anyone else had done so, Jo might have resented it, but, in fact, it felt right somehow.

'Mind? You're joking – it sounds brilliant, especially the bonfire tonight – and the procession.' But then she began to have doubts. She looked at Eve. 'Do you think you'll be all right standing for so long, though?'

Eve smiled. 'I'll be fine, I'm sure. As long as I've got you to hang on to on the walk back – I can't see myself making it up the hill too easily without you!'

It took much longer to walk down to the seafront than usual, because Eve could no longer move quickly. As they walked, Jo stole a glance at her now and again, dismayed at the changes the latter part of pregnancy had brought about in her friend. She looked older, and a weariness had settled about her features; she'd lost her glow and that spark of energy that made her seem as though she was always on the verge of something – about to smile or laugh, about to sing, about to leap up and start painting a new mural on one of the walls. Jo hoped the change wasn't permanent. Then she remembered poor Pat, just eighteen and the mother of twins, careworn and frumpy. But she hadn't known Pat pre-pregnancy, so maybe she'd always been like that.

The celebrations were in full swing when they got down to the front. They stood for a while watching a mime artist, then they wandered further along to watch the morris dancing and then a team of junior acrobats. They didn't fancy the re-enactment of the battle that was happening up near the castle, so they went onto the pier in search of tea and doughnuts before the main parade began. Jo hoped the break would revive Eve enough to get her through the next couple of hours. They made their way to the part of the beach where the bonfire would be lit and stationed themselves where they'd be able to watch the fire, but also have a good view of the parade. Over the last week or so, the organisers had been building the huge bonfire from broken furniture, driftwood, bits of old fences and other unwanted materials. Because of the weather, they'd had to work under a tarpaulin, but now the structure was revealed, there was a great deal of excitement about lighting it. The whole thing was cleverly constructed to resemble a ship; a galleon. Its size and shape couldn't fail to impress – and it was all made from rubbish.

SUSAN ELLIOT WRIGHT

The parade was colourful, noisy and wonderful. Jo felt like a child again, out for a day at the fair or the pantomime. Enchanted by the spectacle, she watched what seemed like a never-ending parade of morris dancers, brass bands, the Boys' and Girls' Brigades, the drum majorettes, and scores of children and adults in medieval costume on their way up to the castle for the next re-enactment.

By the time the parade finally thinned out, it was beginning to get dark. The castle, illuminated against the sky, looked magnificent tonight, and Jo marvelled at the fact that it had stood there, nine hundred years before, looking down on the proceedings just as it did now. The crowds lining the road started to disperse now it looked like there was nothing more to see, but as pushchairs were wheeled away and fathers lifted tired toddlers onto shoulders, Jo could just make out a deep rhythmic thudding in the distance. 'Listen,' she said to Eve. 'Can you hear that?' But almost before she'd finished speaking the sound had become much clearer and was unmistakable.

'Oh goodness, I love the sound of drumming,' Eve said, 'especially when it gets really loud and you can feel it in your belly.' She smiled and looked down at her bump. 'Listen, baby, can you feel that?' Then she looked up. 'Oh, look, here they come!' The drummers were part of a torch-lit procession that was snaking its way down to the promenade and along the coast road. The flickering flames of the torches made a fiery 'S' shape in the darkness, and the smoke that swirled around the procession added a sense of drama. The drummers were led by a tall, thin man wearing a black cloak and a top hat – he reminded Jo of the very first time she saw Scott. The man's face was painted white and his long hair flowed out behind him as he walked. The others, mainly men, were walking three or four abreast, beating drums of varying shapes and sizes. They all had wild hair and painted faces; some drummed with their hands, others used drumsticks, but all were grinning manically and throwing their arms around elaborately as they passed, some of them dancing and making mad faces at the crowd like demented court jesters. The drumming was so loud now that that Jo had to shout to tell Eve that she could indeed feel the sound reverberating in her guts. Behind the drummers, the torch bearers followed at a slower, steadier pace. There were women as well as men, and all wore long white robes and solemn expressions as they held their smoking torches aloft. They too had white-painted faces.

As Jo watched them making their steady way along the route, she was suddenly aware of a dark chill of sadness that replaced the excitement she'd felt only moments ago. There was something about the drumming, about feeling it physically at her very centre, that stirred up a profound sense of grief, not only for her mum, but for her granny, for the cat they'd had when she was a child; even for the baby she'd briefly imagined she might be carrying. But stranger still was the intense sadness she felt to be connected with the here and now, as though she was grieving for something she had not yet lost.

Eve was still smiling, clearly enjoying herself. The drummers were spreading out to form a semicircle around the bonfire and the drumming was getting faster and louder. The torch bearers took up position next to the drummers and held their torches high in the air, the orange and yellow flames flickering dramatically against the night sky while the drumming reached a fever pitch. Jo could feel the adrenalin pumping around her body and she felt Eve's hand grab her arm. She didn't feel sad any more but the sound was again stirring something in her and she fought the urge to cry. Then the drumming stopped. It was so sudden and so complete that the shock of silence was like a slap. Then, at a signal from one of them, the torch bearers all threw their flaming torches into the structure amid shouts and cheers from the crowd.

At first, it was a bit of an anticlimax. Nothing seemed to be happening and people started to murmur that maybe the damp had managed to get in under the tarpaulin after all. But then the fire started to catch, slowly at first, then more certainly as it took hold and began to warm the air. Before long the flames were streaming upwards and then out in all directions as they were caught by the wind. 'Wow,' Jo said. 'It's breathtaking, isn't it?' Eve nodded as she watched with an almost reverent expression. Jo thought it strange to see a huge fire in such close proximity to the sea. In fact, now it had properly taken hold, she thought how closely it resembled the enormous waves she'd seen crashing over the sea wall during a storm a couple of days ago. There were huge, rolling waves of flame, pouring from the structure like seawater through a gap in the rocks. She looked up into the night sky and saw a blizzard of dancing, swirling flakes of flame, like a million fireflies dancing on a summer evening. Then there was another, stronger gust of wind and the fire roared as though it couldn't stop itself from bellowing in delight as it consumed most of the main substance of the structure, leaving a black skeleton flaming and smoking against the sky.

The heat was becoming quite intense now, and Jo could feel it burning her face. 'It's fantastic, isn't it?' She turned to smile at Eve, then returned her gaze to the fire.

'Jo,' Eve said, gripping her arm again. 'I have to go.'

'Oh, just a bit longer.' She knew Eve was tired from being on her feet for so long, but she couldn't bear to leave just yet.

'Jo . . .' It was a strangled sound, and when she looked at Eve properly, she could see that there was something very wrong. Eve's face, clearly lit up in the firelight, was full of tension; her eyes were screwed shut and her mouth was set in a hard line.

'Oh God, what is it? Are you all right?' What a stupid thing to say; Eve clearly wasn't all right. 'Eve?' she said again. But Eve didn't answer, didn't even open her eyes, she just carried on gripping Jo's arm so tightly it was beginning to hurt.

Shit, Jo thought. This couldn't be it, could it? It wasn't due for another couple of weeks. Then at last Eve relaxed her grip and opened her eyes. 'We need to go,' she said. 'Now.'

They began to push their way through the crowd, Eve leading the way and Jo following close behind. 'Excuse me,' she could hear Eve saying. 'Can we get through, please? Excuse me.' Her voice was clear and strong, and she sounded very much in control. Jo started to feel less worried as she followed Eve through the last clusters of people and out onto the main road where there was more space. They crossed the road and began to make their way slowly up the hill towards the house. Just as Jo had begun to think that nothing more was going to happen, Eve stopped walking and clutched Jo's arm. She made a sort of 'oooh-oww' sound and her grip on Jo's arm again tightened almost unbearably. Jo stood still and allowed Eve to hang on to her. 'Is it really bad?' she asked. 'Can't talk,' Eve said in a quick burst, and when Jo looked at her face, she was staring ahead with a really scary look in her eyes.

When the contraction had passed, they started walking again. 'I thought they were supposed to build up gradually,' Eve said. 'But that really bloody hurt.'

Jo tried to think of something encouraging to say, but she'd gone completely blank. Eve didn't say anything else, either, so it felt strange as they plodded up the hill in silence. It can only have been two or three minutes before another pain came. This time, Eve whimpered as they again stood still on the pavement while the contraction seemed to take over her body. The whimper turned into a cry as Eve began to double over. Oh my God, Jo thought. Please don't let it happen here. She glanced around. They still needed to get up the steps before they would be in sight of the house. She wondered if she dare run ahead to get Scott, but how could she leave Eve in this state? She could feel the panic starting to rise when Eve straightened up again and said, 'Come on, we need to get home fast.'

They managed to get up all the steps and almost to the house before the next contraction kicked in, and Jo started to feel more hopeful that this baby wouldn't be born in the street. And once they were back in the house, there was only one more contraction before everything stopped and they all began to feel sure it must have been a false alarm.

Eve went to lie down in the living room while Scott helped Jo to prepare dinner. He picked the last two cauliflowers from the garden; they were small and the heads were yellow rather than white – a result of too much sun, Eve said – but they tasted fine, and after Scott had soaked them in salt water to kill off any cabbage worms, he cut them into florets and arranged them in a dish with some shop-bought broccoli. Jo made the cheese sauce and topped the whole thing with more grated cheese and some breadcrumbs to make a crispy topping. Cauliflower cheese was Eve's favourite meal, and they ate it with grilled tomatoes and French bread, laughing at the fact that they'd been so convinced the baby was coming. 'Daft of me,' Eve said. 'Because I was only reading a couple of days ago that Braxton Hicks contractions can be pretty powerful.' She yawned. 'I'm absolutely shattered. I think

I'm going to leave you two to the washing up and go and lie down again.'

*

'I'm glad it was a false alarm,' Jo said as they stood at the sink, he washing the dishes, she drying. 'I thought we were ready, but when those pains started tonight, I was bloody petrified.'

Scott handed her a dripping plate and began washing another. 'Why petrified? We *are* ready, aren't we? I mean, there's nothing else we need to buy or prepare, is there?'

'I know, but I mean *mentally* ready. It made me think, that's all. There's so much that could go wrong—'

'I thought we'd been through all—'

He was cut short by Eve calling from the living room; her waters had broken.

CHAPTER THIRTY-FIVE

They took it in turns to sit with Eve. Her labour kept stopping and starting, and each time it stopped, she fell asleep quickly and slept deeply, as though soaking up sleep and storing it like a camel storing water. Even though the contractions kept easing off, it was fairly clear that the birth would happen soon. While Eve was awake, even though she was in pain, they were able to stay calm and focused, but it was Eve who reassured them rather than the other way round.

Eve was sleeping again now, but Jo felt restless and couldn't concentrate on her book. She paced up and down the room, trying to still the frenzied movement of the butterflies in her stomach. Scott came back with two cups of nettle tea, but when he saw how agitated Jo was, he sat down and rolled a joint. 'Here,' he said. 'Go and have a few tokes of this. It'll help you calm down.'

Jo hesitated. 'I don't know. We need to keep a clear head, don't we? I mean, what if . . .'

'It's not very strong,' he said. 'I'm saving the good stuff until afterwards.'

She took the joint, grabbed her long cardigan and went outside for some fresh air. It was a mild night, still and quiet with a big, fat full moon, bright enough to cast shadows on the deserted street. She walked to the end of the road, sat on a wall and looked out across the town, which lay sprawled in front of her with no tall buildings to interrupt the view. It was almost three in the morning so there were hardly any lights on in the houses, but it was still a pretty scene. The golden lighting around the castle, the moonlight making a carpet of silver on the dark water, and the little orange pinpricks of artificial light coming from the houses that stood facing this way and that on the staggered levels of the town.

Scott was right, the joint wasn't strong at all; she didn't feel spaced out or giggly, just pleasantly calm and even; able to face what lay ahead. As she walked back along the silent road, a movement to her left made her jump, despite her sense of tranquillity. It was a seagull, silently worrying at something under the hedge. There was a squawk and a flutter of wings and another seagull appeared, screeching and flapping its wings at her. The two seagulls flew off and she crouched down to look under the hedge. When she saw what was there she jumped back; it was a third seagull, obviously dead and with blood on its chest and wing feathers. It had probably been run over. But what had the other two been doing? Surely not trying to eat it? She shuddered and walked back towards the house.

Eve was having contractions again and was sitting up, hanging on to Scott's arm and making a long, low sound as she rode the wave of pain. When it passed she flopped back on the pillows, exhausted. 'My God,' she said, managing a brief smile. 'No wonder they call it labour.' She paused to catch her breath. 'I think you two had better go and scrub up. It's definitely happening this time.' They took it in turns, thoroughly soaping their hands and arms up to the elbows, and they both put on the brand-new cheap cotton nightdresses they were using as gowns. Now it was actually about to happen, they'd fallen silent, perhaps each wondering what the hell had made them agree to this in the first place.

It was only another few minutes before the next contraction, and this time Eve grabbed both Jo's arm and Scott's, shouting, 'Lift me up, lift me up, lift me up.' Jo wasn't sure how they were supposed to lift her considerable bulk but between them they managed to get her up high enough for her to pull her legs around so that she was kneeling rather than lying down. Jo remembered a conversation they'd had about it being unnatural and more difficult to give birth lying on your back. 'Eve,' she said, but Eve had her eyes closed and, although it was clear that the last pain had passed, she seemed to be gearing herself up for the next one. 'Eve,' she said again, 'what position do you want to be in? Do you want us to try and stand you up?' But Eve still didn't answer, just sagged against Scott's shoulder with her eyes closed. Her face was drawn and pale; she looked drained.

Jo looked at Scott. 'Do you think she's all right? Is this normal?'

For the first time since he'd come home, Scott looked worried, too. 'I don't know,' he said. 'It's not like I thought it would be. Eve, are you okay? Evie? Say something to me, babe, please.'

She opened her eyes and looked at him, but as she was about to speak her face contorted. Jo placed her free hand on Eve's belly. The intensity of the contraction surprised her. 'Bloody hell – feel that!' Scott put his hand there as well but then Eve pushed both their hands away as she struggled to cope with the pain. 'Oh, shit!' Scott said, a note of panic in his voice. 'Shit. Shit. Shit! We're supposed to be timing them, aren't we? I forgot. I completely forgot to time the fucking contractions.'

Eve let out another long, low cry and then slumped again, breathing heavily. 'Don't panic, you idiot,' she said. Jo had never heard her talk to Scott like that before. 'That's only so you can tell if I'm actually in labour, and I think it's pretty obvious, don't you?'

'Oh right. Sorry.'

When the next pain came, the sound Eve made was like nothing Jo had heard before. Jo and Scott looked at each other. 'Shall I go to the phone box?' Jo said.

But before Scott had time to answer, Eve had pushed them away and thrown herself forward so that she was on all fours. 'Don't,' she yelled. 'No ambulance. I can do it I can do it I can do it.'

Scott stroked her hair. 'Okay, shush; it's okay, Evie.'

316

THE SECRETS WE LEFT BEHIND

'It's coming,' Eve said, and began pulling her nightdress up and making a deep rumbling sound, almost like a growl.

Jo tried to remember what she'd read. She looked at Scott, but he had his arms around Eve's back, supporting her while she gripped his shoulders. Then she heard Eve's voice in her head saying what she'd said again and again when they'd discussed this. *Just be there, Jo. You shouldn't need to do anything but catch the baby as it's born.* And there was the baby's head, a mass of black hair and a scrunched-up purple face.

'Not too fast,' Eve was telling herself. 'Gotta pant.'

Panting helped the mother avoid the urge to push, Jo remembered from the book, *giving the attendant time to check that the cord isn't around Baby's neck.* 'It's all right, Eve.' Jo tried to keep the tremor out of her voice. 'It's safe to push.' She grabbed one of the new cotton towels that lay folded up on the table. 'I'm ready.' And with another long grunt of effort, Eve pushed her baby into the world and then collapsed, exhausted, onto her side. Tears sprang to Jo's eyes as the little purple child slithered into her waiting arms. 'It's a girl!' she announced, crying and laughing at the same time and completely overwhelmed by the magnitude of it all.

'Hello, baby!' Eve cried, and then she and Scott were both crying and laughing too. But the baby hadn't made a sound yet, and was a still a deep purplish colour. The sound of laughter died away as it dawned on everyone that she wasn't breathing.

Whether Jo was remembering something she'd read or whether she was acting on instinct, she didn't know, but she laid the baby over Eve's bare legs and began rubbing her back with a rough towel and saying over and over, 'Come on, baby, breathe for your mummy; come on, sweetheart, come on.'

After a moment of seeming both stunned and bewildered, Eve pulled her daughter towards her, opened her nightdress and held her child to her breast while keeping up the massage that Jo had started. 'Come on, my gorgeous, darling Lily, please breathe.' After what felt like hours but was in fact no more than thirty seconds, the baby made a choking, spluttering sound and let out a long ragged cry, at the same time as her skin turned from purple to pink, at last filling up with life.

Jo couldn't help herself; she burst into tears which she made no attempt to check. It wasn't only relief at what had just happened, it was also a release of all the tension of the last few months. She sobbed like a child for a few moments, aware that, although Eve and Scott were in tears too, she was the only one who was making a noise. She felt so much better afterwards; perhaps this was what was meant by 'a good cry'. Soon, the tears abated and all three of them were smiling broadly. She watched as Scott cut and tied the cord and tenderly placed the baby in Eve's arms.

As she looked at the little family, Scott with his arm around Eve's shoulders and the two of them gazing in wonder at their child, she felt the tiniest flicker of loneliness.

*

It took a bit longer than they'd expected to deliver the placenta, which Scott then wrapped in newspaper and took outside to bury in the garden. Eve had mentioned the idea of cooking and eating it – something she'd read about in one of the natural-birth books – but Scott and Jo had thought the idea revolting and had talked her out of it by persuading her that burying it in the vegetable patch would at least make good use of the nutrients.

After drinking what she said was the best cup of tea of her life, Eve fell into a deep sleep, her hand still resting on baby Lily who was sleeping in the crib next to her. Jo gently lifted Eve's arm and tucked it back under the covers, then she and Scott collapsed next to each other onto the settee at the other end of the room, tired but exhilarated. 'Wasn't it amazing?' Scott kept saying, keeping his voice low so as not to disturb Eve and the baby. 'And so fucking beautiful! Man, I just can't get over it.' Jo agreed that it was the most awe-inspiring thing she'd ever seen in her life. The amount of pain had shocked her a little, but the way Eve dealt with it, and the way she instinctively knew what to do . . . it made her even more of a goddess.

Scott sighed, a happy sigh, then turned to look at her, right at her. 'You were great, Jo,' he smiled. 'Thanks. It was a lot to ask.'

'I was terrified something would go wrong.' Jo sighed too, tipping her head back and looking at the ceiling. She hadn't noticed before how beautiful that old cornice was; such a shame it was damaged. 'When you think of all the things that could have . . .'

'You worry too much. It was all cool, wasn't it?'

Jo felt a flash of irritation. Hadn't he been worried too? 'Scott, did you even read that book? The baby could have been breech – bum first or even feet first; the cord could have been round her neck; her shoulders could have got stuck. And what about Eve? What if she'd needed a Caesarean? What if she'd haemorrhaged? What if she—'

'Jo, Jo, Jo! Keep it down, man – she needs to sleep. And relax. None of those things happened; it all went well. We have a lovely little daughter – you have a lovely little *almost* daughter – we should be celebrating. In fact—' He held up a finger indicating she should wait and tiptoed out into the hallway where she heard him rummaging in a carrier bag. 'Here we are.' He opened two bottles of cider and passed one to her. 'Not champagne, I'm afraid.'

Jo smiled, took a swig from the bottle, then another. It tasted so good after the rigours of the night; it might as well have been champagne.

'Tell you what I have got, though.' He took a small bag of grass out of his jacket pocket and held it up. 'I have it on good authority that this happens to be the finest marijuana in Sussex. It's a bit trippy, apparently, but I reckon we could both do with a treat.'

'What about the baby?'

'She's too young.' He chuckled as he took Rizlas and a pouch of tobacco from his pocket. 'Sorry, couldn't resist that. It'll be okay; we'll just keep it down this end. I think they're going overboard with all this scaremongering, anyway. My family has always smoked and it hasn't done them any harm. My dad still smokes weed and even my grandad smokes twenty Weights a day, and he's over eighty.' He reached for the cover of *The Dark Side of the Moon* and rested his hands on it while he rolled one of the biggest joints Jo had ever seen. Normally, she'd probably have refused anything 'trippy', but she didn't feel like her normal self, she felt elated, excited; a little bit reckless. Eve was always saying she should open herself up to a wider range of experiences. 'What the hell,' she said, taking a deep draw on the joint and immediately feeling the room spin. 'Wow.' She lay back against the cushions. 'That's really strong.' Her legs started to buzz and she felt a bit sick. She needed to get to the loo, but when she tried to stand, her legs crumpled beneath her.

Scott helped her up and sat her back on the settee. 'You okay?' He smiled. 'Powerful stuff, isn't it? Nice, though. Makes your legs float. Probably best to stay sitting down. Just lie back and let it take you where it takes you.' He took another toke, tipped his head back and closed his eyes. He was still smiling as he passed the joint to Jo again. She took a smaller toke this time, but automatically drew the smoke down and held it in her lungs. As she did so, she watched Scott's smile grow wider and wider until it couldn't possibly fit on his face any more, but stretched out across the whole room, curling around Eve's bed and enfolding her and the baby as though his lips were actually big pink arms. Jo started to giggle; it was obviously the grass that was making her see things, but she'd never experienced anything like this before and, now she'd stopped feeling sick, she was fascinated, and drew on the joint a couple of times before passing it back. She looked across to where Eve was sleeping with the baby next to her, but she could see her face close up, as though she were right next to her, and as she peered at Eve's face, she saw that her eyes had become two little diamonds, turning circles and sparkling away. Jo chuckled, although she didn't know whether she'd chuckled out loud or just inside her head. Her body had shut down to allow her mind to break out, and she had the sensation that her mind was a mischievous entity that had finally been released from captivity and was determined to have some fun.

She may have slept for a while then, but whether it was a few minutes or a few hours, she couldn't tell. Scott's face had disappeared and all that was left where he had been sitting was a six-foot-wide smile, its lip glistening. It's the dope, she told herself. Just blink and the smile will go away and Scott'll come back. She blinked but it took an hour or so for her eyelids to close and open again, and when they did, Scott had changed back to being Scott again, but with his long hair spread out all around him like a silky black swimming pool. She wanted to reach across him for the cider, but she knew that, if she did, she'd be sucked down into the pool and was likely to drown in his hair. She tried to reach out, but sure enough she fell into the pool, only now it was red, not black, and it swirled and gushed and pushed and pulled her with its unexpected current and as she struggled to keep afloat, a baby rushed past her. Eve's baby! She tried to grab it but it slipped through her fingers, and then Eve was there, too. At first Jo thought she was smiling; Eve always smiled. But then she realised that Eve's eyes were closed and her face was blank, there was no expression at all, and she was sinking deeper and deeper into the red pool. Jo tried to reach out so that Eve could grab her hand, but she couldn't move her limbs any more; in fact, she wasn't sure she actually *had* limbs any more. Her head was spinning; she wanted this to stop now. It's just the dope, she told herself again; it'll pass. It was probably best to keep her eyes closed, because then her brain wouldn't be able to mutate what she saw. But when she closed her eyes, she became convinced that the house was the wrong way round, and she had to force her eyes open again to prove that it wasn't. If she could just get to the kitchen and splash some water on her face, she might straighten up a bit quicker. Yes, that's what she must do. She hauled herself off the settee but she couldn't stand, so she began to crawl on all fours. But the rug had become a deep red pool again, and it was getting bigger and bigger as she looked at it. If she went any nearer, she would surely drown. She turned back to the settee, pulled herself up onto it, then curled up and waited for the drugs to wear off.

CHAPTER THIRTY-SIX

When Jo woke, it was daylight. There was a crick in her neck where she'd slept curled up, and she was cold, apart from her feet which were resting against Scott's leg. He was still in a sitting position although he'd keeled over to the side with his head on the arm of the settee. His mouth was open and he snored as he breathed in. She'd never seen him look so unappealing. Slowly, she sat up. There was a weird smell in the room, metallic, like cold copper pipes. Then she remembered that it had finally happened; Eve had given birth, here in this very room.

Right on cue, Lily made a little mewling noise, and Jo felt a sudden rush of love. Maybe it was because she'd helped deliver her, but she felt an incredibly strong connection with her already. Perhaps she could pick her up and give her a quick cuddle before Eve or Scott woke. She tried to uncurl her legs and stand up without disturbing Scott, but as she moved her feet away from the warmth of his leg, he made a snorting noise, then opened his eyes and stretched. His eyes were so bloodshot they looked almost completely red. Hers probably did, too, come to think of it. That grass was ridiculously strong. She stood up a little shakily and started to make her way across the room, but then she stopped, her brain unable to quite grasp what her eyes were seeing.

Blood. Everywhere. So much blood. It was on the rug, and on the floorboards as well as the bed. Jo couldn't move; she felt like the bottom of her stomach had fallen out. Eve was lying in the bed, still covered with the new bedding they'd bought specially, sheets and a continental quilt, all now sodden with dark blood. Jo tried to speak but the sound that came out was more like a cry of pain. She heard Scott leap to his feet behind her. 'Fuck!' he yelled, and rushed over to Eve. 'Don't just stand there, you stupid cow!' His voice was high with panic. 'Go to the phone box and call an ambulance.' He almost fell on Eve and started trying to give her the kiss of life. Jo didn't move. She'd only needed that one look at Eve's rigid, greyish-white face to know that she was dead. It was the same thing she'd experienced when her mum died. The body was there, the person's face completely recognisable as the person you knew them to be, but with something missing; with the soul gone.

Scott was sobbing now; he'd lifted Eve's head and shoulders and was rocking her back and forth saying, 'Eve, oh Evie, Evie.' He didn't ask Jo to go for an ambulance again. 'She's dead, Jo. She's fucking dead.' He looked around at all the blood and gestured helplessly at it, then buried his face in Eve's hair again.

Jo was still standing uselessly in the middle of the room. She willed herself to move but her knees started to feel shaky and she was afraid she was going to be sick, then she heard a buzzing sound in her ears, and then everything went black. She came to a moment later, lying on her back on the floor, and it was a blissful millisecond before the horror of what had happened came flooding back. Scott was crouching next to her and offered his hand to help her up. 'You fainted,' he said. He didn't look at her as she sat up, but she could see his utterly stricken expression. 'Oh Jo,' he moaned. 'How can she be dead? How *can* she be? It was all okay, she said so; she said she felt all right.'

She had. In fact, she'd said she felt wonderful, more alive than she'd ever felt in her life. 'This is what I was meant for, Jo,' she'd said as she'd held Lily to her breast.

'She must have started bleeding after,' Jo said, then cursed herself for the ridiculously obvious statement. 'I mean, maybe some of the placenta didn't come away, or—'

'But why? I mean, why the *fuck*?' And he banged his fist down on the coffee table so hard that Lily started to cry.

Scott didn't move, so Jo got to her feet and walked softly across the room, as though afraid of waking Eve. When she glanced down, the sight of the blood, the smell of it, the stark fact that this was something that was clearly meant to be inside someone's body, not outside, sent ripples of horror lapping through her. She paused for a moment and put her hand on the back of a chair to steady herself. She'd never been particularly affected by blood before, not like her mum who'd gone pale every time Jo grazed her knee, and was incapable of watching a blood test. But now she felt sick and faint at the raw, exposed deadness of it.

Lily stopped crying the instant Jo picked her up, but she began squirming and turning her head forcefully towards Jo's chest. Rooting, that was what the books said; she was rooting for the nipple. Jo began to cry at last, a sudden and unexpected rush of sobbing that she could do nothing to control, so she handed the baby to Scott who seemed surprised to find her in his arms and looked at her as though he wasn't quite sure who or what she was.

In the kitchen, Jo sank into the armchair in which Eve had been sitting only hours before. Eve's long green cardigan, the one Jo sometimes borrowed when she was chilly, was squashed down in the back of the chair where Eve had taken it off without getting up. Jo picked it up and held it to her face as she cried. It smelled of Eve, a mixture of patchouli and that slight scent of apples that came from her skin. On the table beside the chair was Eve's knitting, a tangled mess that she'd decided to unravel so she could start again. Next to the knitting, her favourite red mug with the dregs of her tea and the copy of *Baby Beloved* that she'd been reading bits out of

327

yesterday morning. *What does it matter if the nappies are grey, as long as the bottom they're pinned onto is pink and healthy and cherished.* Eve had smiled and passed the book to Jo. 'Sounds painful,' she'd said and they'd giggled together at the clumsy wording.

Lily was crying. Lily. The reality of what had happened was still difficult to grasp. Before the birth, Jo had lain awake night after night going over the things that could go wrong. She'd read that a post-partum haemorrhage could happen any time up to forty-eight hours after the birth, but this was much less common than haemorrhages occurring during or immediately after delivery, so once Lily had been safely born, she'd forgotten about those possibilities. In their stupid, self-righteous, naïve elation, they'd assumed there was no more danger. And now Eve was dead. The whole thing felt unreal, but not unreal enough for Jo to convince herself she was still tripping. She groaned aloud. If they hadn't smoked that vile stuff, Eve would still be alive. She picked up the red mug and hurled it at the wall.

'Hey.' Scott was standing in the doorway, holding Lily who had started to cry more insistently.

'Sorry,' Jo said. Then she looked up at him, her face wet with tears. 'It's our fault, you know. If we hadn't smoked that weed . . .' And then she was crying again. 'Oh God, Scott, what are we going to do?'

Scott stood there, a look of utter bewilderment on his face. There was blood on his jeans where he'd knelt on the bed. 'Our fault,' he muttered. 'Yes, yes, I suppose it is, isn't it?' Tears were streaming down his face now, too, although they were silent tears that just kept falling, running off his chin and dropping down onto the baby.

For a few moments, it was as though they were frozen in their positions, Scott standing in the doorway holding Lily, Jo a sodden, crumpled heap in Eve's chair. Then Lily's cries seemed to rouse them both. Scott walked towards Jo. 'You take her; I need a smoke.'

'You *what*? You can't seriously be thinking of—'

'Shut up, Jo.' He held Lily out to her without meeting her eye. 'I need a fucking smoke.'

Jo pushed herself out of the chair and stood up, jiggling the baby to try and soothe her. 'You can't!' she yelled. 'You can't just duck out of this!' But he was already walking away from her. 'Scott! What are we going to *do*?'

He came back seconds later. 'I can't go in there.' He was shaking his head. His face had paled and there was a sheen of sweat on his forehead. He put his hand to his mouth. 'Oh, God, I think I'm going to . . .' He turned, then ran along the hallway and up the stairs, reaching the bathroom just in time by the sound of it.

Jo looked down at baby Lily in her arms. Lily's face was screwed up and red from the effort of crying. She was still frantically rooting, her little head turning repeatedly towards Jo's chest. Eve had wanted to breastfeed for as long as possible. 'It's the perfect food,' she'd said, 'and the perfect way for a mother to comfort her child.' She'd held out the book so Jo could look at the picture of a golden-skinned mother, naked from the waist up, smiling serenely as she fed a contented-looking downy-haired newborn.

She heard Scott come out of the bathroom and walk along the upstairs hallway, then she heard the door of his and Eve's room open and close. She waited, but he didn't reappear. Part of her wanted to shout and throw things at him – how dare he just disappear and leave her here like this, with the baby – with *his daughter* – crying for a feed, and Eve, lying in there . . . She felt another sob rising in her chest but she fought it down. Perhaps Eve knew Scott would be useless and this was why she wanted Jo to stay and help. She walked back to the armchair and sat down, still jiggling Lily in her arms. 'You need some milk, sweetheart, don't you?' For a moment, the crying subsided, as though in response to Jo's voice. With Lily still in her arms, Jo began opening cupboards. Somewhere, there were a few bottles and two unopened tins of baby milk that had come in a box of second-hand baby equipment. She found the bottles fairly quickly, but the powdered milk must have been thrown away. Maybe cow's milk would be okay just this once? And she was sure she could boil the bottles to sterilise them.

She looked at Lily properly; the perfect little face, the tawny-coloured skin with its fine covering of down, almost as though it had been dusted with powder, the hair dark, like Scott's, and the tiny, shell-like fingernails so thin that you could see her pink fingertips beneath the transparent nails. The baby was looking at Jo with wide blue eyes that were serious and wise. Granny Pawley had always said Jo was 'an old soul', and now she looked at Lily, she finally understood what that meant. As they looked at each other, Lily's lower lip trembled and she began crying again. It wasn't like this was a newborn baby, a creature just a few hours old; it was as though she had a personality and wisdom, and as though she was somehow disappointed in Jo for failing to provide for her needs. 'Sorry, sweetheart,' Jo whispered, and then, almost instinctively, she lifted up her sweater and her bra, and held Lily close to her breast. The sensation when Lily's hard little mouth clamped around her nipple was unexpected and shocking, like an electric current running from her breast through her stomach to her loins; it engulfed her heart and her head at the same time and was both sexual and yet intensely chaste. She'd never experienced anything so unbelievably powerful in her entire life. She touched the baby's cheek. She hadn't even consciously intended this to happen, rather, she'd thought that the nearness of her warm skin might offer Lily some comfort. But Lily's instincts were thousands of years in the making and involved the implicit trust in Jo to provide both comfort and nourishment. She watched Lily's tiny fingers clenching and unclenching as her hand rested against Jo's pitifully small and empty breast. For a few seconds the poor little thing sucked for all she was worth, until Jo was so overcome by horrified guilt that she was about to try and prise Lily's mouth away from her when Lily broke off of her own accord and began crying again in earnest, and this time there were real, actual tears coming from her eyes. Jo's nipple was reddened and elongated, and she quickly pulled her bra and sweater down again so that neither she nor Lily had to see the evidence of her betrayal. She hoisted Lily up onto her shoulder and murmured, 'I'm sorry, baby, I'm so, so sorry,' into her neck, which smelled uncannily of talcum powder, even though there was no such thing in the house.

CHAPTER THIRTY-SEVEN

As Jo was heating up some cow's milk, Scott remembered where he'd put the powdered baby milk, which turned out to be just within date. Carefully following the instructions on the tin, Jo made up three bottles, one of which she fed to a ravenous Lily who fell asleep before she'd quite finished. She was now sleeping peacefully in her cradle, which they'd moved into the kitchen and wiped clean of the blood that stained its rockers. Jo and Scott sat opposite one another at the kitchen table, too stunned to eat, drink or even smoke, despite what Scott had said earlier. 'We should tell someone,' he said. He was looking down at the table and his voice was so quiet she could barely hear him.

She sighed, then nodded. 'Yes. We should.' After an initial period of not being able to think at all, her thoughts had now started to speed up and were darting back and forth across her mind. Of course they must tell someone.

Doctors? The police? But what would happen when they did? One thought kept coming to the front of her mind, shouting at her louder than the others: As soon as they told whoever they needed to tell, it was unlikely that she would ever see Lily again and the one thing she was absolutely certain about was that she loved Lily as surely as if she were her own baby.

'Scott,' she said, but he didn't appear to have heard her. Scott was Lily's father, but even he might not be allowed to keep her, not after what had happened. She reached across and put her hand on the back of his, shaking it slightly as if gently rousing him from sleep. 'Scott, listen. We need to think. Eve's dead, and we were there when it happened – in the same room, for Christ's sake. We were supposed to be looking after her, although I'm not even sure if it was legal to arrange a home birth with no doctor or midwife around.'

He raised his head slowly, revealing a face that was ravaged, a face that had aged ten years in a single night. 'I know.'

'She bled to death while we were tripping our tits off on illegal drugs.' A scene flashed into Jo's mind, a red pool, Eve's white face amid the swirling red that was dragging her under, drowning her. She blinked away the image and looked around at the real solid objects in the kitchen, the ashtray, the tray of cress growing on the windowsill, the rubber plant that Eve had coaxed back to life, the clock on the mantelpiece – it was still only 9.30 in the morning.

'You okay?' Scott was looking at her, and she realised that she was breathing loudly and faster than usual.

'My God,' she said. 'I thought it was just the drugs, but I think I saw it . . . I think I actually saw the blood . . .' Her whole body began to shake and her teeth started to chatter uncontrollably.

Scott scraped his chair back and came round to her side of the table. 'You're in shock,' he said, resting his hand on her arm; 'I think we both are.' Then he picked up Eve's green cardigan and draped it round Jo's shoulders, which made her cry. He boiled the kettle and made them both tea with lots of sugar, and it did seem to help. He rolled two cigarettes, passed one to Jo then struck a match and lit them both. 'What the fuck are we going to do, Jo?'

She smoked in silence for a minute. They'd have to call the police. One of them was going to have to walk to the phone box and dial 999. What words would they say? *My friend is dead. Oh yes? And how did that happen? She had a baby and then she bled to death. And where were you when this occurred? Sitting on a settee about fifteen feet away. And why didn't you* . . . She took a drag of the thin roll-up. 'We'll be arrested for the drugs, definitely.'

Scott nodded. 'But what else? We were in charge, weren't we?'

It was a strange way of putting it and it made Scott suddenly seem very young, not a man at all but a boy, perhaps because it reminded her of when she was at primary school and was part of a group of children who were tidying up the Home Corner; her teacher had told her quietly that, as the most sensible one, she was in charge of making sure everything was done properly. Now it was clear to her that, not only was Scott just a boy, but she was just a girl. They had both behaved like stupid, irresponsible kids. Eve was the only one who'd had any sense, and now she was dead and it was their fault.

'I think we should go.'

'Go where?'

She looked at him, feeling more certain by the second. 'No one ever comes to this house. I think we should clean her up, say goodbye to her, take Lily and go somewhere big, where we can disappear – London. We've got some money, we could find somewhere to stay, get jobs, start again . . .'

'What?' Scott said. 'Are you mad? They'll be looking for us.'

'They won't find us. No one knows our full names, do they? The bills here are in the name of Smith, we both work cash-in-hand, we're not on the dole – we're not even registered anywhere, are we? We can take anything that would identify us with us when we go.'

'You're saying we should just go and leave her here?'

Jo swallowed. The idea of leaving Eve all alone in the house was almost unbearable, but the alternative was worse.

'They'll take Lily, you know. Put her in some horrible children's home.'

'But I'm her dad.'

'Who was so off his face on drugs that he sat and watched the mother of his child bleed to death!'

He flinched visibly.

'Sorry, but it's true.' She was talking quickly now, a sense of urgency and excitement building. 'They'll say you're not fit to look after her. And we live in a squat – people think that makes us drug addicts anyway.' She waited, but he still didn't say anything.

She took a breath and tried to make her voice calmer. 'Look at it this way, Scott, if we go to the police now, we know for sure that we'll be arrested for the drugs, they'll take Lily away, and we'll almost certainly be accused of – I don't know what it'll be, manslaughter, maybe—'

'No! They couldn't—'

'Well, probably not manslaughter, but *something*. We let her die, Scott.' She paused for a moment. 'But if we take Lily and go, there's a chance they may not find her for a while. We could change our names anyway, to be on the safe side.'

Scott stood and started pacing around the room, then he went out of the kitchen and along the hall to the living room where he stood outside the door for a moment before going in. Jo watched Lily sleeping as she waited for him to come out. What if he said no?

Then she heard his footsteps coming slowly back along the hall. He looked weary as he came back into the kitchen and sat down. 'All right. Let's do it.'

*

It was almost two in the afternoon by the time they were ready to leave. They hadn't been able to clean Eve up as much as they'd have liked – there was just too much blood to deal with, and they'd had to keep stopping to give in to bouts of uncontrollable trembling or waves of nausea – but they'd washed her face, brushed her hair, and covered her with a clean white sheet. They packed the old shopping trolleys that they used for transporting stuff to the markets with a few clothes for themselves, but mostly with baby clothes, bedding, shawls and nappies. They scoured the house for papers bearing any of their names, but there were surprisingly few, and they put them in the bag she'd found all those months ago containing Eve's birth certificate, driving licence and National Insurance number. Jo made up more bottles and a bag of cheese sandwiches, and as an afterthought, stuffed a few things from the larder into her trolley – Marmite, some jars of jam, tins of beans, packets of lentils and rice. Her stomach was churning – what if they couldn't find anywhere to stay? They couldn't sleep rough, not with a baby. Maybe they could find a squat? But how many squats would be suitable? No, she told herself, don't think like that; it's going to be fine. Including Eve's money, they had almost ninety pounds between them. That would keep them going for a few weeks at least.

They each went in separately to say their goodbyes, Jo first, then Scott. He was tearful when he came out. 'Right,' he said. 'Ready?'

Jo tucked Lily into the baby sling and kissed her head,

marvelling once again at the softness of her hair. 'Hang on a sec,' she said to Scott. She hurried back into the kitchen and rummaged in the drawer for some scissors. Carefully, she selected a lock of Lily's silky hair and snipped, then she went back into the living room. Tenderly, she pulled back the sheet and placed the lock of hair on Eve's chest, at about the point where a locket would sit if she were wearing one. 'This is your daughter's hair,' she whispered. 'I will love her for you, for ever.' And she kissed Eve's forehead before covering her again and leaving the room, shutting the door quietly as if afraid of waking her.

Jo instinctively pulled on her parka, but with Lily nestling against her chest, it was impossible to zip up, so she took the big tent-coat Eve had bought at a jumble sale and buttoned it easily, keeping Lily snug inside.

'Lily Hannah,' she said as they walked up the hill to the station. 'Did she tell anyone she was going to call her Lily?'

'I don't know. Who would she tell? She's barely been out for weeks.'

'All the same, maybe we should call her Hannah Lily. Just in case.'

*

At the station, they were about to board the train when a porter came hurrying along the platform towards them. Jo couldn't move. This was it; they'd been found out already. But then the porter smiled and said, 'Not long now, eh?' then took her arm and helped her up the step into the carriage. 'Me and me missus have just had our own nipper, so I know what it's like.' He lifted the trolleys in while Scott took the bags. 'When you due, love?' He nodded towards the bump that Lily made under the huge coat.

She hesitated, unsure how to answer, then Scott chipped in. 'Only a couple more weeks. Thanks for your help, mate. Cheers.' He smiled at the man and pulled the carriage door shut. Jo's heart was hammering as they found their seats in the empty carriage. 'You *idiot*,' she hissed. 'What the hell did you say that for?'

'Well, it disguises us, doesn't it? If they're looking for a bloke and a girl with a baby, all he's seen is a bloke with a girl who's pregnant.'

'But what if she'd cried or something?'

Scott looked at her, and for a moment she thought he was going to cry. 'I didn't think of that.'

They sat opposite each other in silence, both still a little stunned by what had happened and by what they'd done. Jo was conscious of the warm weight of Lily, no, Hannah; she must get used to calling her Hannah, asleep on her chest. She unbuttoned her coat so that she could gaze at the little whorl of still sticky dark hair and remind herself what she'd promised Eve. She was now a mother.

Unable to look at Scott, she turned her head to the window and for a few minutes allowed her mind to go blank as the houses and back gardens with their washing lines, bikes and discarded toys whizzed past. Then she became aware of her own reflection looking back at her. She tried to look past it into the gardens, but its gaze became more insistent, as though it were another person. A few spots of rain fell onto the glass but the speed of the train pulled them sideways, so it was as if the rain was falling horizontally. She could feel her own eyes boring into her, like when you stare and stare at someone until they can't help but look back at you. She gave in and looked, and for a split second, it was Eve staring back. She slipped her hand into her coat pocket and allowed her fingers to close around Eve's birth certificate, now *her* birth certificate.

CHAPTER THIRTY-EIGHT

Sheffield, October 2010

I'm on a train to Hastings. It's been raining all morning and the sky is dark and overcast, making it feel like late afternoon even though it's not yet lunchtime. I look at my reflection in the train window, and I try to see Eve looking back at me, but I can't seem to conjure up her face any more.

This is the second time I've been down to visit her grave since I found out where she was. It was strange the first time, knowing her remains were there but with nothing to say it was her. But they put the headstone up last week, so that's why I'm going down today. I emailed Hannah to ask if she'd like to choose the stone and what she wanted on it, but she didn't reply. I write letters now, almost every week, but she never replies to those either.

I chose the headstone myself in the end; it's quite small and made of smooth white marble, with a built-in flower holder at the bottom. I sent Hannah a picture. Then I wrote again to tell her when they were putting it up, and that I'd chosen a simple inscription: *Eve, beloved mother*. I find I'm impatient to see it now.

*

I walk along the straight gravel path past the neatly trimmed grass and the regimented lines of plots. Eve would have hated the way the cemetery looks; this part of it, at least, where there are so few headstones because this is where they bury the unnamed, the unidentified. Eve would have preferred the ancient cemetery in Sheffield. It's not used for burials any more, but it's a pretty walk, a rambling, overgrown place full of worn headstones and memorials adorned with tiny cherubs, chipped Grecian urns, Celtic crosses and weeping stone angels.

As I turn into the row of plots where Eve is buried, I see immediately that Hannah did receive my letter, because there are sunflowers, five big bright blooms, perfectly arranged in the holder. I know Hannah likes sunflowers; Eve did, too. Is that a coincidence, I wonder? I crouch down to touch them. Hannah has put these flowers here; it may have even been today. I wonder if she brought Toby. I wonder if she stayed and talked to her mother. For a moment, I feel unbearably lonely; a gust of wind sweeps across the grass, stripping some of the petals from the sunflowers and somehow intensifying my sadness.

The stone is rather lovely, and its simplicity sets off the beautiful lettering. I trace the words with my fingertips: *beloved mother,* and then *Eve.*

The sunflowers look nice against the white stone. 'These are from your daughter,' I say aloud. 'She's very like you, Eve, in lots of ways. She's kind, and clever, and strong. You'd be so proud.' I pause; I can hear the wind moving in the trees. And then I realise that I want to keep talking, and so I do. I tell her how sorry I am for leaving her; I tell her how much I love Hannah, how much Duncan loves her, too. I try to explain how scared I was back then that they'd take her away. I carry on talking, babbling away with tears streaming down my face, and I don't stop even when a group of people walk past and I can feel them looking, wondering whether they should do anything or tell someone.

After a while, I straighten up and blow my nose. Silly really. I didn't need to come here to talk to Eve; I could have talked to her anywhere, at any time. But there's something about seeing her name on the headstone, something about giving it back to her, I suppose, that makes me feel close to her again, as though she's actually here, rather than it simply being the place where her remains are buried. As I stand here talking to her, I realise that I'm becoming increasingly reluctant to leave. I know it's stupid and irrational, but it feels like the moment I walk away from here, I'll be abandoning her all over again.

I can hardly believe it was over thirty years ago;

strange to think that Eve will be for ever twenty. When Hannah was that age she still seemed very young. At least, she did to me. And yet I remember Eve as being almost a mother figure as well as a friend; she made me feel safe; she taught me things, and she was proud of me. But we'd both needed mothers back then. It was one of the reasons I'd relished the chance to help her when she was expecting Hannah. I wanted to look after her, to take care of her just as she'd taken care of me. But in the end I let her down. 'I'm sorry, Eve,' I whisper eventually, and as I finally walk away, I feel myself give a small, involuntary wave.

*

I'm not ready to go back to Sheffield yet, so after I leave the cemetery, I go walking, and somehow, I find myself standing at the foot of the cliffs at Covehurst Bay, the wind whipping my hair around my face. This is where Eve taught me to swim. It occurs to me that this is another thing Hannah might like to know about her mother, so I allow my mind to drift back so that I can recall the details which, when I get home later, I'll put into a letter.

I remember the first day we came here. It was a half-hour walk from the East Hill down a narrow, rocky path that wound in and out of woodland so that sometimes we were in the shade, sometimes in the sunshine. That first day the sun was so fierce that it made the skin on my arms prickle. The path was dry and dusty, and by the time we came to the painted wooden sign that said *To the beach*, I was beginning to look forward to being in the cool water, although every time I thought of actually swimming, my stomach turned over.

'This way,' Eve said, turning onto another path. I could hear the gentle hiss of the waves scurrying up the beach, but we still had to climb down another steep path, holding on to tree roots and rocks until we came to a clearing where the ground levelled out and we could see the sea, shimmering and glassy in the distance. There was a three foot drop onto the beach, and we both jumped down, sending pebbles spraying up behind us. The beach here was almost empty. It was sandier, not so steeply shelved as Hastings beach, and the waves were more gentle; the sea even looked bluer.

Eve smiled. 'See what I mean? The water's always calm here – probably something to do with the shape of the bay. It's gorgeous to look at, isn't it? Although personally, I prefer it when the sea's a bit more lively.'

Eve was never happier than when the waves were crashing into the sea wall and the spray was going twenty feet in the air and drenching all the traffic on the coast road. I quite enjoyed watching the huge waves and listening to the heavy thuds as they hit the wall, but I didn't like standing too close because when I looked over the wall, I was overcome by an almost physical fear, not so much of falling, or of being swept away, but of what I might do. It was a terrifying sensation that manifested as a sort of effervescence in my ankles and fingertips, as if there were some hidden presence inside me that might suddenly turn against me and make me leap over the wall and down into the grip of the deep, powerful water.

'But this is just right if you're learning to swim,' Eve continued. 'Come on.' She took my hand. 'Let's get started.' She led me into the water and turned to offer me the other hand as well. 'First of all,' she said, tucking her elbows in at her sides, 'treat my hands like a float. Just hold on, and kick your feet up behind you.'

I did as she said, but I didn't want to splash her too much.

'Come on! Kick harder, make some noise. Okay, rest. Now, try again, only try to get your bottom up higher, right to the top of the water, so you can feel the sun. I know,' she grinned. 'Pretend you're trying to get a bum-tan!'

I had to put my feet down, because Eve was making me laugh. But then I tried again, and concentrated on pushing my body up so that it felt almost straight. I nearly panicked when I felt her grip loosen, but she grabbed me again quickly. Then she got me to lie on my front with my arms out while she put her hands under my stomach to support me.

'Look,' she said. 'I'm lifting you, and I'm holding on to your costume so you can't fall, but it's actually the water that's keeping you up. Try and let your body relax, then you'll feel safer.'

I could feel the warmth of Eve's hands against my stomach; I made a conscious effort to relax, and she was right, I did feel safer. Soon I could lie flat on the surface with my face in the water, as long as Eve was supporting me. I was virtually floating on my own, but I loved the feel of her hands, warm and solid, keeping me afloat.

The lessons continued every day, sometimes twice if I wasn't working. Eve showed me how to float on my back, and how to move my arms as if I was doing backstroke. Then she showed me how to do a front crawl and how to coordinate my arm movements and turn my head so as to take a breath, all the time supporting me, keeping me safe. After a week, she said she wanted to take her hands away to see if I could stay up on my own. What followed wasn't real swimming, but frantic doggie-paddle. But at least I stayed up, even if it was only for a few seconds. Then she moved a few feet away from me and held her arms out. 'Come on, Jo. See if you can swim to me.'

There was something about her expression, a look in her eyes that said she wanted me to succeed; that she really cared whether or not I would finally be able to swim. I took a breath, raised my arm and launched forward, lifting my body to the surface of the water. Sweeping down with one arm, I kicked my feet and heard the splashing as I moved forward. Up with the other arm, face towards the shore, breathe, turn, face towards the horizon, breathe, kick, keep going, left, right, breathe, kick. I felt my own strength and actions pulling me forward. And I wasn't even looking at Eve, though I could hear her clapping and shouting, 'That's it, Jo, you've got it! You're doing it!' And as I looked through the bubbles and saw the sun glinting off the blue-green ocean, I felt as though I could plough through the vast expanse of water with ease, that if I kept chopping through it with my arms and kicking with my legs that I would move forward, on and on until I reached the other shore. I was swimming! Wait till I told my mum! It was a millisecond before I felt the familiar surge of grief flooding through me, but then I fought it down, because I could see Eve, smiling and clapping as I swam towards her.

'That was marvellous,' she said, and she beamed at me as she put the towel around my shoulders. 'I'm so, so proud of you.'

CHAPTER THIRTY-NINE

It's very late when I get back from Hastings, but I stay up later still so that I can write my weekly letter to Hannah.

My dearest Hannah

I was at the grave today, and I saw the sunflowers. I'm so glad you've been down there, and I hope you like the stone and the inscription. I know you didn't feel able to decide what should be on it, but if there's anything you'd like to change, it can still be done so just let me know.

While I was in Hastings, I thought of something that might interest you. You may remember me telling you that I didn't learn to swim until I was sixteen. Well, it was your mother who taught me. She was very patient, and she understood how nervous I was. One of the ways she helped me to relax was by making me laugh. Do you remember that holiday we had in Robin

Hood's Bay when I gave you swimming lessons? You were seven or eight, I think. I taught you in the same way that Eve taught me, and I worked hard at trying to make you forget how nervous you were. I even said the same things to make you laugh. I remember telling you to pretend you're trying to get a bottom-tan – your mother had said something like that to me. You thought that was hilarious; you went running up the beach to Duncan, shrieking 'Bottom-tan, bottom-tan, bottom-tan.'

I'm telling you this because, in a way, it was almost as though it was your mother teaching you to swim through me. And you did it; you learned in two days – much faster than me. You were just like Eve after that – a real little mermaid.

With love always,

Mum

When I wake the next morning, the first thing I think about is the grave, and I think about it with relief, relief that it finally has a headstone, and that I've seen it properly in place and with her name engraved on its surface. It's odd how readily I relinquished the name. I've been 'Eve' for thirty-four years, and I never felt uncomfortable with it until I knew where she was. Now, I'm happy it's hers again.

I switch on my laptop and check the letter again before printing it out, ready to post. I still hope Hannah will read my letters at some point, so I type them so they're as easy to read as possible – my handwriting is appalling these days, and I know she can become impatient with illegible handwriting. It takes up too much time, she argues, which is fair enough.

I've been up for a while before I remember that it's Wednesday and my heart gives a little lift, because Wednesday is the day that Hannah usually takes Toby to the swings after his playgroup, and if I stand way back among the trees, I can watch them, unobserved. Sometimes they only stay for twenty minutes or so, but it's all I have, and it's better than nothing. Hannah hasn't spoken to me since the day I told them back in March – almost seven months ago now.

*

After I'd finished speaking, Hannah stared at me for a full minute, and then she got up and walked slowly out of the house, closing the front door behind her so quietly that I didn't even hear it click. Duncan was still looking at me incredulously. We sat in silence, I'm not sure for how long, and then he started to speak. 'Eve, what . . .' Then he shook his head. 'Jesus Christ, that's not even your fucking name, is it?' Then he mumbled something, stood up and went out of the room. I stayed sitting there as though in a trance. I couldn't feel my body. I'd done it; I'd told them.

I sat there, not moving, listening to Duncan walking around upstairs. I heard him speaking on the phone at one point and, when he came back in, he had his car keys in his hand. Monty climbed out of his basket and stretched, wagging his tail and looking expectantly at Duncan. 'Come on, then, boy,' he muttered, then he turned towards the door and said over his shoulder, 'I'm going to stay at my brother's for a bit. I need to think. I can't do it here.'

I nodded. 'When will you bring Monty back?'

He looked at me as though he didn't know me, and I had to look away because instead of the calm, easy love and friendship I was used to seeing in his eyes, what I recognised there now was mistrust and a flicker of dislike. 'He's my dog, Eve.'

I opened my mouth to argue, but there was no point; he *was* more Duncan's dog than mine. When Duncan first brought him home, I had very little to do with him. Hannah had just gone off to university at that point and I was missing her terribly. I was annoyed with Duncan because I thought he'd bought a puppy as some sort of substitute. It wasn't that at all, of course. He just wanted to save the poor little creature after a policeman had found him tied up and dumped in a skip, half-starved, covered in sores and frightened of his own shadow. It was Duncan who nursed him back to health; Duncan who patiently coaxed him into the room with us and talked to him in a soothing voice while the poor thing cowered under the table. It was even Duncan who took him for walks at first, while I stayed at home, moping around because I missed Hannah. That changed, of course. I soon took over the walking and, as Monty learned to trust me, I grew to love him. And now it looked like I was losing him, too. But I didn't have the strength, or the right, I suppose, to argue. So I watched Duncan go, Monty trotting happily behind him.

After a while, a few minutes, possibly, or a few hours – I had no concept of time whatsoever – I made my way upstairs, took off the clothes I'd been wearing all night and had a shower. Yesterday, the weather had been wet and blustery, but this morning there was sunshine streaming in through the windows, and outside, the pink cherry blossom lay like confetti on the pavements. Spring was in the air; it was supposed to be a time of new life, new beginnings, but for me, it was all about endings. I put on a thin black jumper and black trousers that were now loose around the waist and I looked at my reflection in the hall mirror: 'Jo,' I said aloud as I looked at myself. 'Joanna.' I sighed and shook my head. Would I ever really be Jo again? I put my coat on and picked up my keys. The jangling sound usually brought Monty padding into the hall, tail wagging, to look hopefully at his lead, and I felt a fresh stab of loss as I registered his absence. I locked the door behind me and set off to walk to the police station

At that point, I had absolutely no idea what would happen to me; I didn't even know if they'd believe me – it sounded such a crazy story. But they did, eventually, and of course they had to carry out a full investigation, which took months. It was a long, tense summer as I waited to find out whether there would be a trial. The most likely charge was *failure to report a death;* they also talked about *manslaughter by omission,* but that raised the question as to whether I could have been said to have 'a duty of care' towards Eve. Jen, my solicitor, thought not, especially given my age at the time. What I was most afraid of was being charged with kidnapping Hannah, but as my solicitor pointed out, I didn't kidnap her – Scott was her father and he had every right to take her.

Finally, halfway through September, the case was dropped. Jen said they'd decided it 'wasn't in the public interest' to prosecute, given that the circumstances were exceptional, and that so many years had passed during which I'd been 'a good citizen and to all intents and purposes, an exemplary mother'. Jen has been great. Right from the start she was cautiously optimistic, partly because I'd been so young when it all happened, but also because she felt that I may well have saved Hannah from a failing care system. I wish that was more how Hannah saw it.

When Jen told me the charges had been dropped, it barely registered. I felt so tired that I hardly had the energy to thank her. Odd, isn't it? Before all this came to light, I didn't seem to have a minute to myself, what with work, shopping and cooking for Duncan and myself, walking Monty twice a day, helping Hannah with Toby; now I have so little to do and yet I'm shattered most of the time.

I hated Scott when he showed up last Christmas. Over these last few months, I've often wondered what my life would be like now if he'd stayed in New Zealand and never made contact. Would I have told the truth at some point anyway? Maybe, maybe not. Maybe Hannah would have shamed me into it; I've thought a lot about how forcefully she believes in Toby's right to know the truth about how he came to be born. Or maybe I wouldn't ever have owned up; maybe I'd have remained a selfish coward for the rest of my life. At least I'd still have my daughter. I don't hate Scott any more, and it's a shame he was never able to visit Eve's grave because he'd have found some peace in knowing where she was, I think.

*

We tried to make a go of it after we left Hastings, Scott and I. We ended up in south-east London, living above Freeman, Hardy and Willis in Catford. Scott managed to get some evening shifts at the pub round the corner and I worked days in the shop downstairs, trudging back up three flights at the end of the day, exhausted and smelling of shoes. I think I always knew it was never going to work long-term. I could never take Eve's place in his eyes; we were a false family. But we struggled on for eight months, until the day of the newspaper report. *Body Found in Seaside House*.

I was in the launderette at the time, waiting for the dryer cycle to finish and thinking about how that clean, soapy smell reminded me of wash days when I was little and my mum would have the old twin-tub bubbling away in the corner. Then I flicked through the paper and I saw the headline at the bottom of page 5. My insides contracted and I went hot and cold at the same time, as though I was going to faint. Sometimes, even now, I still get that feeling when I smell that soapy, laundry smell. I remember clearly the rising sense of anger I felt when I read the report. I was angry that it was on page 5 – this was Eve they were talking about, not some lonely old tramp who nobody cared about; it should have been on the front page. There weren't many details, just that the body was female, five foot four, and aged between twenty and thirty years. That was it. There would be a post-mortem the following week and anyone with any information should get in touch.

I hated that they'd said the house was derelict; it wasn't derelict, just a bit run-down. It had been our home, a proper, comfortable, loving home. It turned out that the landlord, who'd lived in Sweden, had died and left the house to his nephew. The nephew had come to England to have a look at what he'd inherited and had found Eve where we'd left her eight months earlier. There was nothing in the paper about Hannah at that point.

Scott walked out that same night. He couldn't handle it any more, he told me, partly because he feared the knock on the door at any moment, and partly because he couldn't bear the fact that I'd taken her name. At the time, I thought it was the obvious, most sensible thing to do, but he said he would never, ever be able to call me Eve, and it would be best if we never made contact again.

I reluctantly agreed. The funny thing was, although I thought I'd miss him, once he'd actually left I didn't miss him at all. I had Hannah, and I realised that, now Eve was gone, she was all I wanted.

The missing-baby stories hit the papers a week or so later. There were a few more details about Eve, but not many. Dental records hadn't been any use – I remember her telling me she hadn't been to a dentist since she was about six. She had lovely teeth, incredibly healthy, and Hannah has inherited that from her, I'm happy to say. Hannah still only has one filling, whereas I had a mouthful of mercury by the age of twelve.

There were repeated appeals for information, but after a terrifying month or so, other events dominated the news; the story gradually faded into the background and I was able to get on with life without constantly looking over my shoulder.

Over the years since then, I have thought of myself so surely and completely as Hannah's mother that in moments of half-consciousness, moments between dreams and waking, I almost fancy I could describe the sensation of giving birth to her. I heard her heartbeat and felt her movements while she was still inside Eve; I watched her enter this world and I touched her, talked to her before she even took a breath; I helped her to breathe. I even, God forgive me, put her to my empty breast that first day of her life.

I love her as Eve loved her, and she could not be more fully mine.

CHAPTER FORTY

I go out to post the letter as soon as I've showered and dressed, but before I have breakfast. I prefer to make a special trip. After my fingers release their grip on the envelope and I hear the satisfying 'thwack' as it lands on top of the other letters in the post box, I wonder, as I do every time, if she'll read this one. At least they haven't come back with 'Return to sender' scrawled over the envelope. Maybe she puts them straight in the bin, but I hold on to the fact that she hasn't asked me to stop writing. The letters were Estelle's idea. She's been wonderful, Estelle has. She's constantly reassuring me, telling me not to give up hope. Hannah will come round eventually, she says, and so will Duncan. 'Because, deep down, they love you very much, you see. You must just allow them a little time to adjust.'

We've met for coffee a few times now, Duncan and I, although he's still living at his brother's. We've talked a little more in the last couple of months and we've a long way to go yet, but our meetings last a bit longer each time. Last Sunday, we spent the whole morning in the coffee shop like we used to. The only difference is that we used to sit in companionable silence, occasionally reading bits out of the paper to each other; but this time we spent the morning engaged in awkward, slightly anxious conversation. Hannah is much better now, he assured me, and she's coping really well with Toby. But she's not ready to see me yet. He looked at me. 'The thing is— ' I saw the slight verbal stumble as he stopped himself from calling me Eve. 'The thing is, she understands why you did what you did – everyone does; Christ, you weren't even seventeen years old. But what she can't get over is the fact that you lied about it for so long, and especially that you lied to *us*.' He looked down at the untouched Danish pastry on his plate. 'And I don't know what I can say to her to change her mind, because to be honest, that's what I've struggled with most myself.' He sighed deeply and rested his chin in his hand, his eyes still cast down.

'Does she read my letters, do you think?' I asked.

'I don't know. I'd like to be able to tell you that she does, but it's something I can't ask her.' He looked at me. 'You understand, don't you?'

I nodded. Duncan and Hannah have become even closer as a result of all this, which makes me as near to happy as I can possibly be.

Estelle says she thinks Hannah is softening; apparently she listens now when Estelle talks about me, and they even had a conversation about my plan to take an Open

University course. I'm not sure what in yet, but I have become aware quite suddenly of how huge the past is, and how tiny the future. Estelle laughs at me, but not unkindly. She says I'm far too young to be thinking that way.

I don't know what I'd have done without Estelle these past six months. Obviously Duncan had to explain why he'd moved in with John, and at first, he just told her that we'd split up and he couldn't say why. She was devastated, apparently, but she kept on at Duncan to tell her what had happened. He was worried about what the shock of it all might do to her, but she convinced him that not knowing was worse and that it was making her ill, so in the end, he told her. She *was* shocked, she told me afterwards, but, as she'd made clear to Duncan, you got rather used to shocks by the time you reached her age, and as far as she was concerned, there was no point in making more of a drama out of it than it already was.

Once I knew he'd told her, I wrote her a letter, quite a long one, as it turned out, because as I started to write, I realised I'd been longing to talk about Eve for years. I told Estelle about how kind Eve had been to me and about how much I'd loved her. I found myself explaining what had happened to her family, and then I wrote about the lovely things she used to make, what she looked like, the unusual colour of her eyes and the gypsy-style clothes she used to wear. I found myself spilling out everything I remembered about Eve, as if by conjuring up all these details I was trying to bring her back; to make her live again.

I finished by trying to explain why I persuaded Scott

that we should take Hannah and flee, how I was terrified I'd never see her again, and that although I knew now that things probably wouldn't have been as bad for us as I thought they'd be, there was no way of knowing that at the time. I added a PS asking Estelle to forgive my outpouring and saying that I hoped I could still visit her, no matter what happened between Duncan and me.

She rang me the very next day. Of course I could still visit; in fact, would I like to come the following afternoon? 'And, darling,' she said in a low voice, 'I have to ask, although it's a little delicate . . . what should I call you now? Would you prefer we stick with Eve or are you going back to Joanna?'

*

When Estelle opened the door the next day, the first thing she did was to put her arms around me. How was I coping, she wanted to know? Were the police treating me kindly? Duncan is her son, so of course she was upset that he was upset, but she has never judged me. 'Nobody has the right to judge,' she told me as we sat drinking tea in her sitting room with the late spring sunshine flooding in through the picture window. 'No one can possibly know what they would have done in a similar situation, you see. And after all's said and done, you lost your dearest friend, didn't you? It's clear from your letter that you missed her terribly; heavens, you still do, and all these years you've had no one to talk to about it.' At which point I nodded and then crumpled, and Estelle handed me tissues and patted my hand while I cried.

The odd thing was, now everything was out, the person I most wanted to talk to about Eve was Hannah. 'Well then,' Estelle suggested, 'why don't you write to her? Not by way of explanation – from what Duncan has told me, you've already explained very fully – and I think you were so brave to do so.' She smiled and laid her hand on my arm. 'But if you're certain that you would like her to know more about . . . good Lord, I don't know how to refer to . . . your friend—'

'It's okay, you can say *her mother*; or just *Eve*.'

'Eve.' She nodded, looking a little uncomfortable. 'I shall try not to get confused, but you must forgive me if I make a slip.'

I'd told her to call me Jo from now on, but she'd known me as Eve for such a long time it was clearly going to be difficult.

'Now, where were we? Ah yes, writing to Hannah. I'm sure she would be most grateful for any little detail you can tell her about her . . . her mother. And you see, you can make clear to her at the start that no reply is expected.' At this, she looked over the top of her glasses at me in that slightly stern way she has, as if to underline what she'd just said.

I nodded. 'That's a good idea. If she knows I don't expect an answer, she can read what I've written without feeling pressurised.'

I wrote the first letter that very evening. I didn't want to scare her so I kept it brief:

My darling Hannah

You do not need to reply to this, although of course I hope you will read it. I want to tell you some of the things I remember about your mother. I think you'll be interested in her, and especially in the things you and she have in common. It was Grandma who suggested I write it all down, and I thought that was a good idea, so I've decided to try and do a letter each week. You may not feel ready to read them now, but at least you'll be able to keep them so you have them for the future. More to follow!

All my love always,

Mum

I haven't said this to Estelle, but although I truly don't want Hannah to feel pressurised, I find myself constantly checking my texts and emails, constantly waiting for the post. I can't let myself even consider the possibility that this silence will last for ever, so I tell myself that she will read my letters, that there will be a reply; one day.

My darling Hannah

I wanted to tell you how proud your mother would be of you. You're like her in many ways. Like you, your mother felt that there were many non-conventional ways in which we could heal ourselves and others. Back then, we didn't know much about acupuncture and reflexology, but these are exactly the sort of things your mother was interested in, and she would have approved very much of what you and Marcus do.

I know the two of you are keen on aromatherapy, too. Well, I think you get that from your mother. We didn't call it that in those days, but she believed that certain scents had powerful effects, sometimes as a physical cure – oil of cloves dabbed onto an aching tooth; a eucalyptus inhalation for a cold; lavender oil for burns. And sometimes, she'd use a scent to lift your mood. If she noticed I was feeling sad – my mum had died quite recently, remember – I'd go into my room to find she'd sprinkled my bedclothes with rose water. I don't know whether it was actually the scent of roses or whether it was her thoughtfulness, but I always felt better afterwards. Once, when she was pregnant with you, she decided to try and make her own rose water. She sent Scott and me out in the middle of the night to nick roses from the neighbours – she said she was fed up with seeing all the rose petals on the ground going to waste. Anyway, God knows how we didn't get caught, because all the rose bushes were in people's back gardens, so we had to climb over fences to get to them. We came back covered in scratches with a carrier bag full of rose heads, which Eve then tried to turn into rose water. Somehow, she ended up with six bottles of something that smelled like it had come from a drain. She was cross with herself at first – it was unusual for her to get things wrong – but then she saw the funny side.

With all my love,

Mum

Dearest Hannah

I've remembered another thing you and your mother have in common. It's the way you turn the pages down to mark your place in the book you're reading. I used to get told off for doing that at school, but Eve said she liked to see books with turned-down pages, or even with written notes in the margins; she said it showed that the reader had loved the story and the characters, rather than caring too much about the actual book. I remember one time, your mother was reading Wuthering Heights. She'd read it before, but I hadn't, and she was raving about it. It was one of her favourite books, I think, that and Jane Eyre. Anyway, I asked her if I could read it when she'd finished, and she just looked at me, said, 'Yes,' then tore her copy in two and handed me the first half. She said it would be better if I started reading it straight away then we could chat about it while we were both reading it. It was only a battered copy she'd bought at a jumble sale for 5p, but what she did still shocked me. She told me off for being shocked — 'Books are only things,' she'd say. 'It's what they make you feel that's important.'

You liked Wuthering Heights too, didn't you? Do you remember that copy you had when you did it for GCSE? You kept dropping it in the bath and drying it out on the radiator, and in the end, it was almost twice the thickness it should have been. But you didn't want another copy, you said you liked the water stains!

You know, there's something about Catherine Earnshaw that is very much like you, and like your mother. I'm not talking about the selfish, spoilt side of Catherine's character, but the way she loves the outdoors, the fresh air and the wild, open moors. You've always been the same, ever since you were little. And it's a bit like how Eve used to feel about the sea. Never happier than when she was in it or near to it.

My love always,

Mum

My dearest Hannah

I know I've already told you what a good, kind person your mother was, but I thought you might like to know about a rather lovely gift she once made for me. I think I told you how, when I first arrived in London from Newquay just after my mum died, I spent a few nights in a hostel and another girl who was staying there stole a cameo brooch that had belonged to my mother? Well, I told Eve about that, and she knew how upset I was to have lost the brooch. Anyway, she obviously remembered it, because not long before you were born, she told me she had a present for me – an advance 'thank you for helping me with the baby present' she called it.

It was a pendant, a cameo she'd made herself out of shell fragments. She'd used dark blue razor shells for the background and white, cream and pinkish shells for the woman's head. It looked great, but it wasn't so much how it looked that made such an impression on me, it was the amount of work she'd put in. The thought that she would spend so much of her own time, would go to so much trouble for me, well, it just really made me feel special. I wish I could have done something similar for Eve. There were only three and a half years between us, but it made a difference. I took a lot of things for granted and it was only much later that it occurred to me that, if Eve's little gestures had meant so much to me, then a similar gesture from me would have meant a great deal to Eve. But by the time that very simple truth had dawned on me, it was too late.

I'm so sorry that I don't still have the pendant to pass on to you, but sadly, it was one of the things I couldn't find when your father and I left the house.

With my deepest love,

Mum

Darling Hannah

Briefly, I enclose the only items I have that belonged to your mother. I apologise for not sending these before, but it was only as I wrote the last letter that I remembered these things and where I'd hidden them. In my last letter, I told you about the shell cameo your mother made for me; she was always an artistic person. Not exceptionally talented, but extremely competent and fairly committed. She'd always been creative apparently, and when she was about ten years old, not long before her mum died, she made a collage out of postage stamps and sent it to Blue Peter. It was a cameo, oddly enough: a woman's head in pinks and creams on a darker background. They loved it and sent her a Blue Peter badge – this was a much-coveted item in those days! She kept it in a crocheted bag along with a few photos of when she was much younger – one with some schoolfriends, one of a cat I assume she'd owned at some point, and one of her with both her parents – your grandparents. I enclose these and hope you'll be pleased to have them as another small connection to your mother.

I left your mother with a connection to you, too. I've been trying to decide whether to tell you this and I'm still not sure whether it's appropriate or not, but anyway: Just before your father and I left the house we each said goodbye to Eve, and I cut a tiny lock of your hair, which I placed on her chest. I wanted her to have something of you.

With love,

Mum

Darkness is taking hold by the time I go through the gates to the park. I'm glad I brought the car or I'd never have made it before the light goes completely, and if I miss them today, it'll be another week before I can be sure of seeing them again. The irony is painful – most grandmas are at least ten years older than I am, and when Toby was born, I felt grateful that I'd have the energy to do lots of things with them both. But now this is all I have. I park the car and hurry down through the woods towards the play area. Usually, I love being around trees at this time of year; I've always enjoyed autumn's display of reds and golds but nature's beauty seems almost painful to me now. In my haste, I trip over a tree root and stumble, but I manage to right myself. Seconds later, I slip on some wet leaves and have to grab on to a branch to stop myself from falling. I should slow down, take more care – I really can't afford to break anything.

I walk down behind the café to where the stepping stones cross the stream, remembering to take off my scarf in case it makes me more visible. I can't see them at first, and I spend an anxious few minutes waiting, watching a little cat playing with the leaves and trying not to glance at my watch every ten seconds. But then I spot them: it's chilly today, and Hannah is wearing her long purple coat and the black-and-white woollen hat she knitted herself, and Toby is looking adorable in a new red duffle coat. He can sit up on his own easily now, and from where I stand behind a dense cluster of trees and bushes, I can see that he's squealing with laughter as she pushes him in the baby swing, but I'm not quite close enough to hear his little voice. She is smiling, too; at long last, she is taking pleasure in her child, and this is the one thing that makes me happy. Well, as happy as it's possible to be. She's laughing now, too, and I smile as I watch them together. This is as near as I dare be to them now. If Hannah spots me, as she did in the summer, she'll strap Toby back into the buggy and hurry away, so I must content myself with lingering in the shadows for the time being.

*

I can't face going home just yet, so on the way back from the park, I drop in to see Estelle. She's pleased to see me as always, and she's smiling as she ushers me into the sitting room. 'I've just this minute made a pot of tea, so that's fortuitous, and there are spare cups in the sideboard. Now, you look frozen, darling. Come and warm yourself.'

Sitting here by the fire with Estelle I feel almost normal. I couldn't have coped without Estelle; she has supported me unconditionally, right from the start.

'I'm so glad you've called in,' she says. 'Young Marcus popped round on Sunday – I asked him to clear my gutters for me before the weather gets really bad. They were completely blocked with leaves and moss. Anyway, we had a little conversation afterwards, and I managed to get some information out of him.' She chuckles mischievously. 'I've managed to establish that your letters have not been thrown away. It's not a lot, I know, but at least we know that much.'

'Has she read—'

She shakes her head. 'I don't know. Marcus says she's very secretive about it; takes them off and tucks them away somewhere, apparently. But he's certain she's kept them all.'

I nod slowly. 'That's good to know; it's . . . a comfort.'

Estelle looks at me with such fond sympathy that I'm afraid I might cry. Then she gets up slowly and uses her stick to help her across the room to the sideboard, where she keeps the sherry.

*

When I arrive home, I prepare myself for the gauntlet of sadness I run each time I enter this house. The front garden was Duncan's project when we moved in; he dug the fish pond, laid the lawn and made the crazy-paved path. For our first anniversary, he bought me a sundial which stands on a plinth near the pond. I was touched because he'd clearly remembered me telling him how I'd once lived in a rambling old house in Hastings and that I'd loved the old sundial we'd found in the garden. The one he gave me is engraved with the words: *Grow old with me, the best is yet to be.* I can hardly bear to look at it.

Once I'm inside, it gets even worse. On the walls in the hall are photographs of Hannah: there's one of her dressed as a Christmas star in her first year at primary school; then one where she's about eight, with short hair and a missing front tooth; there's Hannah and her friend Vicky looking dark and moody in their Goth phase; there she is at the surgery with Duncan during her gap year, helping to hold a Jack Russell while Duncan examines its paw. Then there's the graduation photo, the wedding pictures – a whole wall of Hannahs, smiling, happy. Looking at them hurts, but taking them down would hurt more. I push open the door to the kitchen, and am confronted with the series of scores cut into the door frame where we measured her height every birthday and recorded the year on the wall next to it. It's funny, but I hadn't noticed those marks for years, and yet now they seem to scream at me every single time I walk past them.

I open the back door for Monty to go out into the garden – Duncan lets me have him for half the week now, although it's been slightly longer this week because he suggested we drive out to the moors on Sunday when he comes to collect him, maybe even stop somewhere for a drink on the way back. It's a step on from coffee, I suppose, but I don't want to get my hopes up.

I fill the kettle for tea and open the fridge to see what there is for dinner. Nothing inspires me, and I can't really be bothered, so I cut myself a chunk of cheese and put it on a plate with a few oatcakes and a dollop of chutney. I nibble at the food as I empty the dishwasher. With just me here, I only need to run it every few days. When I've done that, I wander into the sitting room and pick up the remote control. I find I watch a lot of telly these days. I'm flicking through the channels when the phone goes. I almost ignore it. 'Hello,' I answer with a weary sigh, ready to say no, I don't want to change my phone company, fuel provider or whatever. Silence; probably a bloody call centre. I'm about to hang up when I hear a throat being cleared. The voice is quiet, hesitant, but it doesn't sound angry. 'Mum?' she says. 'It's . . . it's me.'

ACKNOWLEDGEMENTS

There are many people whose confidence in this book and unwavering belief in me as a writer have kept me going through difficult times. I am deeply grateful to them all. In particular, I'd like to thank my wonderful editor Clare Hey for her editorial brilliance, her perceptive and insightful feedback, and her reassuring smile. I also want to thank my agent Kate Shaw for her excellent editorial suggestions and for her support and encouragement which steadies me when I'm floundering. For their generous assistance and endless patience in the face of my questions regarding police procedure, forensic matters and the CPS, my thanks to Kevin Robinson, and to Gary Atkinson. Any remaining errors are my own.

My research around Hastings in the 70s led me to *Bats in the Larder, Memories of a 1970s Childhood by the Sea*, a wonderful memoir by Jeremy Wells. My thanks to Jeremy for the lovely email chats that helped to stir my own memories of Hastings and of the 1970s.

Writing can be a painful business when the words don't come easily. I am incredibly lucky to have wonderful friends who understand, and who don't mind me droning on about various versions of the plot and about how hard it all is. For listening, and for sharing wine, coffee and cake, my thanks to Iona Gunning and Sue Hughes, and especially to James Russell for all the above and for reading parts of the manuscript and convincing me not only that I could make it work, but that it was worth working on.

Finally, the greatest debt of all is to Francis, for so much; for everything.